TONY MO

EDEN

HAILED AS:

"ONE OF THE BEST ZOMBIE NOVELS OUT THERE."
—Horror Bound Magazine

"INNOVATIVE AND BREATHTAKING ... WILL REIGNITE LONG LOST FEARS AND KEEP YOU UP AT NIGHT."
—Bryce Beattie, author of Oasis

"A WONDERFUL, ENGAGING NOVEL THAT WILL CONTINUE TO RESONATE, EMOTIONALLY, LONG AFTER THE FINAL PAGE IS READ."
—HorrorScope

EDEN:

CRUSADE

A ZOMBIE NOVEL BY TONY MONCHINSKI

Permuted Press
The formula has been changed...
Shifted... Altered... *Twisted.*
www.permutedpress.com

For Omar Devone Little
"…the cheese stands alone."

EDEN: CRUSADE

A **Permuted Press** book
published by arrangement with the author

ISBN-10: 1-934861-33-2
ISBN-13: 978-1-934861-33-2

Cover art by Christian Dovel.

10 9 8 7 6 5 4 3 2 1

"When you side with a man, you stay with him. And if you can't
do that, you're like some animal, you're finished."
—William Holden, *The Wild Bunch*

"Some of us…are more broken than others."
—Michael Caine, *Around the Bend*

CRUSADE

The dawn came but it did so unbeknown to an earth below—a
morose land canopied by thick, unforgiving storm clouds layered
one upon the other, unremitting, impenetrable. The morning mist
rose from the ground to the sky above in a seamless veil of wispy
bleakness, cloaking the road to town in a fold of hazy desolation.

And from the brume emerged some monstrosity: a man in
shape and form yet somehow misplaced, as if having stepped out of
the past. An atavism brought forth by some ancient incantation. His
person was clad in a chain mail bymie, head and bulky shoulders
cloaked with a coif and aventail. His face was unseen behind a
splatter mask, the slits between the grill revealing only shadow.
Leather gauntlets protected his hands and forearms and he was
festooned with weapons. Leather pants supported triple pistol mag
thigh rigs; extended clips in the handguns; a chainsaw slung over his
back next to a flanged mace; a brace of knives crossing his chest.
Waterproof Blackhawk Warrior Wear Black Ops Boots with full
grain leather uppers protected the man's feet.

Pressed to his immense chest was a cherubic form, swaddled in
blankets, secured to his person in a Baby Bjorn.

Before him he pushed a two wheeled wooden cart, a wagon
laden with leather saddle bags and crates of ammunition atop which
lay automatic rifles and machine guns and spears. Within reach was
a morning star mace. One of the wheels on the cart protested shrilly
as he pushed it onto the bridge that lead into town. Somewhere
below a stream gurgled. The fog rising from its waters shrouded the
chasm and the overpass spanning it.

As he approached forms took shape from out of the gloom.
The rusting hulks of begrimed vehicles long abandoned. He passed
several of them with his wagon and stopped when he reached an

1

old Hummer, its tires flat, one of its doors ajar. In the distance there was a howl but the man was unconcerned.

He left the wagon in the road and walked around the vehicle, morning star raised in one hand defensively lest something should leap from the mist and shadows. He inspected the Hummer, opening each door to peer inside, closing all but one. The keys were still in the ignition. He didn't bother trying to turn the engine. It would be long dead.

"Shhh, shhh, shhh," he cooed to the bundle as he unstrapped it from his chest. "You rest in this car. It's safer for you here."

The bundle did not protest as the man laid it on the leather front passenger seat. He transported some crates from the wagon to the backseat of the off-road vehicle and placed the chainsaw on the floorboards in the back. He looked in once more on the form and smiled, then closed the door and pocketed the keys to the vehicle.

As he did so there was a steady growl from behind him. Headlights cut through the gloom and alighted on his cart in the middle of the bridge. A Chevy Silverado 2500 jacked up on Baja Claw Radial SLT tires, with Bushwacker Fender Flares and a three inch bull bar, pulled to a stop a few yards from the man and his wagon.

A woman stepped down from the cab onto the running board then onto the bridge. Like the man she was heavily armed and armored. Head to toe black body armor enveloped her trunk and limbs. The chest plate, collarbone pads, shoulder and elbow cups, back plate, and kidney belt of her fully ventilated O'Neal underdog body armor protected her upper body. She wore leather motorcycle pants with Vevlar fabric panels on her forelegs and CE armor on the knees. Altama EXO Speed Waterproof Tactical Boots shielded her feet. The boots were water-and blood-borne pathogen proofed; she knew what was coming.

Pistols were holstered on her hips, at her waist, and under her arms. She cradled a Colt Commando M16A2 assault rifle in her hands, which were sheathed in full-fingered shooting gloves. She approached the man and looked warily into the mist ahead of them.

"The child sleeps," said the man by way of greeting.

The woman nodded. Her head was covered by a leather aviator helmet cap. The clear anti-fog lens of an Uvex Bionic Face Shield covered her face. From somewhere in the distance a wail reached their ears.

The man went about his preparations, taking assault rifles from the cart and bandoliers of ammunition and propping them in different areas about the bridge. The sides of the bridge were waist high rock walls overgrown with moss and weeds and tendrils of green sprouting from the asphalt of the road itself. Several of the stones had come undone and portions of the wall lay crumpled in disarray.

The woman cast one last anxious glance into the shadow and climbed back atop her truck, into the bed. On the roof of the cab before her she lay out a Model 85 sniper rifle and stacked numerous box magazines.

The fog was not as dense as earlier. Other shapes farther along the bridge and the road beyond emerged.

The man returned to his wagon and upended a fifty gallon gasoline barrel. He rolled it down the bridge away from the truck, the cart, and the Hummer. When he went a short distance he was satisfied and stopped. He unplugged the barrel and tipped it onto its side. The thump of the drum on the road reverberated. Gasoline splurged from the barrel onto the bridge. He repeated this process with two more barrels and left a fourth upright next to the emptying ones.

There was more movement amidst the fog somewhere beyond the span. A large sign on the side of the road took shape, with only the words *Welcome to* and *Population* left decipherable.

He returned to the cart to retrieve his Colt M16A2 Commando and a handdful of flares. Passing the Hummer, he paused briefly to peer within. His precious bundle rested peacefully where he had placed it. He walked back to the fourth barrel and lay the flares down before it, well out of reach of the gasoline which continued to spill out, cascading down a barely noticeable decline towards the road. He had placed two bandoliers of 5.56mm ammunition in 30-round magazines near the barrels and he took these and laid them atop the side of one drum within easy reach. He leaned the morning star head-down, its shaft against the remaining full drum.

He turned and looked in the direction of the Hummer with the bundle inside and the woman. She knelt in the bed of the truck, the Model 85's bipod rested on the roof of the cab. The fog had dissipated to the extent that when she gave the man a thumbs-up he perceived it clearly.

He returned the gesture and once more faced the road into town.

She stood and squeezed a shot from the sniper rifle into the air. The crack of the rifle echoed in the still of the morning. Above them the clouds glowed a faint purple and bubbled like broken surf.

The woman racked the bolt on the Model 85 back and chambered a new round. The empty shell casing flipped end over end to rest on the mist enshrouded bridge.

"Bring out your dead," she spoke.

There were screams and chortles and moans from within the brume. The man stood and waited. Within moments the first of the undead broke from the mist on the run, misshapen and hideous, arms askance as the bookers sprinted onto the bridge. When they saw the man standing behind the drum their wails increased in intensity.

The zombie in the lead wore a suit jacket and boxer shorts. Its shirt was stained and its tie hung around its neck like a limp noose. As it ran towards the man a 7.62 mm slug from the Model 85 entered its forehead just above the nose and punched out the back of its skull. It collapsed onto the bridge with its ass jutting up in the air. Soon several more sprinting nasties passed by it.

The man waited. He was not as good a shot with a rifle as the woman for his aim was compromised. He watched a second then a third and a fourth zombie as their heads jerked back and they fell. The cracks of the 85 punctured the morning. He stood there with the M16A2 at his waist. His breathing got heavier. More zombies fell and he stopped counting.

He had done this before and felt no fear. In fact, as their numbers increased and they drew nigh, he felt a rage suffuse his being, an anger grip his person, and he started to shake. They were screaming as they ran towards him, sounding like banshees let loose from some infernal netherworld where the hungry dead reigned.

He grunted and raised the Commando, the stock pressed to his shoulder. He sighted and fired, the flash from the barrel licking out into the morning. A zombie wearing a baseball cap backwards caught the round in its upper chest. It staggered but kept coming. The man adjusted his aim and fired again. The zombie dropped in its tracks.

Dozens of them had broken from the fog and sprinted across the bridge towards him and the woman in the truck. They chose their targets and fired methodically..

He was able to fire out one thirty round magazine before they were on him. The first zombie alighted a barrel and launched itself

4

towards him. He caught it in midair, its head in his gloved hands, and he slammed it back down to the ground, twisting its skull savagely. The pop if its spine was audible above the woman's sniping.

He came up with the morning star in his hand. Wielding it like a club, he crashed it down on the head and shoulders of the closest zombie. The sharpened spikes buried themselves in the thing's skull and deltoid. He yanked the weapon out of the dispatched beast and brought it down on the next creature. Its rotten head collapsed under the blow. The thing dropped to its knees.

A zombie hit him from the side and would have knocked him from his feet if he were a smaller man. He brought his elbow down on its head and it crumpled. Then they were all on him—a shrieking gaggle bearing him off his feet and to the ground.

The woman had been through this with him before. She ignored his situation and fired on the bookers crossing the bridge. They fell unceremoniously, all head shot. She worked systematically: drawing back the bolt, chambering a new round, aiming, firing, swapping out for a fresh magazine. She let the empties gather about her feet in the truck bed.

With a mighty heave the man thrust the zombies clinging to him off and stood. His heavily armored body was unviolated. Zombie teeth and claws were unable to penetrate chain linked armor and leather. The zombies shed from him spilled to the road.

He came up with a Colt Python .357 revolver in his right hand and a flare in his left. He straight-armed the revolver and fired. A devastating blow obliterated a zombie skull. He swiveled and fired on others as they regained their feet, the Python recoiling in his mighty hand as he knocked them down forever. As he killed he was aware dozens more were running at top speed across the bridge.

Two zombies tackled him but he would not go down again. They clung to him and pawed and bit at his armor and splatter mask to no avail. He used his left forearm—his left hand still gripping the flare—to pry the face of one away from his body just enough so he was able to press the muzzle of the .357 to its temple and blast the side of its head off. As it fell from him he dropped the empty revolver and cracked the flare open. With a hiss and violent sparkle it sputtered to life. He reached around and snatched the second zombie from his back, yanking it around to face him. The creature screamed and gnashed its teeth. He plunged the lit flare into its maw. As the thing howled he pitched it over the barrel to the gasoline soaked road beyond.

With a *whoosh* the gasoline went up and scores of zombies were immolated as they raced forward. The sound of their suffering and death filled the air. With the bridge ablaze, his attention turned to the creatures remaining about him. Mindless beasts heedless of the danger facing them. One by one he dispatched them with his hands: a crushing punch caving in a face, a blow to the temple felling another. He gripped one by the hair and the entire scalp came off, revealing white bone. The man brought the bottom of a gauntleted fist down and cracked the exposed skull.

In sweatpants with "Juicy" embroidered on the bottom, the final zombie on his side of the fire screamed and circled. He stalked over and grabbed it by the neck and crotch. It tried to fight as he snatched it from its feet, cleaned it to his shoulders and pressed it, then threw it into the fire. It wailed and tried to escape but could not.

He watched them burn as the woman fired at the mass of bookers beyond the wall of flame. He reloaded and holstered the .357 then swapped magazines in the M16A2.

The man aimed over the fire and the forms that crumpled in it—some still twitching—his Commando's semi-automatic discharge joining the woman's. The zombies beyond the fire roared and cackled and dropped one by one. As the fire burned itself out the man and woman kept choosing their targets and firing. The numbers on the other side of the fire dwindled. Eventually the few remaining zombies were able to risk the road and jetted through the last remnants of flame, closing in on the man, who met them with the morning star.

In moments only the man and the woman were left on the bridge.

He reloaded the M16A2 and let it rest against the remaining gasoline barrel. There were pistol shots behind him. Their gunfire had drawn zombies from outside the town along the road they'd come in on. Zombies that now grouped about the Chevy and the woman. They were slow and she was well out of their reach. She fired down into them with deadly effect from the pistol.

There was a collective groan from the road ahead of him. The fog had burned off considerably at this point and he could make out a mass staggering his way.

The man thought of the town beyond the bridge and the thousands, perhaps millions, of undead within it. As he did so the rage crept over him once more, filling his person. He was sweating behind the splatter mask so he shrugged it off and stared out into the gloom with his one eye.

"Bear."

The woman joined the man at his side. Removing her face shield revealed her beautiful olive complexion, chiseled cheekbones prominent, and a lock of thin black hair sweat-stuck to her forehead.

"Nadjia," he said.

Bear looked to the clouds and a drop of rain spattered his cheek.

"Stay here," he told her, taking up the Commando and slinging it across his back next to the mace. "Watch the child."

He walked across the remainder of the bridge. Sucking noises came from the rubber outsoles of his booted feet as he stepped through liquefied remains. The sickly sweet smell of burnt flesh was pungent. Rain drops fell around him, first a few then more until a light downpour enveloped the bridge.

Ahead an undead army worked its way forward, their ranks innumerable. He stalked towards them, drawing first one Glock 18 from his hip then a second.

The zombies saw him and let out a collective bellow—a roar of hunger and hatred. Their host crowded the road beyond the bridge from shoulder to shoulder and there was no end to their mass in sight.

Bear stopped where he stood and gazed out upon them. They moaned and chortled and shambled forward.

He tucked one Glock under his arm and chambered a fresh round in the second, then repeated the process for the first. They had cut the distance separating them and were now starting across the bridge, which formed a natural bottleneck and only allowed a dozen to pass abreast.

The rain was falling in steady sheets now.

Bear looked at them with blind hatred. From deep within his core he summoned a fierce roar that boomed from the bridge to the town beyond and the heavens above. The zombies, incapable of fear, trod onward to their doom. Bear affixed the splatter mask and resumed his walk towards their front lines.

He stopped less than ten yards from their reaching arms, cracking jaws, and wraithlike moans, extended the Glock in his right hand and started firing. He triggered one shot at a time, chose another target and fired again. When the pistol in his right hand was empty he switched it for the one in his left and fired that one out in rapid succession. At this range, and with the zombies pressed so close together, his aim was accurate. One after another they collapsed to their knees to be bowled over by their gruesome companions, or folded to the asphalt to be trod over by the ones behind.

The rain came down in a steady shower, soaking living and dead.

Bear turned his back to the undead and walked off a few steps, dropping first one spent magazine and reloading a pistol then the other. He cocked back the slides on the 9mms and turned. They loomed before him like the water from some nauseating sea, inexorably surging forward foot by foot. He walked back to their ranks and a collective roar went up. He extended the Glock with the green laser sight and resumed the business of killing.

Nadjia had joined him but dared approach no farther than the barrels where she fired into their midst with a Commando. She fired out magazine after magazine while Bear alternated between approaching the line and turning from it to reload. Periodically Nadjia twisted to guard their rear, picking off a stray zombie that had shambled into sight amongst the Chevy, the Hummer, and Bear's wheeled cart.

Bear reloaded the pistols with the last of his magazines and fired them out into the crowd. Zombies bobbed up and down as they climbed over their fallen, the hunger and determination in their eyes unmistakable. When both pistols were empty he holstered them and unslung the Commando from his back. He flipped the selector to semi-auto and pulled the stock into his shoulder, sighting and firing. The back of a zombie's head came undone like a jigsaw puzzle and it slumped to the bridge surface.

He judged their progress by his distance from the barrels, emptying the Commando, reloading, stepping back a yard or two while reloading. The rain pooled around his feet, mixing with blood and muck.

Nadjia fell back to a position halfway between the barrels and the cars, taking a knee and resuming her fire.

When he reached the barrels he took up his morning star and brought it down with a crash onto the remaining full drum. Gasoline jetted out of the punctures as he wrested the spiked head free. He knocked the drum over and rolled it with his foot. Pushing off with all his weight behind it, he watched it spin towards the zombies, gasoline splashing up into the air, mixing with the rain. Two or three of the undead tripped over the barrel and struggled to regain their footing as their legion reeled forward, unrelenting.

Bear brought the Commando up to his shoulder and patiently fired out another magazine, then turned and walked off towards the vehicles. Nadjia shouldered the 66mm M202A1 Flame Assault Shoulder Weapon and sighted. Bear reloaded on his walk towards her as she fired the first of the rocket launcher's four barrels. The backblast from the rocket motor licked out almost to the Silverado. The rocket zipped past on Bear's right trailing flame, impacting the first wave of zombies. A brilliant splash blinded as the M74 rocket detonated, vaporizing the front ranks of the undead. The gasoline drum detonated and a cloud of flame reached to the sky. Smoking body parts rained down on the bridge.

Nadjia shifted her aim and fired the second and third rockets several hundred yards beyond the bridge. The explosion rivaled napalm detonations. The triethylaluminum agent exposed to the air burned at twelve hundred degrees Celsius. Zombies ignited like dry leaves. Even those nowhere near the points of detonation were seared by the thermal radiation of each blast. She fired the fourth and final rocket into the dark and rain. The light and heat flared in the distance. Zombies wailed as scores of them perished in the annihilating fires.

Nadjia laid the empty incendiary rocket launcher down and took up her Commando with what remained of a bandolier of ammunition. Bear tossed her his M16A2 and she caught in on the run in the rain, trotting over to the front of the Hummer. Bear stalked over to the Heckler & Koch G3 he had leaned barrel-up against the stone wall of the bridge. Two soaked bandoliers of magazines for this assault rifle waited atop the waist high wall.

The rocket explosion and gasoline drum had temporarily halted the zombies but now they advanced. The rain quickly quenched the fire. Several of the zombies staggering forward over pieces of their brethren were charred and smoldering, burnt beyond belief but still ravenous, enraged, moving.

Bear fired out first one magazine then another, the rainfall competing with the barks from his rifle and Nadjia's Commando. He stopped only to clear a jam then worked his way through one bandolier of magazines. He was nearly through the second when the zombie front ranks passed the spot where the empty barrel rested.

He signaled to Nadjia and she fell back to the Chevy, clambering atop the bed to fire from first her Commando then Bear's, reloading when both were fired out then continuing.

Bear reloaded the G3 and chambered a fresh round, then placed it back against the wall as he had left it earlier. He took up his morning star and considered the throng closing in on him. He squinted through the grill of the splatter mask and looked to the sky but the purple-dappled clouds masked the universe and its secrets.

He cocked the morning star over his shoulder like a baseball bat and charged their ranks for the second time that morning, uttering a guttural cry of pure detestation, of loathing and something more—*conquest*. Closing with their ranks he swung the morning star. A zombie's head disintegrated in a red mist of bone fragments and meat. He swung again, from left to right, smashing two off their feet into the others. They shrieked and bore down on him, attempting to encircle as he slew them where they stood.

He brought the morning star straight down with both arms, the spiked ball collapsing an undead's skull in a shower of crimson to the shoulder line. Bear left the morning star stuck in the thing's clavicle and from his back took the flanged mace. He lofted it to shoulder level and swung left and right, sweeping blows that brained zombies and sent them staggering backwards, melting down.

He grabbed an obese zombie by its neck with his gauntleted hand. Manhandling it he wielded it as a shield at his one side, momentarily staunching the press of zombies. With his right hand he swung the mace, felling undead. They pressed on, a veritable wall of necrotic flesh, purple pools of blood under bruised skin, many naked, their bare feet marbled blue and ivory. Others wore the clothes of their former trade—mechanics, maintenance men, soldiers, highway road crew members—all once human beings.

As Nadjia fired into the mass of undead she watched them close around Bear until she had lost sight of him in their midst. She resisted the urge to aim into the crowd and instead concentrated on the zombies pressed against either side of the bridge walls, lest one of her bullets strike the man she fought with.

As she reloaded she watched many zombies knocked back and tumble to the ground. Bear stalked from their midst. A flare in one hand kept the zombies back. The mace swung in his other as he cleared a path to his assault rifle. He took it up and fired into the horde closest to him. When the magazine was expended he took up the remaining bandolier and crossed the bridge to the front of the Hummer.

He leaned one hand on the hood and caught his breath. Nadjia's steady fire zipped by overhead. Bear sighted down the barrel of the G3 with his good eye and fired, caving in the nose and mouth of a zombie, the bullet punching out the back of its head and into that of one behind it.

He retrieved the Stoner M63 Light Machine Gun from the rusted roof of an old vehicle. A box-contained 150-round belt magazine was affixed. He clambered atop the pile of bodies at its low point and stood with the M63 in both hands, the stock pressed tight to the side of his hip. Bear fired at the wall of zombies pressing in, reaching for him. He sprayed ammunition left to right and back again. The Stoner fired more than seven hundred rounds a minute. Plumes of blood erupted from heads and shoulders. A mist of it filled the air to be battered down by the rain. Dozens of the undead dropped in their tracks.

He took his finger from the trigger when the weapon was empty and dropped off the pile of bodies, hustling back to the car, taking a second box-contained belt of ammunition and affixing it to the M63. Bear moved to his left and scrambled atop the bodies there. The ranks of zombies were looking for him where they had last seen him. They were taken by surprise when he unleashed the Stoner a second time. A hail of 5.56mm lead ripped through their front lines. Zombies crumbled in scores to be stepped on and stepped over by the ones behind. Shell casings streamed out of the light machine gun, lost amid the bodies and blood and rain on the bridge.

The Stoner emptied, Bear lay it down and hopped off the bodies, confronting half a dozen zombies that had gotten around the heap of undead and now came for him. Their mouths cracked, their hands groped. He grasped the first by the sides of its head and jerked violently, tearing the creatures' head from its shoulders. The body dropped and he pitched the head at the next closest zombie, knocking it from its feet.

He brought the mace into play and closed with his foes. A mighty swipe of the ancient weapon permanently dented a skull. He took a step forward and snapped a booted foot into the chest of an undead. The creature lifted from the ground and slammed down on its back. Bear brought the mace down, braining the zombie he had knocked from its feet. He adjusted his aim and split the head of the one he'd kicked in the chest.

A zombie grabbed onto his mace and roared. Bear let the weapon go and punched the creature with all he had. The brunt force trauma killed it where it stood. He looked up to see the undead had scaled the bodies packed one atop the other and started down towards him, some walking gingerly, others tumbling head over heels, regaining their feet when their falls stopped. Bear snatched up his mace and made for the Hummer and Chevy, for Nadjia and the bundle.

Bear grasped the grill and clambered atop the front end of the Hummer, his leg slipping once on the rain slicked hood. He stood and looked down upon the mass. The rain pounded their heads and shoulders. He turned and retrieved one of the two weapons he had placed on the roof of the Hummer earlier that morning. He raised the second Colt Commando and sighted down on the zombies gathered around the hood, pressed against it by their sheer numbers. He fired. A flap of skull lifted off a pig-tailed ghoul. They reached for him with rotting hands. Rings not removed had long ago cut into dead bloated fingers. As long as he stood with his ankles close to the windshield he was out of their reach, and able to fire methodically with deadly accuracy.

By the time he'd burned through a bandolier of ammunition the zombies were heaped around the front of the Hummer waist high, temporarily stalling the ones behind which had to clamber over the fallen. Bear laid down the Commando and retrieved the second weapon from the roof of the SUV—a ten foot long Chinese spear. He stepped to the front of the hood, careful of the rain that made it slick. The zombies in the front rows let out a voracious roar as they saw him step close.

Bear wielded the Ji with both hands and drove the crescent blade through the skulls and heads of the nearest undead. They twitched and dropped and those behind them climbed over the fallen to get speared themselves. The red horsehair tassel hanging where the blade met the shaft soon hardened from all the blood it was immersed in.

Lightning flashed and lit the scene. Nadjia thought Bear looked like a fisherman at sea, harpooning into the waters around his skiff.

As the pile of bodies around the Hummer expanded, he was able to step off the hood of the sports utility vehicle and onto them. They provided a cadaverous scaffolding.

Nadjia sniped on the zombies with the Model 85, perched atop the hulk of another abandoned vehicle. The rain pounded the rusted metal under her. She guarded her and Bear's backs as zombies from the surrounding countryside followed their ears to the battle, stumbling across the bridge behind them every now and then.

Bear lost his grip on the Ji when it lodged in a convulsing zombie's eye socket. The thing disappeared under the feet of the ones behind and around it. He drew the Colt Python and fired it out into the crowd, broke the cylinder, reloaded each individual chamber, snapped the cylinder shut, and fired it out a second time. He holstered the .357 and swung down into the crowd from atop the mound of bodies, clobbering heads with his flanged mace.

He felt something on his boot and looked down. A zombie with the side of its head caved in had latched onto his foot and was gnawing on the blood soaked leather of the boot. He yanked his leg free and brought his foot down with all his might, popping the beasts' skull and grinding it into the dead beneath.

He turned from the myriad undead and dismounted the mound of bodies, moving perpendicularly away from the Hummer across the bridge towards one of the stone walls. A zombie staggered towards him from the pile of undead, its stomach cavity decomposed, gaping at him. Bear punched a leathered hand into its midsection, felt for what he was looking for and yanked two feet of its spine out. The undead's head hunched into its shoulders, its mouth fell open, and the thing dropped like a sack of potatoes. He cracked the next closest zombie over the head with the section of spinal column and it too fell.

He reached the wall. Nadjia's bullets whizzed by overhead. Earlier he had placed a twenty foot pike against the wall, where it met the road, and he picked this up now. He climbed on top of the wall and turned to face the first of the zombies that had managed to ascend their dead. He thrust the pike with both arms, stabbing and spearing, piercing their craniums and destroying them. In time he moved along the wall until he stood parallel with the crush. They gazed and gawked at him with edacious mouths open, hands reaching, the incessant moaning audible above the pounding of the rain. Bear stood atop the wall and speared them until the sky darkened more and his arms grew tired.

There was no more lightning that day.

The purple clouds went completely black and the rain continued. Nadjia approached the vast pile of dead corpses and climbed over it to stand at its peak. The zombies below now had two targets to glare at and motion for. She loosed a stream of fire on them from the flamethrower she wore strapped to her back. Those caught in its flame shrieked and tried to escape but were held in place by the impenetrable barrier of the ones behind. She sent more jets of fire into their midst and they burned where they stood, screeching and twitching, the rain failing to abet their cause.

When the flame thrower emptied, she left it among the dead bodies and scrambled back down to the Hummer where Bear waited. Most of the earlier action had taken place directly in front of the vehicle or on its driver's side. Bear was able to unlock the passenger doors and she clambered, exhausted, into the back seat. Nadjia pulled the door closed behind her and her shoulders slumped. She breathed heavily.

He sat in the front passenger seat. His prodigious frame filled most of the front of the vehicle. He had removed the splatter mask and pulled the coif down. His bald head glistened with sweat. He unlaced and removed the gauntlets from his large gnarled hands.

"Are you alright?"

"Yes," she said.

"Have you been injured?"

"No."

He nodded.

There was a thump and she looked to see an undead pressing itself against the driver's side of the Hummer, open palms splayed over the window. She unholstered her 9mm and placed it in her lap.

She fought back exhaustion and watched Bear in the front seat. He reached into the saddle bags he carried and took out a bottle and a zip-lock bag full of formula. The bottle was filled three quarters of the way with water from a brook they had camped beside the night before. He opened the baggy and retrieved the measuring spoon buried under the formula. He measured meticulously and was careful not to let any of the formula or the bottle come into contact with the vast amounts of gunk and muck clinging to his body and armor. He closed the bottle and capped it, shaking vigorously.

A zombie had gotten on top of the hood. It dropped to its hands and knees and leaned over to look in on them. Bear ignored it as he picked up the swaddled form from the seat. He spoke to the bundle in a gentle voice, cooing. The zombies circling their sanctuary moaned a dirge in the dark. Spent, Nadjia's eyes closed and she fell off to sleep.

Hers was a troubled slumber that night. One filled with memories of a life past and passed, of people and places and times that would never again be, of loving brothers and a kindly father affectionately called *Baba*.

She woke to a boom. For a moment she forgot where she was and was almost happy, but then lightening flashed in the sky and she saw zombies, dozens deep, ringed the car in which they rested. The thunder crashed and she gathered her senses. In the front seat he was already gearing up, securing the coif and gauntlets in place.

She couldn't see much from the back seat of the vehicle with the darkness outside and all the zombies massed about, but she could tell the rain had not abated, though the sky did look somewhat lighter this dawn. The zombie looking in on her had lost everything of its face from the nose down. It stared at her, blinking, its tongue moving in the hole that was once its mouth.

"Pass me the chainsaw," Bear said. "Please?"

Nadjia dug around in the back of the Hummer, among the weapons and crates Bear had placed there the day before, until she found his chainsaw on the floorboards next to her. She handed it up to him and he took it with both hands, gently less he disturb his precious bundle. The white cord of his iPod ear buds poked out from under his coif.

"Please hold the little one." He passed the bundle back to her and she took it with all solemnity.

Noticing movement within the SUV the zombies outside pounded on the hood and sides. Bear affixed the splatter mask and pulled the starter on the chainsaw. Inside the confines of the SUV the rattle was deafening. Bear wasted no time sawing through the roof of the Hummer. A few zombies that had settled there screamed as the saw blade cut through them, pitching them off the vehicle into the crowd beneath. Watery ichor dripped from the roof onto his splatter mask as he worked. Sparks from where the saw met the roof showered the interior of the SUV. Nadjia turned her head and averted her gaze.

When she looked up he had most of the roof off the vehicle, revealing the interior to the outside world. The rain and thunder buffeted them. He stood on the front seats and wielded the chainsaw, shearing through the zombies scaling the hood. Nadjia lay the precious bundle down on the seat next to her and stood, bringing the Colt Commando into play. She fired down into the ranks of zombies on either side of the Hummer.

Bear cleaved a zombie in half. As its upper body slipped off the hood, he cut off the gas to the chainsaw and laid it on the seat. In his ears Ozzy and Sabbath were singing about a man who had traveled time for his species only to be turned to steel.

The lightning flashed. Bear and Nadjia stood, revealed to the aggregation of zombies who let off a massive howl. The fight renewed. He fired out one Glock then the second. The furor and appetite of the undead drove them to their own destruction.

Nadjia emptied the Commando and took up a second identical assault rifle, dropping zombies as he turned around and retrieved a crate of hand grenades. He took them up two at a time, pulling cotter pins, letting the spoons fly, and throwing them overhand as deep into the crowd as he could.

The grenades detonated, their blasts muffled by the multitude of bodies. Each explosion flashed briefly and powerfully, rivaling the lightning in intensity, temporarily opening up a brief gap amidst the horde—a gap that was quickly filled by the press of new bodies. Bear threw the grenades as far as he could. After he had cocked his arm back thirty or more times the crate was emptied.

There were gaps in the throng now that were not being filled as quickly as before. This was cause for optimism in Nadjia's mind.

"I want you to take the child and wait in the truck." Bear indicated the Chevy as he reloaded and holstered the Glocks. "Give me those, please."

She handed him the two freshly loaded Commando assault rifles, which he slung muzzle down in opposite directions over his back. He gathered up three bandoliers of ammunition and shouldered them.

She drew her 9mm and picked up the bundle. Its blankets were somewhat wet from the rain.

Bear left the saddle bags where they were and stepped over the front seat into the back of the Hummer, taking up a flame thrower that laid in the trunk. He slung the three-tank backpack harness over one shoulder and gripped the strap with one leathered hand. He fired it up and doused the zombies that had gathered around the driver's side of the SUV. They dropped and burned and a couple tottered off alight, wailing.

"Go."

She opened the driver's side passenger door and made for the Chevy, stepping over the dead.

As Bear fought his way to the town—flame thrower jetting liquid fire, flares ablaze, the barrels of his assault rifles glowing red, knives buried in the undead—time passed but he was unaware, caught up in his battle against the zombie masses.

The lightning flashed and the thunder rumbled and the clouds above were as equally unforgiving as the day before.

...you can hide in the sun till you see the light. Holy Diver was playing on his iPod.

Nadjia secured Bear's charge in the Chevy and returned to the mound of bodies stacked shoulder high in some parts. She watched her step and mounted it, reaching its apex. The tide of zombies had turned their backs from the bridge and was intent on the cracks and muzzle flashes licking out into the downpour some distance beyond, as Bear moved through them. She shouldered the Commando and fired, bringing zombies down. Dozens then hundreds of them turned to face her, aware of another human behind them, reaching for her. The more agile ones attempted to scale the dead barrier but to no avail. She shot them down where they stood.

Thunder crashed and a sheet of fire burst ahead on the street under the feet of several zombies who wailed and went up like dry kindling, even in this rain. Lightning reached down from the sky in a zigzag pattern. Bear spied a figure on the rooftop of the building across from him—a wild man garmented in rags, hair and beard wiry and frizzed. In each hand he held a Molotov cocktail, which he hurled down upon the undead crowds. The man was screaming at the top of his lungs but Bear could not make out what he said over the rain and thunder and moans.

The closest building to him was a three-story residential which he fought his way towards. He thrust and jabbed with the knives, driving them through faces and the sides of heads. A booker bursting from the mass launched itself forward and latched onto his shoulders. Bear brought the knife in his right hand down through the top of the creature's head. Wide-eyed, the thing dropped from him.

Flames burst ahead on the street as the wild man launched bottle after bottle of gasoline into the hordes.

Bear reached the building and brought a thirteen-inch hatchet hammer up into play. Part hatchet, part hammer, part pry bar, he swung it left and right. The three inch hatchet blade and flat hammer side slayed undead. He plunged the pry bar end through skulls.

The ground-floor windows were all broken out and there was no sign of life from within the building. The door was closed but not boarded up. He tried the handle and found it locked. He stepped back, aware that a ring of zombies closed in on him. He drove a booted foot through the knob and the door flew open, the frame splintering.

The interior was dark. He entered a vestibule with mail boxes, some of which stood open, empty. Addressed envelopes lay scattered about his feet. He turned and looked out at the street. When the lightning flashed he saw the zombies in their multitudes inching towards the building. Above them, on the roof of the building across the street, the wild-man continued to scream, unheard amidst the rain and thunder. He threw chunks of concrete and roofing tiles down onto the zombies below.

Bear turned and moved farther into the building. Ignoring a hallway that led to some apartments, he mounted dust-enshrouded stairs. As he reached the second floor landing, he could hear the first zombies entering below, coming for him. Apparently there were none up here, or if there were they were behind closed doors. He didn't wait around to find out. He continued to the third floor landing and mounted the stairs to the roof.

A door gave way to the roof, which was deserted. Rain water had pooled in spots about the flat tar. The building next to this was two stories in height. Bear didn't have to worry about zombies from that direction. When the lightning came he saw the wild man across the way had disappeared. He also saw none of the roofs appeared to have any zombies on them, which would mean all the undead in the town were below on the street and working their way up the stairwell towards him.

He considered his options. The door to the roof opened up five feet from a thigh-high barrier, beyond which yawned empty air: a three story drop. He stood in the doorway and looked down the stairs. He could hear them but couldn't see them yet. He laid down the hatchet hammer, removed the splatter mask and uncapped a canteen of water, drinking deeply. He poured some more of the water out onto his face, squinting his good eye, shaking his head. The rain fell around him.

…what you gonna be, what you gonna be brother, Zero the hero…

Nadjia fired out all the ammunition for her Commando and returned to the Chevy for another bandolier. She couldn't hear Bear firing anymore but figured things had moved to hand to hand combat. She remounted the wall of dead and found the zombies still waiting for her below. In another set of circumstances she could have felt pity for them, but they had taken so much from her. They had taken everything that had ever meant anything to her. In place of sympathy she felt a form of apathy—curiously detached as she sighted and fired, felling them in scads.

When she'd fired out the ammunition for the M16 A2 she tossed the weapon aside and picked up the nozzle for the M2 flamethrower she'd lugged onto the mountain with her. She worked the igniter trigger on the front grip and the firing trigger on the rear grip. The nitrogen propellant spit a stream of flaming petrol a hundred feet deep into the crowd at the rate of a half gallon per second. The zombies were cremated where they stood. Torched and shrieking, some pitched from the bridge to burn alongside the banks of the river below. Others squirmed around in the conflagration, melted lumps of undead flesh dropping off their bodies.

When the flamethrower was tapped out Nadjia kicked the tank backpack away from her, down the mound of undead bodies, and drew one of the 9mms she wore. She fired down into the zombies and emptied the clip. They gawked up at her, mouths agape, until each caught a round in the skull and collapsed. After she'd gone through all the magazines for the pistol she holstered it and turned, intent on the truck, but the bodies beneath her shifted and she lost her footing, slipping. She fell onto her hip and sliding down the undead towards the Chevy, aware of a previously unseen zombie barring her path.

She scrambled to her feet and stood face to chest with the largest beast she'd yet encountered. She decided it must have been a football player or Samoan wrestler in life. It was well over six and a half feet tall and nearly half of that across. The zombie growled and clasped her shoulders with two massive hands, pulling her towards it. Its mouth cracked open revealing rotted, jagged teeth and a hot breath stinking of the grave. Its hair was a frizzy afro encrusted with dirt and brambles.

Her instincts fought her impulse to pull away from the beast. Instead she wrapped her legs around it under the shoulders, torquing her body, her weight and momentum enough that the scissor sweep dragged the clumsy creature forward off its own feet, pitching it down face first. Before it could crash on top of her she rolled to the side. The monster landed inches away. One of her gloved hands went to its quivering throat, holding its masticating jaws back from her person. Her other hand went to her lower back, returning wrapped around a Benchmade 175 CBK backup blade. She drove the dagger-style blade through the creatures face repeatedly, plunging it rapid-fire into the thing's eye sockets and cheeks until it ceased moving.

She turned over and another thing was on her, flinging itself from the pile of the dead. Ghastly and grievously injured, its lower legs had been blasted off. Its champing jaws went right for her face guard, but she gripped it by the wrists. Dropping the benchmade knife, she swung her torso around, planted the soles of her feet in the crooks of its elbows and pushed it back, controlling the creature's spastic paroxysms from a spider guard position. She waited for her opening and let go with one hand, her balled fist cracking it above the ear. The stunned creature collapsed. It lay struggling atop the mound of bodies. Not taking any chances, she retrieved the CBK blade and thrust it repeatedly through the thing's head.

She turned over and got to her feet. Another zombie staggered her way from several yards distant. Nadjia shook herself off and met it in the rain, stabbing the CBK's beveled blade through the skull case at the temple.

...why do you have to die to be a hero? Rob Halford was singing. *It's a shame a legend begins as its end...*

When the first zombies reached the bottom of the stairs and spotted Bear, lightning backlit the gargantuan man. They hissed and moaned with desire and proceeded up the stairs towards him. He affixed the splatter mask and waited until the lead zombie reached the top of the stairs. He cracked it over the head with the hatchet hammer and yanked it forward before it could drop in the doorway, thrusting it out over the roof's wall, into the void.

The undead moved sluggishly and, one by one as they cleared the doorway, he battered them about their skulls and pushed them from the roof. He worked like this for some time while the lighting flashed, thunder boomed as if the storm were directly overhead. A mound of bodies piled up three stories below. And the zombies continued to come, packing themselves into the landings and stairwells. Their bodies were pressed so tightly together movement became impossible at times for several of them. The ones in the forefront found their craniums fractured and were launched into free fall.

The building now thronged with undead, Bear yanked the pin out of a thermite grenade and tossed it down the stairs. He turned his back and walked towards the roof's lip where it adjoined the next building. The detonation immolated untold numbers of zombies on the third floor. The flames caught and spread fast amidst the tight-pressed bodies and walls, creating a nascent inferno. There were muffled wails from within the apartments as Bear hang-dropped to the roof of the two story building next door. He kicked the roof door in and walked down two flights of stairs to the front door which opened out onto the street.

Zombies massed there turned and confronted him. He clobbered the closest one over the head, then returned to the roof of this building, waiting as they poured in from the street in scores. Patiently he drummed the hatchet hammer into the palm of one hand. The building next door was engulfed in flames which would soon spread to this one. He watched water drip from the lip of the doorway and listened to the rain about him. Quiet Riot covering Slade implored him to *cum on feel the noize*. Again, when the zombies reached the roof of this building he drubbed them over the head and flung them below.

There was a series of bright explosions from up the street, back in the direction of the bridge. He knew Nadjia had reloaded the M202A1 and unleashed its hell on the crowds of undead.

With a splintering crash the roof of the burning building next to him collapsed inwards. Bear took this as a signal to hurl another thermite grenade into the building on which he stood. As the zombies burned, flames lighting up the dark, fire battling rain and darkness for dominance, he knocked out the glass of a window in the next building and repeated the process of luring the undead into it then immolating them in droves.

Nadjia spent a second night in the Chevy. Bear locked himself on the roof of a building the next block over. He sat in the rain. An entire block burned as he rested. In the morning when he woke, the rain had quenched the flames and was gone.

Superstructural steel beams reached towards the sky. Bear looked down into a street teeming with zombies. There were significantly fewer this morning. The sky yawned grey overhead.

He considered enticing them into this building and destroying them much like the ones from the previous day but decided against it. Instead he met them on the street in battle and dispatched them with hatchet hammer, knives, and his hands.

Nadjia had reloaded all her magazines and weapons and stood on the mountain of dead. In the distance she saw Bear cutting a deadly swath among those that remained. She joined the fray with the M-85, sniping on the zombies from afar. The rifle fire was clear and piercing with the storm passed over, and a number of zombies turned and started towards her. She racked the bolt and fired and reloaded and fired until she was out of ammunition.

She hefted the twenty-six pound M202A1 to her right shoulder and fired out four M74 rockets in quick succession. As hordes of zombies melted where they stood, she reloaded the incendiary launcher with the last four-rocket clip. She fired these final rockets into the crowds of zombies on the main street, cutting through the town, then laid the launcher on the mounds of undead atop which she perched.

She drew her pistols and climbed down, striding over the cadavers and adding to their number as she closed with zombies, firing only when she could not miss. She stayed clear of the areas where the M235 warheads had detonated. Circles of melted flesh and asphalt from the road bubbled as the thickened pyrotechnic agent burned. The stink of it was noxious, poisonous.

Many of the buildings in the town evidenced structural damage, having fallen into decay given time and disrepair. Some were boarded up. Bear had torched an entire block. Stores and buildings were charred and gutted.

Eventually she met Bear in the street and he nodded his splatter-masked head to her. She wondered how many zombies had perished in the burnt down block of buildings and stores. She passed him a Commando and shouldered her own. They stood back to back and fired out bandoliers of ammunition until the zombies had dwindled. Human survivors from the town joined them on the street.

The rag-clad man from the roofs reached them first. He ran down the road to where Bear and Nadjia stood, passing a few undead stragglers late to the slaughter. He gripped a gore-spattered club. Zombies reached for him and groaned but he avoided their arms and came to an abrupt halt before Bear, his club held loosely.

Nadjia had a 9mm by her side.

The man stared at Bear in awe, as if in recognition of something beyond words. Bear looked at him, past the rags clinging to his wasted frame, beyond the mane of dirty white hair, into the eyes burning with lunacy and revelation that signaled a deeper verisimilitude only hinted at. Some measure of clarity in their derangement. He recognized something within those eyes, and went back to thumbing shells into magazines.

There was a scream from up the street. A group of survivors, little more than skeletons themselves, had emerged from a building and fought three zombies with hammers and screwdrivers. One of them, a man, had been bitten on the shoulder and lay in the street.

Nadjia and Bear, trailed by the wild man, walked to them, skirting around and over corpses. The wounded man lay bleeding out atop zombie bodies. There was no clear part of the street to rest him on. The others stood around him with no clue what to do. They were panting and one looked semi-catonic. Nadjia eyed these newcomers warily. Bear stood over the wounded man as he removed his splatter mask, looking down on him as the guy gurgled and died.

Before he could turn into a zombie, Bear fired a single round from the Commando through his brain.

Nadjia stared at the survivors and they at her. Everyone was quiet for some time. Soon thereafter, Bear stepped over and through the dead with the enfolded child clutched to his chest, the mace in his right hand dripping blood, saddle bags slung over his broad shoulders. He wound his way through the carnage as survivors in the town came in their twos and threes. Nadjia waited for them on the road.

He worked his way down to the stream and set the saddle bags by the water and gently lay his precious bundle upon them. He set the mace head-up in the mud next to him and placed one of the two Glocks within easy reach of the saddle bags, next to the swaddled form.

Pulling the coif from his heads and neck revealed his bare scalp. He removed the ear buds. After unlacing his gauntlets, he removed the protective wear and lay them next to him with the coif. The chain mail was taken off next, exposing a dark t-shirt soaked through black with sweat, clinging to the muscles of his chest and shoulders. He took off the t-shirt and soaked it in the stream, wringing the sweat and stink from it several times. He immersed the t-shirt again and wringed it out over his head, rivulets of fresh water running down his bald dome and hirsute, tattooed back. He pressed the t-shirt to his forehead and breathed deeply, sighing, closing his eyes.

His reverie was broken by a low groan nearby. A horrendous apparition staggered his way from downriver, flesh rotted from its torso, the bone of one leg showing through. It moved slowly with steady determination, reaching out to him with one grime encrusted hand. The other arm bent backwards, broken at the elbow.

Bear retrieved the Glock and stood, walking towards the fiend, extending the 9mm and targeting the zombie with the green laser sight, firing once. The beast keeled over onto its side, motionless, half in and half out of the stream. He approached it and prodded it with his boot. A good chunk of its head had come off and floated away. Looking across the water, he spotted a handful of undead gathering there, none daring to cross the watercourse, motioning and groaning. No threat to him or Nadjia or anyone on this side of the river at this point. He reached down and gripped the zombie by its ankle, dragging its carcass from the water, letting it lie unceremoniously a few feet from the stream.

Bear returned to the saddle bags and his equipment and checked the bundle. Satisfied, he returned to his ablutions.

Fifteen or twenty people had emerged from the town and formed a circle around Nadjia. They were disheveled and emaciated—faces marked by sunken eyes and pronounced cheekbones. Their clothes hung off them and their skin was sallow. Some were yellow-eyed. The men all wore beards of varying lengths.

"…and he wrestled a lion, tearing it limb from limb," the wildman spoke as if not to himself but to an audience, though these men and women largely ignored him. "This son of Manoah on the road to Timnah…"

She sat on a crate among them, her weapons holstered but within easy reach. From her seat she could see Bear squatting beside the stream that passed under the bridge. She looked upon a consumptive woman with ratty hair, two grubby children clinging to either side of her.

"How many of you are there?"

At first no one spoke, as if they had forgotten how. Then a wasted man with brown hair and eyes deep in dark sockets spoke up.

"All of these people here are more than I knew about. We were separated…holed up in different places."

"There were sixteen with me," a jaundiced man said. "Plague killed all of them. Except me. That was early on."

"…and in the valley of flame the mighty red warrior came upon Moon Boy, he of the Small-Folk," said the wild-man, "and together they withstood the onslaughts of the invaders from the sky and their *damned* zoological ministrations…"

"Who is he?" a woman with several teeth missing asked Nadjia, pointing to Bear.

"I don't really know." Bear knelt down by the stream, with the enormous expanse of his back to them. He was a preternatural monstrosity in his own right. "He found me a few months ago. I've fought with him since."

They stared at her, these haggard and pallid faces.

"He's called Bear."

"This is what you do?" another in the crowd asked incredulously.

"Yes."

"…and with nothing more than the jaw bone of an ass this son of Manoah did slay an army of Philistines from Askhelon, and they fell before him in trepidation and disquiet, for his was the wrath of the Lord visited upon them…"

"Incredible."

"Just the two of you?"

Nadjia looked at the man who had asked. "There were more of us…once."

"My wife is back in one of the buildings," a high-voiced man spoke up. "She's too weak to move. Do you have food?"

"How about cigarettes?"

"Toilet paper? God please let them have some toilet paper…"

"How long have you been here?" Nadjia asked.

"Since the beginning," the dark eyed man who had spoken first answered.

The wild-man spoke. "He is in the world and he is of the world, yes, but he is with the world, as are we all. He is a creator and maker of a world, and a destroyer, as are we…"

"Who are you?" Nadjia said.

The rag-clad man looked at her askance and replied, "And he who dared to trick Zeus at Sicyon was chained to a rook in the Caucasus, his liver eaten daily by an eagle, ever awaiting Heracles to free him from his beshaklement…"

Nadjia looked away. "Okay."

"He's touched," a woman offered, not unkind, pointing at her own head with a forefinger.

"He's insane," the dark-eyed man answered matter-of-factly, judgment absent from his voice. "A little worse than some of us, a lot worse than most of us."

"In other words, he's fucking nuts," the yellow-skinned man's voice was bitter as he spoke, his contempt obvious. "We should have done him and ourselves a favor and put him out of his misery a long time ago."

"How long have you been holed up in this town?" Nadjia inquired of the man.

"How long?" He thought it over. "What does time mean anymore?" He threw his hands up. "Here we are."

"It's hard…hard to remember," offered the dark-eyed man. "It can't be forever, but it feels like it."

"There were millions of them in the streets," a woman said.

"Last winter was so cold."

Nadjia couldn't tell if the cadaverous person who spoke was man or woman.

"…seemed like millions."

"What's your name?" She asked the dark-eyed man.

"Kevin."

"Kevin, listen to me. You and your people—"

The jaundiced man interrupted her. "He doesn't speak for all of us lady."

"We didn't come here to argue. All of you need to listen to me. You've got to destroy these bodies. All of them. Figure out a way to burn them and start to do it now."

"Hey lady. Thanks for saving us and all. Don't take this the fucking wrong way, but who are you to start telling us what to do?"

She ignored the yellow man but shifted her position on the crate so the 9mm on her hip was within easier reach.

"There will be more of these things. You're all going to have to be ready for them when they show up."

"Do you have any food?" the woman with the two children asked.

"…only three men could wear the armor intended for this son of Thetis, his beloved Patroclus, his nemesis, Hektor—betrayed by the god in the guise of his fallen brother—and the great runner himself…"

"We have some we'll share with you, back on our truck." Nadjia motioned with her head over her shoulder towards the bridge. Their view was blocked by the bodies stacked higher than a tall man. "You have to organize yourselves. Some of you help unload the supplies and carry them back into town. Others need to dispose of…" She nodded towards the crumpled figures of the putrid dead.

The wild man ran off down the street, hopping from piles of bodies to piles of bodies, screaming, "Secure the gate! He has come. He is upon us! He has outrun the torrents of Scamander…"

"So this is what you two do?" an older man inquired.

"Yes."

"You travel from town to town and city to city killing zombies?"

"Yes."

"And how many cities have you cleared so far?"

Nadjia thought about it. "A few. Our work is just beginning."

"You gotta be shitting me," said the bitter yellowed man. "You don't really think you're gonna kill off *all* these fuckers, do you?"

She looked down at her feet. When she looked up she asked, "What's the alternative?"

"You're crazy. Just as fucking nuts as the windbag over there."

Nadjia gestured towards the river. "I follow him."

"Well, then, he's fucking crazy too."

The wild man had rejoined the group and he was mumbling "the jester leaps across the tightrope walker and alighting on the wire beyond he goes unrecognized for what he is amongst the citizenry of Mad Cow…"

"You, him," Kevin spoke. "You can't destroy them all."

"He doesn't fight because he thinks we can win," Nadjia said.

"Then why?" demanded the bitter man.

"He fights because they're zombies."

"One must imagine Sissyphus happy," offered the wild man.

Kevin thought about what Nadjia had said.

"…and so White-Hairs and Stone-Hand joined the Devil Beast in defense of the Kirby universe…"

"Enough of this bullshit." The yellow skinned man glared at the wild man. "The world ends and this fucker lives through it? If we're going to rebuild, we *aren't* doing it with his kind."

"What are you talking about?" someone asked.

"You know what I'm talking about." The man started scanning the ground for a suitable weapon. "He doesn't have to be here for the second act. He'll just slow us down."

"No one touches that man."

All eyes were drawn to the outside of the circle. Bear loomed there, his abs thick slabs, the muscles of his pecs and shoulders like lumps of clay slapped together by a drunken artist. The saddle bags rested on the road next to his feet. In the crook of one massive arm rested the swaddled bundle. His other arm hung at his side, mace in his hand. The circle opened. People stepped gingerly from him, but he did not move.

"...and from his mountain the god looked and saw two stand against many, the Cimmerian and the archer against the riders of Doom, and indeed he was pleased..."

"Listen to him," the jaundiced man said to Bear, indicating the wild one. "I've had to for the past god knows how many fucking months. Is that a baby you've got with you? For Christ's sake..."

He walked over to Bear to get a better look at the bundle. When he had done so he looked into Bear's face, the dead eye and the live one. He was too foolish to heed what the good one revealed.

"You *are* fucking crazy," he said and turned his back on him, his yellowed-eyes squinting at the wild man. "And you..." He spied a large flat rock several yards away and went to retrieve it. "Gonna take care of this shit right fucking now."

He bent to take it up and stood, turning. Bear was upon him, his speed belying his massive size. The mace came down once, the blow breaking the arm the man raised to shield himself, then continuing unabated on its deadly trajectory to impact his skull. The yellowed body collapsed lifeless to the mud and muck.

Bear stood with the bundle in his arm and the mace at his side. Nadjia had risen and one hand hovered over the 9mm, but none of the townsfolk appeared a threat. Their hollowed eyes reflected apathy and, in some, hope.

"We'll rest two or three days here," said Nadjia, "then we will leave. Any of you who wish are free to join us, but you need to know the only thing on the road ahead of us is more of...this." She gestured with an open palm to the carpet of corpses littered in varying displays of grotesquery.

"...and Emmanuel Santana left the monster in the sky, sitting on top of the world, the general alone..."

The evening crept into the sky and the night was lit by tremendous pyres. Dozens of fires ate the dead. Thick black smoking coils of cremated meat merged with the dark above and around. Everywhere the stink of singed dead flesh loomed. The men and women strong enough worked through the afternoon and night, their faces covered with rags against the noxious fumes as they disposed of the pestilential corpses.

Kevin crossed the street, stepping clear of the puddles of gore and rain that had pooled, his path lit by the flames. He pulled the jacket he wore closer about him, shivering in the cool autumn night. He entered a darkened building and walked up two flights of stairs to the door of an apartment of rooms Bear and Nadjia had selected. He stood in front of the door and paused, considering, then knocked, not too loud. Perhaps they were asleep. He did not want to waken them, nor was he completely sure he wanted to discuss what he had come to talk about.

Nadjia opened the door, backlit from a glow somewhere within the suite of rooms. She had the riot suit off and her hair down and she was the most beautiful woman Kevin had ever seen. The curves of her physique through the jeans and sweater she wore stirred something within him that he had not felt in a long time, something he'd given up on ever feeling again. Then he noticed the pistol in her left hand down at her side.

"Kevin."

"Nadjia."

"Is everything okay?"

"Y-Yes…"

Her eyes scanned the murk of the hallway and stairwell behind him.

"Come on in."

She stepped aside and let him into the apartment. A kerosene lamp burned in one corner where her sleeping bag was laid out. He noted what looked like a prayer mat rolled up next to the sleeping bag.

"Sit down." She nodded to the floor. The apartment was bare. It had been stripped of furniture and anything that might burn long ago by people desperate for fuel in the winter. Most of the windows lacked glass and the cool night air whispered in. The sounds of men and women laboring outside on the street were faint.

They sat across from one another—the darkness of a room behind Nadjia, a cold wall against Kevin's back.

"Is it me," Kevin hunkered down further into his jacket, "or is it really cold in here?"

"It's a beautiful fall night. But you've got no fat on you. So you're going to feel the cold more than me."

"Yeah, no fat on me," Kevin agreed. "My damn feet hurt when I walk. The fat on the pads is all worn away."

"You are Moslem?" He pointed towards the prayer mat.

"Lapsed, but trying."

Kevin nodded.

"And him?" He indicated the darkness behind Nadjia, aware of Bear's presence somewhere in the rooms.

"I think he prays," she said, "or at least he tries. But I don't think his god is mine."

He nodded.

They were quiet for awhile. In the silence his eyes adjusted to the dark enough to discern the immense form of Bear in the room beyond, seated as he was against a wall. It looked like he was cradling something in his arms. Kevin thought he knew what it was. He became aware of the presence of another in the apartment with them and guessed it would be the wild-man, somewhere near Bear, oddly quiet in the presence of the giant.

"What brought you here to us?"

He scoffed in a not-unfriendly way. "I could ask the same of you."

She did not reply.

"Nadjia" He liked the sound of her name as it left her mouth. "Well, first, *thank you*. Thank you both. I don't know how much longer we could have held out."

"We were too late for too many. I looked around this town earlier. There are several too weak to move. They probably will not survive, even now."

"When we heard you out there, we thought it was an army at first. We felt hope. I can't imagine the two of you against, against…"

"This was bad but we've faced worse. Philly was a lot worse."

Kevin realized he was staring into her dark eyes and felt self-conscious about it, so he broke his gaze and looked down.

"You'll—you'll have to forgive me," he stammered. "I'm half-starved and out of my mind. You look like some kind of angel sitting there. You're so beautiful."

It was Nadjia's turn to scoff good naturedly. "Well, thank you. But like you said, you're half starved and maybe a little out of your mind by this point. Plus I'm probably the first woman you've seen in awhile who's had a bath in the past month and *isn't* malnourished."

He made eye contact again and smiled.

"Listen, I was thinking of a couple of things," he continued. "You know what you guys need?"

"What would that be?"

"A monster truck. You know, one of those with the huge wheels. You could drive right over all those..." He tried to think of a word to describe the mounds of undead burning outside but couldn't. "I mean, that road is going to be impassable."

"I like the idea but we haven't come across many monster trucks lately. Would you happen to know where we could find one?"

"As a matter of fact, *yeah*. Obviously no one's driven it for a long, long time, so the battery's dead and the tires are probably—"

"Can you show it to me tomorrow? I know a little about cars and trucks."

"No kidding?"

"My father owned a fleet of taxis and limousines. He did most of the maintenance work himself until he made enough money to pay other people to do it for him. He raised my brothers and me to be comfortable around automobiles."

"That's good. That's *great*. I don't even know how to change my oil. Not that I have a car anymore. I mean, I guess I do, if it's still there but... Sorry, I'm rambling. You're the first...you're one of the first people I've talked to in a long time."

"Kevin, listen to me. I know it was bad here. I've seen this before. But now it's going to be better. It's up to you and everyone else here to work together to make it better."

"Yeah, I...that's the other reason I came here. I don't want to stay here anymore."

She nodded. "Where do you want to go?"

"Well, I...don't laugh, I mean, I know I'm as thin as a stick right now and look like something the wind could knock over, but..."

Nadjia waited.

"...but I wanted to go with you, and with him." He nodded into the darkness.

She sat quietly across from him for awhile, then said, "If you come with us, do you understand what you'll face? If you stay here, you might have a shot at something—I don't know—something more *normal*, more like the old life you knew. If you come with us…"

"They destroyed my life, my wife and my kids." He looked out the window into the night as he spoke. "They destroyed my family, my friends, everything. And I want to destroy them. I want to destroy them all."

She smiled at him. Her beauty in the glow of the kerosene lamp brought him back to the room.

"Revenge isn't enough. These things can't understand your vengeance. They don't care. They wait and eat and that's all they do, and they won't stop until every single one of us is gone. Unless we destroy every single one of them."

"I understand that."

"Understanding…that isn't enough. You can't run on revenge for ever. That fuel will run out. I know." She looked away. "What we do…this isn't…I have a few more fights left in me, but that's it. Then I have to stop or this will kill me. When you do this, it changes you. I can't explain how, but it saps you of your humanity. Does that make any sense?"

"What about him?" Kevin chin-nodded into the dark.

"Bear…" Nadjia considered for a moment. "Bear will never give up."

"Then I will fight with him."

"Kevin, I do what I do because it seems like the right thing to do. This is a war. You know the term *Jihad*? Yes? I never under-stood that word until…But now that's how I see this. I will fight for as long as I can, but I know my fight can't continue forever. There are so many of them, Kevin, so many."

"Nadjia, I'm not religious. I have no god. But you and him—you kill zombies. So I'll stand with you."

"You need to think this through," she counseled. "Get a few good meals in you and think it over. We'll stay through the day after tomorrow, and by then if you still want to accompany us, I'll brook no dissent."

After awhile he rose.

"I have to go. Earlier tonight, one of the survivors…one of us got bitten."

Bear's voice came from the dark of the room beyond. "What happened?"

"We were dragging bodies off to the fire...Robert... One of the zombies wasn't dead. It latched on and bit him on his side before we...before we could destroy it."

"Is he still alive?"

"Yeah, but he's bad. He won't last the night. I have to go and...and be with him."

"How well do you know this man?" Bear stood in the room with them, the floor creaking under him. Kevin saw he was correct: Bear rocked the bundle in his arms. The man had removed the armor from his upper body, arms, and head. He was monstrous.

"Robert? I don't. I mean, we were locked up in separate buildings during the siege. He's got no one. All his family are... Well, he's alone now."

"I'll go to him. Where is he?"

Kevin looked to Nadjia but her face gave no indication of the course he should choose.

"There's a hardware store across the street. Upstairs is an apartment. He's there."

"Nadjia, please, the child sleeps." Bear passed the form to the woman. He disappeared again into the darkened room and when he returned he hefted the saddle bags, mace in one hand. In the glow from the lamp Kevin noticed he had a tear drop tattooed under one eye.

"You should get some rest, Kevin," said Bear. "The days ahead of us are long."

He left the apartment, the wild-man trailing behind him silently like a gangling shadow. Kevin and Nadjia sat and listened to them in the hallway, the stairs groaning under their feet.

"What's the story with that guy?" Nadjia referred to the wild man.

"I don't really know," admitted Kevin. "He was always a bit *off* from when I met him. I think someone said he was a college professor. Political Theory or Philosophy. Something like that. I tried to keep an eye out for him, but he was so bizarre. A few months back he went completely off the deep end. They found him playing with his own feces, smearing the walls. They threw him out of where we were holed-up. Somehow he survived. I don't know how. What's the story with Bear?"

Nadjia indicated his iPod on the floor nearby.

"Pick that up. Listen to it."

He hadn't seen one in awhile. He palmed it and touched the pad with his thumb but nothing happened.

"It's dead. No battery."

Nadjia nodded. "Bear's been listening to that thing the whole time I've known him. And the whole time I've known him, that thing has had no battery."

Kevin looked at the blank screen of the iPod.

"You still sure about what you're doing?" she asked.

"I am."

"Then you're with us now," said Nadjia. "If you wish you can sleep here tonight."

"He won't mind?"

"That was his blessing, so to speak. In the other room you'll find some sleeping bags and blankets. I'll wait here for his return."

That night Kevin slept well for the first time in a long, long while.

When he opened his eyes, Robert was cold and aware that he had shit himself again, but somehow wasn't as bothered as he would have been at another time. The room was dark but the dark was not unfriendly. He realized he was not alone in the room. These others bore him no ill will. For this he was glad and felt somewhat comforted.

"It's you."

In the ambient light cast from the fires outside he recognized the mountain of a man who sat on the room's only chair.

"Hello, Robert."

"And him."

Behind the man in the shadow stood the wild-man.

"Does his presence here disturb you?"

"No. Actually, it doesn't. It never did."

Robert remembered his circumstances then: the wound to his side bandaged but incapable of mending, the stained mattress under him, the musty old comforter tucked over his body against the chill night air.

"I'm glad it's you," he said to Bear.

"Do you mind if I smoke?" asked Bear. "Weed I mean."

Robert smirked, not sure if the men could see it. "Only if I can have some."

Bear retrieved his rolling papers and a zip-lock bag of marijuana from the saddle bags. He flattened a paper on his thigh and crumbled a bud onto it, picking out the stems. He folded the paper in half and tucked one end into the other, rolling tightly with his index fingers, drawing his tongue across the joint when he had it sealed to his satisfaction. He took a book of matches from the saddle bags and lit one. In the sulfur glow Robert watched the man squint his good eye and puff, getting the joint going.

Bear inhaled deeply and held it, then exhaled with a sigh. He stood and handed the joint to Robert. While he toked Bear moved the chair closer to the mattress and sat back down. Robert felt safer with the man looming above him.

"I never thought it'd come to this," Robert said. "I don't mean, *this*, *me*, here, now. I mean, the world, like *this*. I mean, who could have, right? Then you guys came today, and, well, you know what I felt? Something I haven't felt in I don't know how long. *Hope*."

He pulled on the joint and handed it back over to Bear.

"I think what's bothered me the most about this whole experience is how it's brought out the worst in everybody. I mean, Weston, in the street today. Weston is the man who was going to kill…" He looked beyond Bear to the dark where the wild-man stood.

"What you did to Weston—I *get* it. It *had* to be done. What right did he have to try and kill that man? Right? So these last few hours I felt hope. Something I haven't felt in god knows how long. Thank you for that."

"You're welcome," Bear said, passing the joint over to Robert. "But I need you to understand. Weston? He didn't have to die. He died because I chose to kill him. His death is on my hands. I'm accountable. But I can live with that.

"And you know what, Robert? This world has brought out the worst in many, but it's also brought out the best in others."

"It doesn't seem that way sometimes."

"That's because the actions of one bad man often seem to outweigh the good deeds of all the rest. The bad is an aberration from the norm. It draws our attention. Similar situation before all this, if you ask me."

They passed the joint back and forth between them.

"Do you think there's hope for us?" Robert asked. "For humanity, I mean."

"There's always hope. We're conditioned beings, not determined. I fight to bring about a vision—a dream I guess you'd call it."

"Tell me about it, please."

"We have to remake the earth. In place of the greed and competition that marked our former lives, we have to celebrate and cherish the ties that bind us one to the other. We have to work together *for* each other. We have to realize that the individual is nothing without...without the social, without the group. That what makes the individual special and recognizable only comes about—is only possible—through the communal, through the social." He paused. "I know we're high, but I'm serious about this."

"I know you are."

"We have to start to care for each other, Robert, really *care* for one another. Create institutions and systems, political systems, that reflect this."

"I like that vision. Too bad I won't be around to see it."

The pain in his side welled up and Robert gasped, losing his breath. Bear reached over and laid a palm on his forehead. He got off the chair and sat down beside the mattress, his back against the wall.

"There's no rhyme or reason is there?" Robert asked when he finally could.

"We make the rhyme. We provide the reasons."

"Will this..." He tapped the joint and sent the blackened ashes floating to the mattress, "...will this be legal in your future society?"

"*Our* future society," corrected Bear. "And I'd think so, yeah."

He giggled, forgetting his situation momentarily. Then it came back to him in its entirety.

"I'm glad...glad it's you here with me to...to see me through this."

Bear didn't say anything.

"Could you roll another one of those?"

"Sure thing." Bear smiled.

"You were very quiet outside."

"I'm changing," said Bear. "It's tough sometimes. I feel different here with you. Calm. Peaceful. I don't always feel that way around other people. Here you go."

Robert inhaled.

"Why don't you tell me about yourself, Robert. Start at the beginning. Tell me who you were, where you were born, what your life was like."

They sat next to each other and talked well into the night. Robert spoke of his dreams and his person and as he faded his eyes grew too weary to keep open, so he closed them and drifted off. In the middle of the night he passed. When he turned Bear finished it with a hammer, the wild-man standing silent witness throughout.

EXODUS

The tunnel was dark and damp and echoed as unseen water dripped from pipes overhead. There was something more sinister, some presence in the shadow behind. Something pursuing, closing in on him. He ran, fear gripping him, a panic unlike any other, and as he ran he could hear it coming for him, splashing through the water. The orange lights overhead flickered, dimmed, and disappeared. He stumbled along in the dark with his hands raised in front of his face. Some rational part of him told him to stay near the wall. That if he followed the curvature it would keep him from pitching into the mire and dank of the water channel. When the thing called his name from the blackness he panicked anew, racing headlong through the slippery murk.

He bounced off a wall and rebounded, landing on his backside in the water, immediately soaked through. He scrambled to his feet and found the wall and moved as fast as he could, open palms skimming its surface for a guide. The wall curved under his hands and as the tunnel turned in the dark he saw shafts of light some distance ahead. He shuddered as the thing behind him spoke his name in a low growl much too close. He made for the motes of dust swirling in the shafts of daylight—the only illumination in this infernal blackness. There was a ladder and if he could only reach it… But he could feel the thing's hot breath on him, and he knew to turn and fight was useless. That this chase and battle were ones that would pursue him for the remainder of his days.

Buddy.

The cold steel of the ladder was under his hands and he rushed up it. Losing his footing he hung for a moment, his lower body swinging like a pendulum in the abyss. His feet scrabbled and found a wrung and he was up, hand over hand and foot over foot, leaving the echoes of the water below, leaving the thing in the dark. He reached the top of the ladder. The streams of light poured down from perforations in a manhole cover. As he put his shoulder to it he looked down and the thing was there, standing just outside the light, beckoning to him, *speaking his name, a hideous trophy swinging in its grip while it called him down to his fate.*

Buddy.

He pushed with his shoulder and the side of his neck. A mighty heave and the manhole cover was clear, but they were on him in their dozens—little arms and hands grasping him, muted faces staring at him, and perhaps most horrifying of all there was no emotion on the faces of these children who sought to drag him up onto the street. He shrugged them off and pulled back and lost his footing, slipping from the ladder, plunging backwards into the dark, falling, reaching for the shafts of light. The thing below scoffed and shuffled in anticipation, and it was laughing. It was waiting—

"Buddy—"

He woke to arms shaking him violently and he reacted. Instinct. His large hands wrapped around the neck of the man crouched over him, pushing him back and squeezing, crushing—

"Buddy!"

Another man latched onto his wrists, trying to pry them from the first man's neck. In that instant Buddy realized he was choking Mickey and it was Bear who loomed above him in the wintry night, forcing open his hands. The fight went out of him. Mickey fell back gasping and coughing.

"Oh Christ—oh Christ—oh Christ."

He scrambled back away from his sleeping bag and away from the fire around which the five rested that night. Julie and Gwen had been roused from their sleep by the struggle and sat staring wide-eyed in their sleeping bags, not comprehending. Julie had one hand wrapped around the out-sized .357, the other around her .380.

Bear crouched next to Mickey, speaking to him and rubbing his back, and Mickey coughed a few more times, shaking his head.

"Mickey, Mickey, listen, oh Christ man, I'm sorry, I—" He didn't know what to say but he needed to say something.

The moon was full in the sky and their camp in the clearing was well lit. Around them was snow and pine trees and off to the left the train tracks and the sluggish, icy river.

"I'm okay, I'm alright." Mickey said to Bear. Bear looked up from him to Buddy and stared at the latter, thinking.

"What happened?" asked Julie.

"Nothing, it's okay." Gwen assured the pregnant woman, closing one of her hands over the hand Julie gripped the Colt Python in, pushing it down, then doing the same thing for the Taurus .380 she held in the other.

"I was dreaming. They were coming for me…" Buddy was sitting up and pulling on his boots.

"You were whimpering in your sleep." Mickey's voice was hoarse. "I tried to wake you."

"God, I'm so sorry, I'm—"

"Okay, Buddy. It's okay." Mickey sounded like a frog, "I know you didn't mean it."

Buddy paced around the fire. "I…I…"

"I get it. It's okay. I know it won't happen again."

"I swear, I'd—no, you're right, it *won't* happen again. It's *me* man. I'm sorry."

Mickey nodded. Bear continued to crouch next to him, eyeing Buddy.

Why's the big guy eye-fucking you, Jig?

"Oh shut up," Buddy muttered a little too loud, aware that he was answering a voice only he heard. He shook his head and said, "Nothing, never mind," to the group then walked off into the dark away from them and the fire. He silently cursed himself.

When he had his head straight he went back to the others. They were all sitting around the fire but no one was speaking. He knew they must have talked about him, about what had happened. Somewhere in the back of his mind a venomous voice assured him he was right.

"You okay Mickey?" asked Julie.

"Yeah, yeah, I just need a minute," He stood and walked off in the opposite direction Buddy had come from, taking his assault shotgun with him. It was a USAS-12 auto-shotgun, though he never fired it on full auto. No need with zombies. The twenty-round drum magazine added some weight to it, but it was a big, blunt looking weapon, and for Mickey, a guy who didn't know much about guns, its fierce-look was reassuring.

He hacked and spat in the night. His throat was raw.

Buddy had almost killed him. He shook his head. Mickey was scared. The Buddy thing, yes, but…he had noticed the scabs on his chest and stomach the day before when he'd tried to clean himself up at a stream. Small patches of his skin were discolored. He felt okay. He hadn't been bitten. He thought he knew what it was: *plague*. But if it was plague, wouldn't he be feeling worse? He'd seen people in Eden come down with the plague. They'd been quarantined because they were contagious. All of them had died.

Mickey wondered if he was contagious. If he was… If he was then it was already too late for Gwen and Bear and Buddy, for Julie and her baby. Mickey felt selfish. A part of him knew he should have told the others as soon as he'd found the scabs on his body. But he was scared. Mickey didn't kid himself. He could kill a zombie if he had to, and he had. But he was no tough guy. He wasn't like Buddy or Bear. He wasn't even like Harris or Bobby had been. A part of him detested himself. He should have gathered his stuff and walked off as soon as he'd noticed the outbreak on his body the day before. He should have left the group without a word and hoped it wasn't too late for them.

Still… Gwen and Bear, Buddy and Julie, they were all he had. The only people left. *His* people. Mickey felt very alone. He felt like he imagined Josey Wales must have felt after the Redlegs had killed his wife and kid; the way Jeremiah Johnson must have felt… But those were characters in movies, not real people, and Mickey wasn't like them anyway. He was a man who felt alone but wasn't alone. He was a man alone in the crowd.

Mickey breathed deeply a few times, hefted the automatic 12 gauge and walked back to the others. Buddy was talking to them.

"Look, I'm sorry," he said to the group. "I can't explain what happened. I was dreaming, and in my dream they were coming for me. *He* was coming for me. They had me…"

"*Who* Buddy?" asked Julie.

He shook his head and looked down. Julie thought it was the closest she had ever seen the man come to crying.

"Still a few hours before dawn," Bear spoke up. "Everyone should try and get some sleep."

"Yeah, yeah. Good idea," said Buddy, composing himself. "I'll keep watch. I can't sleep anymore anyway. Mickey, you have my nine-millimeter?"

Mickey had been on watch before Bear. When they'd switched and Mickey had turned in he'd handed Buddy's silenced pistol to Bear. Bear hefted the 9mm in his open palm and looked at Buddy.

"I got the pistol," said Bear. "I got the watch."

Buddy considered what he could say, and when he decided there really wasn't anything he could say he simply nodded.

In a few minutes they settled back down, deep in their sleeping bags.

Julie and Gwen slept on one side of the fire, side by side for warmth.

"It's okay, Julie," Gwen assured her friend. She slept on one side, her sleeping bag unzipped enough she could bend her right arm and hold the vertical grip mounted on the hand guard of her M16A4 assault rifle.

"I was dreaming," Julie said. "About Harris."

"Go back to sleep. You need your rest."

Without a word Buddy gathered up his sleeping bag and moved away from the fire, away from the others. He took off his boots and climbed into the bag, zipping it up, turning his back to the fire and his companions.

He knew Bear was watching him.

Bear sat on a log and looked out into the night. It was quiet and still. The moon was a giant white orb in space, reflecting off the snow. He got up to retrieve some branches and feed the fire. When he sat back down Mickey said to him, his voice hoarse: "We've got to keep an eye on Buddy."

Bear nodded. If Mickey saw him he didn't acknowledge it.

They woke at dawn and ate from cans then resumed their march north, following train tracks half buried under snow drifts. They saw many strange and disturbing things on their journey. The Hudson River flowed past on their left, bearing with it debris and decomposed bodies and the hulks of destroyed water craft. Across the watery expanse the palisades of New Jersey towered over the river—a sheer vertical drop of over five hundred feet in places to the icy waters below. Purple Royal Paulownia would bloom at the base in the spring, but now the bottom of the cliffs were a brambles of bare, dead branches. An elevated highway was on their right for most of their trek. At times the natural rise of the land put them at eye level with the road and they could see the thousands of stalled cars and jackknifed trucks. Everywhere on the road the undead, in their ones and twos and threes, wandered aimlessly. Some stood alone amidst the snow and patches of bituminous surfacing.

The five men and women from Eden walked quietly and did their best not to draw attention to themselves. Occasionally a zombie from the road would spy them and begin to gesticulate and howl. Others would look and see them but they kept their gait steady. With time the tracks they followed dropped or the road turned away from the river, replaced by the trunks and limbs of deciduous trees that had shed their leaves and fruit. The howls of the undead receded in the distance.

They met few zombies on the actual railroad tracks except for where the tracks passed the outskirts of a town or small city. They followed four tracks which were mostly buried under the snow, ice, and debris. The electrified third rail collected power at the bottom and was insulated from above, but there had been no electricity flowing through them in a long time. The tracks stretched over eighty miles from the city to Poughkeepsie further north.

In Yonkers the train station was teeming with zombies. They had to abandon the tracks and claw their way through the snow and trees and brush bereft of leaves and foliage, scratching their hands and faces in places where dandelion, goldenrod and Black-eyed Susan had thrived and would return with the warmth and the sun. They kept roughly parallel to the train tracks, emerging back onto the rails away from the platforms where the dead stood in their hundreds.

Buddy volunteered to walk point and stayed well ahead of the others. Bear had handed back his silenced nine without a word. Buddy considered the previous night's situation. He'd almost strangled Mickey. *Mickey* of all people. Mickey, who's most important thing in life were his movies. Buddy imagined it must have hurt Mickey to leave his DVD collection back in Eden. He remembered nights on lawn chairs watching one of Mickey's films under the stars with Harris and Julie and Bobby and Gwen and the others, the intermittent cries of the undead still outside the walls.

Mickey. *Damn.* Buddy pulled his leather jacket closer to his torso and rifled through his saddle bags as he walked. His situation wasn't good. He carried a slew of amber vials and most of them were empty or near so. They'd have to pass a CVS or Duane Reed or some such place sooner or later, wouldn't they? In the week or so they'd been on the road since leaving Eden they had only stopped a few times, holing up for a day or two in various stores and buildings. New York City teemed with the undead, millions upon millions of them.

They'd made their way from Queens to the Bronx to West-chester County then crossed west until they'd reached the river and followed it north ever since. The Harbor gave way to the Great Bays and the Bays would let onto the Highlands in the near distance. The river flowed past them southward to the Upper and Lower Bays then into the Atlantic Ocean, salty sea water pushing up the estuary.

Buddy's memory had been slipping lately. He thought he remembered things but then was left wondering if the things he remembered were true.

It's true, Harris said in his head. *All of it.*

Buddy had been hearing voices for some time. He didn't mind Harris'. It was a reassuring voice—an old friend. But there was another… Buddy realized the voices must only be in his head, but they were so real. Sometimes, like with Harris, they were talking to him. Other times, they were talking *about* him.

He gripped one of the amber prescription vials in his saddle bags and only let go when a low moan greeted him from his right. An industrial chain link fence bordered the tracks here, enclosing the back lot of a construction site. It looked like a cement mixing plant. A zombie gripped the links and leered at him. It wore a back support and had a wrist brace on one arm. Buddy stopped and the thing grew more excited, its body jerking in place as it shook the fence, rasping.

He looked back to the four men and women behind him and signaled everything was okay. He checked the slide on his silenced 9mm and walked over to the fence. The thing there was voicing something, a rasp emanating from whatever was left of its vocal cords. Buddy stuck the silencer attached to the 9mm through the links and pressed it to the creature's forehead. The creature ignored the muzzle pushed up to its skull and focused on him.

Buddy changed his mind, holstered the pistol, shrugged his AK-47 off his back. The zombie had itself pressed against the fence. It wanted him. Bad. Buddy fit the affixed bayonet between the links and drove it deep through the thing's forehead. Its eyes bugged out. When he pulled the AK-47 back and the bayonet cleared, the zombie pitched to the side, bouncing off the fence with a last rattle to lay in the snow. Its eyes still open, it stared up into the wintry sky.

Buddy looked around but couldn't see any more of the things. He walked back to the tracks and waved to his companions and resumed his march north.

"Who would have done something like this?"

Bear and Buddy stood staring down at the horror before them. Someone had dug holes in the wintry earth and planted half a dozen zombies, buried to their necks. The zombies stared back at the two men, their jaws yawning, yearning. They were stuck on the side of the hill that rose from the track line and ran off to the road some-where above.

"This is just terrible," Bear said.

Buddy looked ahead to where the tracks disappeared in a turn, the bare limbs of dormant trees blocking their view. He ushered Bear towards the heads in the snow and earth then signaled to the three behind that had stopped well down the tracks.

"They must have buried them when the ground was soft. No way they could have done it in the middle of a winter like this." Buddy stomped down on the solid ground with one booted foot. "That means these things have been here for awhile."

Bear nodded.

They're waiting for you up there big man.

"What's that?" asked Buddy.

Bear looked a question at him and Buddy realized the man had not spoken.

"Thought you said something. Yeah, that's *exactly* what that means," Buddy shrugged out of his saddle bags and opened one, rummaging around inside. He came out with a pair of binoculars.

"Bear, wait here. I'm going to go on ahead around that bend. See what's to be seen."

"Don't go alone," Bear said, both of them aware other human beings were responsible for this and those others may be nearby. "It's not safe."

"I'll be okay." Buddy threaded the silencer on the 9mm as Bear watched.

"He's right," Julie said as she and Gwen and Mickey caught up to them. "You're not going alone. I'm going with you."

"Oh my God…" Mickey's voice trailed off when he saw the heads buried in the snow. "This is some *Motel Hell* shit here."

"You can't go with him," Gwen said, "so I'm going."

"No," Bear said, and the way he said it made it clear the topic wasn't up for further discussion. "Let's go, Buddy."

Buddy decided it wasn't worth arguing about, and having Bear around for anything he ran into might not be a bad thing.

The five of them moved off the tracks into the thin cover of-fered by the dead trees. Buddy pulled off his leather jacket. It was cold but the cold didn't feel bad. Bear slipped off his pack and chainsaw and unstrapped the disposable M72 rocket launcher from his pack. Buddy raised an eyebrow at the sight of the M72.

"You never know," Bear said, raising the M72's tube-like body.

They stayed to the trees on the hill paralleling the tracks, their boots crunching in the snow. Buddy went first, the silenced 9mm in his hand, AK-47 slung over his back. Larger and slower, Bear followed some distance behind, a Glock 9mm in either hand, the M72 on his back.

Julie and Mickey sat in the snow. Gwen stood with them, her breath pluming in the cold winter air. Julie had her knees pulled up to her chest.

"That's freaky," she said.

"That's sick," agreed Mickey. "That's what that is."

Gwen watched Buddy and Bear disappear from sight then she looked over to the Hudson River as it flowed by, sheets of ice massed near the shore. On the other side of the river were hills and mountains. She wondered if she was looking out at New Jersey or greater New York State, then dismissed the thought, figuring cartography and geography had no meaning any longer aside from day to day survival.

"What's wrong with Buddy?" Gwen asked the question that was on all their minds.

"I don't know," admitted Julie.

"I don't think he was trying to kill me," Mickey said. "I mean, I think he was trying to kill whoever's neck he thought he had his hands wrapped around, but…"

"It's okay," Gwen said. "You don't have to make excuses for him. Let me ask you guys this. Does anyone have any idea where he's taking us?"

"North," Mickey said.

"North. Great." Gwen exhaled. "Where? To the fucking North Pole?"

"If Buddy says there's a good place north of here," Julie said, "then I believe him."

"Okay," Gwen said. "But think of this. Panas and Biden and Sal went with Buddy, right? I mean, Larry too, but he came back when they went farther. Then Buddy comes back alone—"

"What are you implying?"

"Yeah," Mickey said. "Buddy said Sal didn't make it."

"Exactly. The man who tried to strangle you said Sal didn't make it. What the hell does that mean?"

"Panas and Biden are waiting for us," offered Mickey weakly.

"Says Buddy."

"Gwen, Buddy is our friend."

"Friends don't try and kill one another," she said and Julie looked away, wondering if Gwen had Bobby and Harris in mind.

"Look," Mickey said. "Something's definitely up with Buddy. But there's four of us, so even if—"

"What, you think you can protect us if Buddy… What about yourself?"

He didn't say anything.

"That was mean, Gwen," Julie spoke slowly.

"You're right. I'm sorry. I'm just worried. We're not in Eden anymore. We're out here. With *them*." She nodded to the zombie's buried in the ground.

"Hey, Gwen," Julie asked. "You still have that hammer?"

"Yeah, why?"

"Let me see it?"

She retrieved the hammer she carried and handed it over.

"What are you going to do with that?" Mickey asked Julie.

She nodded at the zombies sticking out of the earth. They stared at her, Gwen, and Mickey and their eyes did not waver.

"Really?" Mickey asked.

"Yeah. We can't just leave them there, can we?"

"Why not?"

"Someone else might come by," Julie said. "And I don't want these things here when my baby…"

"We're not bringing your baby back here, that's for sure."

"Give me that." Gwen grabbed the hammer and crossed to the zombie heads. She brought the hammer up and down onto the skull of the closest one, killing it with one blow.

"Damn." Mickey winced.

She moved to the next and brained it. The hammer cracked on the skull of the third. It was only stunned and its eyes blinked several times before Gwen hammered it a second, third, and fourth time. She finished off the others and cleaned her hammer off in the snow.

"There."

Throughout his stay in Eden, Bear had steadily been losing weight, almost all of it fat. He found he could move faster for longer distances these days than ever before. When he reached the spot where Buddy crouched down he was breathing heavily but he was not out of breath.

He shook his head when he saw what awaited them.

Someone had strapped a zombie to a tree. They had gone to the trouble of gouging its eyes out and sewing its mouth shut.

That's some fucked up shit

"It sure is," Buddy remarked and the zombie turned its head in their direction.

Bear looked at him.

The tracks took an extreme turn around a corner ahead. Neither Bear nor Buddy could see what lay around it. Whatever it was, Buddy thought, looking at the zombie tied to the tree, it couldn't be good.

He held up a finger and signaled Bear that he would go on ahead, crawling up the rise amidst the trees for a better view. Bear nodded and squatted where he was on the side of the tracks. Glocks in his hands he waited, watching Buddy crawl off on his hands and knees, watching the eyeless zombie turn its head as far as its neck allowed it, trying to follow Buddy's progress. Bear thought about the undead buried up to their necks back down the tracks. He wondered what any of it meant.

Buddy laid flat and still and waved Bear over. Bear crouch-walked over to the other man and covered the last yards on his stomach, snow and seed cones hidden in the snow crunching under him.

Buddy pointed and spoke very quietly: "There they are."

Bear looked. The first thing he saw was hundreds of zombies standing in place beyond the trees and hill he and Buddy hid on. They were clumped into two groups. One group gathered around the foot of a wooden cross that had been driven into the ground. The other group stood around a wooden wall twenty feet high that bridged a gap between cement block walls of similar height.

"Shit."

There was a man on the wall and a man on the cross. Bear didn't need Buddy's binoculars to see either. The man on the wall was decked out in what looked like football shoulder pads and had sections of rubber tire strapped to his upper arms and thighs. Even at this distance—and the wall was set back several hundred yards from the tracks and the river—Bear could see the man's hair was long and pulled into a ponytail. The guy had some kind of combat shotgun in his hands but didn't look too concerned, staring down into the mass of zombies gathered below his wooden gate.

"That guy's alive," Buddy said.

Bear knew he wasn't talking about the man on the wall.

Indeed, the man on the cross was alive. There were other crosses, four in total, with men crucified on them, but the zombies ignored these crosses and gathered all around the one. That was how Buddy knew the man attached to it was alive. Dead human bodies didn't attract zombies.

"They nailed him to it. Christ." Buddy offered Bear his binoculars but he declined.

"Does he look like he's in pain?" Bear asked.

"He looks out of it. His head kind of lolls from side to side. Christ. What kind of people…" He shook his head. He knew the type of people. He'd dealt with their kind in Eden and elsewhere.

Our type of people, jig…

"Shut up," Buddy muttered.

"What's that?"

"No, nothing."

"How many zombies do you figure?" Bear looked them over and estimated close to a thousand.

"I don't know. Enough I don't want to mess with them head on."

"Yeah. So what are we going to do?"

"Looks like they've got some kind of camp or something behind that wall. Hard to tell. And I don't really feel like changing positions and going for a better look. I'm going to assume they're hostile. You with me on that, right?"

"Bet," Bear agreed.

"Okay. We could double back a ways and try to circle around the whole camp there, behind it."

"That'll bring us into whatever cities or towns are up that way," Bear said. "And we don't know how many zombies they've got milling around…"

"Right. If we cross here we could do it at night. None of those zombies are anywhere near the tracks. If we're quiet, we could probably just walk right by them in the dark."

"If there's no moon whoever they have on the wall won't see us. I don't remember what kind of moon we're in for tonight."

"Or, and hear me out on this one," Buddy said. "If we had a distraction, we could walk right past now."

"That'd have to be one major distraction."

"Yeah."

"Talk to me," Bear said. "What do you have in mind?"

Buddy patted the M72 on Bear's back and Bear said, "Mmmm."

They crouched there, looking over the hundreds of zombies to the man on the wall. Bear finally took Buddy's binoculars and scanned the barricade. He could see smoke rising past it and assumed there were fires going inside for cooking or warmth, which meant there were people, perhaps many of them, beyond that wall. The man on the wall looked unwashed and bored. He shifted his weight from one foot to the other.

The man on the cross was calling out but Bear couldn't hear him from this distance. All he could see was the man's mouth moving. They had him tied nearly naked, his hands frozen into blue claws. Railroad spikes were driven through his forearms, nailing him to a plank of wood that was secured to a telephone pole. The man's lower legs were duct taped to the pole.

Bear handed the binoculars to Buddy and slipped off the M72.

"You know how to handle this thing?"

"I think I can figure it out."

"I'll go back, get the others."

"Grab my stuff, alright? I'm going to crawl a little closer and wait. When I see you over by the tracks, I'm going to put this rocket right through that gate. I'll catch up with you guys. Don't wait for me."

"We won't. Good luck."

"Thanks."

Bear disappeared and Buddy sat with his back against a pine tree, shielded by the evergreen. Funny, he thought, once this tree would have been filled with all sorts of birds. Who was he kidding. It was winter. The birds would have been down in Florida or some shit anyway.

He unsheathed and affixed his bayonet to the AK. He didn't intend to get close enough to go at it hand-to-hand with any zombies or anyone from the camp, but... He leaned the rifle against the tree.

He's gonna kill all them people in that camp.

He doesn't have a choice.

Buddy strapped the M72 across his back and got onto his stomach, crawling forward, staying well on the hill. He figured if he kept low he could probably walk to where he wanted but decided not to take the chance. He thought he was making a lot of noise as he crawled ahead, but knew he was far enough away from the zombies and the gate that he couldn't be heard.

When he got where he wanted he stopped and lay flat, craning his neck. The first of the zombies were to his immediate left, standing around, all intent on the man on the cross. He could make out this man and the man on the wall much clearer now.

Buddy pulled the M72 off and rolled onto his back. He removed the carrier sling from the LAW rocket and extended the inner tube. The tube telescoped towards the rear, aligning the detent lever with the outer tube's trigger assembly. The disposable rocket launcher was armed.

After a few minutes Buddy rolled over onto his side, where he could keep an eye on the zombies outside the wall and the tracks off in the distance.

What are you thinking, jig? You know they left you here.

No, they didn't. They wouldn't leave me.

I won't leave you either, heh-heh-heh…

Buddy forced himself to wait. Some time later he spotted four figures in the distance moving along the tracks. He got up on one knee and brought the LAW to his shoulder. The man on the wall spotted Mickey, Gwen, Julie, and Bear on the tracks, turned, and yelled out to people unseen on the other side of the barrier. Buddy knew he only had one shot so he aimed carefully through the rear peep sight, lining it up with the front reticle. The tube rested on his shoulder and in his left hand.

When he fired the man on the wall still yelled wildly down to those below. The 66mm rocket that shot out of the LAW, with a blast much like a shotgun's, was a HEAT round designed to penetrate light armor. The rocket zipped over the zombies' heads and punched through the wooden wall, detonating on impact. The entire wooden structure exploded in a shower of splinters and smoke. A couple dozen zombies closest to the blast—many had been pressed against the wall—were obliterated and flung aside like so many rag dolls.

The man on the wall was lifted off his feet and tossed backwards into the unseen camp. Buddy wasn't sure if the blast had killed the guy or not. He was just glad he'd made the shot. He crouched there on his knee with smoke trailing from the ends of the spent launcher and watched the scene unfold below.

There was gunfire and screams as the zombies marched through the shards of wood that had once held them back. Buddy still couldn't see into the camp but he could imagine the chaos unleashed within. He tossed the used launcher aside and ran back in the direction he'd come. The gunfire behind him intensified. He wondered how many men, women, and children were in the camp and if they'd survive the onslaught.

He reached his AK-47, scooped it up, and tore ass down the hill. There was no sight of Bear or the others on the tracks so he trusted they'd crossed. He broke from the trees and hustled across open ground, looking over his right shoulder once, satisfied that the zombies—hell bent on the camp and those within—had no idea he sprinted past them a few hundred yards away.

Part of him wanted to wait, concealed around the bend in the tracks, to watch and listen, to hear when the gunfire abated and to know who had won the fight. Part of him considered the fate of the man on the cross and he thought briefly of returning to put the man out of his misery. Instead he reached the tracks and slowed to a walk, the scene behind him disappearing as he followed the railroad, spying the prints of Bear and Buddy and Gwen and Julie in the snow.

"Do we have to spend another night outside?" Gwen asked as they marched through the snow. "It's cold." When Bear and Mickey looked at her she nodded towards Julie.

"She's right," Mickey said. "It's cold as a bitch. Tonight's gonna be colder than a witch's tit."

Bear nodded.

It was somewhere between midday and the time when the sun would go down.

"Julie," Bear asked. "How you feeling?"

She smiled, breathed out a plume of air and gave a gloved thumbs up.

Bear whistled and that got Buddy's attention. He stopped up ahead and waited for the other four to catch up to him.

Buddy had noticed he'd been spending more time on point lately. He figured it was some mix of his knowing where they were going and the others maybe being wary of him, after he'd almost strangled Mickey. He really felt bad about that. It was inexcusable.

He'd been walking point most of the day and thought back, wondering if they'd crossed paths with any zombies and if he'd had to kill any of them. He couldn't remember. He looked down at the hatchet in his gloved hand and noted the dried blood on its blade but couldn't discern how fresh or stale it was. *Whatever.*

Shit was getting harder to keep in check. Buddy had been hearing the voices more. They'd come and go. Sometimes he'd turn around and look towards the others thinking it was them. They were always back there, trudging along behind him, following, but not speaking. It scared him there were times he forgot why he was out here way ahead of the others.

The way they grouped around Julie, protecting her and the baby. From him? The thought didn't sit well. But, at times like this, he could understand and accepted it. And he vowed to kill anything in their path that threatened Harris' woman and child. *Anything*.

Buddy stood and waited for the others to catch up, well aware that the person at the head of the parade was either leading the parade or being pushed out.

"What's up?" he asked when they reached him.

"Let's find someplace we can hole up in for tonight," Bear said, motioning his head towards Julie.

"If you guys are doing this for me—" Julie started but Mickey cut her off.

"I haven't been able to feel my toes since breakfast. Okay?"

She looked from Mickey to Bear then to Gwen and shook her head, but seemed resigned to whatever they had in mind.

Buddy nodded and started off back ahead. Bear plodded along next to him.

Bear was a man of few words and Buddy really didn't have much to say. While Mickey, Gwen, and Julie discussed names for the baby the two men in the front trudged along stoically.

Gonna come visit him tonight.

Why don't you leave him alone?

Me and him got a lot in common.

He's nothing like you, nothing.

Oh, that's where you're wrong. You're so wrong...

They followed the tracks and in time spied a house that was set well back. As a group they approached it. As they got closer they noticed the doors and windows were boarded up and the snow around the home looked untrammeled.

Gwen glanced at Mickey and raised an eyebrow. He stuck his lower lip out and motioned with his palms up. They stood together surveying the house, the surrounding trees and countryside and saw nothing. Though it was still light out the sun had fallen behind the bare tree branches.

Bear slid out of his pack and, with a Glock at one side and his mace at the other, he started forward.

"You three wait here," Buddy said, sliding out of his saddle bags, the silenced 9mm in one hand, the hatchet in his other.

"That a hawk or an eagle?" Mickey nodded to a creature in the air.

"That's an eagle," said Julie.

"How do you know?"

"Eagles are a lot bigger than hawks. Longer wingspan."

"Huh."

Buddy stepped in Bear's tracks. The snow around the house was up to his knees and he was a tall man. They reached the house and looked it over up close. The doors and windows on the first and second floors had been sealed from the inside with planks of wood. Without a word between them they set off in opposite directions, circling the house, giving it the once around. Vinyl siding had fallen off and lay half buried in the snow. They met up again at the back.

"Looks quiet," Buddy said.

"Cellar door around the other side of the house," Bear noted. "Locked on the outside."

"It'll do."

Together they approached the back of the house and Bear opened the screen door. Through glass panes he could see the neatly aligned planks indicating the inner door was sealed shut from inside.

"Doesn't look like whoever's in there ever left," Buddy said.

Bear broke the glass out of one pane with his mace and tapped on the wood behind it a few times, then again, harder.

They stood and listened but couldn't hear anything from inside.

Bear broke the other panes and took a step back. Buddy held the screen door open as Bear swung the mace and splintered the planks. It took them a couple of minutes, and they made a lot of noise, but soon they forced the door open by pressing their weight against it.

Mickey, Julie, and Gwen had joined them in the backyard and stood looking around at the darkening sky.

"We're going to check the house," Buddy said. "There's a chance someone is still in it."

Mickey walked over to a car caked in a thick layer of snow. He brushed a swath of white from the hood and looked at the paint beneath.

Bear had already gone inside the house. Buddy had to unscrew the head of his flashlight a bit and shake it. After jarring the batteries inside the torch lit, and he screwed the top snug into place.

He stepped into a kitchen. Somewhere in another room the floor creaked under Bear, and the other man's flashlight and green laser site tracked.

Buddy looked around. Weak light from the ending day leaked in through cracks between the planks secured over the windows. Dust particles flittered through the shafts of light. The kitchen had been left clean. One of the walls was discolored. Upon inspection he saw it was mold. He considered opening the fridge but decided against it. Whatever was in there was probably decomposed beyond the point of stinking, but he had no desire to see it.

"Buddy," Bear called from somewhere else in the house.

He found the other man in a living room. A couch and two chairs were set around a coffee table low to the ground. The opposite wall was taken up with an entertainment center complete with flat screen television, cable box, DVD/VCR, and stereo.

The remains of four people sat in the living room—one in each chair, two on the couch. The bodies were in varying states of decay and desiccation. They almost didn't look real to Buddy. He stood next to Bear, panning over them with the beam of their flashlights. A thick layer of dust covered everything. The green laser site mounted on the Glock tracked it from body to body.

"What do you think happened to them?" Buddy asked.

"I don't know. Suicide?"

Skeletal hands rested on their laps or beside them, unbound.

Maybe they all took pills?

"Look."

Bear turned his flashlight beam on the coffee table around which they sat. It was bare except for an old *TV-Guide* and a single sheet of loose-leaf paper.

Buddy walked over and picked up the dusty paper. He blew on it and sneezed, then read what was written and showed it to Bear.

"Who the fuck is Ted?"

Don't let Ted out of the basement! Was scrawled across the paper in chicken scratch.

They searched the remainder of the first floor and found a sealed door that led down into a basement. Buddy rapped on it with the butt of his 9mm. He and Bear waited around but there was no commotion or any indication Ted or anything else remained in the

56

cellar. The basement door didn't open from the other side, so they surveyed the remainder of the home, noting the hardwood on the second floor carpeted with a blanket of dust, undisturbed, thinking no one had been moving in this house for some time. The wall in one of the bedrooms, much like the wall in the kitchen, was covered with mold.

Satisfied it was safe, Buddy went and got the others.

Bear shined the flashlight around the room. Even through the thick dust and strands of cobwebs he could see it was a nursery, with the walls papered in a soft pink. There was a dresser and a changing station with a box of baby wipes and a crib.

He walked over to the crib and looked into it, standing there for some time contemplating what it held.

"That's a baby Joey," Buddy said from beside him. Bear had not heard Buddy come into the room and had been unaware the man stood next to him but he was not startled and did not move.

"What's a baby Joey?"

"You know, Meathead."

Bear wasn't sure how to take the comment, or where it came from. "You don't have to be belligerent about it."

"I'm not. Meathead. You know, Archie Bunker."

"The TV show?"

"Yeah."

"I'm not getting you."

"Archie's son-in-law. The Polack. Mike. Rob Reiner."

"Oh yeah. That's what Archie called him."

"Right. Baby Joey was the kid Mike and Gloria had. That's a baby Joey doll."

Bear hadn't seen a doll in a long, long time, and he wouldn't have known this was a baby Joey doll or whatever if Buddy hadn't told him. He wondered if the other man knew what he was talking about. Buddy had periods of clarity, and then he had… He wondered how to categorize Buddy's episodes. Breaks from reality? Dementia?

"We used to watch a lot of re-runs Inside," Buddy said by way of explanation.

Bear was a hard man, had done time, and could recognize other hard men. He had long suspected Buddy had been a guest of the state at some point or other, but it was never anything he'd chosen to broach with the other man.

He decided to go for broke.

"What were locked up for?"

Buddy did not answer. Bear turned and saw the other had gone as quietly as he had come. He turned back to the crib and pondered the baby boy doll lying inside.

"You got a thing for Paul Newman?" Gwen ventured.

"Nah," Mickey said. "I got a thing for Paul Newman movies."

"Mind if I share this room?"

"Come on in."

He was stretched out on a king sized bed in one of the upstairs bedrooms, his booted feet on the mattress. His head and shoulders were propped up on a pile of pillows and he had his portable DVD player on his lap.

Well, I've always thought the law was meant to be interpreted in a lenient manner, Hud Bannon was telling his father and a group of other men out on the Texas range. *Sometimes I lean one way and sometimes I lean the other.*

Gwen sat down on the bed next to Mickey and propped her M16A4 against the mattress near her. She unlaced her boots enough to pull one then the other off her feet. The room was dark, lit only by the glow from the DVD player's screen. Mickey didn't get up but scooted over, giving her some room. He had his assault shotgun on the comforter next to him and it rested between them. Gwen climbed under the covers, turned on her side, and rested her head on one of her hands.

"What I said to you the other day? That was really mean and I'm sorry."

"It's okay," Mickey said.

"I was trying to hurt your feelings because, well, I guess I was scared."

"It's okay."

"What is this movie?"

"*Hud.*"

"Do you think they'll ever make movies again?"

"Jeez. I sure hope so."

"Was it tough for you?"

"What's that?"

"Leaving your movie collection behind. In Eden."

"Hell yeah. I can't lie."

"How many did you bring with you?"

Mickey smiled. "A few."

"The ones you couldn't do without?"

"The essentials? No. A bunch of westerns. I mean, some of them are my favorite movies of, like, all time."

The windows were closed and boarded over but were doing a poor job of keeping the cold out. Still, it was better than spending the night outside in the snow.

"Can I ask you something, Mickey?"

"Shoot."

"Were you married? Did you have any kids?"

"Divorced. One boy."

"You were a dad?" Gwen smiled.

"Sure was."

"How old was your son?"

"Twelve. He was twelve."

The house creaked around them.

"What was his name?"

"Forrest."

"What did you and…Forrest…you know, what did you do for fun?"

"We watched movies."

"What was his favorite movie?"

"Forrest was like me. He didn't have a favorite movie. I mean, how do you pick one movie, right? Or one *anything* for that matter?"

"Well, what kind of movies did he like?"

"Forrest liked westerns."

Mickey watched the movie and Gwen watched him. She thought of her husband Bobby, murdered down in a basement by Julie's boyfriend only several months ago. She felt no anger towards Julie. Harris had deceived her. He had deceived them all.

After some time Homer Bannon remarked that *It don't take long to kill things, not like it takes to grow.*

Mickey looked over at Gwen. Her eyes were closed and she was breathing calmly, asleep. He curled his toes in his boots and returned to his movie.

You know something Fantan? shouted Paul Newman. *This world is so full of crap, a man's gonna get it sooner or later whether he's careful or not.*

The credits rolled and he turned off the movie then the DVD player. The room was pitch-black. He laid the portable player on the bed next to him, well away from the edge of the mattress. He rested there with his head and shoulders propped up and thought about his child, taken from him, of Julie and the baby within her, of Bear and Buddy. He listened to Gwen breathing next to him and sometime later he fell asleep.

Buddy unzipped his sleeping bag and spread it out on the living room floor. His head rested on one of his saddle bags. He looked up into the dark where the ceiling was. Bear was somewhere in the room with him, but he could neither see nor hear him. The dead family was there too, seated in their chairs next to one another, together until the end.

He grew restless listening to nothing and turned over on one elbow, unbuckling a saddle bag then rummaging about inside. Buddy found his mini-mag and switched it on, shining it inside the saddle bag. Boxes of ammunition for his weapons, his bayonet, his meds. He picked up an amber vial and looked at the label. Sesaquel. He shook it and there was a rattle. A few tabs left in the vial.

The Resperdol vial was empty. Two tabs left in the Zyprexal. The Thorazine. God, he *hated* taking the Thorazine. It knocked him on his ass. More vials, most empty, the others almost empty. *Shit*.

Buddy shut his flashlight off, lay back down, and stared towards the ceiling, his hands folded on his chest over the mini-mag. Mickey and Gwen and Julie were up on the second floor. Down in the basement there was probably something that had once been human and named Ted. Here in the dark was a dead family and a one-time bad man who went by the name Bear, with another bad man who went by the name Buddy.

Truth was, Buddy admitted to himself, he was scared.

Something was happening to him. Something he couldn't control and he couldn't understand. It had happened to him before, but not in a long time, and he had sworn to himself it never would again, but…he was scared, scared in a way he hadn't been scared in a long, long time.

Creak

His gaze darted forward, peering into the dark ahead. Was Bear awake and moving around?

Creak-creak

No. It was coming from another room.

Buddy.

He recognized the voice and froze where he lay. He opened his mouth but nothing would come out of it. *Bear*, he had to wake Bear.

His mouth was dry and his breath came to him in short, ragged gasps.

The thing in the dark was walking somewhere down here with them.

Hey boy, thought much about me lately?

It was in the room with them. Buddy tried to move, to roll over for his 9mm, but he was paralyzed.

Creak-creak-creak

It was nearly upon him. He closed his eyes, hyperventilating, and tried to extricate himself mentally from the situation, thinking of Henry and Monique and their smiling little faces, frozen in time. That freed him up enough so his trembling hand could turn the mini-mag around on his chest as his—

It's lonely here, jig, why don't you—

—thumb flicked the switch on, the beam illuminating the room. The corpses were in their seated positions, the room otherwise empty, no nightmare creature skulking through the shadows.

The hand was enormous and it splayed itself on his chest and held him in position. His immediate instinct was to fight but he was pinned to the floor. When he went to scream in fear and anguish he found a second giant hand clasped over his mouth and he realized—

"Buddy, *shhhhh*. Buddy, be quiet. Calm down now."

Bear. Bear, oh god. He relaxed immediately. It was Bear stooping over him, holding him down, Bear's mighty hand across his mouth, stifling his cries.

They made eye contact and Bear saw the recognition in his eyes.

"I'm going to take my hand off your mouth now. But you can't scream. You can't wake up the others, okay?"

Buddy nodded mutely and Bear took his hand off the man's mouth. He gasped and gulped down breaths of air and Bear waited until he could speak.

"Are you okay? Now, I mean?"

"Y-yeah."

"Okay."

He took his hand off Buddy's chest and sat down, his back against one of the chairs in which a corpse was positioned. Bear took the flashlight from him but did not turn it off, aiming it instead at his own face.

"It's only me, got it?"

Buddy sweat profusely but was immensely relieved. Bear's face, he thought, flush with the garish light, one eye unseeing, big head bald, was the most beautiful and most terrifying thing he had ever seen.

"Got it, got it." He rolled over onto his side then sat up, across from Bear, who directed the flashlight beam at the space between them.

"Buddy," he asked after some time. "What's wrong with you?"

He didn't know what to say or where to begin.

"Bear, what happened to Harris? *Exactly* I mean."

Bear nodded but he could not see him.

"Harris got bit. None of us knew."

"*You* didn't know? Julie didn't know?" His voice wasn't accusing, it was asking.

"None of us knew. That afternoon we're outside watching a volleyball game or whatever, and after awhile I kind of notice Harris isn't around, and then we heard a gunshot.

"I was the first one down in the basement, after Julie—what she had to see, what she saw—Harris had it in his head that Thompson was responsible, I guess. He had Thompson staked to one of those poles Markowski had down in his basement. He'd chained himself to the other. Shot himself through the chest, bled out quick, came back."

"How did Bobby die?"

"I don't think Harris meant to kill Bobby," Bear reflected. "I think that was a mistake. I wonder if he even knew…"

"Who killed Harris? Was it you?"

"I didn't kill Harris. I killed a zombie down in that basement. Two of them. Harris killed Harris."

"I'm in a bad way."

Bear waited silently for him to explain.

"When I was Inside—when I was in prison—they kept me correct. I mean with the meds situation and all. But out here…I'm losing it, man."

Bear had had his eye on Buddy for some time. When Buddy came back to Eden to find his best friend dead, and his best friend's woman pregnant, many who knew Buddy had been relieved, thinking him dead and gone all those months. But Bear had detected something was up pretty early on. He'd worked in the health care field way back when, enough to recognize the signs of mental illness, even if he didn't possess the medical terminology to label what he saw.

"I hear voices," continued Buddy. "I hear Harris. I hear...I hear voices. They tell me to, to do things. They aren't really there, are they?"

"No. They aren't really there."

"Part of me knows that, but part of me... They're so real. I can't...I can't explain it. I—"

"Let me ask you a question. What happened with you and Markowski, down in that tunnel?"

Buddy shook his head. "I don't know. I mean, I thought—I think—we fought. He fought hard. I killed him. I *think*. But, I don't know. I keep seeing myself sawing his head off in the dark, not even giving him a...a chance. I don't know which is the real version anymore."

"Markowski one of the voices you hear?"

Buddy nodded.

"Can you hold it together? I mean, the other night, with Mickey..."

"I can't believe I...I mean, yeah I can. I can believe I did that. I've done things, Bear...things..."

"We both have."

"No, I don't think you—"

"*I do.*"

"I would *never* hurt Julie, or the baby, I mean, they're my...they're the only reason—"

"I know you would never purposefully harm Julie. But you need to know, if you ever try and harm that woman or child, I'll end you."

It wasn't a threat and Buddy didn't take it as one.

"You know, one time, me and Harris, we got to talkin'. I told him, I said if I ever got bit, I didn't want him to hesitate. I wanted him to do it then and there. He didn't want to hear any of that, but it was important for me that he did hear it, and finally he agreed. I think he agreed to shut me up, but..."

"If I slow you down," he continued, "and the days gonna come I think, real fast, when I *do* slow you down, just leave me. Keep heading north, cross the bridge I told you about, keep goin'. Don't worry about me."

"Understood." Bear's voice was low.

The dead sat in their chairs and the living sat on the floor.

"Does it help?" asked Buddy.

"What's that?"

"Your religion? You're one of those born-again types, aren't you? I mean, you're pretty low-key about it and all, but…"

"I was."

"Not anymore?"

"Back in Eden…I lost my faith down in that basement."

"*God.*" Buddy couldn't imagine. "What keeps you going man?"

"That woman and her baby. I've got to see them through this."

Buddy nodded but Bear couldn't see him.

"That note, on the table," said Buddy. "What are we going to do about Dead Ted?"

Bear cleared his throat. "What do you wanna do about Dead Ted?"

Buddy thought about it.

"You know what? Nothing. Fuck Dead Ted."

THE CONVOY

"Dude, what the fuck are you doing over there? Oh man." Maurice walked up on Damar in the woods. When he said *dude* it sounded like *doo*. "You're not whackin' off are you?"

"You wish."

"No seriously, doo, what the fuck you doing?"

Damar had his back to Maurice and was obviously handling himself.

"I'm trimmin' my pubes, bro."

"You're fuckin' kiddin' me, right?" Maurice stood next to Damar and leaned forward to look. "You're *not* fuckin' kiddin' me."

"Right. I'm *not* fucking kiddin' you. And you *had* to look."

"Doo, what the fuck? Why are you grooming your pubes?"

"Man's always got to be prepared."

"Prepared for what?"

"Hot date, man. Can't be having at it with some pretty young thang, unleash the beast, and he's lost like a bird in a nest. Ya feel me?"

"You're crazy, doo."

Damar shrugged, made one last snip at his groin with the small surgical scissors, and stood there admiring his handiwork. An AKS rested barrel up against his thigh.

There was a low moan from the trees ahead of them.

"Let's get out of here," Maurice said. "You're attracting an audience."

"Maybe you can help me out, Mo. I got a lot of little wiry hairs back around my asshole I can't get to, but maybe if I bend over—"

Maurice had started to walk off, back to their jeep, and waved a hand dismissively at Damar and his nonsense.

"Peepin' Tom motherfuckers." Damar looked into the foliage facing him, zipped and buttoned his jeans and picked up his assault rifle.

"Doo, you're out of your mind." Maurice said when Damar caught up to him.

"I'm out of *my* mind? Let me tell you what I am, bro. I'm ready for the hot and heavy."

"Uh-huh."

"How 'bout you, Mo'? You ready if Lauren ever give it up to you?"

"You fucked up, doo, you know that?"

"I'm fucked up? World's gone to shit, but a man and woman still attracted to one another. That's a *beautiful* thing to me, bro. I mean, it *would be* a beautiful thing if the woman knew you existed. You gotta talk to her nigga."

"Doo, there are some things I wish I had never told you."

They were within sight of the jeep on the road and could see Steve, Eva and the kid. The kid was standing on a milk crate with the shoulder stocks of the Browning .50 cal. snug against his shoulders. The machine gun had a night vision scope mounted on it.

"Don't worry, Mo. We's cool. I'm just saying, when it comes to Lauren, you got no game son."

"Oh. And you're mister-smooth, right?"

"Well, maybe not as smooth as Steve over there, but I do alright, yeah."

"Doo, you bang blind women."

"Bro, Sonya is a MILF. No two ways about it."

"She's a cougar, doo."

"That too, no doubt."

"And she's blind, doo. Not to mention she's got like fourteen fuckin' kids."

"Three, bro. *Three.*"

"Whatever."

"Mo, don't let Eva hear you talkin' that way about her sister. She'll kick both our asses."

Another moan came from behind them. They turned to see a zombie break from the tree line and stumble towards them and the road. Of the thousands and thousands of zombies they had seen in the months since the outbreak this one looked especially putrescent. It had been a man. Its long, once-blonde hair was matted to its skull and neck. It wore a plaid green and red and black shirt-jacket over cargo pants and combat boots, the tongues of which flapped around.

It saw the two men and groaned.

Eva motioned to them from the jeep.

"Let's go," said Maurice.

"Nah, wait a second. I got something for Kurt Cobain over there."

Damar handed his AKS to Maurice and drew two throwing daggers he wore at his waist.

"You know, throwing a knife at a motherfucker isn't as easy as it looks." Damar took three steps towards the zombie trudging their way and stopped. He closed one eye, squinted the other, and bit down on his tongue. Maurice thought he looked very funny, concentrating like that.

"Doo, you look like you studying for your SATs."

Damar ignored him, drew the dagger back past his ear, and whipped his wrist forward. The dagger flew end over end past the zombie's head to land in the grass beyond it.

"See what I mean?" Damar said. "*Motherfucker.*"

"He's coming over here to do the Seattle stomp on your poor black ass." Maurice laid down Damar's AKS and his own Mini-14 then drew the machete from the sheath on his hip.

"One more. One more." Damar waved him away. "I can do this."

The zombie was about fifteen feet from them.

Damar squinted, sighted, drew his arm back and launched the second blade, which buried itself in the thing's chest. The zombie stopped in its tracks, looked down at the handle jutting from its solar plexus, looked up at the two men, growled and took another step.

"Damn."

"Doo, you just pissed the fuckin' thing off."

Maurice walked up to the beast and, before its rotting hands could grasp him, decapitated it with a swing of the machete. The headless torso keeled over into the grass as its head rolled several yards away.

Damar retrieved his daggers, keeping one eye on the trees in case any more zombies emerged from that direction, and then he and Maurice returned to the jeep.

"How's that fifty suit you shorty?" he asked nine-year-old Nelson.

"I want to shoot it," admitted the boy.

"You fire it and it'll bring out all the zombies for miles," said his Aunt Eva.

From behind the wheel, and his mirrored aviator glasses, Steve nodded to Damar. "Your aim sucks, D."

"Your mother sucks—" Damar started to shoot back, noted Eva's hostile glare indicating little Nelson, and caught himself, finishing his sentence with, "Lemons. And I got big motherfuckin' lemons, Steve."

Steve wore a blue t-shirt with Cookie Monster's face on the front of it.

"It'll be getting dark soon," said Eva. "Let's head back. They'll be making camp."

"This road looks pretty good," noted Maurice.

"Yeah," agreed Steve. "I wonder what the Greeks found?"

Steve started the jeep and made a three-point turn on the road. The sun was out of the sky but the heat and humidity lingered. They all enjoyed the breeze whipping against their faces as they doubled back on the path they had followed earlier in the sultry day. Eva sat next to Nelson with one hand around her nephew's shoulders, the other wrapped around the barrel of an M4 carbine complete with a fourteen-inch M26 under-barrel shotgun system, sound suppressor, and AN/PVS-17A Mini Night Vision Sight. The entire rifle rested barrels up on its telescoping stock.

"When is this summer going to end?" Maurice turned around in the front passenger seat and called to Eva over the whip of the wind.

"What?"

"I said when is this summer going to end?"

She looked at him quizzically, unable to make out his words over the noise of the jeep and the wind. "What?"

"Nothing." He waved it off and turned around.

They followed the deserted four-lane blacktop, overgrown in places with weeds and small saplings, passing the occasional stalled or burned out vehicle on the road. Earlier in their day when they'd passed this way they'd seen no one, living or dead, and they saw no one now.

A few minutes later Eva leaned forward and yelled loud enough for Steve to hear. "Stop for a minute."

"What is it?"

"Just stop."

Steve pursed his lips and slowed the jeep to a halt.

"Come with me, Nelson." Eva hopped out of the jeep, leaving her M-4/M-26 behind. She retrieved a five-foot pole from the back of the vehicle then reached up and took Nelson under the arm, setting him on the road with her.

"We'll be right back," she told the men and, holding one of Nelson's hands, she led him off to the side of the road. A lone zombie had staggered from the tree line and was limping their way.

Steve, Maurice, and Damar watched the woman and the boy walk off towards the zombie.

"Look at the way she moves," Damar said. "Like a cat. A big sexy cat."

"Man," Steve said. "You know how many women I fucked before all this bullshit began?"

"That countin' sheep?" Damar asked.

"Inflatable ones?" Maurice quipped.

"Inflatable sheep. Nigga, I hadn't thought of that one."

"Five hundred and twelve."

"But who's counting, right?"

"Wow. Are we supposed to be impressed?"

"I assume that includes the unconscious ones too?"

"No," said Steve. It wasn't clear who he was answering. "You know how many greasy dead heads I've killed since this bullshit dropped?"

Neither Damar nor Maurice ventured a guess.

"Two-thousand-six-hundred-eighty-six."

Damar let out a whistle.

"Those are Magic Johnson numbers you're posting there, bro," he said.

"And you know how many women I've banged since this shit started?"

Again, neither Maurice nor Damar answered.

"Sixteen. Fuckin' *sixteen* man. Course, that doesn't count blow jobs, but who counts those?"

"Okay, Clinton," Damar said. "So what exactly is your fuckin' point?"

"Zombies man." Steve shook his head. "They're killing my sex life."

"This is a Smith and Wesson revolver, Nelson." Eva dumped the cylinder in her hand and snapped it back into place then passed the hand gun to her nephew. "It's called a Lady Smith but don't let the name fool you. It'll kill a zombie or a man just as good as any other weapon."

He took the gun and looked at it, somewhat in awe. It wasn't as heavy as he'd thought it would be.

"This part is called the grip. Wrap your hand around it. Like that. Your index finger goes in there. Like that. Now squeeze the trigger—don't worry, it's not loaded. No, *squeeze*, don't jerk it. You want to be smooth. Try it again. Good. *Smooth*. Again. Nice.

"See this thing that turns each time you squeeze the trigger? That's the cylinder."

"That's where the bullets go?"

"*That's* where the bullets go." Aunt Eva nodded and smiled in approval. "There's two ways to fire this. You can squeeze the trigger and—"she nodded and the boy squeezed the trigger, the hammer falling on an empty chamber, a loud *Click*—"boom. Or you can cock the hammer back like this—this is the hammer. Pull it back like that and it's ready to fire. All it'll need is a little pull and—"

"I thought you said don't pull the trigger?"

"You're right. I meant to say *squeeze* the trigger. Anyway squeeze the—good. Did you see how easy that was?"

"Yes, Aunt Eva."

"Good. Now these are bullets. This gun you have in your hand, its capable of firing three-fifty-seven bullets and these. These are thirty-eights."

"What's the difference?"

"The power. A three-fifty-seven is a lot more powerful than a thirty-eight. But you know what? It doesn't matter to a zombie. A thirty-eight is good enough."

Nelson smiled, though he watched the approaching zombie warily.

"Don't worry about him, baby." Eva showed him how to open the cylinder. "Okay, these go in this way first, all right? Go ahead, baby, load the pistol. Keep the barrel facing down and away from anybody. That's right, good. This revolver only holds five bullets, so you need to keep track of how many bullets you fire, all right?"

"Okay."

"Okay, now close it like this and keep it down because, now, if you pull—I mean *squeeze*—the trigger, it'll fire."

Eva looked up and judged the zombie's distance from them.

"Okay, baby, in a minute you're going to get a chance to use this revolver. How's that sound to you?"

"Cool!" Nelson looked happy.

"Two things. One, you can't think of these things as people. Because they're not people."

"But they *were* people, right?"

"Right. They *were* people. But not anymore. And we shoot them because if we don't—"

"—because if we don't they'll eat mommy and Nicole and Victor and Aunt Eva and Maurice and Damar and even Steve, right?"

"Right. Now, maybe we wouldn't miss Steve," Eva and the boy laughed, though her nephew's laugh was somewhat nervous now the zombie was almost upon them, "but we don't want anything bad to happen to anyone else, right? *Even* Steve."

"Right."

"Good." She stood and took up the five foot animal control pole with both hands. "Stand here and keep the gun pointed down until I call you over."

"Okay, Aunt Eva."

She strode over to the zombie and hooked the loop of the animal control pole around its head. The beast groaned and reached for the loop but clawed at it futilely. It tried to walk forward but she held it in place, her firm grip of the pole keeping the thing at bay.

"Come over here and stand next to me. Don't be afraid. It isn't going to hurt us."

Nelson went and stood next to his aunt. She had told him to keep the gun aimed muzzle down, but he had seen guns fired and wanted to aim it at the creature struggling at the end of the pole.

"Do you know what a *recoil* is Nelson?"

"Hey, watch this," Steve said to Maurice as Damar walked back to the jeep. Damar had taken a piss on the other side of the road where the boy and his aunt couldn't see him. "Shake my hand." Steve offered his hand to Damar.

"Why?" Damar raised an eye-brow.

"Just trust me."

Damar shook Steve's hand.

"Okay. What?"

Steve smiled. "Smell your hand."

"You son of a —"

"Guys," Maurice said.

"What'd you do?" Damar stood looking at his hand, holding it out away from his body.

"Nothin'."

"*Nothing?*"

"Nothin' much. I just touched myself is all."

"Where'd you touch yourself, nigga?"

"Behind my balls. Been a long, hot day. Smells like vinegar."

Maurice looked like he was going to vomit.

"Well then, I don't feel so bad," Damar said as he forgot about his hand and got back into the jeep.

"Why's that?"

"Cause I just dropped a dooky and wiped my ass with my hand."

If he thought he could shock Steve he was wrong. The driver raised his own hand to his nose and inhaled deeply. "Ahhhh…"

There was a single gunshot and all three looked to the woman and boy off on the side of the road. A zombie lay twitching in the grass, head shot. Eva walked over to it and stomped on the thing's head with her boot until it stopped moving.

"Man," Steve said. "If there's one thing I can appreciate it's a hot broad who can kill zombies. Why does she have to play for the other team?"

"Don't let her hear you talkin' like that," Damar said. "She'll kick your ass."

"I wish." Steve studied his nose hairs in the rear view mirror.

"Here, trim those bad boys bro." Damar handed him the surgical scissors from the pocket of his camouflage cargo pants.

Steve thanked him and started snipping at the longer hairs sprouting from his nostrils. Maurice had to look away and put his hand over his mouth as he laughed.

"Man's gotta keep himself lookin' *GQ*," Damar said. "If he's gonna see four hundred and twelve"

"Five hundred and twenty eight," corrected Steve.

"You a playa."

"I'm not a playa." Steve concentrated on his nose. "I just fuck a lot."

"Somewhere out there," Maurice said, "there's a fat motherfuckin' rapper rollin' over in his grave."

"What are you talking about, Mo?" Steve squinted through his shades in the rear view mirror as he trimmed his nose hair. "Fat Joe still alive. I think."

"Fat Joe?"

"You were quoting Big Pun, Steve-O," Damar said, "not Joey Crack."

"Nah, man, that was a Fat Joe joint."

"Look, Steve." Damar exhaled. "Don't no white man try and lecture the black man on rap."

"Oh, what? Cause I'm white I can't like rap music?"

"Nah, nigga, you can like you your Eminem, your Third Base. Hell, I'll even grant you Vanilla Ice."

"Vanilla Ice?"

"Yeah, now please just shut the fuck up before I get all Suge Knight up on your ass."

"Would you niggas both just shut the fuck up?" pleaded Maurice.

Eva and Nelson climbed into the back of the jeep.

"That was some good shootin' young-un." Damar told the boy and he beamed.

"I'll talk to your mom," Eva told her nephew. "Maybe I can convince her you're old enough now to have your own gun."

The horizon purpled into early evening and cicadas buzzed in the trees.

"Steve, any chance we can get this thing rolling sometime soon?" she asked. "I don't want to be out here on the road at night."

"You ask, I obey." He scrunched up his nose in the rear view mirror one last time, handed the scissors back to Damar, and cranked the jeep up.

Maurice turned and asked Damar, referring to his shaved pubic region, "How's that working for you?"

It took them nearly an hour of back tracking to reach the convoy. When they returned early evening was upon them and the sky was going from purple to a deep dark blue. They crested a rise. There it was before them: dozens upon dozens of vehicles formed into a giant, tight circle in the parking lot of what had been a Wal-Mart or something. Recreational vehicles, mini-vans, jeeps, municipal buses, luxury vans, tow trucks, station wagons, sports utility vehicles, panel trucks, every kind and type of vehicle was represented in the fleet. Flat bed trucks carried a front end loader and cars in various states of repair.

The camp was a flurry of activity. Within the circle of cars, trucks, and vans was a relatively safe area. Children ran around in the pollen and grasses and flowers sprouting up between the tar and cement, chasing one another, playing tag, watched over by armed adults. Smoke from cooking fires rose to the darkening sky. Men and women with rifles were spaced out along the perimeter, outside the vehicles—the first watch. When they had to spend their nights in areas with many zombies, the watch stood atop the vehicles.

Sheets of metal had been welded to the sides of the vehicles to keep the undead from crawling beneath and infiltrating their billet. The metal sheets could be moved and placed on either side of a vehicle, depending on the configuration of the convoy, for any particular evening.

The guards stood watchfully and waved to them as they pulled in. A handful of zombies staggered across the immense parking lot towards the camp. There was only one thing Maurice hated more than pulling guard duty and having to while his hours away dispatching any Zeds that got too close for comfort. And that would be waking up after a relatively peaceful night's sleep to find the convoy surrounded by hundreds of undead, standing around, groaning, motioning, hungry, the air thick with flies and stink.

"*Ya'sou malaka!*" Standing smoking a Newport, Markos greeted them as their jeep pulled to a halt at the front of the line. Steve flipped him the bird and the Greek laughed heartily.

Maurice, Damar, Steve, Eva, and Nelson gathered up their gear and crossed to an opening between a former ice cream truck and an RV.

"Hope you enjoyed your trip out with us today," Maurice said to the boy.

"It was great!"

"Remember, shorty," said Damar, "the only good Zed—"

"—is a dead Zed!"

Damar smiled and held up a palm for a high five. "My nigger. Give it here."

"*Damar,*" she snapped.

"What?"

"The only good Zed is a…?"

Damar showed his palms. "My bad."

"Maurice, maybe you could do me a favor."

74

She wasn't asking. Maurice wondered what she'd need. He wanted to get back home to the van he shared with LaShawn and Demetrius, get some food in his stomach.

"Yeah, what's up?"

"Could you walk Nelson over to Sonya's? I need to go to the council and report in first."

"No doubt." Maurice was pleased. Chances were good Lauren would be over at Sonya's at this hour.

"I'm going to the council too," said Steve. "Come on."

"Nelson, go with Maurice. He'll take you to Mommy."

"Okay. Hey, Aunt Eva, today—thanks!"

"Tell your mommy I'll be home in a little while."

"Yo, Steve," called Damar. "You and your roommates holla at a nigga, yo."

"He's a cute kid," said Steve as they walked.

"Yeah, he is."

"Listen, let's stop over at the trailer for a second. I gotta talk to Mason."

"Okay, but let's make this fast."

Steve nodded.

As they walked he and Eva waved and greeted the children and adults they encountered. It was funny, Eva thought, between the lines of vehicles at night you had no clue the world was inhabited by billions of zombies waiting to tear you limb from limb and devour you.

"Hey. Can I ask you a question?"

"Shoot."

"Sonya talk to you much about me?"

"You mean things like, *Steve, that stallion, I wish he'd stop by more often and give me the high, hard one—*"

"Okay, fine, thanks. A simple *no* would have worked."

"I'm just messin' with you, Steve. Sure, sometime she mentions you."

He smiled. "Yeah, what she say?"

"She asked me once what you looked like."

"And you said?"

"I said despite what you thought about yourself you were most definitely not God's gift to women."

The wind went out of his sail, but only for a second.

"What else did she say?"

Eva laughed. "Well, when I told her that, she said, *consider it a mercy fuck*."

"A *mercy fuck*?" He sounded flabbergasted. "*I'm* a mercy fuck?"

"I'm just fucking with you. She never said that."

He smiled.

"No, actually, you know what she said to me?"

Steve fell for it, beaming, expecting a compliment. "What's that?"

"She said Damar has a much bigger dick than you."

"You're real funny, Eva, you know that?"

"But seriously, Steve, can I ask you a question?"

"Shoot."

"It's nighttime. Why don't you lose the sunglasses?"

He took off his mirrored shades, looked up at the sky. He squinted and licked the side of his lips. "Nah." He put the shades back on.

"Hey, Eva, you listen to rap music?"

"No. Why?"

"Nothin'."

When they reached the Coach bus with tinted windows they went right in. The interior was artificially lit. The windows were painted over inside with scenes from children's books: a very hungry caterpillar, a pig named Olivia, a train named Thomas. When the convoy was on the road during the days, a hybrid school and day care was held on the bus. Most of the children had gone home for the evening but there were still half a dozen milling about with a couple of adults who were waiting for the kids to be picked up.

"Steve-O!" Mason called out to them. "Miss Eva."

"What's going on, Mason?"

"Oh, another day of edification and shaping young minds. Know what I'm saying?"

Three little white boys had spotted Steve and ran over to him, clinging to his legs and trying to climb up his body.

"Oh-oh-oh, easy now, easy now!"

"Steve! Steve! Steve!" they cried out in their enthusiasm.

"Take it easy you little peckerheads!"

The boys laughed and giggled. They liked it when Steve called them peckerheads.

"Buckwheat! Farina! Stymie!" Mason called to the boys and Eva laughed. When the kids responded to the names and climbed down off of Steve she laughed harder.

"Buckwheat?" she asked Mason. "Farina?"

"Funny, right?"

"What do their parents think of the names you've given them?"

"Ah, it's just a joke. The boys know those aren't their real names."

"Yeah, I'm not a Stymie," said the youngest, a tow-headed boy. "I'm a pecka-head."

Eva laughed and patted the boy on the shoulder. "You guys are *bad*." She indicated Mason and Steve.

"You got my Oscar winners?" Steve asked Mason.

"Yeah, right here." Mason unlatched an overhead compartment, reached in, and handed him a brown paper bag. "Thanks."

"No problem. Anything else you want to borrow?"

"You got anything, I don't know, foreign maybe?"

"Foreign how?"

"I'm thinking Asian. Maybe a little Chinese or Japanese?"

"Chinese is hard to come by, but I think I can hook you up with the Japanese."

"You all right. No matter what those roommates of yours say. Or what Sonya says."

Eva laughed.

"Steve," she reminded him. "*Council.*"

"Yeah. Gotta run. We still on for Friday night? Texas Hold-'Em?"

"You bet your a—" Mason stopped himself, looking at the children. "We sure are."

"Okay then."

"Steve! Steve! Steve!" the boys chanted as they turned to leave. He spun and hit a faux-most muscular pose and the kids squealed in delight.

"Remember little pecker heads—"

"Train hard!" one of them shouted.

"Say your prayers!"

"Eat your vitamins!"

They had memorized the litany.

"What you gonna do—"Steve's face turned bright red as he pumped out a series of most musculars and front double biceps shots, spittle frothing from his mouth "—when Hulk-a-mania runs wild on you?!"

The kids cracked up laughing and Steve and Eva left the bus.

"Those boys love you."

"Yeah, little kids and dogs," said Steve. "I would have made a good pedophile."

"You're a sick bastard."

"Thanks. I try."

Council was held out in the open with a few rows of folding chairs set up. Every vehicle sent one representative each night to discuss the day's events and the plan for the morning. The Greeks had arrived before them and gave their report from the road. While he listened to Markos, one of the Greeks he knew better, Steve scanned the council for fuckable chicks.

Life on the road was tough, thought Steve, and it took a toll on broads. Some of these at council looked rough as shit. But he knew they weren't here because they were beauty contestants. They were here, because, *number one*, they were tough enough to make it this far, and *two*, because they commanded enough respect in their own vehicles to be chosen to go to council.

He looked around and wondered who he'd bang if he had the chance. There was Stacey, the Greek chick. But she was always hanging around with Markos and the other Greeks. And Steve thought she had something going on with the one older Greek guy who spoke no English whatsoever and always wore the Kangol. Steve and his friends referred to the guy as *Saki*, as in Socrates. He didn't think the guy took it the wrong way. Anyway, he'd figured out a long time ago that *malaka* meant asshole, and the Greeks seemed to enjoy calling Steve *malaka* every chance they got, usually with smiles on their faces, so he thought they meant no harm.

There was Eva. She was hot as shit. Steve had pleasured himself several times, thinking about her tits, about her with another woman. It turned him on all the more that she was really into women. The night Sonya had been drunk and banged him, he had fantasized about having her and her sister Eva in bed at the same time. He'd felt it was some sick perverted line he didn't want to cross, and was worried about cumming too soon anyway, so he'd immediately banished the image from his head and thought about Chuck Norris in *Invasion USA*.

Nothing sexual about Chuck for him, but it kept his mind off the here and now and allowed him to give it to Sonya hard and good. Or so he believed.

Next to him, Eva listened as the council discussed the Greeks' findings. She looked around at the women in attendance. Eva found herself thinking she was such a dog. She wasn't particularly attracted to any of the women who attended council, but she could find one or two that would do in a pinch. Markos' cousin, Stacey or whatever her name was, she would do just fine. There was that older lady from the end of the convoy—maintained a pretty classy look given the situation and all. Eva didn't know much about her, didn't even know her name, but she noticed the woman wore a wedding ring though there was no husband in the picture. She'd gotten a vibe off the woman once or twice but hadn't pursued it. She filed her away as a future prospect as the council turned to her.

Steve listened as she laid out for those gathered where they had been that day and what they had seen. It all went in one ear and out the other. He had made up his mind that if the situation ever presented itself he would, indeed, join the non-English speaking Greek in a threesome with his leggy woman, but there'd be no gay stuff, no double penetration with his ball sack bouncing against the Greek's shaft. None of that shit. Steve kidded around about *fags* all the time with Mo and Damar and his roommates, but he didn't consider himself homophobic. That said, he wasn't too keen on ever crossing swords with another man.

After her brief presentation there was some discussion and a vote to embark on the road Eva spoke of, as this seemed to harbor less obstructions and undead than the road the Greeks had investigated.

Steve and Eva walked back to their trailers, which were four vehicles apart. Steve shared a Dutchmen Travel Trailer with his roommates, Brent and Chris. When he arrived back home Brent was standing on the roof talking to Sam, the man who lived in the Eco-line van next to their RV with his wife and kid.

"Hey, Steve," Brent said.

"Brent. Sam."

"How'd it look out there today?"

"Good. Quiet."

"Hey Steve," Sam called down. "We're pretty close to Pittsburgh, aren't we?"

"Yeah. I heard them talking about that at council. But we ain't going anywhere near the city."

Sam nodded and stood where he was with an assault rifle resting across his shoulders and neck, his arms bent at the elbows, one hand on the barrel, one on the stock.

"Hey, Brent." Steve had Sam pegged for a modern rock type of guy. "You remember that song *I'm not a playa I just fuck a lot?*"

"Yeah."

"Who sung that?"

"Big Pun. R.I.P."

"Shit."

He opened the door to the Dutchmen and stepped up inside. Chris was spread out on the flip-over sofa bed, watching a wrestling DVD. One of their neighbors, a guy they called married-man Bob, was seated at the dinette plus area, drinking one of their beers, talking. It looked like he was rambling away to himself as Chris was engrossed in a wrestling match between the Ultimate Warrior and Randy "Macho Man" Savage.

Steve had watched the DVD with Chris before. Savage was calling himself "Macho King."

"Hey, you ever tapped that blind chick again?" Married-man Bob asked him without taking his eyes off the screen.

"No. Hi Bob. Hi Chris."

"Steve likes to act like he threw that girl a mercy-fuck," Chris said, not taking his eyes off the screen. "But truth is she's the one who mercy-fucked his obnoxious ass. Watch this!" The Warrior lifted Savage off his feet by the neck and choke slammed him back to the mat. "Whoa!"

"Yeah, well at least I get laid," said Steve, "and don't spend all my time watching old wrestling videos."

He went to their freezer/fridge and took out a beer and a couple of hot pockets. Popping the beer, he drank and put the hot pockets in the microwave.

"Anyway," married-man Bob continued, "like I was saying to Chris here before you came in, I live vicariously through you younger guys now. It's a trade off is all it is."

"How's that?" asked Steve, listening to the microwave hum as it turned. "Strange pussy." Married-man Bob took a slug of his beer and burped. "It's a trade off, and the grass is always greener on the other side and that's all well and good, right? But when I weigh, on the one hand, my wife and kids, and the smiles on the faces of my kids when I come home after a day driving or something, versus—" married-man Bob killed his beer, "the uncharted territory of some sweet young ass, well, shit, it all evens out in the wash."

Steve had heard this *strange-pussy trade-off* spiel on that couch several times before and was just glad he'd walked in on the end of it. He wondered how many of their beers Bob had finished.

Chris yelled out "Hell yeah!" as the Macho King jumped off the top rope. The Warrior caught him in mid-air, placing him on his feet then slapping the man across the face.

"You know," Bob said. "That Ultimate Warrior motherfucker was *the* motherfucker."

"Shit yeah."

"How the spooks treatin' you, Steve?" Bob said.

"We get along just fine. Thanks for asking." He tried to take a bite out of his hot pocket but it was too hot so he had to wait.

"I was just sayin' to Chris, trannies are the next big thing for black guys."

"Trannies?"

"Yeah, you know, chicks with dicks."

"I know what a tranny is."

"Well, trust me. You know how, first, fat white chicks were all the rage with black guys? Then Asians, right? Well, I'm predicting a trend and—"

"Hey," Steve interrupted. "Don't you have a family to get back to?"

"Why do you think I'm here? They threw me out of the van."

He finished one hot pocket and started on the second. "I wonder why."

"I guess I just gotta stop foolin' myself." Married-man Bob shook his head.

"About what?"

"Oh shit, did you see that?" Chris said. Randy Savage leaped off the top rope and landed on a prone Warrior. Steve knew he would do this five times in succession.

"My age, man. I used to tell myself sixty is high middle age, end of middle age."

"Sixty ain't old," Steve said. "If sixty is old what is eighty?"

"Old as dirt."

"You ain't anywhere near sixty yet, Bob." Steve picked up the brown paper bag of DVDs Mason had given him and walked over to the liquor cabinet.

"Chris, where's my Blue Label?"

"Huh?"

"Forget it. I got it."

"Don't underestimate the Ultimate Warrior," an announcer on the DVD said as Steve headed back to the double bed he shared with Brent. Chris had dibs on the fold-out sofa bed.

He took his boots off and lay down. He and Brent took shifts with the bed. Because he had been out scouting all day he'd be able to catch a solid eight hours of uninterrupted sleep or wanking to Eva's tits or whatever he wanted. Then he would get out of bed and trade places with Brent when the convoy pulled out in the morning.

He opened his bottle of whiskey and took a slug.

Chris was all excited up front but hadn't left the couch. Steve knew what was happening on the video. The Warrior was talking to his hands and getting ready to guerilla press Savage.

There was a framed poster of Farrah Fawcett in a red one-piece swimsuit on the wall above the bed. The poster was Steve's. His brother had had one in his room in the 70s. After Steve had been born and grew up in the 80s the poster had still been in the room. An old Navajo blanket formed the backdrop behind the beauty.

He took another swallow of the booze. It was better than Nyquil.

When Eva returned to the RV Winnebago she shared with her sister and her nephews and niece, the bunch of them were seated around the dinette playing a board game. Edward brought his dogs, and Lauren and Maurice were there too.

"Aunt Eva!"

"Nicole!" She kissed her niece's forehead, high-fived Nelson, who gave her a knowing look, and squeezed baby Victor's cheek. The eleven-month old squealed in glee.

"Eva," Edward said. He was sitting in the driver's seat, nodding his mutton chopped head to his music on the stereo, petting one of his two long-haired dachshunds, Ennis and Ellis. Eva could never figure out which was which.

"Edward."

She didn't see what her sister saw in the old guy, with his 70s music, those two flea bags he clung to, and that out of date facial hair. But he was Sonya's flavor of the month and he treated her sister correct, so Eva was cool with him. She placed her assault rifle/shotgun combo on the rack over Lauren's MP-40.

"Evangeline," Sonya said, "what's this I hear you let Nelson shoot at Zed today?"

Nelson gave his aunt a sheepish look and mouthed, "I didn't say anything, Aunt Eva."

She looked at Maurice, sitting next to Lauren, petting one of Edward's dachshunds. Maurice looked down. Lauren had her

Browning Hi Power on the table, the slide locked open, the magazine well empty, the clip lying next to it.

"Hi Sonya," she said. "Nice to see you too."

"I'll buy three houses," Nicole said and handed over the Monopoly money.

I sez Pig-Pen, this here's Rubber Duck an' I'm about to put the hammer down, sang C.W. McCall.

"Eva?" Sonya said.

She crossed the Winnebago to sit behind Edward in the swivel chair. Sonya continued to look at the door where she had been.

"He's not a little baby anymore."

"He'll always be my baby," Sonya said..

"This world doesn't allow extended childhoods."

"Ladies," Edward said.

"We're not done talking about this, Evangeline."

"I'd hope not, sis."

Maurice sneezed and little Victor laughed hilariously, like this was the greatest thing the toddler had ever seen.

"That makes you laugh, little man?" Maurice asked and the kid looked at him with anticipation so he faked a second sneeze, jerking his head and making the noise, and the baby cackled.

"Hey Eva," Lauren said.

"Hi Lore. Looks like your friend Mo' there ratted me out."

"Looks like."

"You must be hungry, Eva." Edward stood.

"Edward made us a wonderful dinner," Lauren said.

Ennis or Ellis splayed on his back and Maurice rubbed his stomach. Eva noticed Maurice still wasn't making eye contact with her.

"Oh yeah, what'd you guys have?"

"Peas and beets and ham!" Nelson said.

"Mommy, pay me. You're on Astor Place."

"Beets, huh?"

"Victor likes beets," Lauren said.

"You're a tough little man, little man." Eva hid her face behind her hands, said "peek-a-boo," opened her hands and said, "I see you!"

The baby trilled in joy.

Edward had crossed to the kitchenette.

"Give me a second and I'll fix you a plate."

"Thanks, Edward. You're a gentleman and a man of honor." She looked at Maurice as she said this. When he looked up at her she gave him a dirty look and he looked away. Lauren nudged him with her elbow.

"No, Mommy," Nicole said. "Those are five-hundreds. These are your hundreds."

C.W. sang about *eleven long-haired friends of Jesus in a chartreuse microbus.*

She sat and watched the Monopoly game. She watched Maurice pet the dog with Lauren next to him, thought about how she'd eat and help Sonya put the kids down for the night, clean her guns and talk to her sister, try to avoid an argument but probably fail. She'd go to sleep, get up, and do it all over again the next day.

THE STRANGERS

Buddy hadn't said much all day. He'd trudged along behind them, always back there, always bringing up the rear, the bayonet mounted on his AK. When he'd gotten close enough at times they'd been able to hear him talking to himself, a low, guarded tone, few of the words coherent, and they'd all seen his eyes darting around in his head, side to side, suspicious, scared.

Buddy scared? Gwen couldn't buy it. She'd been there, in Eden, when he and Harris had come in together. Buddy was the only man who could stand up to Graham and his brute thug Markowski, and he had. Her husband, Bobby, had told her once that Buddy was like a bad dream, but someone else's, not their own.

Bear led them up the road, past the occasional car, through the snow. He walked ahead of their little group, and, she thought, was like Buddy, equally a part of it but apart from it.

It never ceased to surprise her how they could go for hours without ever seeing a zombie then there'd be pockets of them, dozens of them, all gathered in one place. She was used to the walls of Eden, thronged by thousands of the undead, their cries breaking the silence of the night when she'd tried to sleep in bed next to Bobby, her man, her protector.

She laughed to herself. Her protector. A quaint concept. Life in zombie-land had taught her she could care for herself. If she hadn't been able to, she wouldn't have made it as far as she had. Bobby had been kind of old fashioned in a sense, and really saw it as his duty to be her provider and protector, and he did that as best he could in the relatively short time they'd had together as husband and wife.

Who had been there to protect Bobby? Gwen thought. No one. Her Bobby had died down in Markowski's basement. Harris' basement,

85

she corrected herself. Harris and Julie had moved into the Pole's house after, well, *after* Buddy killed Markowski down in the dark of the sewers. What had really happened there, she wondered. She'd heard stories, from Camille when Sal had come back from underground, stories about how Buddy had marched Markowski handcuffed into the blackness. How he'd come back with Markowski's head. She'd seen Buddy execute Graham.

Her Bobby never got out of that basement. She figured it out later. Her man had been concerned about Harris and had gone to check on him. And she didn't think Harris had meant to kill Bobby. He probably just didn't want Bobby to interfere with his plans. But he had killed Bobby, *her* Bobby, and her Bobby was gone from her now.

She thought of this as she walked with Mickey and Julie and contemplated the baby in Julie's womb, Harris' baby. It would be all too easy to bear a grudge against Julie. Julie's man had been responsible for her man's demise. All too easy, and all too human. But she wasn't stupid. She knew Julie had had nothing to do with Bobby's death, and that baby in her belly—that baby was innocent of all this.

"…you see the way they're looking at you…"

"…don't listen to him, Buddy, he's trying to goad you…"

Buddy's face twitched and he sniffled.

"…you want to know something truly fucked up, jig?"

"…leave him alone goddamn you…"

"…you think that's your boy's baby in there, huh? Heh-heh-heh…"

"What?" he asked but the sound he made bore no resemblance to the word *what*.

"…you think that's your friend's child inside that bitch?"

"Buddy." Julie had turned and walked back to him.

"Jule-Julie," he stammered.

"You've got to be cold." She reached out and drew either side of his jacket together and zippered it. He stared at her stomach jutting out under her clothes and coat.

"You want to feel the baby?" Julie saw he was intent on her belly. She took one of his hands and made to place it on her stomach but he drew the hand back quickly, surprising her. "Okay. It's okay. You keep up."

They had left the tracks earlier that day and their trek over the last two hours was slow going, all uphill on a curving mountain path. They lost sight of the river amidst the tree and rock outcroppings and did not encounter any undead. The freshly fallen snow here was unmarked—a reassuring sign that no one, living or dead, had come this way.

They passed a one-story Tudor-style building on their right. Snow had slid free to reveal the steep-gabled slate roof. The roof and the stucco-finished walls looked the worse for wear. Two flag poles were set in the ground at the former toll house.

"Hey," Mickey said. "Let's think of some songs we can sing for him when he pops out."

"Mickey." Gwen shook her head. "Pops out?"

"I was there when my son was born. That's basically what happens."

"For *him?*" asked Julie.

"For him who? Or is it *whom?*"

"No, you said let's come up with some songs *for him*. See, now that's funny, because I have this feeling she's a she inside there." Julie caressed her stomach through her layers.

"You think it's a girl?" Gwen asked.

"I don't know why," admitted Julie. "But, yeah, I have that feeling."

"What does your stomach look like—without your clothes on I mean?" asked Mickey.

She looked at him like he was crazy.

"No, I don't mean that in a weird way," Mickey said. "I mean, don't they say its all how your stomach hangs? Kind of indicates whether it's a boy or a girl? You know, if you look like an apple versus a pear?"

Gwen and Julie laughed.

"Mickey," Julie explained. "I think what you're thinking of is if the stomach is up high or hanging low."

"That whole pear-versus-apples thing is about bodyfat distribution," Gwen said.

"Okay, whatever."

"And that's bogus anyway. Guessing a baby's sex by the mom's belly."

"Oh, but if a mom thinks she's going to have a girl, that's enough of an indication, huh?"

"Call it mother's intuition."

Gwen nodded and said to her, "You've earned that."

"Okay, *songs*," Mickey said. "How about this one? *Tick-tock, tick-tock, I'm a little coo-coo clock. Tick-tock, tick-tock, the clock strikes ONE!*"

"I hadn't heard that one before," Julie said.

"The second verse is easier than the first," Mickey said, and he continued the song, Gwen and Julie joining him.

Bear lumbered through the snow ahead of the others. He heard Mickey and Julie and Gwen behind him singing about the wheels on the bus. Buddy was behind them, following the group.

He was worried about Buddy. As long as the man could put one foot in front of the other, and so long as he wasn't a threat to any of their group…

He crested a rise and saw the span of a suspension bridge across the river ahead in the distance. He'd been up this way a few times before, long ago, on his chopper. The Bear Mountain Bridge. He smiled to himself. He hadn't asked for the nickname. It had been given to him.

The span looked free of zombies from this distance. He looked to the sky and judged they had a few more hours of light. The road wound down from this point to the bridge.

A half hour later the road turned and let out onto the main span which was nearly five hundred meters in length. The cables, pylons and deck trusses were all steel. The two vehicle lanes were twelve feet wide apiece and the shoulders, separated by low concrete walls, added another eight feet to either side. Two massive eighteen-inch cables ran either side of the bridge, suspending the entire structure above the Hudson.

As he stepped onto the bridge he saw he had been wrong. There was a zombie on the span, a little one. It had been a midget and it was naked and it just stood there. When it saw him it opened its mouth and rasped but didn't move and he wondered if the little thing was frozen in place.

He approached the thing cautiously, scanning either side of the bridge, looking for other undead, but this one was apparently alone. How long it had stood here, why it wasn't moving, and why it was naked, he would never know. It growled at him as he stepped up to it and he swung down with the mace, his aim slightly off, knocking the thing's jaw off its face.

The little zombie shook its head and blinked, its jaw laying fifteen feet off in the snow. It made eye contact with him and from somewhere deep inside its core it growled. Bear brought the mace down with greater accuracy this time, clumping the thing on the crown of its head, and it dropped like a suit of clothes slipped from a hanger. He was pretty sure it was finished but just to be certain he clobbered it a couple of more times.

"You ever see a midget zombie before?" Mickey asked the two women as they passed the crumpled naked body.

"I think I saw a dwarf zombie," Gwen said. "Dwarves have the big heads, right? And midgets are, like, perfectly formed, right? Just smaller than other people?"

"I think that's it."

"I saw a black albino zombie once," Julie said.

"How'd you know it was a black albino?"

"You never saw a black albino before?"

"No. And you're not kidding me, right?"

"No, I'm not kidding you," Julie said. "My brother wrestled in high school. He always said the toughest guys he had to wrestle were—"

"Black albinos?" Mickey said.

"No, the blind."

"The blind? You're brother wrestled blind guys?"

"Yeah. What, you think blind kids don't wrestle and play other sports?"

"As long as they're not playing darts."

"Not funny, Mickey," Gwen said.

"My brother always talked about this one blind kid, wrestled in the one hundred and eighty one pound class, a blind albino. State champion a couple of years in a row. Said the kid was tough as, well, he said the kid was *tough*."

"This is a beautiful bridge," Gwen said, looking down into the river, then around at the broad expanses of trees and white. The mountains loomed behind and ahead of them to their left.

"Come on ladies. One-two-three! *London Bridge is falling down...*"

At the opposite end of the span was a New England-style brick house and two toll booths. Bear felt like he was being watched as he approached the small building. He didn't stop but he did sling the mace over his back and draw one of his Glocks. He hoped he wouldn't have to fire it. If he did the gunshot would bring whatever zombies were within earshot.

He heard it before he saw it. It must have been a brain and it lay in wait in one of the two toll booths, in the *EZ-pass only* lane. As he tread closer the thing peeked through the window of the toll booth and quickly dropped down. It made a lot of noise, nearly gleeful in its expectation, and he was reminded that as smart as the brains were, they weren't all that smart.

He decided when it attacked him he would take it out with his hands and forego the pistol, unless there was more than one around.

"—*the ants go marching four by four*," the ladies and Mickey were singing, Mickey the loudest, "*the little one stopped to shut the door, and they all went marching*—"

"Oh shit!" Mickey pointed. "Look!"

The zombie came tearing out of the toll booth up ahead and ran straight at Bear. It was wearing a children's party hat, an elastic band securing it under the chin. The snow, nearly knee deep here, slowed it somewhat. Bear didn't give up any ground. He squared his stance, lowered the hand with the pistol, drew back his free hand, clutched his gloved fist and—

"Oh shit!" Mickey said as Bear punched the thing in its face and knocked its head off its body. "I've seen him do that before! But it never ceases to—Damn!"

The body dropped in front of Bear. Its head and the party hat lay a few feet apart from one another in the snow.

"I'm glad he's on our side," Gwen said.

Julie turned around and looked back at Buddy who had just started across the bridge behind them. If the other man had seen any of what just went down he gave no indication of it.

"Come on Julie," Gwen said.

Bear was moving up ahead and they had to follow.

"*Circle to the left, the old brass wagon*," sang Mickey. "*Circle to the left, the old brass wagon…*"

Julie placed one hand under her belly and moved forward, Gwen next to her.

"*…circle to the left, the old brass wagon…you're the one my darling…*"

"So," Gwen said. "What are you going to call it?"

Julie shrugged.

"I don't know. I hadn't really thought about that."

"Whoa, whoa, whoa," Mickey said. "You're like, what, due in two months and you haven't thought of what you're going to name the baby?"

They sat around a fire on logs Bear and Mickey had dragged into a loose circle. The three of them sat bunched together. Buddy sat across from them on the other side of the fire, his gaze downcast, mumbling to himself, rocking back and forth slightly. He had a Zippo lighter in one hand and was rubbing his thumb over the side of it.

"There's just been so much, so much going on…"

"When that little baby gets here," Gwen smiled, "she's going to need a name."

"What do you think about Hunter or Ethan?" Mickey asked.

"I don't know, not…not my style." She wanted to say *not Harris' style*, but didn't. Harris, she thought, would have preferred what he'd have considered more "common" names, like *Matthew* or *Justin*.

"How about a good solid name, like Michael?"

"Hey," Gwen said. "Isn't Mickey diminutive for Michael?"

"You mean is it short for Michael? Sometimes, yeah, I guess. But not always. Like me. I'm just Mickey."

"Why do you assume my baby's going to be a boy?"

"I don't know. Just a feeling."

She smiled and asked him, "Would you be disappointed if it's a girl?"

"No," he said. "I'd love them both equally."

The three laughed quietly while Buddy muttered something and swayed in place.

"Hey, Julie, you know what I always wanted to ask him," said Mickey. "Was *Harris* a last name or a first name?"

"A surname," she said. "A last name."

"Hey, Buddy," Mickey called over to the other man. "That's a nickname, right? What's your real name?"

They looked and waited but if Mickey's question registered he gave no indication.

"Well." Mickey placed his auto-shotgun barrel up against the log he sat on. "Let me see if I can't go help Bear scare up some wood for the fire. It's gonna be a cold one tonight."

"Okay," Gwen said. "Be careful."

"I got my strap." He smiled, patting his waist line where he had his 9mm tucked between his thermals and his jeans. He walked off beyond the illumination of the flame, into the pines and Atlantic White Cypress, thinking to himself about the *Undying Monster* of Hammond Hall, reciting from memory, "When stars are bright, on a frosty night, beware thy bane on the rocky lane…"

"He's funny," Julie said of Mickey when he was out of ear shot.

"He's got his moments," agreed Gwen.

An owl hooted in the woods.

Buddy cocked one eye towards the darkness and his rocking slowed. The thumb on the lighter froze.

"Ho, friends." The strangers stepped from the night and a site they were. There were three of them—a woman and two men. They were clothed in rags and furs and pieces of coats and clothes stitched together. Their hair had grown out and hung from their heads in clumps. They looked weather-beaten and worn around the edges, grimy and feral. As they stepped into the light Julie and Gwen could see one of the two men was missing most of his hand. In his other he toted a red cooler.

The taller of the two men had spoken. Cadaverous, his eyes looked enormous in his head. His shrunken cheeks and prominent chin were covered with bristly hair, much in need of a shave. He had a rifle of some sort slung over his back, barrel down. His skin was leathery and his eyes were hard. He was older than the others, much older.

Gwen instinctively reached for the M16A4.

"I said *greetings* friends." The taller man's voice was gruff, almost hoarse. "Won't be no need for that." He indicated the assault rifle. "Will there?"

Gwen wasn't sure what to do. The tall man had a rifle but it hadn't left his back. They had announced themselves. If they'd meant herself or Julie or Buddy harm... Gwen made a decision and leaned back, away from the sixteen.

"That's better now." The tall man nodded. "Put Emily here at ease."

Buddy hadn't moved from where he sat, rocking slowly, and though Julie and Gwen hadn't noticed it, he was no longer mumbling to himself. His thumb had started moving back and forth again, polishing the side of the lighter.

"Would you ladies mind if we joined you, warmed our weary bones by your fire? It's a cold night, and it's been a long day."

Before either could answer the tall man motioned with his hand. The one-handed man sat down across from Gwen and Julie, on the other side of the fire, on Buddy's right. The woman sat on his left and the tall man settled down next to her, uncomfortably close to Julie. Gwen shifted her weight towards Julie and only after she had done so did she realize she'd moved that much further from her weapon. She silently cursed herself.

"Much obliged, ma'am," the tall man addressed Gwen, letting her know he'd noted her movement, completely ignoring Julie. It was like he wasn't even taking Buddy's presence into consideration.

"Well, I guess, you're welcome," she said, stumbling over her words, detesting herself for it, for any show of weakness. "You'll have to forgive me. It's been awhile since we've seen any other people."

"Where you all coming from?" the other man inquired. He was just as gaunt as the tall man but looked frailer, weaker. He looked like an overgrown baby bird, a fledgling. Both Julie and Gwen noted the way the tall man looked at him when he spoke.

When Gwen turned her attention back to the tall man and the woman, Julie found herself staring at the second man's disfigured hand. It looked like it had been cut in half two inches above the finger line. He still had a thumb, but beneath that was a wad of dirty, reddish bandages. She had to purposefully take her focus off the man. In doing so she looked at his feet, which were encased in torn boots wrapped with duct tape.

"Now L.A.," the taller man said. "You know it's impolite to interrupt a conversation, and me and the ladies here, we were having ourselves a conversation."

The other man looked down at his ratty boots. Julie noted that the tall man wore the best footwear and the woman and the one-handed man named L.A. wore what looked like cobbler's scraps.

"Indeed, where are you ladies, and your gentleman friend there," the tall, grizzled man chin nodded to Buddy, "coming from?"

"The city," Julie said and the man licked his upper teeth before speaking.

"Is that a fact? You hear that, Emily? These three travelers, obviously much wearied and fatigued like ourselves, have escaped from that great whore of Babylon."

Oh Christ, thought Gwen, *religious fanatics.*

"Oh Christ," said the tall man, nailing Gwen with his stare. "I bet you just thought to yourself that you're sharing your fire with a bunch of religious fanatics. Didn't you?"

"No," Gwen lied. "I was just thinking it's nice to have the company of some other…some other people."

"*Some other people*," the tall man said. "You hesitated when you said that. Well, despite appearances, especially L.A. Munroe's here…" The tall man snickered but L.A. continued to look down.

"The road will do that to you. It wears away at you. Your friend over there. He looks like he knows what I'm talking about. Don't he, L.A.?"

"Yeah, John." L.A. kept looking at the ground. "Yeah."

The man who went by the name of John reached into a grimy bag he wore on one shoulder and retrieved a faded green bottle. Something like Julie's grandmother would have kept olive oil in back in their kitchen.

"Don't think I didn't notice you spying my bag there, pretty lady," John said to Julie. "This here's a five thousand dollar designer bag. *Was.* Ain't worth much now though."

He uncorked the bottle and drank from it. He growled as the contents went down. "Well, if that don't keep the cold off you on a night like this," he looked at Gwen, "I don't know what will."

"John Book," a voice called from the dark.

"Well, look here, we got more guests," John said.

Gwen and Julie looked up as Mickey came walking out of the dark, a worried look on his face, dried tree limbs stacked in his arms. Behind him marched another man—this one also tall and dirty looking, wearing a cape of furs stitched together. The man behind Mickey had a shotgun in both hands, and it did not reassure Gwen that the barrel was pointed down and off to the side.

"Mister Marcus. How good of you to join us," John said. "And look, you've brought company. Well, how lucky for us, we exhausted pilgrims, that we found these nice folks out here in the middle of," John looked around, "well, the middle of nowhere." He laughed.

"Lucky for us," said the man John had called Mister Marcus, and when he said it Gwen noticed he was missing a few of his upper teeth. She wanted to look at Julie but didn't. Instead she looked across the fire at Buddy. If he had any idea of what was going on he gave no indication. Mister Marcus's shotgun had a red sleeve of shells hugging the butt.

She realized they were in deep trouble.

"Sit down," Mister Marcus said. "Right there."

Mickey settled down, kneeling, piling the wood next to him, beside L.A. Munroe and his cooler. His USAS-12 shotgun was still barrel up, but it was between John and the quiet woman and might have well been half way across the world. Mister Marcus settled down next to him and the circle was complete.

Gwen could smell this man, Mister Marcus, and the smell wasn't good.

"Son," John spoke at Mickey. "You planning on praying or something? Settle back, why don't you?"

It wasn't a question, and he sat down in the snow. He thought he remembered a porn star named Mister Marcus, but that guy had been black. This guy was white and filthy.

"Have you a drink." John tossed the bottle to Mickey and it landed in the melting snow next to him.

"Well, thanks." He uncorked the bottle.

"Might not want to thank him 'till after you drink that," Mister Marcus said, a smile of anticipation on his ugly face.

Mickey gasped when he swallowed the liquor inside the bottle. "What-what-what the heck is this stuff?"

"What's it taste like?"

"Brake fluid!"

"That stuff'll make your chest look like one of them chia-pets," Mister Marcus promised.

"Well," John said. "How good it is to have some proper company, some *civilized* company, to while away the evening. The Lord works in mysterious ways, don't he Emma?"

The woman said nothing. She had a glazed, far off look in her eyes.

Against his better judgment, Mickey took another drink from the bottle.

Gwen felt like she had to say something to assert her...*her what?* Her whatever. "Emma? I thought your name was Emily?"

"We call her whatever we want to on any given day," the woman did not answer, "don't we Mister Marcus?"

"We sure do."

"What are some of our pet names for Edith there?"

"Well, I was always partial to *whore*, or *slut*, or *cum-queen*."

John laughed and Mister Marcus laughed but L.A. didn't. The woman just sat there.

"You'll have to forgive our, our blue sense of humor." John wiped a tear from his eye. "This road. Been awhile since we've seen any, any living people that is. Pass that bottle back over here, son." He took another swig. "Our humor may not be politically correct, but it helps us get through the day. Ain't that so, L.A.?"

"Yeah, John."

"Didn't catch that. What was that, L.A.?"

"*Yeah*, John. I said yeah."

"L.A.." John shook his head. "He's a bit more serious than me and Mister Marcus here, or Emma for that matter. Ain't that so? Young man's seen more than any young man should ever have seen. He helps keep us grounded, keeps us on the straight and narrow so to speak. You comprehend my meaning?"

Julie did not like their situation one bit. She had the .357 holstered under her jacket, out of sight, next to her protruding belly. The .380 was at her lower back and she couldn't get to it with her coat on. Where the hell was Bear?

"Yeah, we understand," Gwen said.

"Oh, she knows we're just messin' with her, don't ya' hon?" He reached over and squeezed the woman's flat breast through her layers of clothes and rags, which made Mister Marcus laugh again.

"You two married?" Mickey said.

He turned his head slowly to look at him. "We're all married in the eyes of God, son. You're familiar, perhaps, with the concept of the family of man?" He passed the bottle around the circle, back to Mickey.

"Uh, somewhat," Mickey muttered, then changed tactics. "What you guys got in the cooler?"

John laughed and so did Mister Marcus.

"What's so funny?" Mickey asked, steeling himself, gulping down a mouthful of the liquid.

"Nothing. Nothing son." John composed himself. "And it's good of you to point that out. L.A., don't be stingy. Crack that cooler and let's break bread with our new friends. And look at you there, hogging that bottle."

Mickey handed the bottle to Mister Marcus and the other man uncorked it and drank. He watched the man with one hand open the cooler. There was snow packed inside.

L.A. reached into the snow with his one good hand and removed a few Tupperware containers. He cracked one open and there was meat inside.

"Oh man, you've got *meat*." Mickey started babbling in part because he was nervous and the liquor was working on him. "We haven't had meat in…cans, *always* cans. Canned peas, canned corn, canned cream corn. You ever try and eat cream corn out of the can without a spoon?" he asked Mister Marcus.

"No, can't say I ever did." Mister Marcus had a bemused look on his hard face.

"Mickey," Gwen said, but the other did not look at her.

"My friends tell you we're coming out of the city? Well, it's bad down there. Millions of zombies, *millions* of them. We were holed up in Eden—it's got walls, there were a bunch of us, and every day—"

"Did you say *Eden?*" John asked.

"Yeah, Eden. We called it Eden."

"Well, why'd you call it Eden?"

"Eden? I don't know, it—"

"When we got there," Julie said. "They were calling it Eden. The people who were already there—"

"Pretty lady, pretty lady." John clicked his tongue in his mouth several times. "If I correct L.A. Munroe for interrupting my conversation with you and the other pretty lady there, but I *don't* correct you when you interrupt my conversation with this man, well, that might be seen by some as unfair. Couldn't it, Mister Marcus?"

"Sure could."

"So…ain't she a pretty one though, Mister Marcus?"

"Sure is." The other man drank from the bottle.

"Pass that bottle back this way, Mister Marcus. Now, L.A., tight ain't right. Share our bounty with these strangers."

When L.A. hesitated Mister Marcus reached over Mickey and grabbed two of the tupperwares. He dropped one in Mickey's lap and opened the other, scooping up some meat in his dirty fingers and shoving it in his mouth.

Mickey pried the lid from his container and stared at the meat. Roast beef, hamburger, London Broil, pot roast, prime rib, flank steak…it had been so long since…

"Mickey." If he heard Gwen he ignored her as he mimicked Mister Marcus and followed suit, shoving a glob of meat into his mouth.

"L.A.?" there was a question on John's face.

L.A. stood and walked around the woman named Emma or Emily and presented another Tupperware container to the man named John. Then he returned to his seat.

Julie watched John open his container and start to eat. She noticed how neither John nor Mister Marcus, or Mickey for that matter, offered herself or Gwen or the other woman any meat. John drank from the bottle as he ate.

"Your friend there looks like he's in a bad way," Mister Marcus said between mouthfuls, indicating Buddy.

"Yeah, he's been better," Mickey said. "What did you say this was again?"

"Zebra," Mister Marcus said and he and John immediately started laughing.

This John guy reminded Mickey of someone, someone famous, but he couldn't put his finger on it.

"Zebra, huh? Tastes like chicken."

This caused John and Mister Marcus to laugh even harder. When they had finally stopped laughing John asked Mickey, "You guys keep it up, put me in a good mood, I might grace you with a song tonight."

The woman named Emma or Emily or whatever clapped several times then went still once more.

John looked at Julie in a conspiratorial manner and winked at her. "Emma here likes it when I sing. So, you pilgrims used to live in a place called Eden, eh?"

"Sure did." Ravenous, he continued to stuff his face.

"And you chose to leave? Or were you thrown out?"

"It's complicated."

"So you were thrown out."

"No. That's not what happened," He noticed neither Gwen nor Julie were eating. "Hey, you guys want some?"

"Yeah." John turned his attention to Julie and Gwen. "You ladies want some zebra-meat?"

Mister Marcus laughed.

Someone from the movies, thought Mickey, that's who this John reminded him of. Maybe the old man from *Phantasm*? Nah...

"No, no thank you," Gwen said. "What about her?" She meant the woman who travelled with the strangers.

"She'll eat later," Mister Marcus said.

Lance Henrikson, thought Mickey. That's it. And this whole scene, like something out of a movie with Henrickson... *Aliens*? No. *Pumpkinhead*? No...

"What about you?" Mister Marcus asked Julie. "Ain't you hungry?"

"No, I already ate."

"You know, pretty lady," John said. "In some circles it'd be considered downright rude to refuse to break bread with a man."

"Look, I'm not trying to be rude. It's just that, I mean, you guys didn't even cook that meat. I don't know how long it's been in that cooler or when..."

Mickey thought one of Henrikson's finest roles, aside from his work on *Millenium*, was as Jesse, patriarch of the peripatetic vampire clan in *Near Dark*. Jesse, screaming out the window of the Hide-A-Way hotel in his tinted goggles as he unloaded on the law with a big automatic. Jesse, who, when asked how old he was, replied, *Let's put it this way. I fought for the South. We lost. Near Dark*, starring another of Mickey's favorites, Bill Paxton, long before that man was chasing tornadoes or battling aliens. A cocksure six-gun totin' spur-wearin'...

"It's not tartar," John said. "You can trust me on that."

"It's just, I have to be real careful, what with the baby and—"

The woman who had not spoken looked up at her.

"The baby?" John stopped eating and Julie immediately regretted saying it. "Are you with child, pretty lady?"

Gwen forced herself to move away from Julie and towards her M16A4.

"May I?"

Julie wanted to scream no at him, to tell him to keep his dirty hands the hell away from her, but she was petrified and sat as still as she could will herself as John leaned over and unzipped her jacket. He pulled the flap of her coat back, revealing her belly. John whistled and sat back.

"The woman *is* with child. Cause for celebration. Mister Marcus, where's that hooch?"

Mister Marcus passed the bottle back to John and the tall man drank deeply. "That'll do the trick.

"None for you, pretty lady," he said to Julie. "What with the baby and all. Drink Emily."

The woman sipped from the bottle.

Deadman, thought Mickey, *that's* what this whole scene reminded him of. Jim Jarmusch's western. The critics had been unfair. The movie had rocked! Johnny Depp, Robert Mitchum's last big role, Neil Young soundtrack. Gary Farmer as the fat Indian—*Stupid fucking white man*—and Lance Henrickson as Cole Wilson, who, after emptying his revolver in fellow bounty hunter Conway Twill dumps the cylinder and tosses the empties at Twill, growling at him, *Here, eat 'em.* But that scene didn't make the final cut, thought Mickey, you had to have the extras on the DVD for that.

"Course," John was saying, "there are those who would question the wisdom of bringing a vulnerable child into this zombie-ridden world of ours."

And then it hit him, the familiarity of their situation and Jarmusch's film. Henrickson's Wilson character was a legendary bounty hunter who had fucked *and* eaten his own parents. *Eaten.* After Cole Wilson killed Conway Twill he cooked him up and *ate* him, even with that perpetual toothache that—

"*Uhhhhhh!*" He tossed the Tupperware away, rolled over on his side and stuck two fingers down his throat. Mister Marcus and John started laughing demonically and Gwen moved a few inches closer to her M16.

"No," John said. He stopped laughing and moved his furs aside to reveal the handle of a pistol holstered snug against his stomach. It was a Desert Eagle .357. "Don't go and ruin our evening, okay?"

Gwen froze where she was.

"Ahhh, you sons of bitches—motherfuckers." Mickey gagged.

"Looks like the devil got up into him." Mister Marcus said.

"Looks like."

"You bastards." Spit dripped from Mickey's mouth. "What the hell did you feed me?"

Mister Marcus smiled. "Zebra meat, wasn't it?"

"The man said it himself." John didn't take his eyes off Gwen. "Tastes like chicken."

"Motherfuckers, bastards." Mickey dry heaved. "Was that—was that human flesh?"

"Human flesh?" John looked amused. "What do you have to say to that, Mister Marcus?"

"Well." Mister Marcus picked a piece of meat out of the space where a tooth had been. He stared at it. "I guess it was human, once." He popped the meat back in his mouth.

"*Zombie*," Mickey said. "You're *eating* zombie?"

"You're eating it too," Mister Marcus said with a straight face but John laughed hard, holding one side of his torso.

Mickey vomited in the snow.

"Now come on, son. Mister Marcus here is just messin' with you. Do you really think you can eat dead human flesh?"

Mickey squinted from the tears his purge had brought out and stared down at the chunks of meat in his vomit.

"Why don't—why don't you tell me?"

John Book drank from the bottle and sighed. "Come to think of it, lot of things one can do that people never considered."

"Speak, John," Mister Marcus said.

"You all ever heard of a penile bisection? When a man cuts his willy in two, make it look like—aw, forget it.

"Take L.A. there. Ya'll have noticed by now, no doubt, that L.A. is missing him a large part of his left hand, yes? Show 'em L.A."

"Come on, John," the man mumbled impotently.

"I said *show 'em*, L.A.. Show 'em, son."

He held his bandaged hand up for all to see but continued to look at the ground.

"Now, any guesses how L.A. lost that there hand of his? None. Try this on for size. Zombie nibbled the tips of L.A.'s fingers off. A death sentence, right? *Wrong*."

"What do you mean?" Gwen asked, thinking if she could keep this man talking… Where was Bear? She looked over at Buddy. There would be no help from him.

"As soon as L.A. got bit, I got me my saw, and like Abraham draped his son Isaac over that rock, I lay L.A. down—"

"I held him," Mister Marcus said.

"—with Mister Marcus's assistance, and I removed the offensive members, like that." John moved his hand back and forth in a sawing motion. "Boy been alright ever since, ain't you L.A.?"

"Never better." L.A. didn't sound convincing.

"See, we arrested the spread of that zombie's poison in this boy's system. And like I was sayin', there's things known, and there's things unknown."

"Speak, John."

"And there's secrets a man," John looked at Julie, "and a woman," he addressed the group again, "keep close to their hearts." John looked directly at Mickey. "You got you a secret, don't you son?"

"Huh? What? What do you—"

"Don't equivocate with me, son. I am John Book—"

"*Amen!*" Mister Marcus shouted.

"…And I am the Lord!"

"*Halleluiah!*"

"And I have seen deep into the hearts and souls of man and I have seen all that was and all that will be—and, *dammit*, I feel good. I feel good enough…good enough for a song!"

"*Glory come!*"

John Book stood up and started to sway to a tune only he heard. The woman clapped sporadically and had a gleeful, crazed look on her face, though she continued to stare at Julie. Mister Marcus watched Gwen and Julie and Mickey and said, "You are in for an extra special treat now."

"*I knew a girl named Nikki*," John sang, his voice gravelly. "*I guess you could say she was*—no, no, no." He slugged a mouthful from the bottle. "That song don't suit the mood. How 'bout a song, for your women?" John looked at Mickey. "I mean, I can tell they ain't *your* women, but, well, just sit there and if you want to, why don't you join Emily, and clap your spank hand?" The woman hadn't ceased clapping, "Without further ado…

"*Guuuuuuuuuuuuuurrrrrrrrrrrrrrllllllllllllllll*," crooned John—

"Dung-dung-dung-dung," intoned Mister Marcus.

"—*you'll be a woman, soooooooooooooooon*—Damn!" John sat down. "Sometimes, sometimes the spirit just *moves* me."

Mickey sat staring. This was all so unreal. Like a David Lynch film.

"You should close your mouth, son," John said, "before the flies move in. Cigarillo, Mister Marcus?"

He produced a shiny silver cigarette holder from his furs and popped it open. He took out two short, narrow cigars and handed one over to Mister Marcus.

"Let me see that." Mister Marcus reached over and took the lighter from Buddy's hand. Buddy did not protest. "Thanks."

He lit his cigar, "Nice lighter," and then passed the Zippo to John who did the same. He tossed the lighter back to Mister Marcus and Mister Marcus rolled the wheel, toying with it.

"So, pretty lady." John turned his gaze on Julie. "This baby of yours—"

"*Never!*" The woman who travelled with the three men spoke for the first time.

"What's that Emily?" John said. "Listen up, all. The little woman has something she wants to say."

"Never." The woman's eyes looked drugged, Gwen thought. "That child must not be."

"*What?*" Julie said.

"Yeah," Gwen said. "*What?*"

"This world," said Emma or Emily or whatever her true name was. "No child must be brought into this world."

"It is sort of inhospitable," Mister Marcus said, dislodging another gob of meat from a gap in his teeth. He held his thumb out to Mickey and when the other man blanched he shrugged and dipped it back into his own mouth. "You gotta admit."

The lighter had disappeared somewhere in his furs.

"Excuse me," Gwen said. She was angry now. "You have no fucking right to decide for my friend—"

"No sweetheart," John said. "*You* have no anything. And the language ain't no call for."

"I were you," Mister Marcus said, "I'd just sit there and shut my dick hole."

"Fuck you, you—"

"Mister Marcus, Mister Marcus. You heard me reprimand the lady for her tongue just now, didn't you?"

"Come on, John," L.A. spoke up. "Let's leave 'em alone…"

"What have I told you about addressing me, boy? Did the Mayans dare to gaze directly upon the mighty Atahualpa?"

"You're crazy," Gwen said. "You're all fucking crazy, aren't you? Do you really think you're some kind of God?"

"Language." John shook his head. "You really don't get it, do you? This is going to end bad for—"

"John, come on—"

"L.A.."

There was wrath in his voice. As John reached over to take the bottle from the woman, Bear materialized from behind him like a bad dream come from the night, pressing one Glock to the back of the man's scraggly-haired head. In his other hand was a second Glock, the one with the green laser sight, and there was a green dot on Mister Marcus's chest.

"Do it," Bear said. Mister Marcus took his focus off his rifle and stared at the shadow looming behind John.

"Well," John said, and he didn't sound scared. "I don't think we've had the chance to be acquainted. Judging by the look on Mister Marcus's face, you must be a sight to behold."

"Shut the fuck up," Bear said.

L.A. sat, frozen, frightened.

"If you shoot me, you'll bring every zombie for miles around to your camp fire. Ya'll can sing—"

He cracked John over the head with the Glock. The man groaned and leaned forward but remained seated.

"Like I said, *friend*, we ain't been acquainted. My name is John Book, and these good folk here with—"

"*John Book?*" Mickey shouted. "John Book was Harrison Ford's character's name in *Witness*. Your name isn't John Book, you bastard!"

"He sure is," Mister Marcus said, watching Bear, "and *we're* his witnesses!"

"Here's how this goes, you sick bastards." Gwen had retrieved her M16A4 and stood. Julie was behind her, the .357 and .380 drawn. "One at a time, you're going to stand and you're going to take off your coats, nice and slow. Any weapons you have, *anything*, you're going to dump them right here."

John Book was the last of the four to shed his furs and weapons.

"I'm gonna miss that pistol," he said as he lay the Desert Eagle down reverently. He turned to face Bear behind him for the first time. "Well, you are a big one, ain't cha'?"

When they were done they stood, the four of them, L.A. and the woman shivering in the cold. Bear continued to loom behind John, one Glock to the man's head, the laser sight on Mister Marcus.

Mickey picked up the green bottle and drained the contents in the snow. John Book shook his head as the last of the liquid flowed out.

"Now, you're going to walk off, into the dark, away from us, and you're not coming back," Gwen said. "If you do, I'll kill you."

"I'll kill you," Julie whispered, looking at the woman.

"Well," John said. "This ain't exactly neighborly behavior, is it?"

"You like getting hit in the head?" Bear asked.

"Hear me out for one second, okay friends? Hear me this: You'll look back on this night with regret. You took me and Mister Marcus and our companions here for a threat, yet I implore you, ask yourselves, what threat did a starving old man and his three friends ever pose you? You can't be serious believing that was actually zombie meat—"

"You threatened my baby!" Julie snapped.

"I merely advanced an opinion, pretty lady—"

Bear cut off the conversation by smashing the man in the head again with the butt of his pistol. John Book almost went down but remained standing. He blinked several times until he was finally able to speak.

"Okay, okay, okay, *friend*." He looked at Julie. "See you later, pretty lady." Then he looked at Gwen and he winked at her.

"Go, now," Gwen said to Mister Marcus. He exhaled, and she couldn't help but think for a man who should be scared, who should be very afraid, this guy wasn't. He was taking his cues from John Book, and that guy was cool as a —

"Wait," L.A. protested with his one hand. "Can I—"

"L.A., shut up! Come on." Mister Marcus took Emma and L.A. each by an arm. "Let's get."

He led them off into the dark.

John stood there with Bear's 9mm pressed to the back of his head. They waited quietly for several minutes, listening to the receding crunch-crunch-crunch of Mister Marcus, the woman and L.A.'s feet in the snow. When they couldn't hear them any longer Gwen turned to John.

"Now, *you*. Go."

"You sendin' them out there without their coats."

"You too." Gwen said.

"You know what that means, don't you?"

"Go figure it out."

Bear propelled him ahead several feet by shoving the barrel of his Glock against the man's head.

He went to reach for the cooler but Mickey yelled, "No!" and kicked it off into the night. "No!"

"That's the problem with the world, today," John said as he walked off after his companions. "Everybody's so damn un-friendly."

They listened to him leave. Buddy hadn't moved the entire time.

"Are you okay, Julie?" Gwen turned.

"Yeah, I'm—I mean, I'm shook up, but I'm okay."

"Bear, oh thank God. How long were you there?"

"Long enough. I wasn't going to let them hurt any of you."

"Then you heard, you heard that guy's song?"

He nodded.

"Crazy," Mickey said. "They're crazy, aren't they?"

"Whatever they are," Bear said, "they've made it this far. Mickey, do me a favor. I left a whole bunch of wood for the fire over here. Come help me get it."

Julie went over to Buddy and crouched down next to him.

"You okay?"

He either didn't hear her or ignored her.

Gwen stood looking in the direction the four strangers had gone, one hand wrapped around the vertical grip of her M16A4, the other around the pistol grip, index finger resting on the trigger guard.

Julie reached out and put her hands on Buddy's shoulders, then touched his cheeks.

"Oh, you're so cold." She grabbed a rolled blanket strapped to the top of Mickey's backpack. She unfurled it and draped it over his shoulders, tucking it in around his chest.

A few minutes later Mickey and Bear returned with the wood. They stacked most of it and fed the fire the rest. The flames rose and the circle of illumination spread further outwards.

"You should think about getting some sleep," Bear spoke to the group. Looking at Julie he added, "Especially you."

"I don't think I can sleep after that."

"Me neither," Gwen said.

"Think about the baby," Bear said.

That was the problem, Julie thought. She *was* thinking about the baby. And so was that strange woman with those…those men.

"I'll keep watch. You guys try and rest."

"I don't know," Julie said.

"It's okay. I won't let anyone hurt you or the baby."

She believed him.

"What about you?" Mickey asked.

"You guys sleep for a few hours. I'll wake one of you to trade places with me."

Within a half hour the three of them were bedded down around the fire. Only Buddy and Bear remained awake. Buddy sat on his log and stared at his empty hands. Bear had moved beyond the glow of the fire to the shadows and stood with his back to a tree.

He watched Buddy from his vantage point. He thought about the man and his situation, worried for him. He was just beginning to wonder if Buddy could physically relieve himself, or if they'd be forced to change him when he soiled himself, when he stood and walked away from the fire.

He was gone for some time. After awhile Bear thought the man might have wandered off and was gone for good. He might freeze to death out there on a night like this. But Bear had no intention of leaving the dark outside the glow of the fire, of leaving his three friends alone here. He had promised Julie.

When the sounds of footsteps plodding through the snow reached his ears, a warning immediately went off in his head. This was not Buddy returning to camp. He could not have made that much noise if he tried to, could he? Whoever was coming wasn't taking any precautions to minimize the racket they were making.

He moved from his position against the tree to intercept who-ever it was, confident that so long as he kept himself from being backlit by the fire he would remain unseen in this moonless night. He hoped he was wrong and it was Buddy. He had the Glock with the green laser sight in one hand and wished he hadn't left the mace back at the fire with his other possessions. If he had to fire with the pistol he would, but then, like that man John Book had said, every zombie within hearing would be on them.

The other man was moving through the dark, his step unsteady. He slipped to one knee in the snow, righted himself, moved on.

Bear took L.A. from behind. One mighty hand wrapped around the scrawny man's neck, lifting him up to his tippy toes then off the ground. L.A. reached for Bear's wrist and forearm with his one good hand and the half that was the other, gasping, blurting out, "way-wait-wuh—" before Bear's other hand clamped around his jaw. L.A. tried to shake his head free but with a mighty twist Bear broke his neck.

The body went limp in his hands and he let it fall to the ground. He stooped and found his Glock. He wiped the snow from it and stared out into the darkness. Nothing. He left the body and circled back around to the other side of the camp. If the four of them were coming they'd have split up and would attack the camp from opposite sides.

Bear waited in the dark where he could see the campfire and the three people sleeping around it but no one could see him. Why would John Book have sent L.A. all by himself? Even if they had planned a coordinated attack… Bear realized there was no coordinated attack coming. He waited in the dark and watched the camp, realizing L.A.'s body was out there somewhere in the dark where he had left it.

With the coming of dawn, Bear saw Buddy seated on his log by the fire much as he had been the night before. How had he gotten back to the fire without Bear seeing him? Satisfied they were as safe as they were going to be, he trudged over to the fire. Mickey, Gwen and Julie lay in their sleeping bags. Mickey had a troubled look in his sleep, a frown on his face.

"Bear."

"Buddy."

He breathed out. Buddy was a mess. His hands and the blade of the bayonet he gripped were caked with dried blood. The sleeves of his leather jacket were slick with more blood. The man sat there on the log, somewhat coherent, arms resting on his knees.

"What happened?" he asked, but he knew.

Buddy rubbed his finger on the wheel of the Zippo lighter.

"Oh…." Bear sighed. He went to his backpack and opened it, digging around inside until he found the container of handi-wipes.

"Gotta clean you up," he squatted down next to Buddy, "before the others wake up. We don't want them to see this."

He took one of his blood stained hands in his own, removed the bayonet from it, and started rubbing his fingers and palm with the wipes.

"Bear," he said. "Thanks."

His one good eye looked into Buddy's and he was sure the man was there today, unlike yesterday.

"Yeah. You're welcome."

He was apparently "with it" enough that when he volunteered to walk point no one protested. The day was cold and grey and the landscape around them was stark and dead.

"Did we do the right thing?" Gwen asked the question Julie was thinking.

"What do you mean?" Mickey asked.

"I mean, we were freaked out by those people last night, by—"

"You're talking about the other day?" Mickey said. "That compound or whatever it was?"

"Yeah."

"They had people crucified outside their gate," Mickey said it gently. He wasn't looking for an argument.

"Maybe they were zombies?" Julie asked and Gwen looked at her gratefully.

Bear shook his head. "They weren't zombies. Zombies were gathered around the crosses. That meant those people on those crosses were human beings. That guy on that cross, he was alive. He was human. Like us."

"Maybe they were bad men," Julie said.

"Bad men." Mickey mulled it over. "Like Graham. Like Markowski." He would have added *like Diaz* but didn't out of respect to Julie.

"Yeah," Julie said. "Maybe they were."

"Well, look what happened to *them*," Mickey said. "They're dead."

"Because Buddy killed them," as she said it, Gwen looked ahead at the big man with the saddle bags plowing his way through the snow.

"Because they were evil men," Bear said. "I would have done the same. I should have done the same. The point is, Buddy killed them, but he didn't crucify them."

"We blew their gate," Julie said. "We let all those zombies in there."

"*Buddy* blew the gate," Gwen whispered.

"Listen," Mickey said. "If we plan on 'repopulating' the earth or whatever, what kind of people do you want on it? I don't mean you, Julie or Gwen. I mean *you* in general. Do we want assholes? Assholes that crucify their own kind?"

"What did Buddy do to those people last night?" Gwen asked Bear. "When we woke up you were cleaning him off."

"I don't know and I don't want to know." Mickey looked away.

"They were going to hurt Julie."

"Do we really know that for sure?" Gwen said. "No offense Julie."

She nodded. "That woman…"

"Gwen, come on. You can't doubt that now, do you?" Mickey asked.

"I'm just saying I think maybe we acted too hastily, blowing the gate back there. Those people…"

"That fucker John Book got into your head, Gwen!"

"No he hasn't."

"Yes he has."

"I know you are," Julie said, "but what am I" and they all had to laugh, even Bear.

She licked her upper lip. "That guy with one hand, he was kind of quiet. He wasn't like the others…"

"We'll never know," Mickey said.

Gwen spoke, "What the hell is going on with Buddy?"

"He's sick," Julie said.

Mickey thought of himself, of the plague, the scabs spreading across his torso, across his body.

"He's dangerous," Gwen said.

"Not to us," Julie said.

"We don't know that."

"He almost killed you, Mickey," Gwen said.

He had nothing to say to that.

"Don't worry about Buddy," Bear said. "I'll take care of him."

"He looks okay today," Julie said.

"I bet if we just stopped he'd keep walking," Gwen said. "I bet he wouldn't even miss us."

"Buddy came back for us. He came back for you and Bobby and Harris and me and the baby—"

"Yeah, I know that, but…"

"No, Gwen. No *buts*. And please don't get me all excited. You know, early labor and all that?"

"He doesn't look so good right now," Mickey said, grateful to get his mind off the disease eating away at his body.

Buddy had stopped ahead of them and was sitting in the snow.

"Oh great," Gwen said.

The four men and women reached him and stood around him.

"Buddy?" Bear asked.

His eyes were open but they had no idea what he was seeing.

"Well?" Gwen asked.

"He looked good this morning," Mickey said.

Bear thought about what Buddy had told him back in that house a few days ago.

"Mickey, grab his bags. Gwen, take his rifle."

"What are you going to do? Carry him?"

"Yeah."

Bear adjusted his packs and gear to free up some room.

"Oh, you've got to be kidding me," Gwen said. "Come on."

"I am." Bear knelt on one knee in front of the man. "Buddy? Buddy. I'm going to help you man."

He mumbled something unintelligible.

"I can't leave you here, brother."

He grabbed him by the front of his leather jacket and pulled him up, leaning his shoulder into Buddy's waist, standing up with him.

"How far do you really think you can get with him like that?" Gwen said.

"Let's walk," Julie said.

"Suit yourselves." Gwen sounded disgusted but slung Buddy's AK over her shoulder and raised her own M16A4, moving past Mickey and Julie to the front.

THE MAN FROM NANTUCKET

The digital watch he wore beeped and Steve woke up in the RV. He fumbled with the tiny buttons on the side of the watch and groaned but the watch kept beeping. Finally he slammed his wrist against the mattress three or four times and the watch went quiet.

"Shit," he muttered. Steve reached up and parted the shades with a finger. Sunlight peeked in at him and he groaned. A half empty bottle of whisky lay on the pillow next to him. "Hello darlin'."

There were flies on the window, which meant there were dead people probably pressed up against the side of their RV. Always the fuckin' flies.

Steve sat up. He scratched the back of his neck then reached inside his boxer shorts and rummaged around behind his balls. He yawned. He could hear a few faint engines outside already.

Farrah smiled down on him from the wall above the bed.

"Wake up," Brent called from up front. "I'm going over to Bob's for a few."

"Hey, yeah, look man, Mason gave me back your DVDs. He wants to borrow some more."

"Hook him up," called Brent.

"He wants some Asian shit. We got anything good?"

"What's he like? We got some bukkake vids, some schoolgirl shit. Hey, you know what? Give him that Japanese enema video."

"*Give* it to him?"

"Yeah, I been meanin' to get rid of it. That shit's nasty, no pun intended. See you later. Hey, wake Chris up why don't you? He's gotta drive today."

After a few minutes Steve got out of bed and pulled his jeans and socks on and his boots over his socks. He took off his Cookie Monster t-shirt and pulled on another shirt that said "What happens at Grandmas Stays at Grandmas." He shrugged into his shoulder rig and secured his Beretta Model 93-R under his arm.

Steve walked up to the front of the trailer. Chris was passed out on the couch. He shook his head. Brent had made a pot of coffee so he filled a Styrofoam cup.

"Hey, Chris. Wake up."

Chris snored louder.

"Wake the fuck up, man."

He muttered something in his sleep and rolled over.

Steve put a booted foot on his shoulder and shoved him a couple of times until the man stirred. "All right-all right-all right. What the fuck?"

"Wake up. You driving."

"I'm driving."

"Right. Wake up and crank this bitch up."

"Yeah-yeah-yeah."

"Yeah." Steve took an M-16 down off the gun rack near the door. He popped the magazine, inspected it, slid it back home and pulled the bolt back. He checked the safety. It was on.

"Hey, Chris, you like rap music, right?"

"Some."

"You remember that song, *I'm not a playa I just fuck a lot?*"

"You mean by Big Punisher?"

"Shit."

He sipped his coffee and opened the door to the outside.

It was early morning. There was activity around the camp as people went about their business, securing their rides, preparing for the day's convoy.

"Steve!" one of the three little kids—he couldn't be sure if it was Stymie, Buckwheat or Farina—called out to him, passing by holding his mother's hand.

"Morning," he called back loud enough for the kid and his mother to hear, then under his breath, "you little pecker head."

He squinted and put on his shades.

"Nice shirt." Harold, a guy Steve knew from the convoy, walked by. Harold was wearing a t-shirt that said *I am the man from Nantucket.*

"Likewise."

"You white boys sleeping late again, biatch?" Damar came past.

"Waited all night for you to come and tuck me in, D," Steve shot back.

"*Kalimera, Stavors, esai malakas!*" One of the Greeks strolled by, a backpack slung over his shoulder next to a rifle. "You see my cousin tell him we couldn't wait for him, okay?"

"Yeah, you too." Steve climbed up onto the roof of the RV. He didn't speak Greek but he recognized *Stavros* or *Stratos*, his name, and figured the Greek was probably fucking with him, calling him an asshole or something.

There were five or six of the Greeks and they all stuck together and he couldn't tell them apart except for the woman, Stacey, who had long legs and was smokin' hot, and that one Greek who couldn't speak any English.

"Morning," he said to Sam on the next roof over.

Sam didn't always acknowledge him, because Steve and his sense of humor often rubbed people the wrong way, but this morning the other man did.

"Morning. Maybe camping out here wasn't a good idea."

Steve looked and saw what the man was talking about. The vast parking lot in which their convoy had spent the night had been relatively empty except for themselves when he'd turned in the night before. The vehicles were pressed bumper to bumper forming an impenetrable barrier. This morning hundreds of zombies had massed against the northern half of the cars and dozens more were staggering into the lot.

"Shit. Where they coming from?"

"City bit north of here," Sam said. "I knew we shouldn't have spent the night here."

He unzipped his fly and pissed off the side of the RV down onto the upturned faces of the undead standing below. A few of them moaned and motioned impotently towards the men on the roof. Sam lifted his upper lip and shook his head.

Steve finished his business and tucked himself away in his jeans.

"Damn, look at the ass on that zombie." Steve indicated a female zombie in jeans whose hips were wider than her shoulders. "Lotta junk in that trunk, huh?"

His neighbor didn't answer.

"She's a whooty if I ever saw one. Whooty? You know, Sam, a white girl with a booty."

"Well, better get below," Sam said. "Long day ahead of us."

"Yeah, see you."

The RV beneath him shuddered as Chris cranked it up, causing Steve to stagger back a couple of steps. "Whoa, you bastard." He righted himself and flipped the bird to the zombies below.

He stood on his tip toes and stretched. He turned his back to the hordes and the direction of the city and looked out on the space between the vehicles. It was nearly empty now as everyone got into their vans, cars and trucks. The convoy started to pull out up ahead.

Chris must have opened a couple of windows because he heard *WASP* blasting from their stereo system, singing how they fucked like a beast. It was Chris' favorite song and everyday it was his turn to drive he blasted it or Europe's *The Final Countdown* as his first song.

The vehicles at the front of the convoy were pulling into a line. A group of zombies that saw them rolling away started to get all excited and lurched in their direction.

The explosion caught them all off guard.

He felt a wall of heat at his back and before he could react he was swept off the RV roof to the pavement of the parking lot below. Instinct brought his hands out in front of him, trying to break his fall. Landing awkwardly on one foot, his ankle snapped under him, pain bolting up his leg. Rolling forward, he scraped his palms on the asphalt. His M-16 clattered off out of reach.

Other men and women who had been standing on the roofs of vehicles, looking out over the zombies in the general direction of the city beyond, were blinded by a searing light that flashed and burned their retinas. Some of them were knocked backwards off their perches to land on the road below, sustaining injuries ranging from bruises and scrapes to broken bones to fractured skulls. Others tumbled in the opposite direction, perishing almost immediately in the outstretched hands of the undead massed along that side of the vehicles.

A wave of hot air buffered the vehicles and tipped several of them up onto two wheels. Many of these toppled with rending crashes onto their sides and a few unlucky humans close enough were crushed. Other vehicles were shifted askance and suddenly gaps between the vehicles that had not existed before were opened. Into these gaps the first and the fastest of the undead poured.

"*Fuck me-fuck me-fuck me.*" He grasped his ankle and pain welled up his body. "*Shit-shit-shit.*"

Gunfire began around him, first sporadic single shots then heavier fusillades. There were screams too.

He blinked back the tears of pain behind his shades and drew his Beretta. He jacked back the hammer and chambered a fresh round while everything around him descended into immediate and general chaos.

The door to the van behind their RV slid open and Sam jumped out, a pump shotgun in his hands. Steve watched as a trio of zombies came running around the back of the van.

Sam fired and blew the arm off one of the bookers. Before he could pump a fresh shell into the chamber another of the speeding zombies was on him, bearing him to the ground. The third pounced through the still open sliding door of Sam's van, and his family shrieked in frenzied terror.

He watched as the zombie on top of Sam ripped a huge chunk of flesh out of his neighbor then came running right at him. He extended the 92-R and fired three-four-five shots until it dropped.

The armless zombie leaned down and took a bite out of Sam then ran off in the other direction, lost amidst the dozens of people who abandoned their cars and trucks and scampered about frantically.

"Fuck, fuck." Steve winced as he placed too much weight on his injured ankle.

The door to their Dutchmen opened. Chris stood there bristling with weapons and—Steve thought he'd never forget this if he lived long enough—multi-colored tassels around his arms and calves, just like the Warrior. He'd even hastily painted a red, green and yellow mask on his face.

"Steve!"

"Chris!"

"Let's kick some ass!"

"*Shit.*" He grimaced again.

"Shit," Edward said. He had been listening to ZZ Top, the bearded trio, singing about a house of ill repute in La Grange, *ah-ha-ha-ha-ha, ah-ha-ha-ha-ha*, when the explosion had knocked their Winnebago a few feet sideways and the CD stopped. Something wasn't right and it took him a few seconds to realize what it was. The Winnebago was in drive and he had taken his foot off the brake when the blast had surprised him, but they weren't moving. The whole Winnebago was dead.

Lauren blinked and got her bearings.

"What the hell was that?" Sonya called from the back of their RV.

"Look." Edward pointed out his window. Lauren looked and saw a mushroom cloud boiling up into the sky off on the horizon.

"Oh my God," she said.

"I'm fucking blind," Sonya said. "Would someone tell me what the hell just happened?"

"Looks like a nuclear explosion," Edward said.

"Oh…"

"Mommy!"

The door to the RV was yanked open from the outside and Eva leaned in, her hands filled with the M-4/M-26 combo, a pack slung over her back.

"Let's go," she said. "*Now.* Lore, get the kids together. Sonya, come here to me."

She stepped up into the RV and closed the door behind her.

"Go where?"

"We've got to get out of here."

Massive amounts of gunfire filled the air.

Edward was trying to turn over the engine. Ellis and Ennis were hopping up and down in place as much as their elongated hairy bodies allowed, all keyed up.

"Forget it," Eva said. "It won't work. Electro-magnetic pulse."

"Electro-magnetic pulse?" Edward said. "Oh, that's some bull-shit there."

"Move, now!"

"Kids, grab your backpacks like Mommy and Aunt Eva taught you." Sonya tried to remain calm but the truth was her children's lives were at risk and she was terrified.

"Do like Mommy says and get your stuff," she instructed the kids. "Lore, *water.* Bring plenty of water."

"I got the water," said Edward.

It took them a minute or two to gather up their packs, supplies and weapons. Outside the gunfire rippled up and down the convoy. There were screams and the bizarre, other-worldly caterwauling of the dead.

"Okay, listen to me," Eva instructed the group. "We need to stick together outside. Stay close." She looked at Nicole and Nelson. "I won't let anything happen to you." She addressed the adults, "We're going to make for the fields directly south of us. We just want to get the hell away from all these cars. Okay?"

"Okay," Edward said.

"Let's do this." Eva went to open the door but it was yanked open from outside. Without hesitating she unloaded with the pump shotgun mounted under the barrel of the M4. The blast lifted the thing on the other side off its feet and slammed it facedown on the road, unmoving.

"Fuck!" Eva said.

"Oh my god—" Lauren clapped a hand over her mouth and pulled Nicole closer to her.

"Go. Let's go," Edward said.

They stepped out of the relative safety of the RV and into the shouts and screams and gunshots of the morning, with Eva in the lead. Lauren was overwhelmed. Around her all was in disarray as the finely ordered, well-established routines of their lives descended into pandemonium and death.

"Oh my god," she muttered, vaguely aware that with one hand she gripped Nicole's, temporarily forgetting about the Browning Hi-Power 9mm pistol in her left.

Around her a flood of commotion and noise, complete bedlam. Their group instinctively crouched as gunshots zipped by overhead. Vehicles had been knocked out of their tight formation, some completely overturned. A pair of legs jutted from underneath an upset panel van, and as Lauren watched one of the sneakered feet twitched. A man raced past their group screaming, batting at a zombie that had latched onto his back and crunched into his shoulders and neck. A woman stumbled by, her eyes seared shut in their sockets, hands held aloft in front of her as she staggered about confused and blinded, overwhelmed by the agony. Zombies streamed through the breaks between the vehicles and were shot in the head by lone individuals and groups in their twos and threes, yet still more undead exploited the breeches and pushed their way into the midst of the confused, scattered human beings. None of the vehicles were moving; all were stalled where they stood.

"Lore, move!"

Eva had come back and grabbed her by the arm, propelling her ahead through the middle ground between the cars, trucks and buses. Lauren didn't let go of Nicole and though she was aware on some level that the child was sobbing and covering her eyes, she concentrated on placing one foot in front of another and coaxing her body forward in the direction Eva demanded. Sonya clasped eleven-month old Victor to her body, the baby screaming, her other children milling about her person. Lauren assumed Edward was still somewhere behind her. She flinched as a bullet passed close enough for her to hear the *zip* it made as it cleaved the air above her head.

Married-man Bob hurried past their group, shepherding his family.

"Lauren!" Maurice was beside her, snatching up Nicole, the little girl wrapping her arms around the man's neck and burying her face in his collar. "Go-go-go!"

A black zombie with a shiny chrome motorcycle helmet still strapped to its head ran at them. Someone shot it in the middle of the head, the bullet ricocheting off the helmet, stunning the creature. The thing collapsed to the ground.

"Ennis! Ellis!" Edward yelled. His dachshunds were on the felled thing, attacking it, biting at its neck and face. The old man ran over to his dogs.

Maurice hustled Lauren and Nicole after Eva, who had reached Sonya, Victor and Nelson and directed them towards the wall of stalled vehicles fronting the southern edge of what had been a circle. Maurice looked and saw the circle had been broken down at the front of the line where half a dozen or more vehicles had pulled out. The vehicles cut off following the detonation. Zombies came around those cars and were gunned down but more followed, stumbling over and past their fallen.

A group of men and women had popped the hood on a mini-van. While three fended off zombies with rifle and shotgun fire, two were frantically at work under the hood. A man wrestled with two zombies on the ground.

"Look out!" Eva cried.

Lauren looked up. A booker came loping across the parking lot, ignoring everyone else around except her. It screamed as it ran and had murder in its eyes.

Maurice straight armed his 9mm and unloaded on the beast, holding fast to Nicole. The creature caught a slug in its chest and shuddered but kept coming; a second and third round from Maurice's pistol rocked it.

"Fuck you!"

Eva fired the shotgun mounted under her M4. Everything above the beast's shoulders disappeared in a red spray. The legs went out from under it and the creature pitched to the ground, skidding a few feet forward on sheer momentum.

"Where's my mommy? Where's my mommy?"

Maurice looked down. It was one of the kids from around camp—he thought the kids' nickname was Buckwheat—tugging on his arm.

"Come with me," he shouted, trying to grab the kid but his arms were full.

"My mommy!" the boy screamed and would have taken off into the chaos except for Eva, who snatched him by the arm and dragged him along with them, yelling:

"Come on now, kid!"

The boy allowed himself to be pulled along, his cheeks streaked with tears as he continued to cry for his mother.

Gasoline cascaded across the parking lot and splashed over their feet. The smell was overpowering. All Lauren could think was one of the tankers spilled itself out.

"Through the truck! Through the truck!" Eva pulled back the bolt on the M-26 and pushed Maurice towards the cab of the nearest truck. Its passenger side door was ajar.

Maurice hopped into the cab and slid himself across the seats to the driver's side door, banging his thigh on the gear shift. He looked through the window. All he saw was more barren parking lot and beyond that a field where reeds grew chest high. He opened the door and stepped down onto the parking lot. Eva ushered Sonya and her children through the passenger door.

As Lauren waited her turn she held tight to Buckwheat, and watched Eva snap the M4 to her shoulder then fire once, dropping a slow-moving zombie that had been intent on them. She thought she saw Steve scuttling away like a crab on his hands, one foot under him, the other dragging behind. One of the mechanics at the mini-van clubbed a zombie over the head with a wrench. Before she knew what was happening, Eva bodily pushed Lauren up then through the passenger door and into then through the cab.

"*Vre! Ella etho!*"

Maurice looked up. The Greek—the one who didn't speak any English—was running over to him, looking confused, holding on to a pump action Remington 870 like he didn't know what to do with it.

"Yo, Greek dude. Whatever your name is." Maurice was relieved to see him. They both reached up and helped Sonya out of the truck then helped her kids.

"Maurice, can you tell me what's going on?" Sonya tried to keep the panic she felt out of her voice.

There were small groups of people escaping under and through the vehicles around them, tearing off into the field. Maurice wrinkled his nose and looked down. Gasoline pooled from underneath the truck. He imagined the space between the cars and trucks must be a virtual river of the stuff by now.

"We're on the other side of the trucks," Maurice said.

"My babies—are my babies all here?"

"Your kids are fine. I got Nicole, and here comes Nelson."

"What about Eva? Where's my sister?"

"I'm here, Sone, I'm here." Eva was the last one through the cab, having pulled the passenger side door closed behind her then slamming the driver's side door shut.

Lauren looked around and realized Edward was not with them any longer. She wondered where they had lost him.

"Let's go!" Eva yelled at the group. "Into the field! Stick together!" She grabbed the Greek by the shoulders and pointed. "Through the field. We're going through the field!"

They reached the reed bed without incident, the gunfire behind them building to a crescendo.

"What now?" Maurice asked Eva.

"We stick close. We stay together."

"Wait! Help me! Take me with you!" A man they recognized from the convoy, but did not know, staggered out of the field towards their voices. It was evident from the way he clasped his eyelids shut and held his hands out in front of him that he couldn't see.

"What's your name doo?" Maurice demanded.

"Zach."

"Zach." Maurice grabbed the Greek and put one of his hands on Zach's shoulder. "You stick with my friend Saki here, okay? Do everything he says and keep quiet."

The man said nothing, but a look of immense relief washed over his face.

An explosion from somewhere within the convoy drew their attention. As they watched, the vehicles were engulfed in fire from left to right and began detonating one by one.

"*Panavia' mou!*," the Greek said, pulling his Kangol back and scratching at the bald spot on the top of his head.

"What the hell just happened?" the blind guy asked.

They looked back before plunging into the field. The clear sky above the convoy filled with a roiling black smoke. There were screams and howls as the living and the dead perished in the fire, entire families trapped and burnt alive between and inside the cars. A few of the sturdier among the undead shambled out of the conflagration ablaze, toppling to burn in the parking lot. In the distance a huge plume of smoke from the city billowed and dissipated outwards.

The field gave way to trees. They moved quietly through the foliage. Eva walked at the front of the line with her assault rifle/shotgun combo at the ready. Lauren held Buckwheat's hand, leading Sonya who had one hand on her shoulder. Nelson and Nicole stayed close to their mother and Lauren.

"Come on, doo." Maurice did his best to keep up with the women. He took turns with the Greek, half-leading and half-dragging Zach along. The blind man moaned and rubbing at his eyes periodically. "You too. Don't drag ass, Stymie."

The boy protested, "I'm Buckwheat."

"Whatever. Move your little white ass, doo."

The Greek brought up the rear spooked, constantly looking back over his shoulder.

By mid-day they reached a point where the red shoots and flowers of the maple trees gave way to another road, a six-lane highway, its asphalt cracked and grown over with weeds. There were no vehicles in sight and the road stretched on in either direction. The mushroom cloud was behind them. If it still hung in the sky they could not see it because of the tree line.

They stopped and ate a small lunch from cans and drank some of the water they had taken from the convoy.

"Maybe we should put all our food in one knapsack and all our water in another?" Lauren asked.

"No," Eva said.

"Give all the food and water to one person, even two people," Maurice explained, "then what happens if we lose those people?"

Lauren understood his point and nodded.

"Evangeline," Sonya asked. "What happened to Edward?"

"I don't know."

The children were especially tired, but it was decided without much debate they needed to continue and would follow the road, heading in a general direction away from the city, putting the caravan as far behind them as they could.

They spread out along the road and moved along silently, meeting no one.

"You okay?" Maurice held Buckwheat's hand and walked beside Lauren and Nicole.

"Yeah, I'll be okay."

"Okay." Maurice thought of Damar and his other friends and wondered where they were and what had happened to them and if they had perished back at the convoy.

"I think I'm getting my vision back." Zach said. The Greek cursed at him and pulled him along.

Eva crested a rise ahead and held up a hand, waving them forward, signaling the group to keep quiet. Lauren with Sonya and the kids were the last to reach the rise. Lauren looked down upon what had stopped Eva.

"What is it?" Sonya asked.

"Cars," Lauren said. "Tons of them."

From where they stood it looked like a parking lot. Thousands of cars of all makes and models stretched as far as the eye could see, carpeting all six-lanes of the highway, covering the grassy median separating one direction from another, covering much of the shoulders on either side of the road.

"Where the hell did that come from?" Maurice asked.

"*Apo' pou sto thia lo? Erthe aufto? Po po?*" asked the Greek but he knew no one understood a word he said.

"I don't like this one bit," Eva said.

"I don't see Zed," Maurice noted.

"Just cause you don't see any zombies don't mean they're not there," Zach said. "What am I missing anyway?"

As Lauren filled him and Sonya in on the scene Eva and Maurice debated the next move.

"We could circle it," Maurice said. "Stick to one of the tree lines."

Eva looked over either shoulder. There was a seamless melding where the cars, packed from the highway to the shoulder, disappeared into the trees. It didn't look like they'd be able to skirt all the vehicles and Eva wasn't comfortable doing so. *Anything* could be lurking in those trees.

She pointed this out to Maurice and he nodded.

"Want to camp here for the rest of the day?" he asked.

"Do you?"

"No."

"Can't tell how long those cars go on for. Where they hell are we? Is there a town or a city nearby?"

"I don't think so."

"This is a weird fucking place for this. I think we have another hour or two of daylight."

"We get stuck down there," Maurice indicated amongst the cars, "we can find a couple vans or something. Spend the night in them."

"Or on top of them." Eva had no intention of being trapped inside a vehicle with who knew what gathering around in the night.

"Or on top," Maurice echoed.

"Okay, listen up," Eva called to the group. "We're heading down there. We don't see anything but that just means we have to be extra careful. I'm going first. Lauren I want you to follow me with Sonya and the kids, including Farina there."

"I thought he was Stymie," Maurice said.

The kid laughed and said, "Buckwheat."

"Greek, listen to me." Eva signaled with her hands then explained what she wanted him to do. "You stay on our left flank, near the median. Keep an eye on the road over there and the treeline up on that shoulder."

"*Pragmatika katalava lexi apo ti epeis.*"

"Shit. Okay, Maurice, you get our flank on that side. Greek," she pointed as she spoke slowly. "You-bring-up-the-rear, okay?"

"*Den milao-Anglika. Den em ai vlakas.*"

"He's not retarded, Eva," Sonya said. "He just doesn't speak English."

"And you're blind and I'm standing right over here, so shut the fuck up. I mean, I'm your sister and I love you and all, but right now we're in some shit, so I need you to listen to me so we can all get through it, all right? Greek, go, now. And take this other blind motherfucker with you."

"I'm getting my vision back," Zach said. "I think."

"You're flash blind," Lauren said. "You were looking towards the city when the nuke went off, weren't you?"

"Dammit, that's what it was, wasn't it? *Shit.*"

"Shit is right. We better get our asses moving," Eva snapped. "I don't feel like standing here chatting and waiting to see what reaches us first—a radioactive cloud or a bunch of fuckin' zombies."

"Let's go." Maurice started forward, walking off towards the left.

The Greek looked at Zach.

"*Me vlepeis?*" He waved a hand in the man's face.

"I see shadows. Light and dark. It's an improvement over what I saw before."

"*Ga mi sou. Ako lou tha me.*"

The cars, trucks, buses and vans stretched out around them, tightly packed in places, scattered haphazardly in others. Some doors stood open and the interiors were empty. In other cars skeletal remains cluttered the seats: clothes that had once hung from flesh and muscle and bone pooled about them. Other skeletons and parts of skeletons lay strewn outside the vehicles, often in proximity to a weapon of some sort: guns and knives, a tire iron. All of the tires were flat.

"Lauren, what is that I'm stepping on?" Sonya could feel whatever it was crunching beneath her shoes.

"It's glass Mommy," Nelson said.

"From a car window," Lauren added.

"Something must have broken in," Sonya said.

"Or something broke out."

Eva led them, picking a path between the vehicles. Two or three spots proved impassable, cars pressed bumper to bumper, so it was up and over, crossing hoods to the highway on the other side. Lauren was especially cautious with Sonya in these areas, her work doubly difficult as Sonya clutched baby Victor to her chest the entire way.

Like a rabid dog locked in its owners' car, the zombie smashed itself against the glass of the driver's door and Maurice involuntarily jumped back into the side of another car, pointing the barrel of his Mini-14 at the window.

"Holy shit."

The thing was trapped inside. Tufts of its hair were missing and it looked like they had been torn from its scalp. Maurice wondered how long the beast had been locked in the car like that, if it had grown bored and pulled its own hair out. Its teeth and rotten gums were pressed against the glass and the thing snarled at him, just like a dog.

"Damn." Maurice shook his head and started walking again, turning his head a few times to check on the thing in the car, which pushed up to the windshield and watched him go. He walked with the 14 secure to his shoulder from that point on.

"Damn," he repeated, when he had put enough cars between himself and the zombie he could no longer see it.

"Eva, wait. Don't shoot!"

She lowered the twin barrels of the M4/M-26. "Maurice. Fuck."

He wound his way through the cars towards her.

"I asked you to walk up there for a reason, didn't I?"

"Stop being a bitch for a second and listen, aight? There's zombies in some of these cars."

"Motherfucker."

"Yeah. I've passed three of them now. They can't get out."

"We're lucky these dead bastards are so fuckin' dumb."

"Yeah, we are. I guess they crawled into those cars and died, came back. Now they can't get out."

"Like I said, we're lucky. Now do me a favor and get your ass back up there. I don't like that tree line."

"I don't like it either," Maurice said over his shoulder as he trudged off.

He let out a low whistle that only he could hear. He thought of the possibly thousands of people who had been trapped here at one point, like the skeletons and zombies in the cars. But most of the cars were empty and he couldn't have imagined the occupants had all met their ends out here on the highway. He pictured them streaming up into the trees on the hills and down the road, fleeing whatever it had been they'd been scared of.

The sun was going down when he stopped and climbed atop the hood of an old Cadillac. He stepped onto its roof and from there reached out and up with one foot, alighting atop the cab of an 18-wheeler. He reached up and swung a leg over and pulled himself from the cab to the top of the cargo container then stood and surveyed all he could.

The cars stretched out in all directions, for miles. He wondered how far they'd come. Had it been a few miles or more, or had it only felt as such because of the constant maneuvering between dead vehicles?

Sonya had an arm out-stretched and was holding onto Lauren's shoulder. It felt like a flock of children moved with them.

Eva was well ahead of the group, the assault rifle/shotgun tensed on its sling. Maurice thought again how bad ass Eva was, how he wouldn't want to fuck with her.

The Greek and Zach had fallen behind but were in sight. Maurice couldn't hear him but he could see the Greek was saying something. He imagined he was prodding the other man, hurrying him forward.

Maurice squinted and looked as far ahead as he could into the slowly gathering dusk but he could not see any zombies…

Sundown was upon them and soon it would give to night. Eva knew it was time to stop and find someplace suitable amongst these cars to wait for morning. She looked behind her, could see Lauren with Sonya, her niece and nephews and that other little boy winding their way through the vast collection of stalled vehicles. She knew Maurice was following off to her left somewhere, closer to or on the median. She could not see the Greek and Zach.

Eva figured they had gone several miles at least. She had noticed a couple of things about the vehicles on the road right away. First, they were all facing in the direction in which her little group was headed. Even the cars across the median on the other three lanes had been headed in that direction. She assumed these vehicles and their passengers found themselves here sometime soon after the immediate zombie outbreak so many months back. She thought they'd been fleeing a city, maybe Pittsburgh, where she guessed the nuclear explosion—what else could that mushroom cloud have been?—had originated.

As she walked among the still cars and trucks, the M4-shotgun combo tensed on its sling, she considered where all these automobiles had been going and why they had stopped. She thought they'd been headed away from the cities, towards the countryside, headed for areas with lesser populations. Though an eleven-month-old like Victor would be too young to remember it, she recalled all too well how the cities had quickly become death traps, teeming with millions of the undead, survivors trapped in apartment buildings and malls and supermarkets and anywhere they could get to.

There was a buzz in her ear. She swatted away something she dismissed as a gnat.

But why had the cars stopped? What, she wondered, was up ahead? And how far was it? Maybe a military blockade? Eva remembered how, early on, the National Guard and the Army had set up barricades and tried to quarantine entire towns and cities, murdering citizens, the infected and uninfected alike, not allowing them access to the areas that had not yet been contaminated. In the end all areas had become contaminated and the barricades had fallen. The soldiers and police officers abandoned their posts, seeking safety and their own families. The ones who had not run had died at the barriers.

She passed a yellow school bus and had to go around it. A van had been parked flush against the side of the bus, directly behind the door where she imagined kids not much older than Nicole and Nelson had gotten on and off every day on their way to and from school.

That was another thing she had noticed about the cars. There had been numerous fender benders and small accidents. It looked like some drivers had tried to drive *through* other cars, attempted to push them out of their way, all to no avail. At times she and the group had to circle around small groups of vehicles that were joined bumper to bumper.

She swatted at the gnats again.

Eva thought they'd be safe enough if they spent the night out here on the road, maybe inside or on top of some of the higher trucks. Inside would be better. If something or someone passed by in the night there'd be less of a chance of them being spotted. They'd spent months in the relative safety of the convoy. Their numbers and the sound of their band had drawn zombies nearly every day, but it had also kept them safe from other human beings. Eva had heard enough stories from people who had joined the convoy to know that not everyone you met on the road was a friend. At the very beginning of this thing she had sworn to herself she would do whatever she had to do to protect Sonya and Nelson and Nicole and Victor.

If she had allowed herself the luxury she would have felt how terrified she was. But she didn't. Instead she imagined how Sonya must feel, blind, three kids in tow, now that little kid, Buckwheat, and Sonya's husband dead and gone.

It was at that moment something in the back of her head clicked and she stopped where she was. The sun was down behind the trees but there was still a great deal of light in the sky. Off in the distance there was the buzz of cicadas.

She looked around in all directions and didn't see anything amiss. The cars and trucks stretched on as they had. To her left, beyond wherever Maurice was, the shoulder of the road angled up through waist high grass and ended at the tree line.

She got down on one knee then lay flat and looked under the car to her right then the van to her left. She didn't know what she expected to see but seeing nothing did not assure her.

Eva got up and climbed on top of the hood of a car then the vehicle's roof. She looked back and saw Sonya, Lauren and the kids and she signaled to them to stop. Lauren said something to Sonya that Eva could not hear but their small group halted where they were near the bus Eva had passed a few minutes ago.

Maurice saw her signal to the other women and he stopped too.

Eva squinted in the growing dusk and looked around and saw nothing, but, no, that wasn't quite right, there was *something* up ahead three or four cars. She watched it but couldn't figure out what it was. A growing sense of unease welled up inside her. She turned back to her sister and Lauren, signaling to them to stay where they were. She carefully stepped down from the roof of the car onto its hood, and from the hood to the trunk then roof, then to the hood of the next one, and so on until she had crossed three cars this way. Now she stood on the roof of a Volkswagen Rabbit looking down on a mess.

A man was lying there on the road between the car on which Eva stood and the next. His face was ravaged, a mask of red and raw muscle and sinew laid-bare. From his neck up the only identifiable parts were a tongue and an eyeball. The man's nose, ears, lips, the entirety of the skin on his face, most of his scalp, was all gone. There was some hair plastered to the back of his head and the road.

A few things hit Eva at once. The blood was fresh. This was a recent kill. He wore a blood-stained t-shirt that said *I am the Man from Nantucket*. She knew this man. He was from the convoy.

And those weren't gnats, they were *flies*. There were hundreds of them, many buzzing around the man, but too many to be drawn by the corpse alone. Eva knew where there were flies there were—

"Uggghhh!" the man uttered a gargled cry. She jumped back and lost her footing, slipping on the hood of the Rabbit, her ass slamming into the windshield, her body rolling off the car. She hit the road with one hand out to break her fall then quickly scrambled up. As she did so she heard a gunshot from somewhere behind followed by "*Ska ta!*" and more gunfire. She knew the Greek and Zach were in trouble.

"Eva!" Sonya screamed but she couldn't see her sister. She backed away from the space where the mess lay and wondered if the man in the t-shirt was still alive, or was coming back from the dead, when Maurice yelled out "Fuck!" She looked up. There were dozens of bookers sprinting down from out of the tree line towards him and the cars. He turned and ran, disappearing from her view.

"*Raaaaaaah!*"

The growl turned her around. A zombie, one of the smart ones, squatted on the roof of a car, looking down at her. As Eva watched, the thing cracked its mouth open and a gob of bloody spittle descended from its maw to the road surface in an unbroken line as it tensed to pounce.

She hit it with a slug-load from the shotgun mounted under her carbine. It wasn't a head shot but the blast lifted the creature off the car roof and deposited it somewhere on the other side of the vehicle. She didn't stick around for it to come back. High-tailing it between the cars, trucks and motorcycles back towards her sister and the others, she screamed: "Get in the bus! Get in the bus!" She was aware of movement from many sides now, more things like the brain she had just blasted moving amongst the vehicles, coming for her, shrieking and hopping on and over cars.

Two vehicles over a zombie popped up from between a couple of cars like a jack-in-the-box and howled at her.

As she ran she pumped the shotgun, chambering a double-ought shell. There was gunfire from amidst the cars now and the Greek was still cursing. Eva looked up. The bookers were all gone from the hillside, which meant they were amongst the cars on the highway. Sure enough she caught a glimpse of a head and shoulders blur past between a couple of cars.

Eva reached the bus at the same time the Greek did.

Lauren stood in the doorway of the school bus, the MP-40 submachine gun in her hands. Eva could see Sonya and the kids inside the bus.

"Where's Zach?" Lauren yelled at the Greek, who motioned futilely with one hand and yelled back something none of them understood.

"Get in the bus! Get in the bus!"

Eva brought the stock of the M4 to her shoulder and sighted around the front of the bus, firing. A windshield spider-webbed. The zombie rushing past it did not flinch. The creature disappeared from view. The Greek fired behind her. She turned and there were a quartet of bookers loping towards them from around the side of the van pushed up against the bus.

"In the bus!" Eva fired the shotgun and the buckshot spread, knocking two of the four zombies down momentarily. The third and fourth tore past the other two, mouths wide open—

The Greek fired his Remington, pumped and fired, dropping both.

Eva was the last one in the bus. The Greek worked the lever, slamming the door shut. Immediately there was a zombie outside the door, looking in, slapping at the glass , jerking its head around to catch sight of each of them.

"*Esai vromikos poustis*!" The Greek extended his 12-gauge towards the door but he didn't fire, and the door held.

The sound of thumps on steel came, and Eva looked out the window to see the front of the bus surrounded by zombies, at least a dozen of them.

"Shit."

"Eva? Are you okay? Where are my babies?"

"We're here Mommy." Little Nicole hugged her.

"Where's your brother? Where's Nelson?"

"He's right here Mommy. He's okay."

The baby cried at the top of its lungs.

"Eva," Lauren said. "Where's Maurice?"

"I don't know. What happened to Zach?"

"Ask the Greek." Lauren shook her head. "I don't understand a word he's saying."

The Greek was babbling on heatedly, pointing through the window back up towards the tree line.

"Oh shit," little Nelson said and while his mother scolded him—"Nelson what have I told you about your language?"—in a harried tone, Eva and Lauren looked where the Greek pointed. There were dozens of zombies shambling down the hill towards the vehicles on the highway, towards the commotion about the bus.

"*Shit*," Eva said. "Shit. Shit. Shit."

"I want my mommy!" Buckwheat cried.

The Greek was cursing at the zombies outside the school bus, pointing at each one of them and yelling, his face all red.

"In two minutes we're going to have hundreds of them swarming us," Eva said. "You've got to listen to me."

"What? What are we going to do?" Sonya asked.

"There's an emergency exit at the rear of this bus," Eva said, making it up as she went along, which was their only chance. "There's also one in the ceiling. I'm going to climb out onto the roof and draw their attention. Most of them are gathered around the front of the bus. When I start shooting you guys get the hell off the bus, get out the back and head that way—" She pointed where she meant, realized Sonya couldn't see where she directed, so she caught Lauren's eye. "Get off the road. Get the hell out of here!"

"What about you?" Sonya demanded.

"Don't worry about me!"

"I'm your sister! Of course I worry about you!"

"Sonya, you've got to get the kids out of here! Now! Greek! *Greek*, look at me!"

He stopped cursing at the zombies massing outside to look at Eva. He had spittle flecked in the corners of his mouth.

"Give me a hand up!" She stepped onto a bench seat and fiddled around with the emergency exit hatch mounted in the roof. She figured it out and disengaged it. The hatch slide back and open.

"Lauren! Sonya! You have to all stick together—do you hear me? It's getting dark outside! Get off the road and don't stop. I'll catch up! Greek, give me a boost!"

He didn't understand a word she said but apparently understood fully what she wanted. Eva stepped into his clasped hands and he boosted her up and through the roof.

"Rifle," she called down and he passed it up to her, wishing her luck, "*Kali-tixi, na exeis.*"

She stood on the roof of the school bus and looked at what was unfolding below. There were fifty or sixty zombies gathered around the front of the bus and scads more stumbling towards it through the parked cars on the highway. The sky was purpling and soon it would be impossible to see. She hoped the night would help her sister and the others steal away unnoticed.

"Hey! Dead fucks!"

She fired the M4, the 5.56mm round punching through the chest of a zombie in a suit jacket. The creature staggered back two steps and looked up at her. The undead around it looked at it curiously. When the second shot from the assault rifle cracked, removing the top of the chest-shot zombie's skull, they again looked up to the roof of the bus at Eva with anticipation in their eyes.

"Yeah! *You* dead fucks!"

She started screaming at them and firing down into them. The zombies pawed the air for her, hissed and cried out in frustration and hunger and dropped, head shot.

The bolt of the M4 clicked open on an empty chamber. Eva dumped the magazine and slid a fresh one home.

"Eat my pussy limp-dick!" She fired the shotgun mounted under the barrel, racked the bolt, fired, spraying the massing zombies below with buckshot and slug loads. When the shotgun was out she chambered a fresh five-round magazine and started back into them with the M4.

On her third magazine for the assault rifle, she paused briefly to look over her shoulder. She could just make out someone—the Greek and one of the children—crouched over, disappearing in the shadows amidst the cars. Hundreds of zombies were streaming towards her position but she breathed a sigh of relief. Sonya and the kids might just get away.

"Eva!"

She looked up.

"Mo!"

Maurice had climbed atop the cab of a standard 8x4 dump truck several vehicles away. At the sound of his voice many of the zombies looked up and cawed at him. The ones gathered directly around the front of the school bus looked from Eva to Maurice, confused, unsure who to go for.

"Get the fuck out of here!"

"Maurice, you crazy—"

"Go on! Tell Lauren—"

"Fuck you!" She fired down into the mass of zombies, scoring a headshot, aiming at another, "And you!"

A second assault rifle entered the fray, as Maurice fired his Mini-14 down on the zombies gathering around him and over their heads at the exposed zombies near the bus. As Eva swapped out another magazine she watched several of the creatures grouped beneath her turn and head towards the dump truck.

She stepped back and squatted down, out of sight of the zombies below.

"Eva!" Maurice stopped firing long enough to reload and call out to her. "Wait a minute then get the hell out of here! Take care of your sister! Tell Lauren—tell Lauren I love her!"

She didn't say anything. She would not risk Maurice's sacrifice. There were hundreds of zombies coming down off the hill, through the cars, and as he resumed firing they congregated around the truck on which he stood.

She waited and reloaded the M4 and the M-26. When she peered off the side of the bus and didn't see any zombies below she rolled off onto the roof of the van flush against it and from there dropped to the highway.

Maurice fired behind her, out of sight. She knew there were hundreds, maybe thousands of zombies back there, only several yards away from her at most, so she kept low and ran as best she could in the general direction she thought Lauren would have led Sonya and the children.

Eva reached the shoulder and the tree-line on the opposite side of the road without incident. She didn't look back as she plunged into the woods, breathing heavily, listening as best she could. Maurice continued to fire and as she moved through the woods his gunshots diminished.

After fifteen minutes of wending her way through the trees and dark she started to wonder what she would do if she had lost them out here in the night. Then from somewhere up ahead she heard the cry of a baby and she sped ahead.

"It's me," she called, risking the noise less someone accidentally fire on her. "It's Eva!"

"*PoPo, piga na se skotoso*," the Greek said, lowering his Remington. "*Nomiza pos esouna zobi*"

"Eva!" Sonya clutched her sister with her free arm, the other holding Victor. Her kids grasped Eva's legs.

Nelson cried: "Aunt Eva! Aunt Eva!"

"Lauren." She caught the other woman's eye. Lauren's eyes were puffy like she had been crying. Eva noticed someone was missing. "Where's Stymie? Where's that kid?"

"I don't know." Lauren looked down. "We—I lost him, somewhere on the highway. I told him to stick close..."

"We have to move," Eva said. "There are thousands of those things back there."

"How did you get away?" Sonya asked.

"Come on, I'll explain on the walk."

"The kid," Lauren implored.

"He's gone, Lore. Deal with it, okay?"

They moved through the dark for an hour or so until they could go no farther. It was a moonless night and the gloom was impenetrable. Eva had a flashlight and did her best to light their way but soon it was evident they would have to stop. She called a halt and said they'd spend the night here, beneath the trees. The children lay down around Sonya, exhausted, little Victor at the breast, and were soon asleep.

Eva leaned against a tree, the barrels of her assault rifle pointed towards the pine needles littering the ground, and she listened to the night.

Lauren lay there thinking about Stymie or Buckwheat or whatever his name was. How had he become separated from them? Where had he gone? Was he still alive out there? Alone, with all those zombies? The little boy… The thought made her want to vomit.

The Greek was snoring and she couldn't sleep. She stood up and walked over to him, prodded him awake with her foot.

"*Ti? Ti? Ti egine?*"

"Greek, you're snoring." He pulled his Kangol up off his eyes and looked at her without understanding. She mimicked the sound of snoring and pointed to Sonya and her kids huddled nearby. "You're gonna wake the kids."

"*Den mou pirazi katholou.*" He waved his hand, yawned, rolled over and went back to sleep.

Lauren didn't lay back down. She walked over to where Eva stood in the dark.

"You should get some sleep," she told Eva. "I'm tweaked. I can't sleep now."

"I can't either. But you should try."

Lauren yawned and stretched.

"Listen, Lore, you did good back there."

"You're welcome. I can't get that kid out of my mind."

"Did you tell him to stick with you the entire time?"

"Of course I did."

"Then he should have listened."

"You can be a real harsh bitch, you know that?"

"I need you to understand something. All that matters to me in this, the *only* thing that matters, is my sister and her kids. Not *you*, not *me*, not that snoring-assed Greek over there. Got it?"

"Yeah."

"You want to hear some fucked-up shit? When we were in the RV, when we were getting ready to leave it, remember when the door opened and I fired at the zombie there?"

"Yeah."

"That wasn't a zombie, Lore. That was Mason."

"Oh shit, Eva…"

"Oh shit is right. I killed him. I thought he was a zombie and I killed him. But I thought he was a zombie and I thought he was coming for my sister and my niece and my nephews and I killed him. Do you understand me?"

"Yes."

"Good. If I'd thought you could draw their attention I would have left you on the roof of that bus, like Maurice."

"Damn, you are cold—what? *Maurice*? What are you talking about?"

"Maurice showed up. He drew them to him. That's the only reason I'm here."

Lauren closed her eyes.

"Oh Jesus. They got him then?"

"Unlikely."

"What do you mean, *unlikely*?"

"Last time I saw him he was standing on top of a dump truck shooting it out with them."

"Oh my God."

"He told me to get out of there, to catch up to Sonya and—"

"So he's still back there? Alive on that road?"

"Yeah, I suppose. He told me to tell you—"

"You *suppose*?"

"Look, that shits not my concern. My concern is right *here*." She nodded towards her sister and the children.

"You're a cunt. You know that?"

She didn't say anything.

"I can't believe… Well, fuck you."

"Where are you going?"

"I'm going back. To get Maurice."

"You can't be serious, Lore."

"Fuck you. I am. And if you don't shut up we're going to wake up Sonya and the babies."

"Think about what you're doing," Eva took a step towards the woman. "It's crazy. Maurice sacrificed himself so—"

"Maurice may have sacrificed himself, but we don't have to sacrifice Maurice."

"He's dead."

"Maybe he is, maybe he isn't."

"*Yet.*"

"Fuck you, Eva. Goodbye."

"Wait. If you come back, keep heading in this direction. We'll stick to this path. Here, take this."

Eva threw something to her. It landed in the dark near her feet. Lauren considered ignoring it and continuing on but her curiosity got the better of her. She paused, crouched down and ran her hands over the earth until she came up with it.

The flashlight.

"The batteries don't have much left in them," Eva warned.

"Thanks," Lauren said, her tone softening. "But you're still a major league cunt."

Eva didn't say anything to her. She listened as Lauren went back off into the night, in the direction in which they had come, and very quickly she could hear her no more.

Lauren stumbled through the night, trying not to use the flashlight, using it more often than she wanted to. She worried about draining the batteries and she feared drawing the attention of anything out here in the dark. From her experience, most zombies were none too delicate and made a good deal of noise, but the ones they called brains... Brains had set the trap back on the highway— the trap they'd walked right into.

As she walked she listened to the nighttime and thought about Eva and Sonya and Sonya's kids and a little boy who had gotten separated from their group, who might be wandering in the night just now like she was. She thought of Maurice and wondered what she would do when she got back to the highway, if she could even find him.

She came out onto the road in the middle of the night. There was no visible moon. Around her came the sounds of nocturnal things, things that might have scared her once, but she knew there were other things out here in the dark, things worthy of fear.

She considered the wall of cars stranded on the road, stretching out in both directions. She wondered where she had emerged. Had they left the road farther to her right or to her left? She listened to the night but it gave her no clues. After a few minutes she decided any action was better than none, so she turned to her right and walked, sticking to what pavement was left, overgrown as it was with grass and weeds, the clear demarcation of the road and its shoulder eroding.

She had gone far enough to wonder if she had gone too far when she heard them. Faint at first, but no mistaking the source of the clamor. *Zombies.* She proceeded with more caution, aware of her surroundings. The cars cast dark, ominous shadows. Lauren wondered if a brain might be lurking between them, waiting for someone like her to pass by in the night.

Silly. She banished the thought from her mind. Even the smartest of the undead found whatever rudimentary intelligence they still possessed trumped by their hunger. If Maurice were still alive, all the zombies in the area would be where he was.

It took her another ten minutes of walking, drawing closer to their calls and chortles, to confirm her suspicion. She became aware of movement ahead so she stopped where she was and stared off into the gloom. She could not discern details but she could see a bit. A mass of them circled a vehicle that was higher up off the ground and bulkier than others surrounding it. Eva had said a dump truck or something.

Lauren climbed on top of a station wagon as quietly as she could. She stood on it and looked around. She had a better view of the undead throng ahead. To her left she could just make out a sole shape atop the bulkier vehicle. That had to be the tow truck or whatever Eva had said she'd last seen Maurice atop of.

She held the flashlight above her head at arms length and flashed it repeatedly. There was a stirring among the undead and their noise picked up, the flashing light drawing their attention. First a few then several broke from the group, staggering off to investigate. Lauren was down and moving away from the station wagon as quickly as possible, stopping only when she was on the other side of where she presumed Maurice was, again climbing on top of a vehicle and signaling with the flashlight. More zombies hissed and cried out and left the main group, heading in this direction.

She circled around Maurice's position, close enough to hear zombies stumbling through the nighttime towards the spot she had just vacated, close enough to yell out to the man if she'd wanted, but she knew to do so would bring hundreds of zombies down on her immediately so she kept her mouth shut. When she'd reached a position directly across from him she flashed the light and rested it on the roof of a luxury van, leaving it on. It was a calculated move and she continued her progress in the pitch black of night, praying she wouldn't walk right into a brain or a booker coming out above Maurice's position on the hill that led to the trees. The hill she'd watched all the zombies pour down earlier the day before.

She couldn't see the zombies in the dark but she was equally certain they couldn't see her. She knew they were down there. Maybe thousands of them. It sounded like thousands. Grunts, cries, screeches. And that only from the ones that made noise. If she could avoid them she might be okay. They had an advantage in the night: their sheer numbers. She steeled herself for what she was going to do next and switched the selector on her M-16 to full-auto.

"Maurice!" she screamed, hoping he could hear her from the distance and above the clamor of the undead. "Get ready to run!"

Lauren aimed up into the sky and depressed the trigger and the M-16 spit out a stream of shell casings, the muzzle flash lighting up the night, and in the space of a couple seconds she had spent an entire magazine.

She didn't wait around to see what the undead did next. She ran back towards the cars and into their midst, sticking farther to her left, farther away from where Maurice was, reloading on the run, then putting one hand out and feeling her way through the cars. She had a general sense of where she was and the cries and yelps of the zombies were uncomfortably close, but seemed to be moving away from her.

Lauren hoped they were confused, moving towards her former position on the hill or one of the places she'd flashed the light. She hoped enough of them had dispersed to allow Maurice to escape. She heard no gunfire from his position which could mean he was dead or out of ammo or purposefully not firing, and she wondered if he was still alive, if he was down among the cars as she was, creeping through the night.

She stretched across the hood of a car and fired out another magazine, aiming slightly above the roof line of the vehicles. If Maurice was somewhere out there she didn't want to accidentally cap him. The screams of the undead closed fast but she was moving again, reloading as she went, passing over the thicker grass of the median, not stopping until she reached the other side of the road.

She turned, facing the silent wall of cars, and the lack of visibility was disconcerting. *Where was he?*

"Maurice!" she called his name as loud as she could. As she did so she knew she shouldn't, she knew they would come for her en masse, drawn by her voice. And though she could not see them yet, sure enough, she could hear them. They were coming for her, bouncing off the cars, off each other in their greed to reach her.

"Maurice! Over here!" she held her ground and got ready to shoot it out with the first zombies but then she heard him. It was Maurice and he was calling out *her* name.

"Maurice!"

"Lauren!"

"Over here!" She aimed the muzzle of her rifle into the sky and fired one round.

"It's me! It's me! Don't shoot!"

In less than a minute he was standing next to her. She wanted to embrace him but there was no time. They turned together and ran as fast as they could, sticking to the shoulder of the road for awhile. This allowed them to put a little distance between their nearest pursuers. Then when they both sensed the time was right, they slowed slightly and plunged through the trees.

"I had a flashlight," she said.

"Here. I got one." He handed her the one he held.

They ran. When running in the night became unsafe they slowed to a fast walk and felt their way through the trees and brush, the howls of the undead receding behind them. She used the flashlight sparingly, fearing it would draw the undead right to them.

"Lauren, here!" They had become separated by only a few feet in the dark and she made for his voice, finding his hand reaching out in the blackness. She took Maurice's hand in her own and they continued together in this way.

After some time he spoke and there was a weariness in his voice and something else. "Let's stop here...for awhile."

"Here?" Lauren looked around. They were in the middle of a copse of trees. She had no idea where they were headed. She just knew they were heading in a general direction away from the road and back towards the course Eva and the others were following.

"Yeah, here." Maurice didn't wait to talk with her about it. He sat down in the dark and she could barely see him.

"Maurice," Lauren felt about and found him sitting against a tree. He was panting. For the first time she noticed she was out of breath herself.

She turned on the flashlight to get a look at him but he immediately covered the beam with his hand. "No, they'll see it. Keep it off."

"Right, okay."

"Water?" He passed her a two-liter bottle from his knapsack and she drank greedily.

"I think," he said. "I think we're safe here...for a little bit."

"Okay," she agreed. She tried to hand him back the bottle of water but he said, "You keep it."

They sat side by side in the dark for a bit. Maurice said, "Lauren. Thank you."

"You don't have to thank me."

"I know I don't have to. I want to. Thank you."

"You're welcome."

"The others?"

"Eva and the Greek are with Sonya and the kids."

He asked about Zach.

"I don't know what happened to him. He's just...gone."

"Damn." He sounded dejected.

Impulsively she leaned over and hugged him tight. At first his body was rigid but it quickly loosened in her embrace and he hugged her back, pressing her to him.

"I didn't want—I didn't want to just leave you out—"

"It's okay. You *didn't*, you didn't. Be quiet. Just hold me, okay?"

They sat in the night clasped in each other's arms. When they finally disengaged she sat back, her shoulder and arm pressed against him, and she became aware that she was wet, the whole front of her shirt and jeans. She brushed a hand over the wetness and smelled it, but couldn't see what it was. Before she could turn the flashlight on Maurice spoke.

"I got bit." In his voice was a resignation devoid of hope.

"Bit? Where?" She turned to face him and she was near hysterical.

"Lauren, *shhh*. Sit back down next to me, okay? Here, hold my hand. Please?"

Maurice had been bitten. Lauren didn't want to think about it. She resumed her position at his side and clasped his hand in both of her own, sobbing silently.

They'd been resting for several minutes but, if anything, he was breathing heavier. He squeezed her hands and she squeezed his back.

"What about," he spoke through a cotton-mouth. "What about the boy? Stymie?"

Lauren knew the truth wasn't something he needed to hear.

"Farina? He's with Eva and Sonya and the other kids. He's okay."

"Good." He snickered slightly about the whole Farina-Buckwheat-Stymie thing and it hurt him when he laughed.

In the distance came the faint rustle of foliage.

"I need you to listen to me now, okay?"

"We've gotta go—"

"No, *listen* to me first, 'aight?"

She held back her tears and mumbled okay.

"That shit in the sky? Avoid it. Stay the hell away from it. Get yourself away from here, as far away as you can, 'aight?"

The rustling amongst the trees was still far off but closer now. She knew it was the undead come for them.

"You have to keep yourself safe, okay?" Maurice said. "But more than safe. You need to be happy, too? Right? Do you understand me?"

She let go of his hand long enough to wipe the tears off her face. Part of her felt selfish to be crying around him, knowing he was the one bit and dying. Part of her wanted to throw herself on him like a child and cling to him and tell him how she really felt for him and how things could have been different for them if only—

"*Happy*, right? Do you understand me?"

His voice was clear and calm but there was great pain behind it.

"Y-Yes. We've got to get out of here."

"Okay. Hey, get my machete for me." He squeezed her hands again. "I dropped it over there."

He said "over there" and she assumed he motioned but she couldn't see anything in the dark. She let go of his hands and leaned forward on her hands and knees, feeling around for the machete, even turning the flashlight on briefly. While she did so Maurice stuck the barrel of his pistol in his mouth and blew the back of his head off.

"Mo—Maurice!" She scampered back to where he was and couldn't talk. Her throat went hoarse. The voice gone from her, she hugged his limp body, vaguely aware of the pistol still clutched in his one hand.

A nearby growl in the dark made her sit up and take notice.

Zombies. Out there. With her. In the night. She rubbed the snot off her upper lip with the back of her wrist. She ran her hands up and down Maurice's body, but it was a mechanical action now, bereft of any emotion. She unbuckled the utility belt he wore with extra magazines for his pistol and pulled it off his body. She found the machete he spoke of and pried the pistol from his dead fingers.

She shouldered his pack and took up her own rifle and left his body alone in the dark, the undead closing in. She bit her lower lip and didn't look back.

CLAVIUS CITY

The path was unmarked. As they trekked through countryside the snow was almost as high as their knees in places. A bitter wind blew wisps of white stuff in their faces, obscuring their vision.

They heard the first of the bookers before they saw it. The thing screeched at the top of its festering lungs, hidden from them by the falling snow. Mickey shouldered the USAS-12 and sighted, looking for a target.

"No," Bear said, pressing a palm to the barrel of Mickey's auto-shotgun, hefting his mace in his other hand.

"Where is it?" Julie asked, anxious.

"There!" Gwen pointed through the swirling snow.

The snow slowed the thing. As they watched it came at them in giant strides, like it was moving through molasses. It wore a neon rain slicker and stood out in the white. Suddenly it roared and changed paths, loping away from them, back in the direction they had come.

"Buddy!" Julie yelled.

He stopped in the snow well behind them, stood there, saddle bags draped over his shoulders, hands at his sides.

"Dammit." Bear scuttled through the snow towards him. The booker closed in on the other man.

Gwen's M16A4 fired once and the 5.56mm slug caught the booker above its ear, exiting the opposite side of its head. The echo of the shot reverberated as the body slouched to the powdery white.

"Shit," Gwen said.

Bear looked back at her. He knew if she hadn't taken the shot the zombie would have reached Buddy before he reached the zombie.

There were screams and whoops and more bookers came for them.

"It's on, now," Mickey said. "Gwen, stay here with Julie. I have to cover Bear!"

"No." She was already rushing as fast as she could past the man. "Wait here for us!"

"Gwen!" Julie called after her.

"Can you hear me?" Buddy stared blankly at him.

Gwen fired her M-16 from behind them.

"Damn." Bear slung the mace over his back and drew the Glock with the green laser sight. "Come on." He bent over and put his shoulder to Buddy's hips, then stood with the big man and all his equipment draped over his shoulders.

"You're heavy. You know that?"

Buddy didn't say anything. He lay across Bear's shoulder as Bear plod back towards the group.

The snow fell heavily—thick flakes from the lowering sky.

"Bear, behind you!" Gwen screamed and he turned. Two book-ers were making for him and Buddy. He extended the Glock and depressed the trigger slightly, the green laser sight lighting up on the chest of the closer of the two beasts. He corrected his aim and loosed three quick shots. The first undead dropped.

Mickey was discharging his shotgun on automatic up ahead. Gwen turned and saw half a dozen bookers streaming towards her, staying clear of Mickey and Julie. Though she did not comprehend why they ignored Mickey and Julie she was grateful they did so. Mickey managed to drop two of them as they passed. Gwen con-centrated on the remaining four, sighting through the snowfall, shooting, missing, shooting again. A zombie head jerked back. The thing landed on its face in the fresh powder.

Bear stood beside her with Buddy on his shoulder and fired his Glock, as she blasted another zombie with the M16.

"I'm out," he said, dropping the clip from the Glock then re-loading, the task made all the more difficult with Buddy on his shoulder.

Gwen dispatched the last of the charging zombies.

Julie screamed something at them. He squinted at her through the falling snow. She was shouting—"Look out!"—and when he turned to look behind them the zombie hit him head-on, knocking him to the snow. Buddy flopped off to the side, nearly catatonic, helpless.

"Bear!" Gwen fired the M16 as the bookers descended, emptying the final rounds of her magazine in the chest and head of the nearest. Then she was also born to the ground by two of the things clawing and snapping at her.

The zombie on top of Bear cracked open its mouth mere inches from his face and the fetid stench that roiled out of it was nearly overwhelming. He jammed the Glock in the things' maw and it bit down on the locked open barrel. He made a fist and his gloved hand punched the grip of the pistol, ramming it through the creature's head, the barrel rupturing out of the back of the thing's neck. It crumpled and he rolled over in the snow. Shadowy streaks showed in the snowfall as more bookers charged them.

He reached out and grabbed the foot of one of the things that had knocked Gwen down and pulled it towards him. The undead let go of the woman, shrieked and twisted and sat up, intent on munching on Bear now, but he punched it in the face, stunning the beast. While it blinked and its mouth hung open, he reached his gloved hand in and ripped the jaw off its face.

"Fucker—motherfucker!"

Gwen stabbed the zombie she wrestled with repeatedly. Unlike a human being the thing did not try and protect itself. It kept reaching for her and its groping hands absorbed several of her knife blows. Finally she managed to stab it through the forehead and it stopped struggling.

There was a sputter and a roaring buzz. She looked up and Bear stood with his chainsaw. He looked something fierce. As she watched he raised the chainsaw above his head and bellowed at the zombies hurtling towards them. As he brought the saw down on the nearest booker, she found her M16A4 and quickly reloaded. She pulled back the bolt and chambered a round then started picking off targets.

Buddy laid in the snow near her feet.

Bear buried the blade of his chainsaw in the head of a zombie, forcing it down. The saw's roar muffled, a mist of red filled the air. The zombie's hands shot up spastically like a marionette's then dropped to its sides as he yanked his saw free and swung it horizontally. There was a sheer of sparks and then red as it cut through another monster's skull.

She fired, felling a zombie. As the head of a zombie next to her disintegrated in a scarlet spray she felt like she had been punched in the shoulder. She was knocked off her feet for a second time.

"Shit." She scrambled to a seated position despite the fact her right arm wasn't responding. She drew her pistol with her left hand and tried to figure out how she could take the safety off with one hand.

Bear's saw cut off as abruptly as it had started. Mickey frantically called her name, "Gwen! Gwen!"

"Gwen." Bear was down beside her. "Are you okay?"

"Yeah, I—my arm, I can't move my arm." Adrenaline coursed through her system.

"Oh Gwen. Oh Jesus, I'm sorry." Mickey had a forlorn look on his face and was near tears.

She realized what had happened. Mickey had blown the head off the zombie next to her. Some of the buckshot had caught her, enough to knock her off her feet.

"Mickey, shut up. I'll kick your ass later. Help me up."

"You get her," Bear said. "I got Buddy."

It was slow going through the snow and the path wasn't clear. As they walked Mickey tied his belt around her upper arm and pulled it tight.

"We'll stop somewhere up ahead," Julie said, "and check that arm out. Somewhere where it's safe."

"Where'd they all come from?" Gwen grimaced in pain. "What are all those zombies doing here?"

"Keep moving," Bear said. "The bookers always come first."

"Listen," Julie said.

"Oh, Gwen, I'm sorry. I'm so sorry. I didn't—"

"Shut up. I know you didn't mean to shoot me."

There were faint groans and protests around them, but visibility was limited in the falling snow. Zombies were out there, the slow moving ones.

Bear hadn't been eating the way he should have these last few days. Their rations were limited and he wanted to make sure Julie got the sustenance she needed for herself and the baby. He would forego most of his own rations in such a way that no one would notice, making sure Julie got more than the others because she needed it.

He pressed on as far as he could but knew he would soon collapse in the snow from exhaustion. He couldn't let it come to that. Better to turn and face the undead hordes while he still had some strength. A few minutes later the snow let up. They faced a wooded hill, and he made his decision.

"We stop here," he said.

"*Here?*" Mickey asked.

"We've got to keep going," Julie said.

"I can't." Bear breathed heavily. "Not with him." He crouched and shrugged Buddy off to the ground. He stood and arched his back, trying to draw his elbows together.

"There might be thousands of them out there," Gwen said. "Let's leave him and—"

"No!" Julie said. "How many times do I have to go through this with—"

"I don't mean we leave him on the ground," Gwen said, feeling woozy as she settled herself on the snowy hill. "We'll put him up in a tree or something."

Bear shrugged out of his equipment and gear, laying his weapons side by side on the snow near where he stood. He buried the mace handle up in the snow at his feet. He looked at the Glock in his hand and holstered it.

"Mickey, let me see that shotgun of yours."

"Well, this should be interesting," the voice belonged to a female and came down off the hill.

Bear turned.

There was a black woman seated on the rise several yards away from them. She had an enormous afro and a scar down one side of her face. She was dressed in white camouflage fatigues that helped her blend into the hill, but on top, incongruously, she wore a waist length Red Kangaroo fur jacket. Next to her was a backpack and she had an M-16 with an M-203 grenade launcher attached resting across the pack, the 16's butt in the snow.

"You're planning on fighting those zombies all by yourselves?"

"Who—who are you?" Mickey asked, aware his hands were without a weapon, as were the woman's.

"You can call me Tris," she said. "That's what they call me. And I get real uncomfortable with your friend aiming that street sweeper at me."

"No offense," Bear said. "Make your intentions clear and we'll decide where I bury the buckshot."

"My *intentions?* Take a look at this." Tris raised her hand slowly. She was gripping a hand grenade. "See this? Fragmentation grenade. And that's the pin hanging off my neck on the chain. I wear this for the day my time to check out comes. Planning on taking as many of those dead motherfuckers with me."

"Like Blaster," Mickey said under his breath, thinking of *Uncommon Valor*.

"It was Sailor," said another female voice behind him.

He turned and there was a woman with an MP-40 submachine gun there, decked out in white from head to toe. Even her boots were taped up with white duct tape or something to help her blend in.

"See Tris? He knows the movie I was talking about."

"Yeah," Tris said, her focus on Bear. "My friend Lauren there told me about the grenade around the neck thing. You know, I get real nervous when people aim anything larger than a .45 at me. And when I get nervous, my palms get real sweaty, and when my palms get sweaty…"

Bear lowered the muzzle of the USAS-12 but kept watching Tris.

"I'm going to stand up now, so don't any of you get jumpy with those bang sticks."

Tris stood and Gwen could see she was tall, at least as tall as Julie, and the afro added another eight to ten inches on her. Tris replaced the cotter pin in the grenade and secured the explosive device around her neck, tucking it under her fur.

"You're right," Mickey said. "It was Sailor. Tex Cobb." He turned to Tris. "What's with the pimp jacket?"

"That how you talk to a woman when you first meet her? Well wise-ass, let me assure you, I keep my pimp hand strong."

"Sounds like you brought all of them this way," the black woman added, referring to the moans drawing closer.

"The tall one looks pregnant."

"You pregnant girl? *Damn*, big man, there you go with that shotgun again. I just asked your friend a question. You don't have to go and get all hostile on my ass."

He lowered the muzzle.

"Shit," Tris said.

"Yeah, I'm pregnant," Julie said. "You a farmer? What's with the sickles."

In addition to the various pistols she wore on her person Tris had two hand-held sickles strapped to her back.

"Tris isn't into agriculture," Lauren said. "She's like death. The other one don't look so good," Lauren indicated Gwen.

"Fuck you, you skinny bitch," Gwen managed.

"What is it with you people?" Lauren asked. "I meant you look like you're bleeding to death right here and now. It wasn't a comment on your looks."

"What are you two doing out here all alone?" Mickey asked.

"We're not alone." Tris raised a hand and waved it forward. Figures materialized from the hill, camouflaged against the snow in white parkas, holding assault rifles wrapped in white tape and cloth. One by one the figures came down the hill, fanning out, and Bear figured if he had to he could take out one, maybe two, before they lit him up.

"That big mean looking motherfucker hits me with that shotgun," Tris said out loud, "you blow him in two, okay Lore?"

"I got your back."

Lauren had her hands on the pistol grip and stick magazine of the vintage German submachine gun. She kept it aimed at the ground but appeared ready to bring it up into play if she had to.

"Bear?"

His good eye darted to the man who had called his name.

"Bear? Is that—Buddy! *Buddy*, no way, I—"

"Panas?" Mickey was overcome with joy. "Panas, is that—"

"Mickey! Julie and Gwen—Gwen what happened?"

"I shot her," Mickey said sheepishly.

"Oh," Panas said. "It's okay, Tris. I know these people."

"These the people you're always talking about?" asked the black woman. "From the city?"

"Yeah. I can't believe it, but yeah." Panas reached them and hugged each in turn, starting with Mickey. "Julie, my god, you're—"

Gwen lay down on the snow, exhausted.

"I am," she heard Julie say.

"We got a couple hundred Zeds coming to play," a man's voice.

"Well, Steve, let's get ready to rock," Tris spoke.

Gwen's head felt thick.

She watched Panas embrace Bear. He couldn't get his arms around the man.

"Damn, bro, you're a big one," she heard someone say. "Anyone ever tell you you reminded them of a wrestler or somebody? My roommate is going to friggin' love you…"

"Gwen, can you hear me?"

Panas.

"Y-yeah," she said but it felt like someone else was spoke for her.

Bobby? Was that her Bobby leaning over looking at her?

"Okay, this woman is going into shock," a voice, seemingly from a distance. "We've got to get her back to…"

And then all was black.

When she opened her eyes she was in a warm bed in a softly lit clean room. Her Bobby was no where to be seen. Instead, Mickey was sitting next to her bed in a chair.

"Gwen." An expression of pure joy swept over his face.

"Mickey…"

"Thank God you're okay. I feel so bad, I can't—how do you feel?"

"I feel…fine, I think. What's this?"

She raised her arm. A tube disappeared in her forearm.

"An IV. Dr. Malden said you lost a lot of blood. It was my fault, Gwen. I shouldn't have taken that shot. Not from so far away. Not when the zombie was so close to—"

She held up a hand for him to stop.

"Where are we?"

"Gwen." He leaned forward. "This place is amazing! It's just like Buddy said. You know who's here? Panas, Biden—those guys from Eden. You're never gonna guess what they call this place! Clavius City—you know, like Clavius Base in Kubrick's—"

"Okay, Mickey," she cut him off. "Julie?"

"She's fine. She just stepped out."

"The baby?"

"Not here yet."

She managed a weak smile.

"And there's this woman. Man, she's so friggin' hot and I think she digs me. She likes the same movies I like, can you believe that?"

She couldn't believe it but thought there was someone for everyone. "How long…how long have I been like this?"

"Since yesterday afternoon. We had a huge battle, hundreds of zombies. You should have seen it. These people can fight! They've trained and they know how to deal with zombies. That black chick—the one that looks like Erica Badu? She was fucking Zed up—"

"Zed?"

"That's what a lot of people here call them. The zombies. Zed."

"Oh."

"And Bear? He was a maniac. He cranked up that chain saw and sprang right into them, and then when it ran out of gas he was tearing them to pieces with his bare hands."

"Buddy?"

"He's…well, hopefully he's going to be okay," He leaned closer. "The doctor says it sounds like Buddy was on some serious psychoactive meds or something. He's got issues, Gwen."

"That's an understatement."

Mickey laughed. "But he was right. I mean, look at us, we're here." He swept his arms out to encompass the place, "Well, I mean, you haven't seen yet, but you will. This place is so cool, Gwen."

"We're safe?" she asked him, noticing he wore a pistol.

"Yeah, this place is locked down."

"I see my patient is awake." Dr. Malden knocked as he entered the room. "How are you feeling Ms. Evers?"

"I feel…fine, I think, and…and it's Gwen, doctor, not Ms. Evers."

"If you don't mind." Dr. Malden leaned over her and pulled one of her eyelids up, shining a small light in her eye. "Uh-huh, now the other."

"Gwen!" Julie rushed to the side of her bed and grasped her hand.

"Julie, I'm—"

"You're okay. You're going to be okay, and wait until you see where we are."

Bear loomed in the background, between the door and the bed.

"Well," Dr. Malden said, standing up and stepping back, pocketing his stethoscope. "That arms going to be in a sling for awhile, but you're friend is correct. In the long-run, no major damage. You got lucky."

"Thank you, doctor." Gwen hadn't said those words in so long. She couldn't remember how long ago she had seen a real doctor. "How did I get in here? All I remember is a bunch of voices and then, nothing."

"Mickey carried you in," Julie said.

"Thanks."

"It was the least I could do." He blushed.

"You're right, you bastard." She smiled. "Next time aim farther to the right with that scattergun."

She noticed everyone was wearing a side arm, including the doctor.

"Stacey." Dr. Malden signaled and a woman entered the room. "Gwen, this is Stacey—"

"Hi."

"—she's one of our nurses here at the medical center. She'll be in to check on you frequently, given that you're only one of three patients we have here."

"Medical center? Are we in a hospital?"

"Well," the doctor said. "We're a little smaller than our name implies, but we're expanding every day and pretty soon we'll live up to our name."

"The doctor is just being humble," Julie said. "This place is everything we could have hoped it would be."

"I'm glad to hear that. Doctor, you remind me of someone, from television…"

"*Little House on the Prairie,*" Julie said. "Doctor Malden looks like the doctor on the show."

"My girls used to watch that." Malden smiled. "I caught it with them once or twice, and from what I remember, the doctor was a noble character. So thank you. Well, why don't you and I—" he addressed Julie, "—go next door and run that sonogram I promised you?"

"Sonogram?" Gwen asked, brightening, "You're going to find out—"

Julie nodded her head and her smile was all excitement.

"I'm going to run down the hall for a couple of minutes," Stacey said. "Can I turn the TV on for you?"

"Television? You've got lights and television here?"

"Solar and wind power," Mickey said. "They're on the grid."

"Yes," Stacey said, "but all we have are a bunch of TV re-runs on DVD from the 70s and 80s. Our television station isn't up and running, yet. I'll bring you some DVDs to choose from."

"Okay, thanks."

"Gwen," Mickey said, "Dr. Singh—he's another of the doctors here—he was going to show me and Bear around today. Will you be okay by yourself for awhile?"

"I'll be fine. Hey, Bear. What, no hello?"

"Hello," said the big man from across the room.

"Hello, Bear. If you boys get a chance, stop by later on. Fill me in on what I missed."

"We will," Mickey promised.

Where Dr. Malden was older and avuncular, Dr. Singh was young and good-looking, like a doctor from a soap opera. There was another man in the room with him who wore an automatic pistol in a chest rig.

"Hey, how are you guys feeling?" he asked as Mickey knocked on the doctor's office door, Bear in tow.

"Pretty good," Mickey said. "Happy to be here."

"That is good." The doctor stood and shook both men's hands. "This is Sonny. He works in defense here at Clavius."

"Among other things." Sonny was about Mickey's height and ruggedly built.

"It's an amazing coincidence that you guys ran into Tris and her crew outside. Though from what I hear," Dr. Singh looked at Bear, "you might have been able to fend them all off by yourselves."

Bear didn't respond to the intended compliment.

"You giving them the tour, Kip? Mind if I tag along?"

"I don't mind. Well, like I promised last night, you gentlemen want the tour first or your examinations?"

"Let's start with the tour," Mickey said.

"Follow me, gentleman."

Singh led them through the two floors of the medical center, showing them the various rooms and equipment.

"We don't have everything we'd like here, not yet. But we've got a fairly sophisticated facility available to us. You have heart palpitations, we have a Holter monitor. Echocardiogram, heart stress-test. Need your vision corrected? We have a LASIK surgical laser. MRI, ECMO machine, all sorts of acronyms. Adenoids act up, we can remove them."

"You know how to use all this stuff yourself?" Mickey asked.

"Most of it. Malden and I specialized in internal medicine."

"There are other doctors here in Clavius," Sonny said. "Malden and Singh happened to be on duty when you came through."

"We've got three patients here, currently," Singh said. "Two of them are your friends. Let us introduce you to Michael. May we come in? I want you both to meet Michael."

A man sat up in a hospital bed reading a book. Most of his head and face and hands were bandaged.

"Hi guys," he said, then looked at Singh and Sonny. "Did you explain to them why I'm here? I don't want to freak them out…"

"Michael has the plague," Sonny announced like it was no big deal.

"Whoa—" Mickey forgot about his own condition and backed up a step.

"See?" Michael aimed the question at Singh.

"Michael is not contagious," the doctor explained. "The plague is something we're studying here. Not everyone who gets it can pass it along, and not everyone is vulnerable to it."

"Interesting," Mickey said "Sorry I…"

"Nah, its fine. I get it. I'm just lucky I've got the doctors and nurses here who are helping me out."

Mickey noticed that the bandaged hands resting atop the book on Michael's lap—the title of the book was *The Pugilist at Rest*—were missing fingers and he thought of the thin man at the fire that night.

"How is your family, Michael?" asked Singh.

"Everybody's great. Max's birthday is tomorrow."

"Well, we'll have you out of here by the morning."

Out in the hallway Mickey said, "Hey, uh, doc? Sonny? The plague? How can you keep him here?"

"Well, that's the thing about the plague," Singh said. "In some people it's clearly contagious and remains so throughout the duration. That is, until the person expires. But we've seen others infected who haven't been contagious, who live for remarkably long periods."

"How long?"

"Well, take Michael back there. He had the plague when he arrived in Clavius City. We briefly quarantined him and determined he wasn't contagious. And he's been here, what Sonny? Six-seven months?"

"Yeah. Just to be clear with you guys, not everyone is happy with that."

"What do you mean?" Mickey said.

"Look, me, the doctor here, we work with people like Michael on a daily basis. We're in close personal contact with them. If they were contagious we would have been infected by now, right? But we're not."

"What about what you said to us inside there?" Mickey said. "How some people may be immune to getting it in the first place?"

"Too many of us work here for that to be the case," the doctor shook his head. "Michael isn't contagious."

"We do have a vocal minority who don't want anyone with the plague here," added Sonny. "*Anyone.*"

"Well, is that a major issue?"

Sonny was about to address Mickey's question when Singh put his hand on the other man's arm. "You know, I'd like to show them something now."

"Sounds good," Sonny said.

Mickey and Bear followed Singh and Sonny down the hall towards the elevator.

"We try not to keep any secrets here," Singh explained as he pressed the button for the elevator. "So, I want to be open with both of you. Before the outbreak, I was very active in college, and even in med school, as an animal rights activist."

"PETA?" Mickey asked.

"A similar organization. I was out there on the picket lines, protesting the cosmetics industry, KFC, the things they do to animals. And I want to be clear with you both, I still believe in what we were fighting against, and *for.* So, what I'm going to show you downstairs—"

The elevator door opened with a *bing.*

"I'm not trying to sound unfriendly, doctor," Bear spoke up for the first time in a while, "but we're not getting on that elevator until you cut to the chase."

"What Kip is getting at," explained Sonny, "is that this is a joint military-medical facility, if that terms means anything. That's part of the reason I'm here."

"You'll have to forgive me," said Singh. "We're experimenting here, on the zombies. Downstairs, I mean. That's what I want to show you. But I wanted to warn you first, because some of what you might see, it can be disturbing."

Sonny added, "And you've probably never encountered zombies in anything but a hostile environment, right? Their presence can be...startling."

"They're not running loose down there, are they?" asked Mickey.

"No, of course not," assured Sonny. "They're secured."

Bear looked at Mickey and although he did not look happy he stepped on the elevator.

The doors opened two floors down. Singh and Sonny led Mickey and Bear down a short hall and introduced them to a female guard seated at a desk flipping through a magazine. They next entered a suit of large rooms. The first contained several desks and computer consoles and there were five or six men and women working at various stations.

Sonny introduced them to Mickey and Bear—"and this is Greg, and Hayden there is our I.T. tech—" but Bear had stepped forward to a large glass window that looked out onto the next room where three zombies were secured vertically to gurneys.

"…and those three," finished Sonny, joining Bear at the window, "are Bill, Al, and Hilary. We're trying to learn everything we can about them."

"You named them?" asked Bear. "Like pets."

"No, not like pets," Singh said, as he and Mickey joined Bear and Sonny at the glass. The three zombies, which had been looking elsewhere, all looked up at the glass, causing Sonny to remark "Interesting."

Singh finishing his thought, "We never want to forget as we experiment on them that they were human. They were us. And we could too easily become them. One bite, yes?"

"As strange as this is gonna sound," Sonny said. "We don't want to forget their…*humanity* I guess you'd say. So, no, we don't name them to belittle them."

"You don't feed them, do you?"

"Of course not," said Dr. Singh. "They're zombies. They don't need to eat. All they would eat is human flesh, and we're not going to indulge that here."

"They eat other animals too, right?" asked Bear.

"Yes, but as plentiful as everything might appear here, we can't afford to sacrifice a deer or a cow for them. We have living human beings who need that protein."

"Uh-huh," Mickey said. "Bill, Al, and Hilary, huh? Someone with a Red State sense of humor around here."

"We're equal opportunity offenders," Sonny said. "The last couple we worked on we called Ron and Nancy."

"So, what have you learned from them?" Bear asked.

"For one thing," Sonny said, "they track us with their sense of smell."

"Smell, huh? They can smell humans?"

"No, they can smell *blood*," Singh said. "If you have an open wound, they will find you. From miles away. It's uncanny really. We don't know how they do it."

"I don't get it," Mickey said. "In so many ways, once a person turns into a zombie, they seem so...*dumb*? But..."

"But their olfactory sense is somehow heightened," the doctor said. "Yes, we don't *get it* from a scientific standpoint either, but we're working on that."

"Another thing about them?" Sonny said. "They won't go near plague victims. Or the autistic."

"They won't go near the autistic?" Bear asked.

"I know, *strange*," Singh said, "and again, we don't know why."

"What's that about they're not being attracted to plague victims?" Mickey asked.

"Once someone is infected," Singh explained, "even before the plague is showing, zombies will not attack that person. A plague victim, like Michael upstairs, could freely move among a crowd of them. It's quite remarkable actually."

"Interesting," Mickey said.

"Is this one-way glass?" Bear asked.

"It is."

"Funny," Mickey said, "they're looking like they know we're here."

"We'll show you something interesting," Singh said. "Hayden?" He gestured to one of the people in the room with a motion like he was turning a knob.

"You'll note the wires connected to the sides of Al's head." Singh pointed them out. "They're connected directly to the parietal lobes."

"What's that?" Mickey asked.

"It's part of your brain responsible for language," Bear said.

"Yes, it is." Singh was pleased. "One of the reasons we chose these three over others available to us outside is because of the viability of their throats, vocal cords, and mouths. Dysarthria—or something like it—seems to set in as the bodies decompose. Something we've found, well, let's just show you. Okay, Hayden? One hundred fifty, please."

The young woman in the white lab coat Singh spoke to cranked a knob on a console and the zombie nicknamed Al shook as electricity coursed through its head and down through its body. As Mickey and Bear watched it went rigid, lifted its neck, opened its mouth and said, "The rain in Spain falls mainly on..."

"Holy shit," Mickey said. "What the fuck was that?"

"Again, Hayden, please" Singh said. When Hayden turned the knob a second time the zombie went rigid and blurted, "I've been slimed…"

"Unreal," Bear said.

"Once more," Singh said.

"Tea and crumpets, governor…"

"That's crazy," Mickey said.

"No, like your friend said, it's *remarkable*."

"Nah, I agree with Mickey," Sonny said. "That is crazy. Never ceases to amaze me."

"What's causing it?" Mickey asked. "I mean, I get the electrical stimulation or whatever to the brain, but…"

"Does it know what its saying?" Singh asked. "We don't think so. Does it repeat itself? Occasionally."

"That's very disturbing," Bear said.

"I can see why," agreed the doctor. "It's so human, so like us. And yet, one look at them, and well, they're nothing like us, anymore. You do know they will eat until their stomach bursts, right?"

"And keep eating," Bear added.

"Yes, and they *will* keep eating. They seem quite impervious to pain."

"Except burning," Bear said.

"Except burning," agreed Sonny. "There's something about fire Zed don't like."

"You know what probably freaks me out most about this whole zombie thing?" Mickey said.

"What's that?"

"It's how right the movies got it. I mean, directors like Romero and Argento, Fulci and de Ossorio, right?"

"I'm unfamiliar with most of those. I've seen a couple of the Romero films," Singh said. "You're correct. It'd be like if something happened and vampires suddenly became a reality, only to conform to the Anne Rice ground rules."

"There's no explaining it," Sonny said wistfully. "Not yet at least."

"You think there will be one day?" asked Bear.

"I have to hope so. I mean, there were what, six or seven billion people on Earth when this happened? How many billions of them are Zed now? So what's our alternative? I mean, we either find a way to, I don't know, live with them, or we have to kill all of them."

"You think that can be done?"

"Again, what's the alternative? I've got a daughter, Torrie. You'll meet her later. She's almost seven. All she can remember is this bullshit. Is that what the rest of her life is going to be like? Not if I have anything to say about it."

"In the interim," Singh said, "we live our lives here as best we can. All things considered, it really isn't all that bad."

"No, it doesn't look like it is," Mickey said. "So, this is the secret lab, huh?"

The doctor grinned. "We purposefully try not to keep secrets here. This lab is open to all. No one's told them about the job complexes yet I assume?" Singh looked at Sonny who shrugged. "Well, you've been here less than a day. Let's just say, if this interests you, you can have your chance to work here too one day very soon."

"That's okay," Mickey said. "Quite honestly, I don't like being around these things."

"Understandable," Singh said. "Why don't we go upstairs then for those physicals?"

"From what I hear you guys are invited to a little party tonight," Sonny said.

"Yeah," Mickey said.

"Well, I'm going to say goodbye for now but I'll see you tonight, and you guys will get to meet Torrie."

"Cool."

Ten minutes later Mickey was stripped down to a towel around his waist in Dr. Singh's office, the door closed. Singh stood back with his arms folded, studying his torso.

"How long have you known you've had the plague?"

"I don't know. A few weeks. I'm not contagious, am I?"

"I'd say not. You've been with your friends for a considerable amount of time, first in that place, Eden, you told us about, then on the road, and they're not infected."

"Thank God," he said. "I didn't think I was, but..."

"No, you're not contagious. Your friends, they don't...?"

"No. They have no clue."

"Hmmm. Maybe better to keep quiet about this for awhile. But you saw how the zombies downstairs reacted to you when you walked up to the glass, yes?"

"Yeah. You saw that too, huh?"

"Yes. As, I'm sure, Sonny did. And the others downstairs."

"Shit."

"I'll talk to Sonny and the others, but you tell no one," Singh said. "And let me tell you why. Remember earlier Sonny was telling you and your friend, Bear, that not everyone here believes that the plague infected are benign?"

"Yeah."

"And you noted there was only Michael here, only one man with the plague?"

He nodded.

"Well, there have been others."

"What do you mean, doc? Where'd they go?"

"I don't know. They disappeared. I mean, I have my suspicions, but until I have proof…"

"What do you think happened to them?"

"I think they were forcibly exiled, let's say."

"Forcibly exiled?"

"Thrown out of here. One morning myself or Malden or another of the staff show up for work and they're just gone. And no one knows where they went. They're never seen again."

"You think someone is killing them?"

"Killing them? I'd hope not. That's part of the reason Sonny was here today. He's a military man you know. We're reconsidering security around this facility. I think someone is sending the plague-infected packing, threatening them to never come back."

"Hmmm."

"Yes."

"Doc, what does this mean, for me I mean?" He gestured to the bruising and scabs on his torso.

"You said you first noticed these a few weeks ago?"

"Yeah."

"It started out as some slight discoloration, like bruising? Like these spreading to your upper arms and thighs?"

"Yeah, exactly."

"Well, let me speak frankly, yes?"

"Please do."

"Most people who contract the plague are contagious and have to be kept from the others. They don't last long. Others, like yourself or Michael, are not contagious and can move about freely—"

"How long, doc? How long I got?"

"Could be a few weeks, a few months. Maybe a year. Maybe more. We just don't know."

"Shit."

"We have people here, people you could talk to."

"I'm talking to you, doc."

"And I need to be honest with you. You understand?"

"It's all I'd expect."

"Have you seen what happens to plague victims?"

"It's bad, right?"

The doctor shook his head, "Well, it's not good, but... Look, you're here now. When the time comes, we can keep you comfortable. And you've got time. You might have plenty of time. But I wouldn't tell anyone about this if I were you."

"I'm so glad to hear you say that," he said. "When I first suspected, I felt so selfish keeping quiet about it. I mean, there was the fear I'd infect the others, especially Julie and the baby, but, but I didn't want them to, to..."

"I understand. And as it turns out, your reticence didn't lead to any harm."

"Well, I did shoot Gwen in the arm."

"Yes, you did. And you also secured that tourniquet much too low, but we'll keep that between us too, yes? After all, Gwen will heal."

"What about our other friend—Buddy?"

"Malden and I were talking about him. He was near catatonic when Bear carried him in here. And you say he'd been like that for a couple of days?"

"Yeah, but he...he got worse fast, really fast."

"You know, Malden met Buddy here once before. When Buddy arrived with Panas and the other two. How long has it been, you said, since Buddy returned to your place, to this Eden?"

"I don't know. Three weeks? Maybe a month tops. Bear will remember better."

"I came here six months ago, Mickey. And I never met Buddy."

"Well, you've got like what, two thousand people living here?"

"No, that's not what I mean."

"What do you mean then?"

"According to Malden and Panas and the others, Buddy left here to return to Eden six or seven months ago."

"But that—"

"That means it took him five or more months to return to you and this Eden place."

"That's—then where the hell was he all that time?"

"That's the thing. He was wandering around, out there, with those things, with the zombies."

"For months? Jesus."

"Yes. And he wasn't alone. Hhe left here with another man—"

"Sal…"

"—who wanted to get back to his wife—"

"Camille…"

"—in Eden. You said he arrived back in Eden unaccompanied, yes? Well, your friend is very sick, and his sickness is not physical. Now, you've gotten a chance to look around a little? Well, sometime in the next day or so someone will come and give you the longer tour, explain to you how things work here.

"It's really quite, well, I guess I'd have to say it's amazing. Participatory economy and all that. Now, I should be taking a look at your friend, Bear, out there. Does he have a name other than Bear?"

"I don't know. You'd have to ask him." Mickey, buttoned his shirt. "I'm worried about him."

"What about him?"

"He is getting, I don't know, *quieter*. He's…I guess I'd say he's withdrawing."

"I'll talk to him. Why don't you go and check on Julie and Gwen?"

"I will." He stood. "Hey, doc, one last question?"

"Shoot." Singh held up his hands like he was warding off a blow. "No pun intended."

"Oh, you're a funny one. One of the women we met yesterday when we…her name is Lauren."

"I don't know her. Like you pointed out, there are close to two thousand people living here. I know a lot of them, maybe most of them. But not her. Why, is she cute?"

Mickey smiled. "Heck, yeah."

The doctor smiled. "Take care of yourself. Come and see me in two or three days or I will come and see you." He opened his door. Bear was sitting in one of the chairs in the hall, dwarfing it. "Come on in, please."

Bear entered silently and Singh shut the door.

"Why don't you start by stripping down to your underwear?"

The doctor made some notes on a clipboard while he disrobed.

"You probably get a lot of comments about your size," Singh said when he stood in his drawers.

He shrugged.

"Don't feel uncomfortable. I did not mean that in a sexual way. What are you, about six-two?"

"Yes."

"You have a name, aside from Bear?"

"Yeah."

"What is it?"

"Jimmy."

"*Jimmy*. Well, Jimmy," Singh frowned, "you look more like a *Bear* than a Jimmy to me. I guess that's why they call you Bear.

"These tattoos. You were part of a motorcycle club at some point in your life?"

"Yeah."

"Which one? Angels? Mongrels? No, I see, Pagans."

"How'd you know that, doctor?"

"This tattoo." He indicated the ink on his back. A deity sat on the sun holding a sword. In red, white and blue the word *Pagan's* was above the god and the initials *MC* beneath. "This is Surtr, fire-giant. I used to read about one-percenters when I was a little boy in Mumbai. I was a big Chuck Zito fan. Was he as bad-ass as was claimed?"

"I wouldn't know. I never crossed paths with him. But I wouldn't mess with him."

"Few would."

"You know what that tat on my back means, then you know what the tear drop under my eye and the spider web on my elbow mean."

"You've killed men."

"I'm not proud of that."

"You carry this much muscle naturally?" He noted how the doctor deftly changed the subject. "Insipid question, yes? Of course you do. You're a natural meso-endomorph. Were you a bodybuilder?"

"Powerlifter."

"Well, looks like you could have had a career as a bodybuilder if you'd wanted."

"I used to be a heavier than I am. Fatter."

"Lost a lot of weight, have you?"

"Starvation will do that to you."

"Well, no one starves here," Singh said. "What do you think about our town?"

"It's...it's great."

"You're a man of few words, huh?"

Bear shrugged.

"Your friend, Mickey? He's worried about you. Told me you've been getting quite taciturn of late."

"That's what you were talking to Mickey about? *Me*? Isn't that against doctor-patient confidentiality or something?"

"I was talking to Mickey five minutes ago. Five minutes ago you weren't my patient. Now you are. I won't talk to Mickey about you any longer. You look fine, by the way, physically. Those scars on your torso, multiple stab wounds?"

"Somebody took me for a pin cushion once."

"How do you feel?"

"With my hands."

"Oh, very clever, yes. No, really?"

"Tired."

"You slept well last night?"

"I slept twelve hours last night. I slept like I haven't slept in a long time."

"That's good. So when you say you feel tired, it's more a physical or an existential feeling?"

"Both."

"Let's discuss the existential aspect then. You can sleep another twelve hours tonight."

"You an M.D. or a shrink?" he asked in a neutral tone.

"I'm an M.D., but I'm also a human being who cares."

"That must be nice."

"Why, don't you care?"

"I used to, a lot more than I do now."

"What do you mean?"

"I don't know. I don't feel the same anymore. I don't feel...I don't feel like I used to."

"How so?"

"I can't really say. I used to feel, I don't know, *closer* to people."

"Which people?"

"My club. The people in my church."

"You're a religious man?"

"Not much anymore. If at all."

"You don't feel close to anyone anymore?"

"The woman, Julie, I guess. The baby."

"You carried Buddy in here yesterday. I'm told you'd been carrying him for two days."

"Off and on." He shrugged.

"Maybe you're depressed. Maybe you're just exhausted. When we were downstairs, you knew about the parietal lobe of the brain. You have some background in medicine?"

"I was a home health aide for a long time."

"A caring profession if there ever was one." Singh smiled. "What kind of clientele?"

"The elderly. I've seen old men and women with parietal lobe strokes, not able to say a thumb is a thumb."

Singh nodded. "Agnosia."

"Yeah."

"That kind of work still interest you?"

"Why? You need another nurse around here?"

"Actually we do. But most of the men and women who work as nurses in this center are also interning with Malden and myself to become doctors."

"No kidding?"

"We're teaching them everything we know and they're teaching us and each other everything they know."

"What if someone doesn't want to be a doctor? Only wants to be a nurse."

"Then they can be a nurse. No one's forced to be something they don't want to be. Julie and the baby—you or Mickey or Buddy the father?"

"No."

"It's tough," Singh said. "For Julie. She's lucky she had you to get her here."

"I started to wonder if we really were going to get here."

"I'd like to talk to you about your friend, Buddy."

"The way you talked to Mickey about me?"

"Yes. The way I talked to Mickey about you. Your friend Buddy has had a major disconnect with reality."

"He's psycho, isn't he?"

"We're trying to figure that out. He's schizophrenic, that's for certain. Those empty medicine bottles he had in his bags? They contained psychoactive medications. Panas said Buddy made a few comments over time, things that made him—*Panas*—think Buddy might have been imprisoned, yes?"

"He told me he was Inside. I don't know for what."

"Well, let's assume your friend was in some kind of prison before the zombie outbreak, yes?"

Bear nodded.

"You know, it wasn't uncommon for men and women in prison to have mental issues."

"I've been there, doctor. I know."

"Either they developed their issues in the institution or they were there because of them. Who's to say? The rates of mental illness, drug addiction, HIV infection, all that was quite high among prison inmates, compared to people outside of prison.

"So it's not inconceivable that Buddy was, one," Singh held up an index finger, "imprisoned before the outbreak, and, two," he held up his middle finger, "is suffering from a severe mental illness. Yes? Now, one thing that the state or federal government would have done for him while he was in prison would have been to medicate him—"

"And then he gets out of prison and no medicine."

"No medicine, *correct*. So what happens to your friend? Well, once the meds are out of his system, he's gripped by whatever mental illness the medications were keeping at bay."

"Damn."

"Yes."

"So, what's he, what's he experiencing?"

"Right now we're trying to figure out what medications he needs. It's a process of trial and error, really."

"Is he, does he *know*?"

"Here's some of the things your friend has probably been dealing with. Dr. Malden knows a lot more about this than me, so you should talk to him later. He's probably experiencing auditory hallucinations—voices in his head."

"Does he see things?"

"Visual hallucinations are rare, except in cases of brain damage, but Buddy doesn't seem to—"

"He tried to strangle Mickey."

"I know. Julie told us. It's uncommon among schizophrenics to harm other people. They're much more likely to be self-injurious. Which is what makes Malden and myself think there's some co-morbidity at play here."

"Co-morbid with what?"

"You asked me before if Buddy was a psychopath? I think he might be a sociopath."

"A sociopath."

"No regard for others. No sense of remorse or guilt. Sociopaths appear to lack what we call conscience. Their activities are completely self-serving. They exhibit a disregard for rules, for social mores and laws. They put themselves and others at risk."

"But he's so…nice. Usually, I mean." He thought of that night he had to pull Buddy off Mickey.

"Yes, well that's where Malden and I are trying to figure it out. Are his symptoms more typical of a sociopath or a psychopath? A psychopath can mimic behaviors that make them appear normal, but they have no empathy. Some are outright sadistic."

"No," Bear said, thinking of the Buddy he knew, the way he treated people, treated him, treated Harris, the way he had come back to Eden for them. "He was…He is genuine. He isn't fake."

"Which may be his real personality," Singh pointed out. "Or it may have been the medication covering up his mental health issues. It's hard to tell."

"Man…"

"Yes. I should also point out that delusional thoughts are very common among schizophrenics. Very *involved*, intact beliefs that bare no semblance whatsoever to reality but seem very real to the person having them. Stress can trigger them."

"Is that why he tried to kill Mickey?"

"I don't know. Maybe he was having a delusion. Maybe he had built up a delusion. Maybe he thought Mickey was someone else. We'll do what we can for him here. The good news is we've stockpiled lots of different medications."

"The bad news?"

"No one's making these medicines any longer."

"Yet."

"*Yet*. Exactly."

"You know they invited us to this party or whatever tonight?"

"Yes. I think you should go. I think you should all go, including Buddy."

Bear looked at Singh.

"It won't hurt him to be around people. He can't lay in that bed down the hall all day and night."

"That guy, Michael, with the plague? He's going to die one day, right?"

"We're all going to die one day," Singh said. "It's the way of all flesh. Let me reassure you, we're doing everything we can for your friend, and we're going to ensure the remainder of Julie's pregnancy is as stress-free as possible."

"Thanks, Doctor Singh."

"It's Kip, Jimmy, or do you prefer Bear?"

"I haven't been called anything else in such a long time."

"Well, you think about it and let me know. And like I said before, if you decide you might like someone to talk to, I can help you with that too. Introducing you to someone to talk to, I mean. It doesn't have to be me. God knows I have enough of my own issues."

He smiled. "Thanks, Kip."

Julie knocked on his bedroom door in the dorm and leaned her head in. "You coming with us?" Her stomach was so large she could not wear the .357 holstered anywhere on her waist. Instead she had tucked the .380 at her lower back beneath her sweater and jacket.

"I don't think so." He was stretched out across the bed, his lower legs hanging off the end. "You guys go ahead without me and have a good time."

"Bear." She shook her head, entered the room, and sat on the bed where he lay. "What's the matter?"

"Nothing."

"Why don't you want to go?"

"I don't know. The idea of a party…"

"It's not a *party* party. I mean, I don't think anyone's going to ask you to sing karaoke. It's Tris and her girlfriend and a bunch of their friends, just saying hello, welcoming us, getting to know us. No one's going to ask you to dance."

The corners of his mouth rose.

"What if no one wants to dance with me?" he asked.

"Then I'll dance with you."

"What's the doctor say about the baby?"

"The baby is fine. Malden asked me if I wanted to know if it was a boy or a girl…"

"And?"

"And I didn't want to know."

"Why not?"

"I guess I like pleasant surprises, and, well, this will be the first pleasant surprise in a long time."

Julie touched her stomach.

"You're getting big."

"You should see my belly button."

"Innie become an outtie?"

"Exactly." She smiled. "You know, I think I have some idea what you're feeling. I mean, it was pretty bleak out there…on the road. There were times I really didn't think we would make it. And when Buddy started losing it… Now we're here. It all seems, I don't know, too good to be true."

"I don't know if it's too good to be true," Bear said. "I just don't know if I can deal with it. With people."

"I feel the same way. But, one of the things I know, I can't sit in my room here all night. I'll think of Harris…"

"He was a good man."

"If he could see what was happening…what was happening with Buddy…"

"They're trying to help him, Julie. I was talking to one of the doctors about it earlier. Buddy must have had some major clinical issues we didn't know about."

"I know. Harris always said Buddy had his past…"

He nodded.

"I want to ask you a favor."

"Go ahead."

"Be the godfather to my child."

"Julie, I…" He sat up on the bed, the springs creaking beneath his frame.

"It would mean a lot to me. It would have meant a lot to Harris."

"Wow." He tried to get his head around the idea.

"If anything ever happens to me, a godparent would be responsible for—"

"No, no, I know what a godfather does, Julie. It's just, I don't know where I am anymore, with God I mean. I don't know what I believe any more. I don't even know if I think there is a God or gods or anything, other than this…"

"Your religious belief or disbelief, or whatever, that doesn't matter to me. I'm asking you to help me raise my baby, and if something ever happens to me—"

"*Nothing* will ever happen to you." He swung his legs over the side of the bed and put his feet on the floor. "Not while I'm around."

"Then be the godfather of my child."

"I don't know what to say, I'm…"

"Say you're honored and you'd be happy to be godparent to this kid."

"I *am* honored." Bear beamed in a way Julie had never seen him smile before. "And there's no greater happiness I can imagine than for me to be godfather to your child, to Harris' child."

"Thanks." She stood up. "Your responsibilities start now. So get your boots on and let's go. I need a big strong man to lean on, make sure I don't slip outside."

"Okay, give me two minutes." He patted his bald head. "I've got to fix my hair."

"What's he doing here?" Steve asked Lauren and Sonya.

A group of them were in a big carpeted room of the recreation center. Buddy, freshly bathed and dressed but still looking mostly out of it, was seated in the center of the room on the floor. A bunch of little children were playing duck-duck-goose around him.

"Who?" Sonya asked.

"One flew over the coo-coo's nest over there, that's who."

"Singh and Malden thought it'd be good for him to get out and be around people," Lauren said.

"Singh brought him here?"

"Yeah."

"Then Singh can keep an eye on him. Does that guy even know he's here?"

"Sure he does." Singh walked up to them. "We're trying him out on some new meds and we'll see how they work."

"I don't know," Steve said. "Is it safe to have him around children?"

Several of the smaller kids splayed their palms atop Buddy's kinky head and ran around his seated form.

"We're all here, Steve," Sonya said. "What's he going to do? And if you're worried about the mentally ill, what's up with your roommate?"

Chris was in a small group over on the other side of the room, decked out in his arm bands and face paint. He hadn't taken them off since the day he rescued Steve at the convoy. Every time he showered he reapplied the paint.

There was a stereo playing in another corner of the room.

"Hey, he just bit Victor," Steve said.

"Very funny." Sonya, rolled her blind eyes. "Not."

"I mean, you should have seen this guy going at it with those zombies," Isaak told a bunch of men and women. "You ever seen someone chainsaw zombies before?"

"Son of a bitch," Chris said. "I knew he was bad just lookin' at him."

"He tougher than Tris?" Danny asked. His twin sister, Hayden, scoffed.

"Tougher than Tris?" Isaak said. "I don't know about that, but he was tearing limbs off those zeds like, like, like—"

"Who's tougher than me?"

Tris sauntered over with her arm around Eva's shoulder. She wore her Red Kangaroo fur jacket.

"The big guy."

Sonny nodded at the four men and women who had just walked in. He held his daughter's hands while she walked up his thighs and flipped over backwards to stand upright.

"Bear," Biden said.

"Bear," Tris said. "Yeah, he *is* a tough one."

"Not as tough as you, baby," Eva said, looking up into her scarred lover's face.

"You know what the statistical probability of you ever running into your friends again was, Biden?" Hayden asked him.

"No. Do you?"

"No, but it's got to be enormous."

"They're still down there," Biden said, thinking of others. "In the city."

"Tris, we gotta go down there," Isaak said. "Rescue those people. Bring them back up here."

"Hell yeah," Danny said. "Time to bring the pain to Zed himself."

"No you don't, Tris," Eva said. "You need to stay right here with me." She leaned over and kissed her woman on the cheek.

A few feet away from them Chris elbowed Brent, none too subtly, causing Brent to blush and ask, "What do you want man?"

"I'm thinking about that," Tris said, ignoring the two men and Eva. "But tonight let's try and have some fun."

"Damn, that woman looks like she's ready to pop," Hayden noted of Julie.

The newcomers were welcomed and introduced to everyone. Bear noticed how people eyed him, somewhat warily, somewhat respectfully. He stayed close to Julie while some of the women talked to her.

"When are you due?"

"Doctor Malden says in about five weeks."

"Do you know if it's going to be a boy or a girl?"

"You'll love it here. This is a great place to give birth. Mary just had her baby three weeks back and everything went fine…"

"Hey, big man." Chris walked over to Bear with three cans of beer hanging from their plastic webbing. "You want a beer?"

"No, thanks."

"Daddy, what's this man's name?" Torrie asked her father.

"Introduce yourself, sweetie," Sonny prodded her.

"I'm Torrie. What's your name?"

"Bear."

"Bear? That's a funny name."

"Yeah, I guess it is. Why don't you call me Jimmy?"

"Okay, Jimmy, look what I can do." Torrie walked up her father's thighs and flipped herself over in a flash of skirt and little flowered purple panties.

"*Wow*," Bear said, "that's cool."

"Watch me do it again—watch me do it again!"

"Hey man," Chris said to him, "let me be blunt with you. You ever think of being a professional wrestler?"

"Once or twice, a long time ago."

"Look, Jimmy, look at me!"

"Ah man, let me tell you, if Vince McMahon was here and he could get a load of you…"

"Your friend is very kind," Lauren said to Mickey, "to humor Chris like that."

"Yeah, what's up with that guy?"

"He's…I don't know, he marches to a different drummer than most of us. But he's a good soul."

"Yeah, he's good people," Brent said as he joined them. "But you know what he wanted to play on the stereo?"

"*Wasp?*" Lauren laughed.

"Yeah, *exactly*."

"What's so funny about Wasp?" Mickey didn't get it.

"You ever hear the song, *Animal?* Chorus goes—"

"*I fuck like a beast.*" Mickey laughed .

"Speaking of singing," Lauren said. "Singh introduce you to his little choir over at the med center?"

"Yeah. That's something, ain't it?"

"That's *crazy*," Lauren said.

"This place is incredible," Julie said. "You rely on ditches for protection?"

"You saw them when you came in, right? They're fifteen feet deep, vertical on our side. We expand them when we have to in the warmer months."

"Real bitch digging ditches in the earth when the grounds frozen like this."

"Danny," Hayden said, "you never built a ditch with your hands." She explained to Julie, "We use earth moving equipment. I don't even know what the stuff is called—"

"You guys had walls around where you were staying?" Danny asked Julie.

"Yeah."

"Walls suck."

Lauren continued, "Clavius is always expanding and we can't be spending half our time taking down and rebuilding walls."

"Only problem with a ditch," Panas said, "is they're meant to protect against Zed, not other human beings."

"Those people you told us about were scary," Hayden said. "To think there's people like that out there…"

Not anymore, Bear thought.

"Jimmy, look what I can do—"

"Honey, leave Bear alone. Go play with the other kids and Buddy, okay?"

"Okay Daddy."

"We get Zeds in ones and twos," Sonny said, "but sometimes we get them by the hundreds, couple of times in the thousands. Where they're coming from, I don't know. Why they come here, I can only guess."

"They don't get past these ditches?" Bear asked, his eyebrow raised quizzically.

"No. We've got men and women stationed every couple hundred yards. If a zombie makes it to a ditch, they're taken out."

"Zed don't surf!" Danny spat and Mickey wondered if the kid even knew what movie the original line came from.

"You said *if a zombie makes it to the ditch?*" Bear asked.

"We've got teams of people out there," Sonny clarified. "They go out in teams of four and stay out for five days to a week."

"I'm going out next week," Danny piped up. "Gonna light Zed up."

Hayden scoffed, pouted her lips and rolled her eyes.

"He's a young gun," Sonny noted sardonically. "Wants to kill zombies, don't you? You'll get your chance, kid. When the teams spot any movement, if it's something they can handle, they take care of it. If it's not, they radio back and alert us."

"What are we talking about when you say it's something they can't handle?" Mickey said.

"Zed, man," Danny said. "Zed in his glorious hundreds and thousands."

"We've had droves of them come up through here," Sonny said. "We either go out and meet them, like Tris and her crew the other day were doing, or the team will lead them to a specified area where we've got an advantage."

"It's like a duck shoot," Danny said. "Hundreds of the damned things just standing in a draw—like one of the trenches—and we blast 'em."

"Then we burn them, bulldozers come in, cover up the remains."

"Yeah, this place is friggin' enormous," Mickey said. He was going to say *fuckin' huge* but there were children within earshot and he didn't want to curse in front of them.

"We've got several square miles covered," Sonny agreed. "But you can imagine even that starts feeling small after awhile."

Brent killed his beer and looked at the can. "How long is it safe to drink a beer after the expiration date, anyway?"

"I think as long as it doesn't have any dents in the can it's okay," Mickey said.

"Sounds good to me. Time for a refill. Later."

"Later, Brent."

"Hey, Lauren. That's a museum piece you carry there, isn't it?" Mickey said of the MP-40 on her back. "Nazi weapon?"

"Yeah."

"Schnauzer or something?"

"*Schmeisser.*" She laughed, not sure if he had been kidding around.

"I noticed outside yesterday, you guys all carry the same weapons?"

"Pretty much. We usually go out with the same kind of rifle and at least one pistol in common. Helps with the ammunition. Instead of everybody having a different kind of weapon, different ammo."

"Makes sense."

"But we also carry any personal pieces we want. For me, that's this." She snapped the strap of the MP-40.

"Everyone here is armed?"

"All the time."

"You ever have zombies get in?"

"Never. The perimeter is patrolled twenty-four seven."

"And you haven't blown each other away?"

Lauren laughed and Sonny said, "Gun control, or whatever it was called, meant a whole other thing before...before we were here. Before this. Yeah, we all pack, but we're not killing one another."

"I guess that was one of the good things about America having so many guns," Mickey said. "When the zombies came you could literally find a machine gun on the street if you looked long enough."

"Yeah, Charlton Heston would have been proud," Sonny said.

"*Soylent Green!*" he fake yelled. Lauren nodded and laughed. Then he asked, "What is this, some kind of utopia?"

"Seems that way, sometimes," she said. "But it's not. I mean, it's really great. But let's face it. There are people here who don't really get along. There are people," she looked at Steve in his sunglasses across the room, "who are still assholes. And we've got probably four or five billion zombies beyond the walls, out in the world. So, utopia? No."

"Yeah, but it's so much better than being out on the road."

"I haven't been outside for awhile. Hey, want to get some fresh air?"

"Yeah."

"Let's grab a couple more beers. Take them with us."

"I'm one of your doctors," Singh told Gwen, "and in my professional opinion, one beer won't harm you, even with the pain killers for your arm."

She smiled and held the can out. Singh hooked the pull ring and popped it for her.

"*Gracias,*" she said.

"*De nada.*"

They were standing next to Steve, his roommates and a few other people and could hear their conversation.

"She's pretty hot for a pregnant woman," Steve said. "I'd do her."

"You keep talkin' shit somebody's going to shut you up one of these days," Biden observed.

"I love it when you talk dirty to me, Biden, I really do. Hey Mother, want another?"

"Are you an asshole?" Gwen broke away from Singh, confronting Steve.

He looked at her with her arm in its sling.

"Depends on who's asking." He winked.

"Doesn't depend on who's asking," Brent said. "He *is* an asshole. I live with him. I know."

"Don't mind Steve," Singh said. "He's just…he's just Steve."

"I didn't know they made those t-shirts in that size," Gwen said. Steve was sporting his *what-happens-at-Grandma's-stays-at-Grandma's* t-shirt.

"Yeah, for the developmentally disabled," Brent said.

"That's me. Gifted and talented."

"That what they're calling it these days?" Hayden said.

"That isn't what they meant when they told you you were *special* Steve," Brent said.

"What was Singh talking about when he mentioned 'job complexes' this morning?" Bear asked Sonny.

"What we're establishing here in Clavius is a participatory economy. Have you ever heard that term?"

Gwen, Julie and Bear all shook their heads.

"I hadn't either. The way things were done in this country, and most of the world before all this, right? We called that capitalism, right?"

"Right," Gwen said.

"This stuff bores me." Danny faked a yawn and his sister shot him a dirty look.

Panas inserted himself into the conversation, "We called our political system a democracy. But what did that mean? That you got to go out and vote once every couple of years? Meanwhile, things continued the way they always were."

"The golden rule, Arnold called it," Danny said.

"The golden rule?" Julie asked.

"He who has the gold, *rules*."

"Now, you can feel free to *disagree* with me," Sonny continued, "but let me see if I can't make you *agree* with me that our democracy was extremely limited, if it was even a democracy. And I say that to you as a one hundred percent god-fearin' U.S. of A. good-old boy."

"Believe him," Danny said. "He's a superpatriot."

"We're listening," Bear said.

Panas looked at Sonny and when he gestured with his open hand Panas picked up the conversation. "Democracy is a way of life, not just a political system. You know who said that? John Dewey. Dewey also said that the democracy that limits itself to the political sphere is a democracy that denies itself."

"What does that mean?" asked Gwen.

"Well, consider your jobs before all this, okay?" Panas said. "Were your jobs democratic? Was the economy democratic?"

"I don't even know what that's supposed to mean," Bear said.

"Did you get to decide what was produced, or how it was produced, and how the profits were spent or re-invested? I doubt it. That's what we mean. Here in Clavius we're setting up our work places so that the workers have a great deal of autonomy and say in what goes on."

"In other words," Danny said, "there are no bosses."

"No bosses, yes," Sonny said, "but we organize councils around each work place."

"How does that work?" Julie asked.

"Let's say—Mickey, he's like Lauren. He likes movies, right? So he gets a job in the new TV station we're trying to get off the ground—"

"TV station," Bear said. "You're kidding me, right?"

"No, no joke. He gets a job with our 'entertainment industry', if you will. Well, everyone in his particular part of that industry will vote to send a representative to a larger council that meets weekly—"

"Or whenever needed," Panas said.

"—or whenever needed. At that council all the concerns of the particular workplaces are shared, progress is reported on—"

"This is some boring shit just to talk about it," Danny muttered.

"The kid's right," Sonny said. "It'll make a lot more sense when you can kind of see it in action. Otherwise it risks being very academic. Maybe tomorrow if you're all up to it we can have you visit some workplaces, see what we're talking about."

"How do you get to work in a certain industry?" Julie wanted to know.

"Well, if you've got an aptitude for something, we're not stopping you."

"Except me," Danny said. "All I want to do is kill zombies, and they won't let me."

"All in good time, kid," Sonny said. "And if you've got an interest in something you can receive training. But another important thing, and I'd be remiss if I didn't tell you about this, is that within a workplace it's not all the same people doing the same tasks."

"What he means is," Panas said, "if Mickey were working in the TV station, he might be writing scripts and directing them, yes, but he'd also spend his fair share of time cleaning the toilets and such."

"Why's that?" Julie was genuinely curious.

"Why should all the empowering work fall on one or two people or a select group?" Panas asked rhetorically. "What we strive for here are balanced job complexes, meaning you do a certain amount of empowering work and a certain amount of more humdrum, needs-to-get done stuff."

"One of the other beautiful things," Sonny said, "is he wouldn't have to work in the TV station all day. If he has another interest—"

Mickey with another interest outside of film? Gwen and Julie looked at one another.

"—it can be arranged for him to pursue it."

"It's like Marx wrote," Panas paraphrased from memory, "*...society regulates the general production and makes it possible for me to do one thing today and another thing tomorrow, to hunt in the morning, fish in the afternoon, rear cattle in the evening, criticize after dinner, without ever becoming hunter, fisherman, critic or shepherd.*"

"You've got that memorized, huh?" Julie was impressed.

"Pretty much. Not quite word for word."

"So zombies take over the earth and the remaining humans turn to communism?" Bear asked.

Panas shook his head. "Communism, socialism. Those words are tainted, my friend. Forget everything you knew about the Soviet Union, about Cuba and China and North Korea. What we're talking about here is decentralization and direct workplace democracy."

"It's not as bad as it sounds," Danny said. "It's actually pretty cool."

"What about you guys?" Bear asked. "You guys work?"

"Of course we work," Sonny said

"I'm off today," Danny said.

"We're part of the committee that welcomes new arrivals," Panas said. "Haven't had a lot of work lately, but the committee still exists. Usually we're doing something else when there's no one to show around."

"Uh-huh." Bear nodded. "What's your work week like around here?"

"When I first arrived in Clavius," Sonny said, "we were working fourteen hour days. Those were the initial days, when we were still spending a lot of time excavating the trenches. Then twelve hours, ten. Now eight. As more people—like yourselves—arrive and are trained, we're looking at a six hour day in the near future."

"Four hour work day isn't out of the question," Panas agreed. "And everybody gets a couple days off a week."

"What do you do with your free time?" Gwen asked.

"There's classes. People educate themselves, learn things," Sonny said. "Best part about it for me is I get to spend a lot of time with Torrie."

"What kind of classes?" Bear asked.

"Everything from martial arts to history to science," Panas said. "There's a lot of talent here in Clavius City and people want to share."

"Panas and a couple of others teach Greek," Danny said.

"Greek, huh?" Gwen asked. "Big turn out for that?"

"You'd be surprised."

"What about people who can't work?" Bear asked. "Or won't?"

"Well, not surprisingly, to me at least," Panas said. "We haven't had many slackers. Everyone seems to want to contribute. Those that don't? That hasn't been a problem, at least not yet. But I suspect if and when someone gets it in their head to slouch, it'll be tougher for them to do so when everyone around them is contributing and genuinely enjoying doing so."

"And those that can't, the infirm, the disabled," Sonny picked up. "They're provided for, taken care of. But we've had very few here that can't do anything at all. There's usually something someone can do, even if it's reading stories to the kids at daycare. And I'm not saying that task is any less worthy than the others."

"Which ones are yours?" Julie asked Sonya, sitting down next to her.

"Julie, right? The kid with the dark hair, you see him?"

There was a swarm of children running around and over Buddy, climbing over him where he sat cross legged on the floor. The big man had a goofy smile on his face.

"I see two boys with dark hair."

"Nelson's wearing a Disney t-shirt," Sonya said. "At least that's what Eva told me. She helped pick out his clothes. My daughter, Nicole, has the long hair."

"Wow, her hair is long. She looks like you."

"I've been told. The little one is mine too. Victor is almost three."

"Oh, I see him." The kid was playing with Sonny's daughter, Torrie, who was popping up and down behind Buddy, saying "peek-a-boo" to the toddler. "He's a cute one too, wow."

"Thanks. He's got a thing for stairs. Put him on a staircase and you'd think the kid was at Disneyworld. He loves walking up and down them."

"That's funny."

Hayden knelt down to play with Victor. "Want to play fish?" She bent her index finger and put it within an inch of the toddler's mouth. The kid immediately went for it. "You got the fish hook, you got the fish—*oww!*"

"Tris told us your friend is really good at killing zombies," Sonya said.

"Well, I guess everyone's good at something."

"Sonya." Eva came over and put her hand on her sister's shoulder. "Lore and I have to go. Tris will help you and the kids get home tonight, okay?"

"Okay. Thanks, Eva."

"Love you sis," Eva kissed her sister, nodded over to Julie.

"It'll be spring in a few days," Lauren said.

Outside the rec center it was cold and their breaths plumed. The moon was full. The rec center sat in the middle of a strand of trees. Occasionally a sentry walked by, armed with a rifle, making her rounds.

"Yeah," Mickey said. "I always liked spring. Fall too. Winter is *too* cold. And summer…"

"You don't like the heat?"

"I like the air conditioning."

"What do you miss the most about your old life?"

He didn't hesitate. "My boy."

"Oh. I'm sorry."

"No, it's okay. It's funny, you know? I couldn't talk about him for a long time. I mean, I *always* thought about him, but… Only recently could I talk about him. Maybe it has something to do with Julie and the baby."

"Yeah, that's a good thing, isn't it? And now that you're all here…"

"Can I tell you something, Lauren?"

"Sure, go ahead."

"Singh told me not too. He said—"

Lauren looked at the man standing with her. "Ohhhh, Mickey. No, you don't have to tell me it's—"

"I have the plague," he blurted it out, then looked to make sure no one else had been around to hear him. He couldn't look at her while he waited for her to say something, so he stared up to the white "cool roof" of the rec center, designed to reflect heat in the summer.

"Singh told you not to tell anyone?"

"Yeah." He looked into her green eyes.

"You need to *listen* to Singh. You can't tell anyone. You *shouldn't* have even told me." She looked away.

"I know, I just… I get this feeling, like I can talk to you. Not trying to weird you out or anything."

"No, you're not weirding me out." She sighed but then her spirits lifted. "Hey I know, let's play a game."

"A game?"

"Yeah, I'll name one thing I liked about things beforehand, and you name one thing you *didn't* like. And then we'll switch. Got it?"

"I think so."

"Okay, I go first. *Penne a la vodka.* I really liked *penne a la vodka.*"

"Oh man, me too."

"No, you're supposed to name something you—"

"Oh yeah, right, I got it. Fried bologna."

"Fried bologna?" Lauren scrunched up her nose. "Yuck."

"Yeah, *yuck.* When I was a little kid one of my grandmothers used to eat that crap. On toast. It was disgusting."

"What I'd give for some over-priced caffeinated beverage," she said.

"Yeah."

"No, you're supposed to—"

"Oh yeah, umm, you know what I don't miss? The way—like when you're chewing gum, okay?—the way a cold drink will make the gum harder in your mouth, but a hot drink, like coffee, will make it soft."

"Reality television shows. Man, do I miss those!"

"What do you miss about them?"

"They were so entertaining. I mean, there's something very compelling about watching a bunch of celebrity has-beens…"

"Yeah, hey, I don't have to name a TV show now, do I?"

"No, anything you want."

"Good. *Any* movie starring Nicolas Cage."

"Even *Face Off*?"

"*Any* movie starring Nick Cage," he repeated.

"Well, I don't know about that—"

"Yeah, well, you're a girl," he corrected himself, "*woman*."

"But I do think John Woo's Hong Kong stuff was way superior to anything the MPAA allowed him to get away with here."

He wanted to ask her if she'd marry him but figured that *would* weird her out, so he just said, "Agreed."

"You know what I liked?" She looked wistful. "The top down, the wind in my hair, Don Henley on the CD player…"

"Bicyclists," Mickey said.

"Bicyclists?"

"Yes. What is it with those guys? They take up a whole lane of traffic all to themselves like it's their god-given right. I mean, you ever drive behind one of those guys or a group of them? If you went that fast in a car, cop would pull you over and give you a ticket for violating the minimum speed limit. But those motherfu—excuse me—those *bastards* think they're entitled or something."

"Wow. I never met someone who hated bicyclists so much."

"Well, I mean, where do they think they are? Holland? Seattle? What about you—what's something you miss?"

"My deck. I had a really cool deck out back on my apartment. In the afternoon, I could lay out in my lawn chair, settle back and read a book, sip some iced tea."

Mickey got caught up in an image of Lauren in a bikini on the deck of her apartment.

"Your turn," she said.

"My turn."

"Sorry to break up this little party, Lore." Eva came outside. "We have work to do."

"Damn." She had forgotten.

"You gotta go?" The disappointment in his voice was obvious.

"Yeah." She felt the same way he did. "Hey, one last question before I go."

"What's that?"

"One thing you miss, about the world I mean."

"That's easy. All those things I said I *didn't* miss, things I couldn't stand?"

"Yeah?"

"*Those* are also all the things I do miss."

"Let's go, Lore." Eva looked impatient.

"Damn. Hold your horses. We'll continue this game some other time, okay?"

"You got it." He nodded.

Lauren waited until they were out of ear shot and then turned to Eva. "You have to be a bitch about it?"

"We've got work to do. It is what it is."

"You had to stand there and wait for me while...?"

"Look, let's do this then you can get back to your little boyfriend there, okay?"

"*Bitch*. You know who you are? You're the female Steve."

"I've been called worse. Not much, but worse."

"They're hitting on your friend, aren't they?" Sonya asked Julie. Julie laughed because for a blind woman Sonya didn't miss much.

"Yeah, I guess they are."

Gwen was talking to Isaak.

"How'd you know that?"

"I'm a woman. You're a woman. They're men. I may be blind, but the pheromones are overpowering in here. Let me guess which ones."

"Go ahead."

"Steve."

"Yep."

"Well, that was a given. Who's she talking to now?"

"One of the younger guys. I don't know his name. She's been talking to Singh a lot too."

"Hmmm." Sonya nodded. "Good for the doctor. And good for your friend, Gwen, right?"

"Yes, Gwen."

"Well, a few more weeks," Sonya gestured at Julie's belly, "they'll be hitting on you."

Time passed and the alcohol flowed. Several people bid their farewells and left, having to get up early for work. Someone had turned the stereo off.

A loose circle formed. Bear's frame swallowed a chair next to Julie. Chris, in his Ultimate Warrior garb, was on Bear's other side. Steve, with a couple of six packs in him, noticed Gwen was sitting next to Singh and considered this a challenge. Steve was sitting between Biden and Brent, and Tris was next to Sonya. Nicole slept on a chair aside her mother and had her head in Sonya's lap. Sonya stroked her daughter's hair. Hayden and Danny were part of the circle as well.

Victor was fast asleep on the other side of the room in his pack and play. Nelson had curled up on a bench and had his eyes closed. Torrie was knocked out on a couch, her little dress ridden up over her flowered purple bloomers. Panas remained standing, holding a fifth of vodka by the neck of the bottle. Isaak and Sonny stood on either side of him.

Remarkable, thought Mickey, seated next to Buddy, how children were able to sleep through so much noise. He figured it probably wasn't that noisy. He was just tired.

"I knew an old man, before this," Sonny was saying. "World War 2 veteran. Pacific theater."

"Pacific thee-a-ter." Danny was drunk and happy.

"Told me once he was in a foxhole with a few other guys. Grenade lands in the foxhole—"

"Hey, Danny," everyone ignored Steve, "How's your man hole?"

"—told me they'd trained them to grab the grenades and throw them out. But this one guy in the fox hole with him, he jumps on the grenade."

"Yikes," said someone.

"Yeah, but the grenade don't explode right away. It doesn't detonate for a few seconds. So this guy is hunkered down on it, waiting. He looks up, into the eyes of the old man I knew. And the old man told me, the look on the guy's face... He knew he should have thrown it. He knew he didn't have to die. Then it detonates. He's gone."

"That's a messed up story," Brent said.

"You know what I wish we had?" Isaak said. "Some marijuana."

"Hey, Bear," Panas asked. "You still carry bud?"

Bear reached into one of the pouches on his web belt and withdrew a small baggie with marijuana in it.

"Oh shit!" Isaak's face lit up.

"Bear." Panas laughed approvingly.

"I knew you was alright, big man," Chris said.

"That was a messed up story, Sonny," repeated Brent.

"You want to hear a messed up story?" Tris had a few too many in her. "That story ain't shit. I'll tell you a messed up story."

Mickey, Gwen and Julie looked intently at the woman.

"Tris—"

"No, Sonya, let me tell the new guys my story. I was stationed down in Bragg when all this started. My husband was at home, in Raleigh, with the kids. I jumped ship. I'm not ashamed to admit it. A.W.O.L. I wanted to get home to my babies."

Bear had rolled a fat joint and Mickey reached over to an unresponsive Buddy, pulled the Zippo lighter from Buddy's pocket, leaned forward, lit Bear's jay.

"Well, I got home. My kids, my husband, they'd all been bit. They were all lying around together in one room, waiting, dying. And there I was, come all those miles, unharmed."

Sonya had heard the story before and pulled her sleeping Nicole closer. As Tris talked, Sonny walked over and smoothed Torrie's dress down over her purple flowered panties. The joint made the rounds. Only Julie and the sleeping children did not partake.

"One by one, they turned," Tris spoke slowly and quietly. "And one by one, I did what needed to be done. I knew, from Bragg, from the road, from what we'd seen on the TV while the TV was still working... I knew what had to be done. And I did it."

Panas stared at the glowing tip of the joint.

"Anyway," Tris finished, "from what I hear, Bragg didn't last much longer."

Gwen got up to go get herself another drink.

"What about you, big man?" Chris said. "Where were you when it happened?"

"Yeah, big man, what's your story?" The way Tris said it came off as a challenge.

Bear thought for a moment then spoke.

"I was working in a nursing home."

Buddy mumbled something and Mickey leaned closer to him. "What's that Buddy?"

"A nursing home?" Chris asked.

"…C.H.U.D., Mickey…"

"Yeah, Buddy, C.H.U.D.." Mickey was drunk and high and happy, remembering an old conversation with Buddy.

"Let the man tell his story, Chris," Brent said.

"Yeah, I was working in a nursing home. I went home one afternoon and by the next morning…things had gone to hell. I'd watched the television, listened to the radio. I had a pretty good idea what was going on out there."

"…who was in that Mickey…"

"Well, John Goodman, before Roseanne, before he became famous…"

Chris looked at Bear, all expectant, waiting to hear some story about Bear battling scores of zombies.

"So, I got up and went to work the next day. I stuck to the side streets and when I saw groups of people that looked, looked like they might not be people any more, I stayed away from them. Anyway, there was this old couple I used to visit every day up on the third floor, Mr. and Mrs. Sullivan.

"The old man, he liked to read the *Post*. The woman liked the *Daily News*. I used to pick the papers up for them, in the morning. There was a newsstand across the street from the home. Well, that day I show up for work, the newsstand is shuttered. But the papers are lying outside, bundled up. So I grab a *Post* and a *News*, and I cross the street, and as I cross the street I see them, standing in the windows, all those old people…"

"Mickey," Buddy whispered.

"What's that?"

"Adlard. I saw him one night."

"Okay."

"At first, I think to myself they're zombies. They're bit and they've changed," Bear unfolded his tale. "But they're not. They were old people, and they were scared, and they were staring out the windows just to see what was going on. No one had evacuated them….

"So I cross the street, and I'm walking to the front door, and some of them must recognize me, because they're waving to me, and I think to myself, what am I going to do? That place must have had, I don't know, a hundred elderly? The whole city, the whole country, is falling apart around me. There was no one else on that street with me, no one living. Only one zombie, standing all alone, in front of the doors...like...like it was guarding the place. It looked up at me and screamed as I got closer.

"I'm crossing the street, and I'm thinking I could wait it out with them, in the facility. But, you know what I did?"

"What'd you do?" Chris asked.

Tris nailed Bear with her gaze.

"I turned and I walked away. I left that zombie standing there. I left those old folks in their home. That's what I did."

"Well, you didn't have no other choice," Chris tried to rationalize.

"*No*," Bear answered quickly. "I had a choice. And I made my decision. And those people died in there because of me."

"You don't know that—"

"I know it. When I was walking away, I refused to turn around and look at them in the windows. You know why? Because I was scared. Because I was ashamed."

"It's okay." Julie put a hand on her friend's arm.

"No, it's not okay. Those people are dead because of me. I live with that. I'll always live with that. That zombie... I'll never forget what that zombie looked like."

"Then live with it, big man," Tris said. "If that's what keeps you going, fucking run with it. The man I saw outside, yesterday, killing Zeds? I didn't know better I'd swear you were born to kill zombies. And I got news for the rest of you—" Tris addressed the circle.

"We're going back, aren't we?" Biden asked.

"Spread the word, ya'll. We're going back down to the city, back down to this place these people are from, place Biden and Panas told us about. We're going to find this Eden and if there's any people left there, we're going to bring them back here with us."

"Hell yeah!" Danny said.

"Let's go and kick some motherfucking zombie ass!" Chris pumped a fist in the air, the tassels on his arm flying.

"You're drunk, Tris," Singh said.

"You are," Sonya agreed.

"I'm drunk, yes. And I got my head up behind this weed, true, but I know what I'm saying and I mean what I say."

"I'm in, Tris," Biden said.

Isaak nodded. "Me too."

"And me," Brent added. He looked at Steve but Steve looked away.

"You guys are crazy," Julie said. "Listen to me. I'm *from* there. There's no way you're going to get—even if you make it to Queens—"

"She's right," Sonya said. "What about your jobs? You'll need council approval for this."

"The council can kiss my ass," Tris said.

"We are the council, Sonya," Isaak said.

"The council will approve this," Panas said. "We've got proof there are still people alive down there. They'll approve."

Gwen was sipping her last beer of the night by the cooler, listening to the conversation from across the room. Steve walked over to her and got himself a beer.

"They're going to do it, aren't they?" she asked him.

"Yup, back to Brooklyn." He guzzled the beer and let out a huge burp.

"You're disgusting. And it's Queens. You're bent, you know that?"

"No, I'm Steve. My roommate is Brent.

"So." Steve extended the index finger of the hand gripping his beer and touched Gwen's ring finger. "Is there a Mister Evers?"

"No…not any more."

"Oh, hey, I'm sorry."

"No, it's okay."

"No, really, listen. I'm not the big asshole you probably think I am. I'm not the big asshole these guys will tell you I am. Don't get me wrong. I am an asshole. I'm just not that big of one."

A smile crossed her face.

"Are you going down to the city," she asked, "with them?"

"Fuh-uck that."

"That's how I feel."

"You're not going, are you Daddy?" Torrie was awake and stood tugging on her father's hand. "You're going to stay here with me, right?"

"Nothing's going to hurt your daddy, baby." Sonny picked her up and held her in his arms, "You don't worry."

"But there's got to be, what, millions of zombies out there?" Mickey said.

"No." Panas shook his head. "Probably *billions*."

"We can't let that stop us," Danny said.

"Now that's what I'm talking about!" Chris agreed.

"Sometimes you sound so much like Tris it's scary," Hayden told her twin brother.

Singh opened his mouth and started to say something about "council" but Tris cut him off, "Council will approve this."

"Look," Julie said, "I know we're new around here, but how can you be sure about this?"

"In addition to the security teams stationed around Clavius City," Sonny said, "we send out search and rescue groups."

"Search and *rescue?*" Mickey asked.

"There's other people—survivors—out there," Sonny said. "In the towns and cities. We try and find them and bring them back if they want to come back. If they can come back."

"What does that mean, if they *can* come back?"

"I've been out there guys," Panas said. "It isn't pretty. We had it relatively good in Eden."

"We had it good in Eden, Panas?" Mickey said. "We were starving to death, man."

"At least we weren't eating each other."

"*Ohhhh.*" A look of disgust crossed Mickey's face.

"We find people out there..." Sonny gestured beyond the walls of the recreation center, beyond the sentries and trenches and security teams of Clavius City. "You'd barely recognize them as human."

"Doesn't take someone too long to go native again," Danny said.

Hayden looked at her twin. "How would you know?"

"Look at Steve."

"And they're not all friendly, either," Singh said, "like those people you met weren't."

"That's why Tris was so ready to throw down with you the other day," Sonya said. "Aside from her sweet and calm disposition I mean."

Tris mouthed *fuck you* to the blind woman.

"Listen to all of you," Bear said. "You sound like you're getting ready to go down to the city with an army. This is a rescue mission, am I right? Or is it a war?"

"We're going down there to see if there's anyone left in Eden," Tris said coolly. "We expect resistance."

"Yeah, but better to go in with a small team, make as little noise as possible, and get out fast."

Even though Tris was drunk she didn't look upset that Bear had challenged her because she knew he was correct.

"Okay, then here's how it's gonna go," she spoke up. "Here's how I'm gonna' *suggest* it go at council, and I hope you all agree with me. We go in—no more than seven of us. Any married men or women, anybody with children, you're out. Sonny, you're out—"

Sonny looked like he wanted to say something but looked at his daughter.

"Danny, you're out."

"No, Tris—"

"Danny!" Hayden grabbed his arm.

"No, Danny. There were millions of people living in Manhattan. We've gotta expect most of them are zombies now, and we have to expect casualties."

"I'm in," Biden said. "I lived there. I know the people and the place."

"Fuck that. I lived there too," Panas said. "I'm in."

"No, not both of you," Bear said. "I'm going so at least one of you is staying behind. Preferably both."

"Bullshit, Bear," Panas said. "Come on."

"Flip a coin," Singh said. As Biden and Panas were both drunk it sounded like a good way to solve their conundrum.

"Bear…" Julie tugged on the man's arm and looked in his eye. They had just got here and they were lucky to be alive. What the hell was he thinking?

"Call it, Panas."

"Heads."

"Tails, sucker. I'm in!"

When the three roommates walked back to their place that night, they were worn-out and in varying states of drunkenness.

"Hey, Steve-O," Chris said. "You ain't going with us, to the city?"

"No, I'm not going."

Brent didn't say anything.

"But you don't go you're like breaking up the fellowship. The three amigos, man."

"Look, you're going, Brent's going. Zeds gonna have his hands full. Plus think of this: you guys go, who's gonna clean the apartment?"

Chris considered it but thought it was a little strange, as Steve rarely lifted a finger to clean the apartment.

"Besides, I got a chance at number five hundred and forty-five." He stuck his tongue out and flicked it up and down.

"Oh, that Gwen-chick." Chris nodded. "She's real pretty."

"Yeah, she is, isn't she?"

Brent knew if the shoe were on the other foot, if he or Chris were staying behind, Steve would be the first to bitch about *bros before hoes* or some bullshit. But Brent also knew that this was about more than a woman with a broken arm. Brent would never call him on it, but he knew Steve. Steve was scared. He'd been scared since that day at the convoy when he'd been scampering around on his hands and one broken ankle like a retarded crab and Chris had saved his ass.

"Yeah, might be good you stay behind," Brent said. "You go away for a week Gwen might be moved in with Singh by the time you get back."

"Oh, hell no."

Brent didn't think badly of Steve for not wanting to leave the safety of their haven. He would miss his roommate on the road, but if Steve's heart wasn't in it, there was no need to drag him along.

"Mark my words. By the time you guys get back, I'm in like Flynn."

"Walk, Michael." Eva prodded the sick man forward, away from the Jeep, through the snow.

Michael cried openly. He was not ashamed.

Eva and Lauren had come to the hospital and woke him. They'd told him to get dressed quickly and come with them, assuring him his wife and child were okay. He had done what they had said and they had walked him right out of the hospital, past a security guard who had nodded at them, into the Jeep and through the gates, out of Clavius City. The crew manning the gates had waved to them and as it dawned on Michael what this was about he realized the two women were not alone in their sin.

"I'm not going to beg you, Eva," he stammered between his tears, plodding through the snow.

"Then don't."

"Think of Patty. Think of Max, for God's sake."

"I am. *Move.*"

He walked through the snow, his ankles cold and wet because he wore no socks and his pants rode up over his sneakers. Lauren had parked the Jeep such that the headlights illuminated their path through the woods. She walked slightly behind and next to him, loosely gripping that MP-40 of hers. Michael couldn't see Eva but knew she was behind him.

"Stop here," Eva said when they had gone a couple of hundred yards from the road.

He halted and breathed, the tears streaming down his cheeks. Above him the trunks of the trees reached to the moonlit sky.

"Eva—" started Lauren but the other woman cut her off with a look.

"Will you take care of Patty and Max?" He managed to ask as calmly as he could.

"Yes."

"They'll be fine," Lauren said.

"Good." He nodded and looked out into the dark. He thought about his wife and how they had met in high school. The day Max had been born, all pink and wrinkly and screaming and Michael had cried and—

Eva raised her M16/M26 to her shoulder and sighted down the barrels.

—when he had started pre-school when he was three. They had bought him a little lunch box with the *Teletubbies* on it and he had—

She fired the assault rifle once and the bullet punched through Michael, knocking him face down to the snowed over earth.

He made a noise and started praying, *Our father who art in heaven—*

"Shit."

He was down but not out. As she walked up to him he was crawling forward.

—*hallowed be they name, thy kingdom come thy will be done on—*

She leaned over and fired another 5.56 mm round point blank into the back of his head. She stood up and turned around. There was no remorse in her eyes that Lauren could see, no anything.

On the ride back to Clavius City, Lauren drove.

"That's it, Eva." She mustered up her courage to confront the other woman. "He was the last one."

"He was the last one for now," Eva said. "There's always some-one else."

"No, I mean, that was it. For me. Forever."

"Uh-huh." Eva dismissed her.

"You've heard Singh and Malden. The plague isn't always contagious. We're safe. Sonya and the kids—"

"Sonya and the kids are *my* concern. And that's why we do this. What, your conscience is bothering you all of a sudden?"

"It's been bothering me for a long time. People like you—"

"Well, you know what, Lore? Wake up in the morning and go to your little work council or whatever and do your job assignments and *people like me* will continue to do what has to be done to keep you and everyone else in Clavius safe so they can wake up in the morning and—"

"You are such a self-righteous, bitch. *God.*"

"It works for me," Eva said, staring out into the night.

That night, long after most everyone else had gone to sleep, Eva and Tris lay in bed in the house they shared with Sonya and her kids.

"You're really thinking of going," Eva asked, "back down into that city?"

"I'm not thinking about it, trick. I'm going."

"You have a death wish?"

"Girl, you know I ain't met no-one tough enough to take me out of this game yet."

"Yeah, what about me?"

"What are you getting at?"

"Stay here. With me."

"Eva, Eva, Eva." The moonlight coming in from the window reflected off the scar on Tris' face. "It's good, what we got between us. But you know what the difference is between us?"

"I'm a dyke and you're a diva?"

"No."

"Remind me then."

"Before you, I wasn't into women. At all. If my man was still in the picture…"

"Yeah, I know. If your husband was still alive we wouldn't be here together like this. But here we are, Tris, and what we got, come on—"

"What we got, it's good, I know, but…"

"No, Tris. No buts. You want to know the real difference between us?"

"Go ahead."

"I'll kill those things. I'll kill anything that threatens my sister and her kids. But you? You *live* to kill zombies."

Tris was quiet, then she said, "I hate those dead fucks."

"I know you do."

"And, yeah, if I could I'd kill each and every single one of them. That's what they'd do to us."

"Fuck them," Eva said. "This right here? This is about you and me. This isn't about them."

"Yes it is. Don't kid yourself, trick. From the first day this has been all about them, and until they're all gone, that's all it's ever gonna be about."

"God, I thought I was a thick-headed bitch."

"You are, trick. Let me ask you a question. If it was a choice between me and your sister and her kids, who'd it be?"

"That's not a fair—"

"There's no fair anything. Just be a woman and answer the question. If it was between your sister and her kids or me?"

"My sister and her kids," Eva's answer was subdued. "That's what it's about for me."

"And I *get* that. I'm cool with that. But you have to understand, baby, that for me, it's all about making Zed dead."

A few minutes went by and she thought Tris had fallen asleep until the other woman spoke.

"Eva."

"Hmmm?"

"You have anything to do with those people disappearing from the hospital?"

She feigned sleepy annoyance. "You're keeping me awake to ask me that? *No.*"

"Good." Tris pulled her closer in the crook of her arm. "That's not what this place is about, you know?"

"Mmmmm…"

She lay there until she was sure Tris had fallen asleep, and then she lay there for some time afterwards, thinking about Lauren's bullshit speech in the Jeep tonight, about Sonya and Victor and Nicole and Nelson with the peach fuzz on his upper lip, and though she tried she was too jacked up to sleep for a long while.

"We're very lucky to be here," Gwen said. "To have found this place."

The next evening, following a day taken up with a long council session, a group of men and women sat together in the dorm four of them temporarily shared. They had their friendship and the months they had shared together behind Eden's walls in common.

Panas brought over a bottle of Baileys and they all partook in a nightcap with the exception of Julie and Buddy.

"Buddy knew what he was talking about," Bear said.

"He did," Gwen said. "I'm so glad we're here. For you, Julie, and the baby, especially."

"And I'm happy for you," Julie said. "That doctor, Singh? He seems like a nice guy."

Gwen blushed. "What are you getting at?"

"Nothing."

"The good doctor putting the moves on our Gwen, is he?" Mickey asked. "I think Steve might have something to say about that."

"God," Julie said. "Is that guy Steve as obnoxious as everyone told me or what?"

"Oh, I don't know," Gwen said. "He's kind of cute."

"Gwen!"

"He's got a certain kind of charm. But enough about me. What's going on with Lauren, Mickey?"

"What's going on? Nothing. She's a nice girl."

"Nothing? Bull. That girl's all you."

"She does know about Ty Cobb," Julie said.

"Tex Cobb," Mickey corrected, smiling like a cat with the bird.

The council session began with various people presenting, talking about Eden and New York City and what they knew of the world that could impact any mission sent there. Biden stood and laid out the location and layout of Eden. He spoke of the refuge known as Jericho and what had transpired there.

"Awful quiet again tonight, aren't you Bear?" Gwen said.

"Bear," Julie confronted him. "You can't go."

"I have to."

"Don't go."

"Yeah, don't go" Mickey said. "Panas *and* Biden could go." *He should go. He had the plague. Zombies would avoid him. If he were with whoever went, they stood a better chance. But he was scared. He had no intention of leaving this place.* "They could show them…"

"Those guys came through the sewers with Buddy," Bear said. "There's no way they're getting back in that way."

At council, Panas had talked about the sewer and subway systems they'd traversed when he'd left Eden with Buddy and Biden and the others months ago. After brief discussion it was agreed that the sewers would be impassable, and that even if they weren't, it was better to operate on the assumption that they were.

"There's no way you should go," Julie said.

"Bear," Gwen said, "I get it. If I could go," she shifted her arm in its cast, "I'd go."

"You're crazy." Mickey looked at her. "You'd give this up? You'd leave here?"

"Think of the people we left behind. Fred, Keara—"

"Hey, I'm sorry for them. But this isn't about them—"

"Sure it is."

"Bear." Julie reached out and put her hand over one of his. "Please don't go. The baby."

"I've got to go. And I will be back."

"Yeah, like Arnie in *Terminator 2*," Mickey said, "and you know what happened to him at the end of that movie, right?"

Julie looked into the giant's one eye. What she saw there convinced her that continuing was futile.

"I'll be back before the baby is born," Bear promised. "Gwen and Mickey and everyone else here will take good care of you."

Different people had spoken at the council. One of the technicians Bear and Mickey had met briefly on their first full day down in the lab, Stephanie, described the effects of nuclear weapons detonations. Before worldwide communications media had failed, it had been established that thirty nuclear weapons had been detonated around the world, six of them in the continental United States. Most of the nukes had been deployed by countries against their own domestic targets. It looked like only India and Pakistan had traded missiles. Israel had wiped itself out less its neighbor's compromised its territorial integrity.

Manhattan, which many felt would have been a likely target for a nuclear strike, was spared because the United States Government had used nerve agents on the city early on. This had effectively annihilated the civilian population but had done nothing to the undead.

Stephanie spoke about the short-term and long-term effects of nuclear explosions, about first and second degree burns in people six or seven miles from the blast site, about the travel distances of thermal radiation and the expected future spikes in fatal cancers among human survivors. She explained that fallout in the form of a thin layer of dust was the greatest threat, how electromagnetic waves were caused when nuclear radiation was absorbed in the air or ground, and how these EMPs had effectively killed any vehicles and electronic equipment for miles around each blast.

"I'm going to miss you," Gwen said. "You too, Biden, but I mean..."

"Don't worry. I understand."

Bear looked touched.

"Thanks," he said. "I'm going to miss all of you guys too."

"Bear," Panas said, "keep yourself safe and get your big hairy ass back to us as soon as you can."

"That's the plan," acknowledged the big man.

"How you feeling?" Biden looked to Buddy. Buddy's face was impassive at first but then something like a lopsided smile appeared.

"Bear," Julie said, "I gave Mr. Vittles to Fred..."

"I'll get the cat," he reassured.

"Here, you should have this." Julie broke the cylinder on the Colt Python, emptied the six shells into the palm of her hand, and passed the .357 over to him butt first.

"But that's Harris'. It's yours—"

"It's too big for me." She smiled. "It fits you better. And Harris would be happy about you having it." She pressed the bullets into his free hand.

"A toast?" Biden stood with his glass.

"Toast!" Mickey and Gwen said in unison.

Everyone raised a glass in their hand except Buddy. Julie was drinking water.

"To old friends, reunited," Biden said.

"To old friends," Julie said and everyone sipped.

Mickey couldn't hold his liquor like everyone else could and when he stood he was a bit wobbly.

"Forever and forever farewell, Brutus," he recited. "If we do meet again, we'll smile again. If not, it's true this parting was well made."

"*Hamlet?*" Panas asked.

"No," Mickey said. "Hackman doing Hamlet. *Uncommon Valor.*"

Gwen and Julie looked at one another and laughed.

That night when Bear lay down he was plagued by nightmares. The zombies were on him, their teeth were ripping into his arms and shoulders and thighs. He was screaming at them, his voice shrill and terrified, unable to fight. They were pulling on his limbs, which loosened in the sockets and—

He sat up in his bed panting.

He hadn't dreamed in a long time. Correction, he thought. He hadn't been able to recall a dream in some time.

He got out of bed and padded across the room in the dormitory he shared with Gwen, Julie and Mickey. There was a faint hum somewhere in the building as something electric did its work.

In a few hours he'd be waking and embarking for Eden. It felt like they'd just left there…Julie and the baby… He walked down the hall and looked in on the woman. She slept on her side, looking so peaceful. He vowed to himself in her doorway that he'd be back for her and the child.

THE WAY OF ALL FLESH

At almost 23 tons, not counting the seven men and women riding inside and atop her, the AAVP-7A1 armored personnel carrier knocked most of the cars and trucks on the roads it ran across out of its way. It was cold and grey out but most of those aboard had opted to sit atop the amphibious assault vehicle or in one of its hatches.

Tris sat behind the M2HB .50 caliber heavy machine gun in the gunner's hatch of the turret, scanning the road on both sides for any signs of survivors. Isaak's head poked out of the driver's hatch. Bear sat on the AAVP-7A1 with Chris and Brent. Biden and the seventh member of their party, a woman named Carrie, slept inside the AAV.

The AAVP-7A1 was capable of carrying 25 fully equipped combat troops in addition to three crew members. On the open road it could exceed 40 miles per hour, but Isaak kept it to nearly half this speed for most of the first day they were on the road. The roads would stretch for miles with nary a car or zombie in sight, and then they'd round a bend or crest a rise and there would be abandoned vehicles and dozens of the undead. The zombies got excited and made for the personnel carrier when they saw it.

Tris told Chris to save ammunition and not fire on the undead, as who knew what awaited them down in the city. The temptation to unload on them was great, but Chris didn't want to piss Tris off. The zombies unlucky enough to get in the way were mowed down under the treads. He looked with some satisfaction on their crushed, still writhing forms in the wake of the AAV.

Bear noted that Tris' crew was well disciplined. When she told Chris not to shoot, he didn't. The AAV, camouflaged for the desert, stood out against the wintry landscape. They had foregone white fatigues in favor of cargo pants and jackets that would keep them warm but not impede movement. Tris had pointed out that once they were down in the city, it wouldn't be white on white, so the snow camos were unnecessary.

They carried an assortment of personnel weapons—Mickey had given Bear his USAS-12 gauge and the last two drum magazines he had for it—but each was armed with an identical M16-A2 assault rifle. Thirty-round magazines were taped together or joined with dual magazine connectors. Bandoliers of magazines hung from their persons and a couple cases of ammunition and pre-loaded magazines were housed inside the AAV. Some had underslung M-203 single shot grenade launchers attached to their M-16s, others had flashlights and laser mounts affixed to the carry handles.

The AAV was capable of travel in water and they had considered the Hudson River. In the end the seven of them had decided they'd stick to the open road south for as long as feasible. The AAV was fully fueled when they'd left and they had extra fuel stored inside the transport.

"I hope you don't think I'm queer on you or nothin'." Chris pulled one of his iPod earbuds out of his head and said to Bear. "It's just, you really do look like one of them wrestling fellas to me."

Bear laughed. "No, I don't take it the wrong way. You're really into wrestling, huh?"

"Hell yeah. Me and Daddy would sit and watch the Pay-Per-View specials, Wrestlemania, Summer Slam, Survivor Series, you name it."

"I was into it in the mid-80s," he said. "The Road Warriors, British Bulldogs, Hercules Hernandez, Bobby the Brain, those were my guys. People used to say I looked like Bam Bam Bigelow."

"Nah man, he was kind of fat, man," Chris said. "You ain't heavy like that."

You should have seen me a few months ago, he thought. He wondered if Chris knew that wrestling was "fake." That it was sports entertainment.

"What are you listening to?" Bear asked.

"Oh, I got me some Dokken, some Sabbath, Maiden—"

Bear was impressed. "Maiden? You got *Flight of Icarus* on there?"

"And *Run to the Hills*."

"I haven't listened to Maiden in," Bear thought about it, "in a long time."

"Yeah, well, later on you want to listen you can borrow this," offered Chris. "Got some Ratt, Judas Priest, Europe—"

"*Europe?*"

"Europe," he said. "*Final Countdown.*"

"Well, with the exception maybe of that last one," Bear smiled, "you got yourself some righteous music there brother."

Brent said, "Chris is a big 80s-hair guy if you ever—"

A rock bounced off the side of the AAV and Chris immediately raised his M-16 to fire.

"No," Bear grabbed the barrel and jerked it upwards, "Look!"

"Isaak, stop this tank!" Brent yelled.

A little boy, no more than eight or nine, caked in dirt and in a patchwork of clothes sloppily stitched together, was staring at them from the trees. The kid held a sling shot. The band was drawn back with a stone in place.

The AAV ground to a halt.

Chris and Brent jumped off the AAV and Bear climbed down.

"Hey, little fella," Chris called out to the kid.

"Look out, Chris. He's gonna—"

The kid fired a second stone, turned and ran. The rock thunked on the hull of the AAV, no threat to its 45 mm armor.

"What the fuck was that?" Tris asked from atop the personnel carrier.

"Wild child," Brent said.

Bear stared into the trees and snow but the kid was gone.

"We gonna stop and look for him?" Chris asked.

"And do what?" Tris asked. "Make him our pet? Get back up here and let's go."

"Little fucker could have taken my eye out." Chris took a few steps towards the tree line, the barrel of his M16 lowered. "Hey, little fella. Hey! Little boy!"

"Let's go," Brent said.

"Kind of feel weird leaving him out here all by himself."

"Something tells me that kid's okay." Brent looked suspiciously from tree to tree. "He's survived this long…"

"Come on," Bear said.

Chris looked one last time into the trees, held his assault rifle aloft and screamed "Wolverines!" at the top of his lungs.

"Fucking zombies," Tris muttered, "fucking plague, fucking wolf children. How good does this shit get?"

A decision was made to ford the river. Isaak drove the AAV into the ice and water, the cold wash flowing over the sides of the amphibious assault vehicle.

Brent and Tris went below and traded places with Biden and Carrie. Bear sat cross legged on the hull of the AAV, watching the miles of dead trees and bleak wintry landscape pass them by at roughly eight miles per hour.

"Spring will be here in the next week or so," Carrie said.

"About goddamn time," Chris said. "I hate the winter."

"Look at that." Carrie pointed.

A cherry picker was stranded alongside the river, the bucket fully extended. In the bucket a zombie rasped down at them.

"Fuckers too stupid to figure out how to get down."

"Wonder how he got up there in the first place?" Carrie said.

Bear sat with his legs drawn up, his back to the hull of the AAV, the automatic shotgun across his thighs.

"Tris, look at this," Carrie called down into the hatch sometime later and Tris poked her afroed-head out.

Carrie pointed up to the grey sky where a balloon floated past in the distance.

"A fucking balloon," Chris said. "What do you think is up there in it, Tris?"

"I don't know," she answered. "It's going the other way. Maybe they haven't seen us."

"Maybe they're dead," Carrie said.

"Yeah, maybe."

"Hey, big man," Tris called to Bear. "Your name really Jimmy?" He wondered where she had heard that. "Yeah."

"You don't look like a Jimmy to me."

"What about you? *Tris* your real name?"

"Tristan," said the woman with the scar on her face. "Tristan Nicole Lee. My father had a thing for the Knights of the Round Table, even if it was a boy's name."

"Hey Tris," Chris asked. "Why your daddy give you three names?"

"Because I'm so much goddamn woman I need three names."

Sometime later Isaak yelled from the driver's hatch, where his head was visible, "Heads up back there."

"Shit," Chris muttered.

There were thousands of zombies standing on the shore nearest them as the AAV churned its way down the river. A collective moan and excited screams went up as the AAV drew close and started to pass the first of the undead.

"Fucking look at them," Chris said.

"Good thing for us they can't swim," Carrie said.

"Damn, I wish we could light them up." Chris gestured to the .50 cal.

"Keep it cool," Tris said

"Yeah," Bear said, looking out upon the ranks of the undead. "We're gonna need it in the city."

"It's gonna be bad down in the city, ain't it?"

"Yeah. It's gonna be real bad."

"Gonna kick us some zombie ass." Chris was all excited.

The throng of zombies, in some places packed six or seven deep, stretched for a good three quarters of a mile then just ended. There was a bend in the river. When the AAV turned it the zombies were gone from view.

The afternoon was ending when the AAV went back up on shore and pulled to a stop near a small brick municipal building. A gigantic Komatsu excavator was besides the building, its articulated arm drawn up. The AAV's ramp opened and the men and women inside climbed down, stretching cramped limbs.

"What are you listening to now?" Bear asked Chris, eyeing the terrain warily.

"Dio."

"Righteous."

"I gotta take a shit," Chris said, heading off to the building with a roll of toilet paper and his assault rifle.

"Keep an eye open," Tris said.

"Gonna crack my brown eye open." He laughed.

"Your roommates spending way too much time with Steve," Carrie said to Brent.

"Did you see the little boy they're talking about, Bear?" Biden asked.

"Yeah."

"How'd he look?"

"He looked…rough."

"Poor kid. I guess it's good to know there's other people still alive though. Right?"

Bear was going to answer but there was a loud curse and several three-round bursts from an M-16. Chris came stumbling out of the brick building—"Mother fuckers! Mother fuckers bit me"—bleeding profusely from the shoulder and arm. He stopped and turned, firing out his M-16 in short bursts into the doorway he'd just exited. He stumbled backwards a few steps, fumbling with the magazine and fell down on his back in the snow.

"Chris!" Brent ran to the man and Bear followed, bringing the stock of Mickey's USAS-12 to his shoulder. Tris reached Chris first.

A zombie shrieked at them, standing there gripping either side of the doorway. It had no nose. In the center of its face was a small hole surrounded by pieces of cartilage. Tris straight armed her 9mm and fired it-*pop-pop-pop-pop-pop-pop*-until the thing collapsed.

Three more of the undead rushed from the building and Tris fired out her pistol, dropping two of them. She reached behind her and unsheathed the two hand held sickles she wore, bringing one up behind her head, the second in front of her face.

The third zombie of the trio stopped a couple of feet from her. Chris was between Tris and the undead thing. It looked at the wounded man still trying to reload his assault rifle and the black woman with the enormous hairdo. The zombie raised its hand, pointed a finger at Tris and shrieked.

"Your mother—" She brought the sickle above her head down. The pointing finger and the hand it was attached to dropped to the snow. The zombie raised its stump to its face and looked at it.

Tris swung the second sickle and caught the beast through the neck, yanking it forward, towards her—

"Come 'ere motherfucker!"

—bringing the first sickle up and back down—*thunk*—right through the top of the thing's head. She yanked her sickles out of the monster as it fell.

"Fuck!" Chris cursed on his back. "Goddamn it!"

The empty windows of the building filled with the straining arms and leering faces of the undead as they sensed prey.

Bear stopped and fired the automatic shotgun. Some of the arms disappeared backwards into the building. He emptied one drum magazine while Tris and Brent dragged Chris back towards the AAV.

A lone zombie bumbled into view from behind the Komatsu digger. Topless, it wore cowboy boots and was missing its nipples.

"Gat that fool!" Tris yelled. Bear turned at the hip and fired three rounds, tearing whole chunks out of the zombie, knocking it backwards and down.

Carrie was in the gun turret and let rip with the .50, a stream of lead zipping into the building, pulverizing brick and mortar and the zombie flesh behind it. Brick dust and a bloody mist hazed the air. Carrie raked the entire lower level then did it again.

"Motherfucker," Chris said. "Man can't even take a shit with-out—"

"*Christ*," Brent, said holding a hand up to his forehead.

"Get him in the back of the AAV," Bear said. "Let's get out of here and patch him up."

Tris looked at him.

"No," he said. "We're taking him with us."

"But you know—"

He felt his anger rising. "It's not your call."

"And what makes it yours?"

Carrie sent another devastating hail of lead into the structure.

"It's Chris' call," Brent said. "It's none of ours. Chris, what you want to—"

"Like the big man said." Chris grimaced through the pain. "Let's get the fuck out of here."

She gave Bear a look and the look wasn't friendly. He ignored her and helped Brent carry Chris into the AAV.

They stopped several miles down the road for the night. Bear had staunched the bleeding and bandaged Chris' wounds.

"You get some rest, brother," he told him.

"Thanks man, I knew you were alright the first moment I saw you," Chris spoke slowly. "Hey man, do me a favor, hold onto this for me." He pressed one of his hands into Bear's and he took it with both of his. Chris opened his fist and passed something into his palms.

He looked in his hand. It was Chris' iPod, the cord for the ear buds wound around the device itself.

Bear didn't know what to say and he didn't know if he could say it without breaking down. Somehow he managed a "Thanks brother."

Brent sat next to Chris and talked to the doomed man quietly, keeping him company. Biden sat across from them on another bench, looking distressed. Tris had gone topside. Isaak snored in the driver's seat. Bear thought he would have a difficult time sleeping but he was out like a light within moments of stretching himself out on the floor of the AAV.

His sleep was plagued by another nightmare, the worst. It was daytime and Buddy sat in a clearing in a forest. His hands and arms were soaked with blood and he was talking into his hands, crying. Several yards from the man lay a baby wrapped in a blanket, the blanket resting on Buddy's saddle bags.

He whimpered in his sleep. A mask of pure rage crossed Buddy's face and he stood, cursing his hand, gibberish. He crossed to the child and looked down upon it and it didn't look like Julie or Harris, it looked like…like Markowski. He picked the child up by its feet and he walked up to the nearest tree.

Buddy.

He drew back his arms and Bear whimpered again as he bashed the little bundle against the tree. A red wet spot appeared on the bark. He drew the limp blanket back once more, swung it. There was a crack as it connected—

A single gunshot startled him awake.

"Who-who?" He squinted his good eye.

"It was time," Brent said. He sat on the bench next to his friend Chris, a 9mm in his right hand. The only light came from the glow of the instrument panels.

"Did he come back?" Biden asked from somewhere in the dark.

"I didn't wait. He died."

Bear fought to banish the images from his head: Buddy, Chris, the baby, Julie.

"You know what he said to me?" Brent asked Bear. "He said if he was going to die and come back… He said he didn't want you to see him that way."

Brent lowered his head and his shoulders shook as he sobbed in the dark.

Julie.

"Are you alright?" Biden asked.

He had made up his mind.

"Biden, if you can, get Harris' cat. Fred Turner's got it. How do I open this thing? Let me out of here."

As he walked down the ramp, his gear slung over his shoulders, Tris hailed him from atop the AAV. "Where the fuck do you think you're going?"

"Back to Clavius," he said. "Biden can take you to Eden."

"What?" Tris said. "You're just going to leave here? You're kidding me, right?"

He stopped.

"I *need* to go back."

He started walking off into the night.

"Big man."

He turned.

"Here."

Tris removed the grenade she wore around her neck and tossed it to him. He caught it and considered it.

"Big man. You and me, when we get back, we gonna have a little talk."

Bear ignored her, turned, and continued walking.

Tris watched as the night swallowed the giant.

"Mickey, wake up. Wake up!"

Someone was shaking his shoulder violently. He opened his eyes.

"What-Wh-Sonny? What the—"

"Where is he? Where the fuck is he?" Sonny's voice was desperate and shrill.

"Who? Who are you—" Mickey squinted against the glare of the fluorescents.

"Sonny!"

The other man was fully dressed and wore his assault rifle on his back and his .45 on his chest. "Sonny, come in man!" The voice was coming from his radio.

"I'm here, Danny. Come in. What's up?"

"I got him. He's here! Over."

"Where are you?"

"The commons."

"Is Torrie with him?"

"No, she's not—"

"I'm on my way," ignoring Mickey, he walked out of the room, leaving the light on. "Don't approach him," Mickey heard him say. "Do you hear me? Do not go near this guy." Then the door to the dorm slammed shut.

What the fuck?

"Mickey!"

Now Julie burst into his room. What time was it and what the hell was—

"It's Buddy."

He sprang out of bed and started pulling on his pants.

"What happened?"

"Sonny's daughter is missing." Julie had her winter jacket on over her jeans and a maternity sweater. "Buddy isn't at the hospital—"

"Where is he?"

"One of the guards at the hospital is dead." Singh popped his head into the room. "Come with me. I think I know where they are."

Mickey started to ask "What's going on, doc?" but had to hustle and lace up his boots as Singh and Julie were out of his room and down the hall. His eyes were still half closed as he fumbled with the holster of his 9mm. "Screw it." He pulled the pistol from its leather, leaving the rig in his room.

He hit the front door of the dormitory. The doctor and Julie walked off in the distance under the stars.

"Wa—" he almost yelled *wait* but it had to be three or four o'clock in the morning and he did not want to wake anyone up. So he hustled as fast as he could to catch up with them.

Holding back his tears and fury, Sonny ran across the commons, towards the two figures that stood out in the moonlight. One figure was down, on its back, the other sat slumped a few feet from it.

When he got close enough to see who was who he came up short, huffing and puffing. Slow steps completed the distance between himself and the two men in the snow.

Buddy was half leaning over his saddle bags, his gaze darting around. He looked out of it, but was fully dressed and in his leather jacket.

Danny was on his back, dead. A bayonet had been driven up under his chin and through his head to the hilt. The snow was swept clear in the area around him like he had been struggling.

"Where's Torrie?" Sonny screamed as he approached. "Where's my daughter?"

Buddy sat still as if he didn't hear him.

"You motherfucker." He drew the .45 from his chest rig. He shrugged out of his M16A2 and tossed it to the side. "Where's Torrie goddamn you?"

"Sonny!" Singh yelled."

"*Torrie*, Kip!" Sonny was in tears. "He did something to her."

"What are you talking about? How do you—"

"I *know*, Kip, I fucking know." He walked around Buddy and stared down into the man's blank face. "Where's my daughter? Do you fucking hear me? Where is she?"

"Danny, oh god." Singh knelt beside the fallen young man, checking for a pulse, knowing he wouldn't find one.

"Buddy!" Gwen rushed up to them. "What the…" She saw Danny and stopped. "Oh no."

"Motherfucker," Sonny straight armed his .45 and aimed it at Buddy's head. "You better start talking to me you son of a bitch! Where the fuck is my—"

"Hey, don't aim that gun at—" Julie and Mickey reached them.

"He took my kid," Sonny shouted. "He took Torrie!"

"How do you know that?" Julie said. "How do you know it was him?"

"He killed Danny." Singh stood.

"Oh fuck" Mickey put a hand on his head.

"Fuck this." Sonny pulled back the slide on the .45. "You're going to talk to me motherfucker. You're out of it, is that it?" He was spitting and crying as he yelled. "I'll make you feel. You ready to feel motherfucker!"

Buddy had a puzzled look on his face.

"Last chance, fucker. *Talk*."

Bang.

The gunshot reverberated across the commons into the night.

"Motherfu—" Sonny dropped his .45 and reached for his thigh, grimacing in agony as his leg buckled under him. He collapsed on his side, his right arm going out to break his fall.

"I'm sorry," Julie said, lowering her .380. "I really am."

Sonny looked at her then squeezed his eyes shut. His head shook in frustration and pain.

Mickey stepped forward and kicked his pistol away. "Julie?"

"They're gonna kill Buddy. Look at him," she meant Sonny. "He was going to kill—"

"You should get your friends out of here," Singh said. "Out of Clavius…"

"Julie," Gwen said. "What the fuck are you thinking?"

"…for a few days, until this calms down. Otherwise they'll never be treated fairly." Sigh dropped down next to Sonny and started working on his thigh.

"You can't go, Julie, look at you—"

"I shot him. I shot Sonny. I have to."

"*Nooooo!*" Sonny bellowed in anguish.

"Come on," Mickey said. "Gwen, give me a hand with—"

"No."

"What?"

"I don't want any part of this." She shook her head. "You go and take him with you if that's what you want to do."

"You're serious?"

She didn't answer.

"Come on, Mickey." Julie tried to lift Buddy.

"My daughter, my little girl…" Sonny cried.

"Sonny, listen to me." Singh bound the man's wounded thigh. "If this man is responsible for Torrie's disappearance, killing him won't help you find her. You know that."

"Get out of the way, Julie." Mickey tucked the 9mm in his waistband and pulled one of Buddy's jacketed arms over his shoulders. "Get his bags."

"You're never going to get out of here," Sonny promised between gritted teeth.

"Wait," Singh said, standing and taking Buddy's other arm, "I know a way we can go. Mickey, help me get Buddy there and then you stay. You stay and you help find Torrie. You talk to everyone and make them understand!"

"Yeah, okay," Mickey sounded unsure.

"Kip!"

"Sonny, when calmer heads prevail—"

"Let's go," Julie said. There were voices and lights in the distance.

"Gwen." The two women looked at one another. "Goodbye."

Gwen didn't say anything. She watched them go. Mickey and the doctor supported Buddy. Julie followed a few steps behind.

"*Nooooo!* Not like this—no!" Sonny howled and punched the ground. "Everything we went through—no! All that—not like this! No-no-*nooooo!*"

Gwen sat down in the snow next to him. Danny's body laid a few feet away. She put her elbows on her knees, her chin in her hands, and waited for the first of the people to arrive.

Panas sat in the break room at work the next night, alone at his table with a cup of coffee. Kieran, Sasha, and Mei mostly ignored him, talking low amongst themselves at another table across the room. He had his back to them and the door, alternating between staring into his cup of coffee and the bulletin board on the wall. When Eva entered the room, Kieran looked up at her, nodded, motioned to the others, then they all got up and left the room.

She walked over to the coffee pot and poured herself a mug.

"Panas." She came over to his table and circled it.

"Eva."

She sat down in a chair across from him. Eva placed her coffee mug on the table and unslung the assault rifle, placing it on its butt on the floor, the barrels leaning against the table.

"You like the nightshift?"

"It gives me time to think," he said.

He knew why she was here.

"What do you miss most about that place *Eden*?"

Panas thought about it.

"We used to sit out in the evening, watch movies. Harmon—Mickey, that is—had a huge collection. Sometimes when we'd watch a film, I'd forget where I was. What was going on around me."

"Mickey and his movies. I thought Lauren was bad, but that guy," the door behind him opened and Panas noticed Eva didn't look up to see who it was, "he takes the cake. You know he has the plague?"

"Mickey?"

"Yeah, it's true. Sonny told me."

"Well." He noticed she did not drink her coffee. "Damn."

"Mmmm. Let me ask you a question, Panas. You got a first name?"

"Nick."

"Nick. Okay, Nick, let me ask you a question. You said you like the late work. Gives you time to think. When the doctor and the pregnant bitch carted that baby killer out of here, what were you thinking when you let them go?"

Panas picked up his coffee and sipped it.

"I thought someone would kill them. Kill Buddy. Sonny's daughter?"

"Torrie is still missing. But you and I know, we know, she's not going to turn up alive, is she?"

"I really hope she does."

"Sonny is...He's a broken man," she said. "This Buddy—he that important to you?"

"The Buddy I knew—" Panas said, "if he is responsible—the Buddy I knew *wasn't* a bad man. He came to Eden and he helped us all out. He—Graham, Markowski…" Panas knew she wasn't listening to him. He knew she had made up her mind, so he stopped.

"Your friend, Mickey? He should have run while he had the chance. Nick, let me tell you what I'm going to do when I'm done here talking to you. I'm going to go and wake Mickey up, take him for a ride. Out into the woods. We'll stop and we'll go for a walk. Not too far. And then I'm going to kill him. Do you want to know what I'm going to do after that?"

Panas picked up his coffee cup and sipped.

"I'm going to hit the woods and track down your friend Buddy and his little entourage. They couldn't have gotten too far. Not with your friend the way he is. Not with the pregnant bitch in the condition she's in."

"That's what you're here for now, isn't it?" Panas asked. "You're here to kill me too?"

"No." Eva leaned her chair back against the wall and clasped her hands behind her head. "I'm not going to kill you."

The garrote dropped around Panas' head from behind and Hayden pulled it tight. The wire buried itself in his neck. His hands shot up to grab at it but it was already digging into the soft flesh of his throat and had opened him up. Blood ran down his neck and chest, his hands and forearms.

Eva put her chair back on all four legs, leaned across the table, and grabbed his wrists. She wrestled them down to the table and held them there while Hayden pulled back on the garrote. His face turned crimson, his legs kicked the table, his torso torqued in the chair, and the coffee mugs toppled, spilling their contents across the table top. Eva's M16/M26 shifted and clattered on to the floor.

Hayden cursed between her clenched teeth. The veins in her forearms popped out.

Panas evacuated his bowels and died.

Hayden let him go and the corpse slumped across the table in a puddle of coffee.

"He stinks."

"He shit himself," Eva said. "Spilled my coffee too." She bent over and picked up her assault rifle.

"You need a hand with that other guy?"

"No. I got help waiting for me."

"Eva. *Thanks.*"

She looked at the younger woman.

"I know it doesn't bring Danny back. But, I don't know," Hayden looked at the garrote in her hands, "it makes me feel better."

"Mickey?"

It was the second time in as many nights that he was roused out of bed early, but this time he was pleasantly surprised.

"Lauren?"

"Yeah, it's me." She stood in the doorway of his room. She hadn't turned on the fluorescents, but he could see her clearly from the ambient light in the hall.

"Hey, what's up? What time is it?" He sat up in bed and pulled the sheet over his underwear.

"It's real late. Or early, depending on how you look at it. I'm sorry to—"

"No, it's cool."

"I'd like to show you something, something beautiful."

"Okay." Mickey was eager.

"Put on something warm. We won't be gone long. I'll wait for you out here."

"Okay."

He watched her go. He stood up and stretched, his excitement mounting. *How cool is this?* The chick he was into, a chick he knew was into him, showed up in his room at three or four o'clock in the morning or whatever time it was. She wanted to show him something beautiful. *Awesome.* For a few moments he was able to forget about Julie and Buddy and the missing girl.

He pulled his sweat pants up to his hips and considered. Was she here for sex? He pulled the elastic of his boxer shorts forward and looked down at himself. Maybe he should chub up? *Nah*, no time. And if she was taking him outside in the cold it would defeat the purpose. He pulled his sweat pants up the rest of the way and hastily laced his boots.

He found the 9mm but left the holster on the dresser, sticking the pistol instead in the back of his pants. He slept in a white t-shirt, so he pulled a light flannel shirt on over it.

When he stepped out into the hall it was empty. There was a low electrical hum from somewhere in the dormitory.

"Lauren?"

There was no reply.

Maybe she was waiting for him up ahead or outside in the night. With a smile spreading across his face, he strutted across the hallway like a rooster. The pockets of his sweat pants were inside-out, flopping at his hips like a dog's ears. He passed Gwen's closed door and stepped into the common area they all shared.

The blow to the back of his head knocked him down.

He managed to push himself up, getting most of his upper body off the carpet, his is head throbbing, not comprehending—

The second blow put him down.

When Mickey regained consciousness he was very cold and couldn't see anything. There was something pulled down across his eyes and nose. His mouth was bound with tape. He tried to talk but couldn't. Instead he mumbled futilely, moving his head side to side. They had a hood or something over his face.

He was in a vehicle of some sort. He could feel it moving beneath him. His hands were bound at the wrists. Try as he might he could not free them.

There were two voices talking in front of him but he couldn't make out what they were saying.

When the Jeep stopped, Eva put her hand on his neck and dragged him from the backseat. He tripped and fell from the vehicle, landing in the snow. He protested behind the tape and hood.

"Shut up," she said, pushing him forward with the barrels of her assault rifle.

Mickey staggered forward a few steps unseeing, tripping and falling again.

"Get up."

"He can't see, Eva," Lauren said.

"You want to see? You want to see where the fuck you are?" Eva ripped the hood from his head.

They were standing on the side of a road, trees stretching out on either side of it. Someone must have plowed in the last couple of weeks because there were mounds of snow packed on the sides. Mickey thought this was strange. The sky above and behind them was purple-black. The horizon in front of them lightened with the dawn.

The Jeep was parked in the road. Eva and Lauren stood looking at him. Eva had murder in her eyes and the assault rifle at her hip. Lauren looked bewildered and had the MP-40 at her side on its sling.

"Looking for this?" She held his 9mm in her hand. "Say bye-bye." She winged it off into the trees on the opposite side of the road.

Eva reached to his mouth and tore the tape off. It felt like his lips came off with it and he gasped.

"Scream if you want," Eva said. "No one is around to hear you. No one who can help you."

"What is this place?"

"*Miller's Crossing*," Lauren said before Eva told Mickey to shut up.

"Move."

Eva prodded him forward. This time he kept his footing. He climbed through the piles of snow, unable to use his hands, which were cold and taped in front of his body. His boots had come untied and the laces dragged through the snow. As they walked, he spotted birds in some of the trees.

"Keep walking."

Mickey was terrified. *Miller's Crossing*. He'd seen the movie, god knew how many times. Written by the Coen brothers, directed by Joel. There were three scenes in that movie set out in the woods. In the first Gabriel Byrne walked John Turturro out into the trees on an autumn day, then made him stop. Turturro's character, Bernie, turned and faced Byrne's Tommy Reagan. He fell on his knees.

Look in your heart, Tommy. I'm praying to you. I can't die. I can't die Tommy!

"Here," Eva said. "Stop."

Mickey halted and looked ahead into the new day. The birds were cawing.

"Get down. On your knees."

Slowly, he bent one leg and knelt, then followed suit with the other. He bent over crying. His tears were cold on his face. They dripped to the snow and dirt.

Before he'd followed Bernie into the woods, Tommy had received some advice from Al Mancini's vicious—if short—hit man, Tik-Tak. *You gotta remember to put one in his brain*, Tik-Tak had counseled. *Your first shot puts him down, then you put one in his brain. Then he's dead. Then we go home.*

Eva was behind him.

"Pl-please, please-please-please—"

"Shut up. Shut up! Have some dignity now at least!"

"I-I-I—"

"You helped that baby killer escape. That's what you did. And you should have escaped when you had the chance, stupid mother-fucker."

"No, I." Weeping as he was, he couldn't continue.

Caw caw.

The second scene in the woods brought Tommy's turn to be taken for a walk. Tik-Tak was there, his breath a plume in the autumn day. His sidekick, the much larger thug Frankie, sang in Italian, his voice echoing through the trees. The ferocious Eddie the Dane was with them. Tommy had known he was going to die. He had looked up at the trees and the sky. Then he had leaned against a tree and vomited, fell on his knees. The Dane had taken the hat from Tommy's head and tossed it aside...

Eva leaned over his shoulder and spoke to him.

"I'm going to kill you here, *now*. You should thank me. You ever see what happens to people with the plague? Your fingers, toes and *dick* will fall off. You selfish bastard, did you think you'd keep it secret?"

Mickey sucked in the snot threatening to drip down his face— an ugly, pathetic snort—and stared into the snow before him.

"When we're done here I'm going to go and see your friend, Gwen, and then—"

"No, she didn't know—"

"Fuck what she knew—"

"Gwen didn't like Buddy, she—"

"Then I'm heading back out here. I'm going to find that pregnant bitch and that baby killer, and that goddamn doctor too. It won't be as pretty for them as it will be for you."

Her voice receded. On some level Mickey knew she was stepping back from him, raising the M4/M26, aiming it at his back.

Caw caw.

The third and final scene in the woods occurred at the end of the film, when Gabriel Byrne meets his one-time friend and boss, the Irish gangster, Leo, at a graveside. Leo and Tommy had had a falling out, but Leo was looking to make things good by inviting his former confidant back into the fold. *Good bye, Leo*, Gabriel Byrne tells him. As Albert Finney's Leo walks off down the road in the woods, Byrne's Tommy leans against a tree and adjusts his hat.

"I'll do it," Lauren said behind him.

"Then do it," Eva said.

There were fresh buds on some of the trees. Spring was coming.

Behind him Lauren racked the slide on her MP-40, chambering the first round.

He raised himself up on his knees, straightening out his back, puffing out his chest. He lifted his head and looked towards the horizon, towards the day.

The submachine gun ripped. The birds in the trees took flight, squawking.

"You going to invite me in for a drink?" Steve asked Gwen.

"Not tonight. It's too late."

"Come on, invite me in. Like Billy Crystal says, we'll do things I'm going to tell my friends we did anyway."

She laughed. "I had a good time tonight. Thanks."

"I did too."

"What do you look like without those sunglasses?"

He shrugged.

"Take them off?"

He did so and she looked into his brown eyes.

"You've got nice eyes."

"Appreciate it. So, how's your sex life?"

"You're incorrigible." She laughed. "Get out of here."

"Okay. But if you need anything…"

"I know. I will."

She closed the front door to the dorm behind her. Standing in the common room, she was aware of something in the darkened building aside from herself and Mickey in his bedroom. A presence.

She left the light off and dug her pistol out of its holster. She flicked the safety off and waited, her broken arm pressed tight to her in its cast.

As her eyes adjusted to the dark she discerned a much larger, darker mass among the shadows in the area of the couch.

"Gwen."

"Bear." She sighed. Relieved, she lowered the pistol. She didn't bother to turn on the light. There was a chair near the door and she sat down in it.

"Where are Julie and Buddy and Mickey?"

"Oh God."

She told him about Sonny's daughter going missing. About Sonny heading first to the medical center, finding a dead guard, then finding Buddy and all his stuff gone. She told him of Sonny coming to the dorm and waking Mickey and herself, of the scene in the commons, of Julie shooting Sonny and absconding with Buddy, the doctor and Mickey in tow.

When he asked her how they escaped Clavius City, she told him about Panas being stationed on watch that night—how he let them walk out. She told him how Mickey had stayed behind to try and straighten things out with everyone in Clavius, to try and help to find Sonny's daughter, and how Singh had accompanied Julie and Buddy to care for them. She told Bear the direction they were headed and where they might be found.

She didn't tell him why she had stayed behind; how the thought of leaving had never crossed her mind; how she had no intention of leaving this place.

"Where's Mickey now?"

"What do you mean? He isn't in his room?"

He didn't answer. He must have stood and turned, because she saw the shadows shift, and heard the floor creak under his feet as he walked towards the back of the dorm.

"Bear." He did not respond but she knew he had stopped. She wanted to ask him why he was back—why he was back so soon—why he was alone. Instead she said, "Take care of yourself."

She sat there after he left, thinking and listening. After awhile she holstered the gun and turned the light on in the common room. She checked Mickey's room. Bear was right. He wasn't there. She turned on all the lights in the dorm and thought about going and getting Steve.

Eva was bent over Mickey, whispering in his ear.

Caw caw.

Lauren considered the MP-40 in her hands. Mickey had his back to her.

"And I'm going to find that pregnant bitch and that baby killer," Lauren heard every word Eva said, "and that goddamn doctor too. It won't be as pretty for them as it will be for you."

She stepped away from the man on his knees and raised her M4/M26, aiming it at his back, ready to blast him from behind.

Caw caw.

"I'll do it."

Eva turned and looked at her. Lauren motioned with the MP-40.

"Then do it."

Mickey straightened himself out where he knelt, lifted his chin and looked straight ahead.

Lauren shifted over a few steps behind him. Eva looked on approvingly. Lauren raised the MP-40 to her hip.

She couldn't see his face, but imagined he must look as much at peace with himself and the world as he was ever going to be.

She swiveled at the hip and triggered the MP-40.

Brrrrrrrrrrrrrpppppppppppppppppp

A stream of lead stitched Eva from crotch to clavicle, knocking her off her feet. Her assault rifle landed a yard away from her body.

The birds in the nearest trees took flight.

"Enough," Lauren said it like it was a curse. "Enough already."

Mickey kneeled there. He blinked. Was he dead?

Lauren walked up to him, lowering the MP-40.

"Get up you dumb son of a bitch," she said, tears in her eyes.

Mickey stood and turned. Eva lay there, one leg bent under her, the blood from the ragged holes in her draining into the snow and the earth underneath.

"Lauren, oh Jesus."

"God, you're a dumb fuck," Lauren said. "I tried to give you a fucking hint."

Miller's Crossing. Each time he'd gone out in the woods, Tommy Reagan had walked away.

Eva gurgled and gasped.

They stood and looked down on her.

Eva stared towards space then focused on Lauren's face.

"If you can hear me, Eva," she said. "I'll make sure Sonya and the kids are okay."

Eva convulsed and blood welled up out of her mouth and nose. Her eyes glazed over and she lay there with a blank stare, seeing nothing.

Mickey stooped to retrieve her assault rifle.

Back in the Jeep, Lauren turned the engine over and cranked the heat up as high as it would go.

"Are you okay?" she asked him, putting the vehicle in drive, executing a three-point turn.

"My head hurts."

They drove in silence for several minutes. Mickey watched the scenery pass—trees and the road, the sky lightening as dawn arrived. He thought of Julie in the woods somewhere with Buddy, of Bear atop an armored personnel carrier heading down into the city, of Fred Turner, Larry Chen, Keara and Phil back in Eden, of Gwen asleep in their dorm inside Clavius City, of Eva dead in the snow, crumpled and bloody.

"Stop the Jeep," he said.

Lauren slowed the vehicle to a halt in the middle of the road.

"What is it?"

"Give me a kiss."

She leaned over and kissed him on the mouth. He kissed her back, hard. When they pulled away, she wiped her mouth with the back of her hand.

"That was a smooth line. Hey, where…"

Mickey had opened the door and stepped outside the Jeep.

"This is it for me."

"What do you mean?"

"I mean, this is it. You head back to Clavius."

"But what about you?"

"I'll be fine. Who's going to mess with me? The undead?" He scoffed.

"No, we can go back together and—"

"You know we can't. Even if we could…" He thought of the plague infecting him, of how his end would be.

A lone zombie stumbled through the trees towards the road and their Jeep.

"But what will—what will you do?"

"Me? I'll be okay," he said. "Back in my room, in my bag, I have a collection of DVDs. I want you to have them, okay?"

"Mickey, I—"

"No, Lauren. I love you."

"Don't tell me that." She cried.

"Well, it's the truth. And I want you to know."

"No, that's not what—I love you too, Mickey."

He beamed.

"When you're lying in bed sometime, think about me. Think there's someone out here, in the world, and he's thinking fondly of you."

She couldn't answer through her tears.

"Go now, girl." He slapped a palm against the side of the Jeep.

She nodded and looked at him one last time. She eased her foot off the brake. As the Jeep pulled ahead she tilted the rearview mirror so she wouldn't have to see him standing there alone. Lauren wiped the back of her jacket across her eyes.

When the Jeep was gone, Mickey sighed.

He looked up at the zombie staggering his way. The thing was decked out in a black full length North Face winter jacket. As it broke from the trees and stepped towards him, he considered the M4/M26 in his hands, then heaved it off into the woods.

"Moment of truth, Mickey boy." He walked up to the zombie.

The thing stopped and looked at him, its eyes bloodshot and rheumy. He got up in front of it and stared right back.

A look of disinterest crossed its face and it made to turn away from him, but he grabbed it by the arm. "Wait a minute there, pal." He pulled first one sleeve of the jacket then the other off the zombie. The undead thing protested shrilly but made no move to bite him.

The jacket stunk and was stained with mud and dirt, but it fit well and *damn*, it *was* warm.

The zombie stood looking at him.

"Thanks then." He walked off the road into the trees, striking off towards the rising sun and the new day. The zombie watched him walk off.

It had taken Bear two days and nights of walking to return to Clavius City. When he left Gwen and slipped back outside the walls he raced through the night at a steady pace, shedding gear as he went, keeping only the essentials.

A full moon lit his path. When it departed the sun rose to take its place. He purposefully avoided the few zombies he encountered.

By early morning he stumbled across three sets of tracks in the snow and followed them. His pace quickened. His sense of urgency renewed.

As he drew closer to Julie, Buddy, and Singh he encountered more and more zombies. They staggered through the thick and densely furrowed chestnut trees, all in one direction, and he knew he was heading the right away.

When he broke through the trees into a clearing he saw the doctor swinging a tree branch, batting a zombie in the head. Julie was flat on her back next to a felled tree trunk, bundled up, clutching something. Buddy sat on a tree stump near her, out of it. A small fire burned.

Bear grabbed the zombie Singh battled by its hair and pulled its head back. He swung the flanged mace down and caved in its face.

"Bear!" Singh cried, relieved.

"Julie." He ignored the doctor and made for the woman.

"She's fine." Singh's voice trailed behind him.

"Bear." Julie smiled weakly up at him. A baby wrapped in blankets was pressed to her chest.

He sank down beside her and tears welled up, blurring the vision in his good eye.

"It's okay. I'm fine, the baby's fine—"

"She's okay?" Bear sobbed.

"*He's* okay. It's a boy."

As if on cue the baby started to scream and Julie cooed, "*Shhh, shhh, shhh.*" She looked at Bear. "Little Harris, meet your godfather."

He didn't think the neonate could see him, but damn he looked just like his father. He reached out to the newborn, touching its wrinkled cheek with the knuckles of his hand, and the baby gripped his index finger instinctually.

"Got a grip on him this kid." He was overwhelmed.

"Bear," Singh said. "We really shouldn't be moving Julie and the baby right now, but…" He gripped the tree branch and gestured to the woods at the zombies they could see and the ones they could hear. The doctor had a revolver holstered on his waist.

"I have to feed Harris now."

"Of course."

He strode over to Buddy and opened the man's saddle bags. He rummaged through them quickly, his mind set on one thing. When his hand closed on the butt of the pistol he pulled the silenced nine, then checked the chamber and magazine.

Bear went and stood next to Singh, handing him the 9mm. "Use this if you have to."

He looked one last time at Julie lying peacefully with the baby attached to her chest. She smiled up at him. He dropped all his gear save the mace, whatever guns were holstered, and knives sheathed on his body.

"They're attracted by the birth," Singh said. He had done a good job of cleaning up after the baby's arrival, but the scent of blood and afterbirth gave them away.

"You stay here with Julie and the baby, with him." He nodded to Buddy. "If you need me, fire one unsilenced shot, okay?"

"Got it."

As Singh walked over to check on Julie, he walked up to the nearest of the zombies. It raised its pallid hands for him before he bludgeoned it. He moved to the next one and repeated the process. The mace rose and fell as skulls shattered.

He worked his way from zombie to zombie methodically, stalking through the trees, felling them where he found them.

"What's Bear…"

"You rest now," Singh said. "You and that baby are going to need all your strength."

"Okay." Her bottom still throbbed and she was worn out.

Singh sat next to her with the silenced 9mm in his lap. He looked over at Buddy, who was dazed. He wondered about the dopamine activity in the man's brain today.

There was a cry from the trees. Singh looked up in time to see another zombie crumple. He watched Bear go about his work, moving in ever-widening circles, ensuring the safety of the clearing. Singh lost sight of him eventually.

Julie nodded off. When she opened her eyes the baby slept in her arms. Singh had moved and was across from her, feeding their fire. She propped herself up on one elbow. Buddy was still seated on a tree stump. Bear was nowhere in sight.

The pain in her lower body was intense, but she smiled, looking down on the sleeping Harris.

It would be better if she kept an eye on one side of the camp, while Singh watched the other. She tucked the blankets around the baby and laid it on a clear spot on the other side of the log. As long as she moved slowly she thought she'd be okay, though she was exhausted.

Buddy sat on the blackened tree stump and looked from Julie and the baby to Singh. The doctor noted that he was looking at him.

"Buddy? How do you feel?"

Come on, nigger, let's finish what we started, you and me.

"All right," Buddy tried to say but what came out was garbled. Singh shook his head and turned. He struck. The blow was sloppy but still toppled the unsuspecting doctor.

"Buddy?" Julie looked at him. The fear rose in her when she realized the man looking back at her was not the one she knew.

"Buddy?"

He advanced on her. She barely had time in her weakened, vulnerable state to stand and shift away from the baby to scream "Bear!" before he was on her.

He grabbed her by the neck and slammed her down into the snow, dead leaves, and fir cones. She grunted as the air left her. The pain in her lower body exploded.

He fell on top of her, wrapped his big hands around her neck, and started to strangle the life from her.

She tried to gasp his name but his hold was solid. She could not speak, let alone breath. A torrent of thoughts flashed through her mind, but first and foremost among them was her baby.

She forced herself to pull her hands from Buddy's wrists and reached for his face. Finding his cheeks, she tried to work her thumbs into his sockets. He took one hand from her neck, drew it back open-palmed, and cuffed her in the side of the head, stunning her.

"Buddy!" Singh wrapped his arms around Buddy's head and hauled back, trying to pull the enraged man off Julie.

There was a low moan as a couple of zombies lurched into their clearing.

"Buddy! Get off—" Singh pulled back with all he had and dislodged the man. Julie grabbed at her neck and gasped for air as she sat up.

The baby slept where he was.

He twisted in Singh's grasp and reached around, got a hold of the revolver on the doctor's belt, ripped it free of the holster, and pushed Singh away. Singh staggered back three steps until he regained his footing. "Buddy, no." He moved his hands out in front of himself, open palmed. The gun fired. The slug punched through his palm and into his stomach.

Singh tumbled back a few more steps, holding his middle. A burning sensation rushed through his guts. He looked at his hands and they were slick with blood.

"Buddy?"

His legs went out from under him at the same time Buddy fired a second shot. The bullet zipped by overhead as Singh dropped where he'd stood.

The zombies smelled his blood and stumbled towards his fallen form.

Buddy turned back to face Julie. As he did so her blade entered him low in his side, between his ribs. He let out a mangled yell and dropped the revolver, throwing himself on the woman. Both of them hit the ground. They struggled but he was much larger and stronger and filled with rage. He climbed on top of her. Julie clawed and slapped at him.

He grabbed her around the neck and started to slam her head against the ground. Spittle flew from his mouth as he muttered gibberish.

One of her hands found the knife in his side. She yanked on the handle. He bellowed but reached down through the pain, found her wrist and pulled it from the blade. He gripped Julie's arm in one hand and grabbed the knife handle where it protruded from his torso, wrenching it out of his own body, screaming as he did so.

Her legs kicked and flailed. He stretched her arm out. He pressed her forearm tight to the log and drove the knife through her wrist, deep into the bark of the tree beneath, pinning her there. Julie screamed and cried.

Buddy kneeled over her, bleeding, listening to the sounds she made. He had an erection.

The bullet entered his lower back. His hands shot behind him as if reaching for it. His torso straightened and he went rigid.

Singh sat up with a second pistol in his hand. Buddy looked down the barrel and Singh hesitated momentarily. It was just enough time for the first zombie that lurched into view behind the doctor to reach down and grab him, pulling him back. The pistol fired into the air.

Singh screamed as the zombie's teeth sunk into him.

Bear had a hand on either side of a zombie's head and was squeezing the life out of it. Both its eyes dislodged from their sockets and hung down on its cheeks from the optic nerves. He stopped and listened, ignoring the grunts of the zombie in his hands.

There was a gunshot off in the distance.

The booker launched itself through the air and landed on his back, latching on. He rolled forward, the move tossing the beast from him. The creature slid from the snow and sprang back up, growling at him. Three other zombies shambled towards him as the booker prepared to attack once more.

Julie was still pinned to the tree where Buddy had left her. She rolled halfway over onto her stomach and pulled her backpack towards her, going for something inside. Her clothes had ridden up and part of the Cosette tattoo on her back was visible.

Buddy stuck his booted foot on her chest and flipped her back over. Julie's face was streaked with tears and mucus. Long strands of her hair were sweat pasted across her face.

"Buddy—Buddy, no, please—"

He fell on her again, securing his grasp on her neck and squeezing, his forearms shaking with the effort. Julie clawed at him with her one free hand but he ignored the scratches she opened on his face. Blood ran down his cheeks and neck. Her nails stopped ripping at his face and her legs stopped kicking. Her hand went limp beside her, and he was still unaware.

A gunshot behind Buddy gave him pause. He let go of the dead woman and turned around.

Singh had shot one of the two zombies that were eating him. The thing reached up to its forehead and touched the hole there, then promptly rolled over.

The doctor struggled with the second zombie. The creature tore flesh out of his exposed neck. Singh tried to get the pistol in its face.

Buddy shut his eyes from the pain in his back and side.

He stood and went over to his saddle bags, rummaged around within, and pulled his hatchet out. He limped over to Singh and the zombie and cleaved the beast's skull.

Singh tried to aim the gun at Buddy but he couldn't steady his hand. He wound up bringing the pistol snug against his own belly. His other hand reached up for his neck, squeezing as best he could. He was losing blood, but the zombies hadn't hit his artery or he'd be dead by now.

Buddy looked up. There were more zombies entering the clearing. He limped over to the first and killed it with his hatchet. He had some trouble prying the blade from the thing's head but finally freed it in time to bury it in a second beast's face.

There was someone behind a tree watching him. The thing pulled itself back behind the trunk, out of sight.

No, Buddy thought, suddenly petrified. His wounds screamed at him. He grew aware he was bleeding all over the place. *Had the thing been holding its own head?*

Singh tried to control his breathing.

He watched Buddy standing there, looking out into the woods.

Buddy was talking to himself. Singh watched him stoop with great effort and retrieve his saddle bags, then sling them over his shoulders. Buddy looked around, ignoring or not seeing the doctor lying there. He focused on the sleeping child.

Oh God, no... Singh couldn't move.

A few minutes later Bear burst from the trees. He did not see Singh at first. The doctor watched as the giant spied Julie and the man's shoulders drooped.

Bear looked down on Julie's inert form. He looked up to the sky. There were tears in his eyes. He fell on his knees beside her and opened his arms, imploring the heavens, letting loose a howl of anguish and sorrow.

In the woods beyond Buddy was brought up short by the cry. He heard a rustle and turned. Something was following him, coming for him through the trees...

Markowski? No...how...

When he turned to look back in the direction of Bear's howl, the brain following him stopped and stood perfectly still. The creature lacked anything resembling human intelligence but it could smell blood and it knew fear, and this man it was after was bleeding and very afraid.

Bear reached down, removed the knife from her wrist, and threw it off into the woods.

"...bear..."

He went to the grievously wounded doctor.

"What happened, Singh? Where's the baby? Where's the boy?"

Singh tried to speak, tried to explain what had happened, but all he could manage was a dispirited "...*buddy*..."

A new look came to Bear's eye.

He retrieved his pack, slinging it over his shoulder.

Buddy.

He drew one of his Glocks and walked back over to Singh. The doctor looked up at him, blinking. Without a word he fired a single round through the dying doctor's head.

Buddy.

Buddy lost his footing and went down to a knee. One of the saddle bags landed in the snow, the other draped loosely over his shoulder. He gasped as a bolt of pain shot up his spine. He was breathing hard, sweating and bleeding, and they were talking about him again.

...he can run but it won't help him...

...leave him alone will you...

...you saw what he did with the kid didn't you...

...run Buddy just run...

His bare hand had gone out to break his fall and was buried in the snow. He looked down at it like it didn't belong to him. He didn't feel the cold.

...I'm comin' for you boy...

He turned and looked over his shoulder in time to see something disappear behind a tree. He blinked and looked again but it wasn't showing itself.

He knew who it was coming for him.

...get up Buddy get up and move...

Yeah, Harris. He righted himself, staring at his snow encrusted hand curled up into a claw, his arm bent at the elbow and pulled in tight to his side. He tried to pull the saddle bags back into place with his one good hand, but couldn't quite do it.

...he's going to get you Buddy. Run...

He looked back and saw nothing. But that didn't mean nothing was back there.

...that's right boy. You can run but you can't run forever...

With a huff, he threw one leg in front of the other and continued to slog through the snow, dragging the saddle bags along.

Bear saw Buddy off ahead of him. He watched him stumble and fall and he waited while he knelt there. He had followed the spattering of red in the snow. He wondered when he would collapse from losing so much blood.

A zombie was between himself and Buddy. Because it was tracking Buddy, he thought it had to be a brain. They were smart, but he didn't think it knew he was following it.

When Buddy turned his head to look behind once more, the undead thing darted behind a pine and stood perfectly still.

Bear wondered if he would get back up. *Where was the baby?* He was some distance away, but when he squinted he saw no evidence of the child.

Buddy stood, half bent over, and staggered on, the saddle bags trailing.

Bear gripped the handle of the flanged mace that much tighter through his glove.

Hey Buddy...

Gotta...gotta run, Harris, he's...he's coming for me...

You remember the old man with the boat?

Yeah. Buddy smiled and cleared his throat. He spat. It was a gob of blood, but he was unaware of it.

...nigger...

He stopped and let the saddle bags fall.

Fuck this. It stops here.

He turned to face Markowski.

There was a zombie thirty yards behind him. As he turned he saw it scurry behind a tree. He blinked. The tree was too small to hide the thing and he could see its arm and half its side behind the trunk.

He started to laugh. The effort caused him to double up and grip his stomach. There was blood on his lips.

Fuck. Just a goddamn zombie back there. It wasn't Markowski with his severed head.

...you did the right thing, you did the right thing...

A zombie he could deal with. If it had been Markowski, he would have had problems. He turned and took one step forward—

...you the man Buddy...

When the bullet hit him in the face it snapped his head back, lifting a piece of his skull free and sending it spiraling through the air to land several yards away.

Bear heard the crack of the unseen rifle. He watched Buddy catch the headshot, saw him plunge to the snow. He wasn't moving. Bear hunkered down where he was behind the multiple twisted trunks of an evergreen and waited.

The zombie following was confused. It waited behind its own tree for a minute before emerging then running up to Buddy's limp form. It wore a hoodie. Several thousands dollars worth of diamonds gleamed from the grillz in its mouth. It circled the body and the saddle bags in disappointment.

A second shot rang out and knocked the zombie down.

Bear watched from his concealment as the undead twitched in the snow. He spied four men as they broke from the trees and marched towards the bodies. When they reached Buddy and the fallen zombie, one of the men drew a pistol and shot the undead through the head.

Another used his foot to flip Buddy onto his back. They stood around him and the zombie talking for a bit, after which they gathered up the saddle bags and walked off in the direction they had come, back through the trees.

He crouched and waited for the sun to go down.

"Those were a couple of good shots you made today," Jim told Pete.

"*Ahh*, first one was good. Zed went right down. Second one should have been better."

"My brother, the sniper," John said. "Mom and Dad would have been so proud."

"Yeah, yeah, yeah."

"Not as cold tonight as last night." Sean said. He was seated atop his sleeping bag, kicking absently at a small branch half in and half out of the fire.

"Not yet," John said. "Give it time."

"Nah," Jim said. "Spring is definitely in the air."

"What month are we in?" Pete asked.

"Who knows," Sean said.

"Couple more nights of this and then we head in," John said.

"Shit yeah," Jim said. "I hate being out here in the dark with those things."

"All we seen all week were the two today," Pete said.

"Yeah, so? You know they're out there, somewhere, right?"

"Fuck 'em," Sean said. "I'm turning in."

"What else is there to do out here?" Pete asked.

"Hey, John, put a can of beans on the fire for me, will you?"

"Yeah, you got first watch again."

"Luck of the draw."

"Yeah, luck of the draw."

No one particularly enjoyed sitting up for two hours alone while the others slept, but it was generally agreed among the men that the guys pulling first and last shift had it best. At least they could catch a solid six hours of uninterrupted sleep before or after their own turn.

"Wake my ass when the birds start chirping," Sean said, curling up on his side in his sleeping bag. He had the fourth and final watch for the night.

"Bet you can't wait to get back into Clavius," John said quietly to his brother. "See Mei."

"Yeah."

"When that girl gets done with you, your ass is gonna be sore for a week."

"You be careful," Pete told his older brother. "Or you're going to wake up tomorrow and *your* ass is going to be sore."

As if on cue Sean farted in his sleep.

"Now *that's* funny," Pete said.

Jim had come over with an oven mitt and was getting his can of baked beans from the fire. "You guys want you can stay up and keep me company."

"Screw you," John said. "Goodnight."

Jim walked off to his spot beyond the fire.

"You know," Pete said, "what the best part about Asian girls is?"

"What's that?"

"They got small hands. Make someone like you feel like he's got a big cock."

"Nice," John managed sleepily.

Jim sat away from the snores of the group, watching the dark and stirring what was left of his cold canned beans with a spoon. When the grenade exploded in the middle of the sleeping bodies, he was far enough away that the shrapnel wounded but did not kill him.

The blast extinguished the camp fire.

Bear came out of the trees and walked to the center of the camp. Smoke rose from the glowing embers scattered about. Two of the bodies lay unmoving in their torn sleeping bags. A third was moaning softly and shifting around inside his bag.

He walked over to the severely wounded man and looked down on him. The guy's face was torn and bloodied. The material of his shredded sleeping bag darkened.

"Where's the baby?" Bear stood over him. When the man couldn't or wouldn't answer, he finished him with one blow from the mace.

Jim tried to crawl off into the night, his legs dragging uselessly behind him, when Bear stepped on his lower back and pinned him to the ground.

"Please—Christ—Jesus—"

He reached down and turned him over.

"Please Mister—"

"Where's the baby?"

"Wh-what baby?"

Bear raised the mace.

"Where's the baby?"

"I swear to you—Mister, I don't know what you're—"

He brought the mace down and brained him.

He walked back to the ruins of the fire and searched in the dark until he found what he was looking for. The saddle bags. The grenade explosion had picked them up and thrown them away from the group.

He squatted down next to the bags and undid the clasp of the first. He dug around through it, searching. His hand gripped something small, smooth and cold. When he pulled it free he found it was a Zippo lighter. He rolled the wheel and watched the flame catch. He considered the fire in his hand then threw the lighter away.

He rifled through the other saddle bag. When his hand closed on soft cotton, he drew it out and looked at the little purple flow-ered panties. Drained, he exhaled and sat down in the snow, his head bowed. He felt very alone in the universe.

CRUSADE REPRISE

"Bear."

He recognized the voice and opened his eye.

"Bruce."

"Found this character lurking around…"

He was on his knees in the grass. In front of him was a blanket on which his pistols and weapons were set, freshly cleaned and oiled. Most of his armor and gear lay massed about the blanket as well. Beside him lay the saddle bags.

He rolled back onto the soles of his feet and twisted around to face Bruce and the kid with him.

"Where'd you find this one?"

"Hanging around the line. Wasn't with anyone. He's all alone."

"Is that a fact?"

"What do you want to do with him?"

"Leave him here with me."

He nodded, turned and walked off across the grass for the bushes.

The little boy stood there. His skin was black. His hair was grown out and nappy. He couldn't have been more than ten and he looked like a scrapper. The kid wore pants that were way too big for him. He had secured them around his waist with a loop of rope and cut the bottoms off so they wouldn't drag on the ground.

The boy had a pistol stuffed in his pants.

"Well. You're a young one, ain't ya?"

The boy didn't say anything. He tried to look tough.

"You use that thing before?" He gestured to the butt of the pistol jutting out of the kid's pants.

"Yeah."

"You afraid of Zeds?"

233

"No." The boy tried to sound convincing. "Why? You?"

"Me? Are you kidding? I'm terrified of them."

"But you're…you're the man they call Bear, right?"

"That's what they call me. How 'bout you kid, you got a name?"

"My name is David Lee Roth."

He put his head down and shook. When he looked up the kid saw he was chuckling.

"What's so funny, Mister?"

"Do you know who David Lee Roth was?"

"Yeah. I'm David Lee Roth."

Bear chuckled again.

"Why you laughin'?"

"I say *Jump*, or *Ain't Talkin 'bout Love*, or *Panama*. That doesn't mean anything to you?"

"You making fun of my name?"

He had to admit the kid had balls.

"Kid-kid, listen. You're talkin' to a guy they call *Bear*. You think I'd make fun of *your* name?"

The kid considered it, then said no.

"Let me tell you why I'm laughing." Bear turned back to his blanket. "Come on over here. Sit down." The kid sat down opposite him. As Bear spoke he reached down and assembled a 9mm Glock.

"Back in the 80s—the 1980s—there was this rock and roll band called Van Halen. They had a lead singer named David Lee Roth."

"Van Halen?"

"Yeah."

"And this guy you're talking about, he sang for them?"

"Yeah."

"Did he look like me?"

"No, kid, he didn't look anything like you. He was this tall skinny white guy, big hair—"

"What do you mean, 'big hair'?"

"Kid, you gotta understand, this was the '80s. Guys wore their hair like women. All poofed out and Aqua Netted up."

"Aqua Net?"

"Hairspray, kid. Hairspray."

"What's hairspray?"

"How old *are* you?"

"I don't know."

"You with anybody?"

"No."

"So who named you David Lee Roth?"

"This man and woman I was with for awhile."

"What happened to this man and woman?"

The kid shrugged, trying not to look sad. "Zed."

"Zed." Bear shook his head. He holstered the Glock and went to work assembling the second one.

"If his name was the same as mine why'd they call the band Van-whatever?"

"*Van Halen*. There were a couple of other guys in the band, last name Van Halen."

"Oh."

"David Lee Roth was with them a long time, but not forever."

"Zed get him too?"

Bear looked up from his work. "Probably. But back then, he left the band, worked as a radio DJ and an EMT for awhile—"

"What's an EMT?"

"EMTs were the guys who would show up when you had an accident or something. They helped you out."

"What happened to the band?"

"They got a new lead singer—guy named Sammy Hagar."

"Like Hagar the Horrible."

"You know Hagar the Horrible but you never heard of Van Halen?"

"Nope." He gestured to one of Bear's weapons. "I know what that is. Knights used to use it."

"They did." He picked up his flanged mace and held it for the boy to see. "Want to hold it?"

"It's heavy."

"It is."

"And knights used to wear those too." The boy pointed to his chain-mail.

"That they did."

"But what's that?"

"That's called a splatter mask."

"What's a splatter mask?"

"Tank crews in World War One used to wear them. Protect them from ricochets and all."

"We've got tanks now."

"That we do."

"You liked David Lee Roth and Van Halen?"

"I did. Which is ironic..."

"Why's it ironic?"

"It's ironic because their kind of music—remember I told you the guys all wore their hair big and long like a woman's? That type of music used to be called 'Hair Metal,' and look at me." He ran a hand over his bald head and David Lee Roth laughed.

"What happened to your hair?"

"I cut it all off. Makes me look prettier." Bear chuckled and so did the kid.

He slid into and adjusted his armor.

"He's kind of quiet, isn't he?" David Lee Roth nodded his head towards the wild man who had been standing behind them the entire time.

"He is." Bear holstered his pistols. "Sometimes it's better to be quiet. You can learn something."

The boy nodded and asked, "What happened to your eye?"

"You've got a lot of questions kid, don't you?"

"Sorry."

"It's okay." He slung the chainsaw blade down across his back.

"Is this going to be a long fight?"

"This one? *Months*, David Lee Roth. *Months*."

The boy nodded.

"You ever been to New York City?" Bear pulled one gauntlet on and secured it.

"No."

"It was a beautiful city, a real beautiful city."

"Was?"

"It will be again. Here. I got something for you."

The kid reached out and he handed him an iPod.

"What's this for?"

"Music. You can listen to music on it."

"Really?"

"Well, we gotta get some electricity for it, recharge the battery, but yeah."

"If it's got no battery, what do you listen to?"

"Whatever I want to. Whatever's in my head."

He stood. "Roll that blanket up for me, would you?"

The kid did as he was asked. He slung the saddle bags over his shoulders and picked up his bundle.

"Why do you carry that doll?"

"So I never forget, David Lee Roth."

"Forget what?"

Bear didn't answer the kid.

"You ever ride shotgun, David Lee Roth?"

"What's that mean?"

"Come on, kid." Bear turned and started walking across the grass towards the bushes. David Lee Roth followed him.

As they walked the wild man fell in behind them. He was speaking to himself, "In the beginning, good always overpowered the evils of all man's sins…"

The boy followed him through the bushes and trees. They emerged on a road packed with hundreds of vehicles stretching further than the little boy's eyes could see. The first several dozen vehicles in line were tanks and armored personnel carriers.

"…lay destroyed, beaten down, only the corpses of rebels…"

Thousands of human beings waited patiently around the vehicles. When Bear appeared from the green they cheered—a massive sound that drowned out the wild man.

The boy followed him to a truck that rested on four of the largest wheels he had ever seen.

"…so come now, children of the beast, be strong, and…"

They were at the front of the line. Ahead of them stretched a vast double-decked suspension bridge. The boy knew it was the George Washington Bridge because he had seen all the signs for it, as he'd approached the line of tanks and heavily armed men and women this morning. M67 flame tanks and M4 Dozers had moved across the six lower and eight upper levels, immolating thousands of zombies that had tried to cross to them. Knocking cars and trucks stuck on the bridge out of the way, off to the sides, they had cleared a path down the center of each level.

"Bear!" Kevin called from behind the driver's wheel of the monster truck.

"You ever ride in a truck like this before?"

"No," the boy said, a look of wonder in his eyes.

"Kev, this is David Lee Roth. He's riding next to you today."

"No kidding? Well come on then, David Lee Roth!"

"How do I get in?" The kid looked at him.

"I'll help you."

He walked him to the passenger side and helped him up into the cab.

"You sit there and you listen to what Kevin tells you to do. Okay?"

"Okay."

Bear walked away from the truck, over to the side of the road, acknowledging the armored and armed men and women who greeted him. Some were eager, some wore serious looks, but all showed respect. He walked through and past them and stopped when he judged it a good place to do so.

He lay the doll wrapped in its blanket on the grass beside the road.

Bear walked back to the truck, around to the rear, and climbed aboard, pulling the ladder up with him, laying it in the bed. The wild man was there waiting for him, seated with his back against the cab.

He walked over and stood next to where the wild man sat, checking the MK 47 automatic grenade launcher mounted on the roof of the cab. A belt of 40mm grenades disappeared into a metal box resting in the bed.

He looked ahead, across the bridge where the flame tanks held the zombies drawn to the bridge at bay, trapped on the other side of the Hudson River. There were millions of zombies waiting across there for them, had to be.

He turned and squinted at the line of tanks and armored vehicles stretched out behind them. Men and women had started across either of the bridge's pedestrian paths on foot. They streamed by, their faces hard set as they readied for the task ahead. A few of them waved to him, or shook their fists in solidarity.

He turned back to the MK 47 and looked out across the river and bridge. He peered into the city one final time. Satisfied, he banged on the top of the cab. Kevin shifted the truck into gear and the wheels rolled forward.

"Put on your seat belt kid," Kevin said. "Just in case."

The tanks, assault vehicles, trucks and cars behind them rolled forward across the bridge. They were headed into Eden to take back the earth.

AFTERWARD

"You are satisfying in an indirect, false way your lust to jab and strike." DH Lawrence wrote his once friend, the philosopher-mathematician and pacifist Bertrand Russell, in a letter dated September 14, 1915, citing the latter's opposition to supporters of the first world war. "Either satisfy it in a direct and honorable way, saying 'I hate you all, liars and swine, and am out to set upon you,' or stick to mathematics, where you can be true." Lawrence, who had and would again flirt with fascism and anti-Semitic views, berated Russell for his "sheep's clothing of peace propaganda," accusing him of a general misanthropy, noting, "I wouldn't care if you were six times a murderer, so long as you said to yourself, 'I am this.'"

Lawrence was incorrect in his assessment of the co-author of *Principia Mathematica,* and would have done better to turn his critical gaze upon himself. But, much as Lawrence felt for Russell, I now feel for one Tommy Arlin.

When my own break with Arlin came, it came quickly, though not completely unexpectedly. Tommy had long been attracted to the rogues—the low lives and shady characters of history and his own times. I thought we had much in common when we'd first met years ago: our mutual admiration for the lives of the Beats; our appreciation of women of any and all ethnicities; what I thought was Tommy's progressive political bent.

I was wrong.

Eden's modest success wasn't enough for Tommy. He wanted more, *expected* more. He sent me letters—always by post, the guy avoids email—laying out perceived slights and indignities delivered us by such luminaries as Robert Kirkman and Romero. What the hell was Arlin talking about? These guys didn't even know we, or our book, existed. I wrote Tommy back stating as much and warning him that whatever course he was planning on taking, he risked making a fool of himself over nothing. *Where was our Bram Stoker?* Arlin kept demanding.

Tommy showed up at my door one clear, spring day, a bottle of whiskey in his hand. Dirtbag Brown was in tow. I wouldn't let either of them in my house. I needed to shield my wife and two babies from these besotted, borderline belligerent men. We sat on the porch and drank. Actually, they drank. I merely sipped at a plastic cup-full of Arlin's rot-gut.

"We're riding a tide, Monchinski," he said to me, "and History is the ocean." Tommy abided by his faith that zombies were on the verge of being the next big thing. Bigger than vegetarian vampires and boy wizards. Anyone else emerging on the scene was "stealing our thunder", and he said he was going to go to Hollywood and confront Woody Harrelson personally. I think I managed to talk Tommy out of that one, which is a good thing because I have no doubt Woody would have kicked Tommy's ass.

Arlin sat in the hard metal of my deck chair—I hadn't bothered to bring the cushions out from indoors—spewing half-coherent ideas for any number of stories between swallows of hard liquor. One yarn involved a zombie-like "black widow" virus that spreads homicidal nymphomania among the female population—I opined that his idea was too much like *Y: The Last Man*, even if the male hero of Arlin's plot was, ingeniously I admit, impotent—to a *Watchman* parody, with a character—Dr. Peneii—loosely based on me. Me, Dr. Peneii? I don't know why but I mentioned my idea: a screenplay for a screw-ball comedy, *No Zombie Left Behind.* Tommy and Dirtbag ignored it.

If Arlin had come for moral support he wasn't going to get it from this end. Euripides Brown was drunk as a skunk. When he went and urinated in my wife's tomatoes, in full view of the neighbors' houses, I politely asked them to leave, which they did.

Arlin had fallen in with the wrong crowd. The Wood Nation was an obscure east-coast rap "family," always on the verge of "making it" and getting signed to a label, though as of this writing that hasn't happened for any of their many members. A motley collection of hustlas, pimps, playas, street soldiers, and hood poets, they went by names like Black Jesus, True Soul-Jah, Sweet Daddy Woo-Woo, Killah Skillz, and Ras Supreme.

They met Arlin through Dirtbag Brown, whom they worshipped, placing him in a pantheon among the great Philly gangster rapper Schooly-D; the obscure, not-even-one-hit-wonder Niggerace; and the Geto Boys' Bushwick Bill, though they all referred to the diminutive one-eyed rapper by his longer title—Dr. Wolfgang Von Bushwick the Barbarian Mother Funky Stay High Dollar Billstir. The Wood Nation's A-Suhn and lil' Whut-Whut had met Euripedes Brown when he was selling bootleg DVDs on a blanket in Jamaica, Queens. These aspiring rap stars were working a corner, selling cooked-up rocks. The two had convinced Brown to accompany them back to their flop with promises of crack. Most likely planning to rob him, they wound up adopting him as a spiritual and influential forebear instead, much like Pearl Jam claimed Neil Young.

The straw that broke the camel's back for me with Arlin came at Horrorfind Weekend in March, 2008. Arlin mailed me a letter saying we'd been "invited to read." I have to admit I was very excited. I'd been doing what I could to promote the book, answering online interview requests, and appearing for forty-five seconds on *The Miserable Men Show* with the Reverend Bob Levy and Shully, before my internet phone connection cut out and I was disconnected (thanks, incidentally, to Rich Butters for arranging the call). What Tommy didn't tell me was we *hadn't* been invited; he'd written and asked—begged—we be put on the reading list. Not only that, after arriving there, I found out we'd both have to fork over fifty bucks to get into the convention in the first place.

I showed up in Maryland in high spirits. I have always liked Maryland ever since I'd commute up I-95 from my home in Smithfield, North Carolina (exit 95 on I-95—easy enough to remember!) to my parents' house in New York City. Maryland is home to some good, though wild, friends of mine: the enormous Jim Vest with his twenty-two inch arms; world bench press champion Jeff McVicar—who once dumped 600 pounds on his abdomen going to rack the weight and had two inches of his gut pop out his ass, which he proceeded to push back into place with his thumb—and Brian "Flatline" Weston, called such because he had once died from a morphine overdose but came back, making Weston, arguably, a living, breathing zombie himself. And heck, Baltimore was the setting for *The Wire*, one of my favorite shows of all time.

Well, things in Maryland didn't turn out the way I or Arlin had expected. Scratch that. I really don't know what Arlin was thinking.

He had insisted we share a room, which he made a point of paying for. (Though the sub-prime mortgage crisis had robbed Tommy's rich grandmother of much of her wealth, he assured me that the old lady was still rolling in dough.) What I didn't know was that Arlin had brought a few members of the Wood Nation along with him—Ras Supreme, Killah Skillz, and the inseparable pair of Yagi Bear and Ye-Yo. The latter two never slept as far as I could tell, always hoovering comically-giant lines of cocaine which were heavily cut with baby lax, which meant one of them was constantly monopolizing the room's sole commode. If Grandma Arlin was as blue blood as Tommy always claimed, couldn't she have at least sprung for a suite?

Saturday afternoon and the time for our reading arrived. Arlin was nowhere to be found. I had left the room early in the morning, wanting to get away from him and the other maniacs, and figured we'd meet up at the location of the reading. When I got there, there was no Tommy. As a matter of fact, the only people in the expansive room filled with folding chairs were fellow Permuted author Kim Paffenroth, a friend of mine—James Doller—from work and his buddies, the Parduba brothers. Where was everybody? Dr. Kim read from his *Dying to Live* then I, feeling extremely pathetic, read for an abbreviated five minutes from *Eden*.

Later that night, after wandering the main convention floor with Doller and the Pardubas—surreptitiously leering at Chainsaw Sally; watching Ken Foree talking with Tony Todd; buying an 8x10 from the director of *Ugor,* a little known series of low-budget, soft-porn, cult serial killer films—I went back to the room and confronted Tommy. Where the hell had he been? At the Sid Haig Town Meeting on the first floor with most of the other convention-goers. Did he give a shit that he'd missed our reading? "History, Monchinski," he said, "the tide." Killah Skillz was giving me dirty looks and Arlin was three sheets to the wind, wasted or high or something. I couldn't tell. Yagi Bear and Ye-Yo were snorting lines off the ass of a high-priced escort in the fouled bathroom.

That's bullshit, Tommy, I remember saying to him, but he waved me off, dismissing my concerns.

And then he started the argument that ended our friendship. Arlin knows I am an enormous Robert Mitchum fan—hadn't we included a character in Eden named after him?—and he had the balls to claim that Robert Shaw was a "way better actor" than my man, the original Max Cady. *Bullshit, Tommy,* I told him, and it was on. We commenced a game of one-upmanship, Arlin naming a Shaw character or movie and me countering with one from Mitchum. The original Mr. Blue? What about *Mr. Allison? The Sting?* Try *Night of the Hunter.* "Jaws, motherfucker," Tommy cackled, and I immediately shot back, "*Out of the Past,* cocksucker."

Then Arlin croaked "Gator McClusky," Burt Reynolds' character in *White Lightening,* and I knew I had him beat. As great an actor as he was, Shaw couldn't trump Mitchum, and if Arlin wanted to bring a fast-car-driving-moonshiner into it I wouldn't have to leave the Mitchum oeuvre, so I spat out "*Thunder Road,* fucker." Tommy looked at me, a mix of disdain and drug induced incomprehension, and he started to sing, *Farewell and adieu unto you Spanish ladies*... I felt I had won the argument and made my point. Further, I'm not the confrontational type, and Killah Skillz looked like he was getting ready to shank me. So I gathered my belongings and left the hotel room, leaving Arlin and his entourage to their madness.

I heard later that Tommy and his little coterie—including the escort—had an altercation with security and were tossed out of the hotel and the convention, following a ruckus at Scary-okie that night. I haven't spoken to Arlin since, though I did receive one last letter from him.

A few remarks, then, about *Eden.*

To the people who read it and enjoyed the book, several of whom took further time to email me such, *thank you! Eden was* for you; *Crusade is* for you. I am, like you, first and foremost, a huge fan of the genre. I want to thank Jacob Kier and Permuted Press for publishing *Eden.* Thanks also for all the support the book has received on the forums at Permuted, *All Things Zombie,* and *Zombie Squad.* If the idea of a participatory economy interests you, check out any book by the amazing Michael Albert.

I'd like to thank Permuted's Chris Kaletka for the astounding job he did on the cover of *Eden.* And Leah Clarke receives my gratefulness for the unenviable task she tackled when editing *Eden* (Hopefully *Crusade* proved easier than its predecessor). A few reviews have noted "grammatical errors." Spelling errors I will cop to. So, if for example, I misspelled *looked* as *lookied* on page 5 of *Eden,* that's on me. But writing an action sequence—conveying a sense of multiple lines of action with the use of hyphens—constitutes no grammatical error. Those sequences, which may have been unwieldy for some but seemed well received by most, were purposefully written in that style, and if they are not "grammatically correct" that begs the whole question of standard usage and the political and social determinations that go into ascribing such.

I want to thank Dr. Michael Hardiman for his insight into schizophrenia and other psychotic disorders. Thanks also to Anastasia Katechis for her help in translating the Greek. Crusade wouldn't be what it is without the attention to detail and amazing editing job of Louise Bohmer, whom I wish to thank immensely! To my wife, Myoungmee, and my two children, Tony Michael and Honalee, I declare all my love and gratitude for their inspiration. To you, the reader, I again offer my appreciation for your interest and support. I would love to hear from you, either on the forums (www.PermutedPress.com) or through tmonchinski@gmail.com.

So, this is goodbye then. Goodbye from me the author to you the reader until the third and final installment in this trilogy (the only hint I'm giving is its set about twenty years after the events in *Crusade*). Goodbye from me to Tommy Arlin and his bogus ways. I now realize that my attraction to Arlin was based on my own insecurities and his B.S. His bullshit, because he talked a good game—about his love of zombies and the genre and left-wing politics—but he never walked the walk. If you ever meet Tommy you will find he is charming, even dashing. Tommy will talk circles around you about his love for humanity and the human species, but all he truly cares about is his latest debauch. And if you're a woman, be especially careful.

My own insecurities left me vulnerable to Arlin's influence. Ever since I'd got it into my head that I wanted to be a writer then read about the Beats, I wondered, who would be Neil Cassady to my Jack Kerouac? With time and, I like to think, maturity, I left my attachment to the Beats behind. The myths didn't and don't make up for the men behind them. Kerouac spent his last years as an anti-Semitic drunk; Cassady criss-crossed the country but couldn't take care of his own family; Burroughs killed his wife playing William Tell in Mexico and was a pedophile junkie who would travel to Tangiers to have sex with pre-pubescent boys. Today I am able to write for the sheer joy of it, and like I said above, the occasional email from a reader really does make my day.

Arlin sent me a final missive, threatening legal action against my person should I take it upon myself to pen an Eden sequel. He stated he was working on his own sequel. One that combined zombies, Romanticism, Southern Gothic and time travel (What is he thinking?). *Whatever.* In his 1915 letter, DH Lawrence asked Bertrand Russell why he wouldn't "own" his "perverted, mental bloodlust." Beware, dear readers, of Tommy Arlin and what drives him, and should you meet him, listen to his words, yes, but more importantly, watch his actions. "Let us become strangers again," Lawrence ended his letter, "I think it is better." And to Tommy, if you are reading this, I ask much the same. We are history, Arlin.

Tony Monchinski
Peekskill, New York 2010

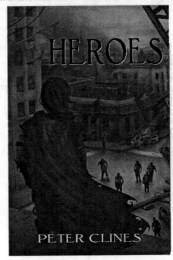
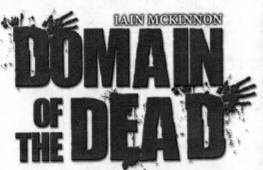

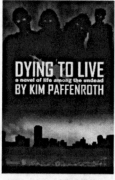
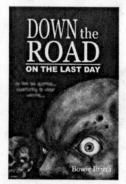

BY WILLIAM D. CARL

Beneath the dim light of a full moon, the population of Cincinnati mutates into huge, snarling monsters that devour everyone they see, acting upon their most base and bestial desires. Planes fall from the sky. Highways are clogged with abandoned cars, and buildings explode and topple. The city burns.

Only four people are immune to the metamorphosis—a smooth-talking thief who maintains the code of the Old West, an African-American bank teller who has struggled her entire life to emerge unscathed from the ghetto, a wealthy middle-aged housewife who finds everything she once believed to be a lie, and a teen-aged runaway turning tricks for food.

Somehow, these survivors must discover what caused this apocalypse and stop it from spreading. In their way is not only a city of beasts at night, but, in the daylight hours, the same monsters returned to human form, many driven insane by atrocities committed against friends and families.

Now another night is fast approaching. And once again the moon will be full.

ISBN: 978-1934861042

EDEN
A ZOMBIE NOVEL BY TONY MONCHINSKI

Seemingly overnight the world transforms into a barren wasteland ravaged by plague and overrun by hordes of flesh-eating zombies. A small band of desperate men and women stand their ground in a fortified compound in what had been Queens, New York. They've named their sanctuary Eden.

Harris—the unusual honest man in this dead world—races against time to solve a murder while maintaining his own humanity. Because the danger posed by the dead and diseased mass clawing at Eden's walls pales in comparison to the deceit and treachery Harris faces within.

ISBN: 978-1934861172

MORE DETAILS, EXCERPTS, AND PURCHASE INFORMATION AT
www.permutedpress.com

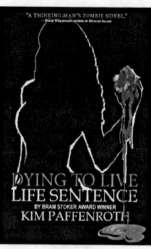

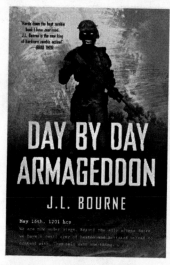

LaVergne, TN USA
08 December 2010
207889LV00004B/168/P